RYAN NORTH | SHELLI PAROLINE | BRADEN LAMB

MIDAS ™

Ross Richie..CEO & Founder
Joy Huffman..CFO
Matt Gagnon..Editor-in-Chief
Filip Sablik.............................President, Publishing & Marketing
Stephen Christy...President, Development
Lance Kreiter.............Vice President, Licensing & Merchandising
Phil Barbaro.............Vice President, Finance & Human Resources
Arune Singh...............................Vice President, Marketing
Bryce Carlson........Vice President, Editorial & Creative Strategy
Scott Newman...................................Manager, Production Design
Kate Henning......................................Manager, Operations
Spencer Simpson..Manager, Sales
Sierra Hahn...Executive Editor
Jeanine Schaefer..Executive Editor
Dafna Pleban...Senior Editor
Shannon Watters..Senior Editor
Eric Harburn...Senior Editor
Chris Rosa...Editor
Matthew Levine..Editor
Sophie Philips-Roberts................................Assistant Editor
Gavin Gronenthal...Assistant Editor

Michael Moccio..Assistant Editor
Gwen Waller..Assistant Editor
Amanda LaFranco.....................................Executive Assistant
Jillian Crab...Design Coordinator
Michelle Ankley.......................................Design Coordinator
Kara Leopard...Production Designer
Marie Krupina...Production Designer
Grace Park.......................................Production Design Assistant
Chelsea Roberts................................Production Design Assistant
Samantha Knapp................................Production Design Assistant
Elizabeth Loughridge.......................Accounting Coordinator
Stephanie Hocutt...............................Social Media Coordinator
José Meza...Event Coordinator
Holly Aitchison.................................Digital Sales Coordinator
Esther Kim...Marketing Coordinator
Megan Christopher..............................Operations Assistant
Rodrigo Hernandez...............................Operations Assistant
Morgan Perry.........................Direct Market Representative
Cat O'Grady...Marketing Assistant
Breanna Sarpy..Executive Assistant

BOOM! BOX™

MIDAS, May 2019. Published by BOOM! Box, a division of Boom Entertainment, Inc. Midas is ™ & © 2019 Ryan North. Originally published in single magazine form as THE MIDAS FLESH No. 1-8, & BOOM! BOX MIX TAPE 2014. ™ & © 2013-2014 Ryan North & Boom Entertainment, Inc. All rights reserved. BOOM! Box™ and the BOOM! Box logo are trademarks of Boom Entertainment, Inc., registered in various countries and categories. All characters, events, and institutions depicted herein are fictional. Any similarity between any of the names, characters, persons, events, and/or institutions in this publication to actual names, characters, persons, events, and/or institutions is unintended and purely coincidental. BOOM! Box does not read or accept unsolicited submissions of ideas, stories, or artwork.

BOOM! Studios, 5670 Wilshire Boulevard, Suite 400, Los Angeles, CA 90036-5679. Printed in China. First Printing.

ISBN: 978-1-68415-359-6, eISBN: 978-1-64144-342-5

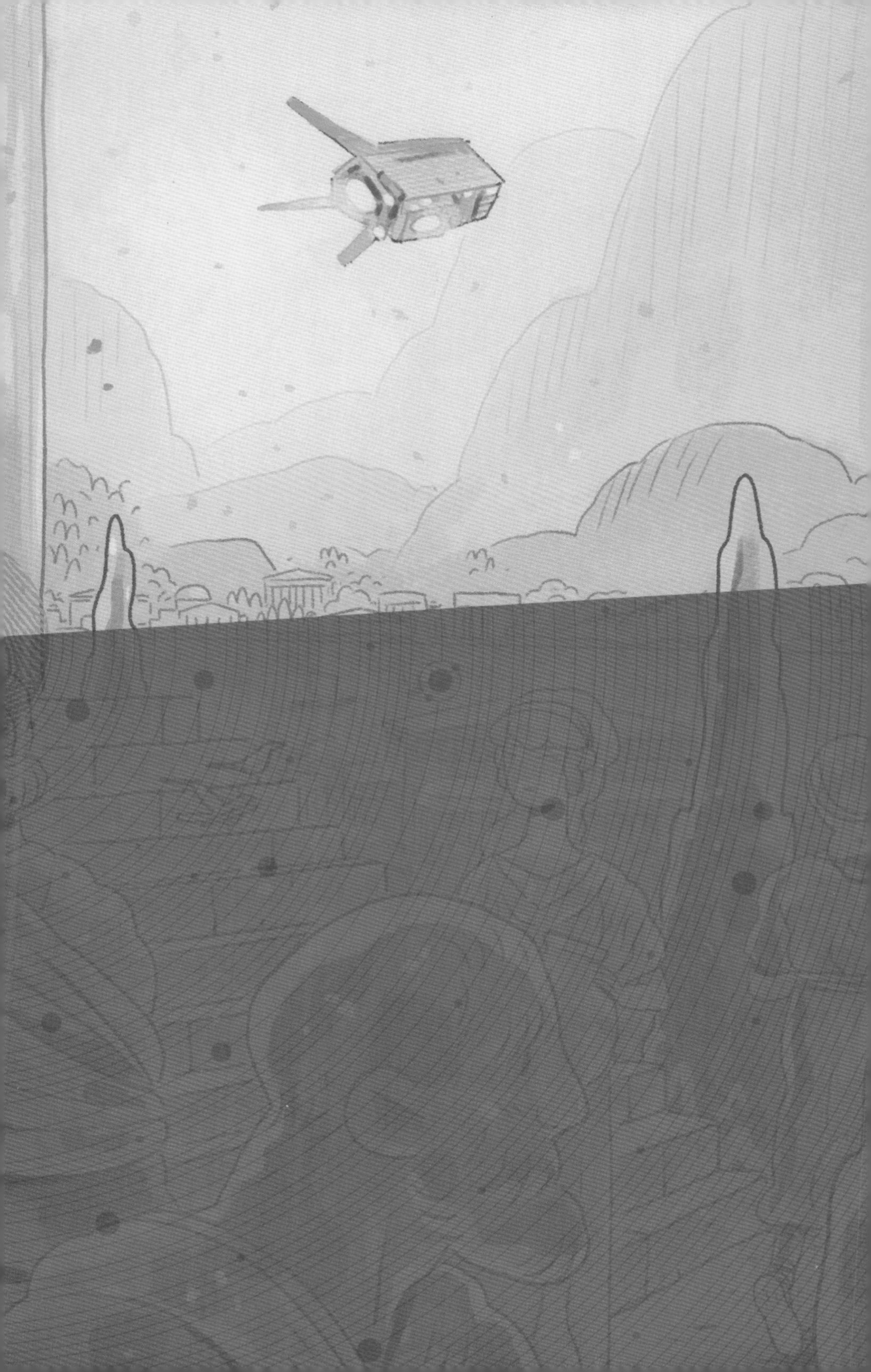

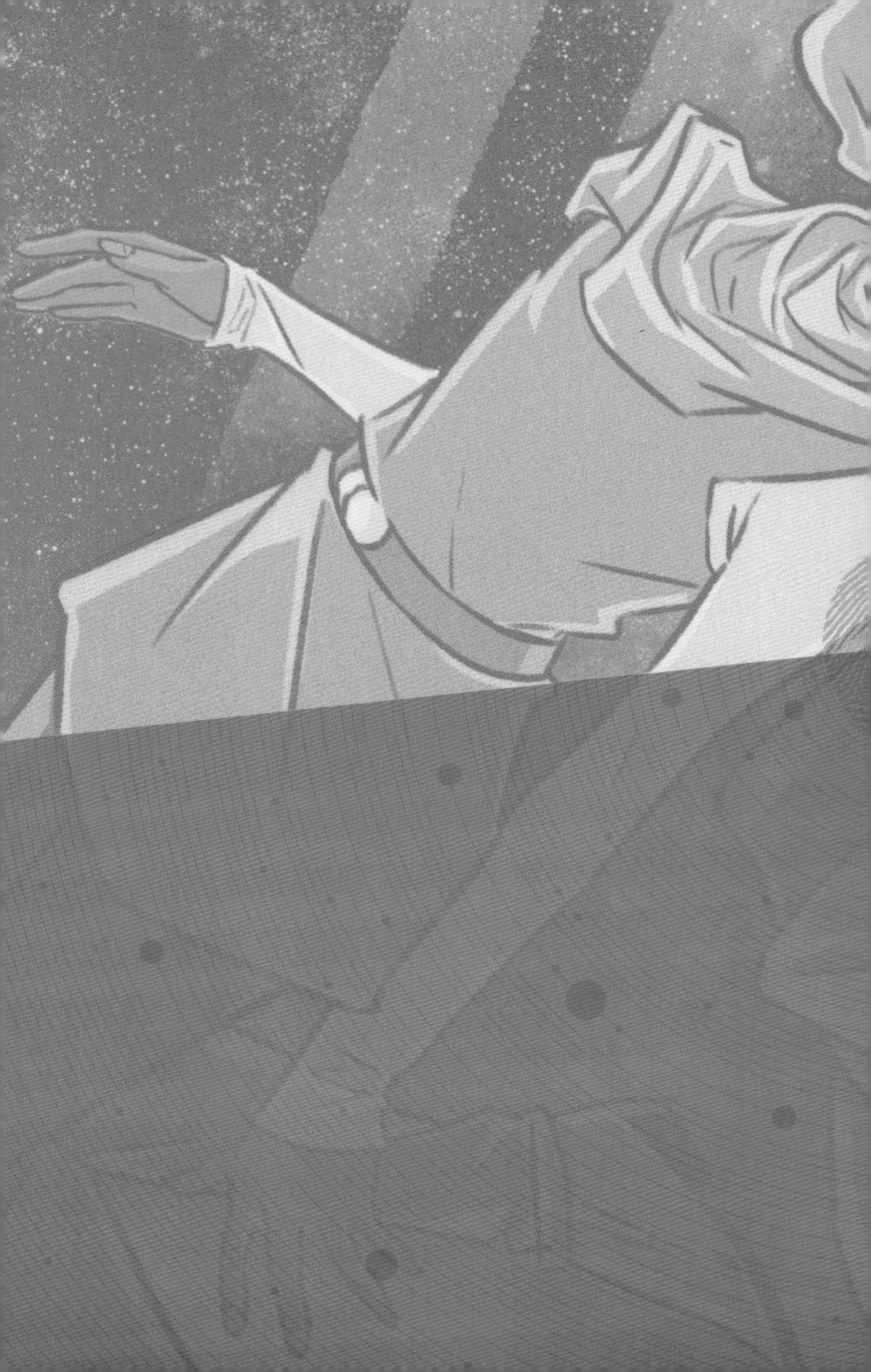

CREATED & WRITTEN BY
RYAN NORTH

ILLUSTRATED BY
**SHELLI PAROLINE
& BRADEN LAMB**

LETTERED BY
JIM CAMPBELL

COVER BY
**SHELLI PAROLINE
& BRADEN LAMB**

DESIGNER **JILLIAN CRAB**

ASSISTANT EDITORS **JASMINE AMIRI
& SOPHIE PHILIPS-ROBERTS**

EDITOR **SHANNON WATTERS**

CHAPTER
ONE

MIRACLES: EVENTS SO RARE, SO UNLIKELY, THAT THE FACT THEY EVEN HAPPENED SEEMS INCREDIBLE. EARTH'S FIRST MIRACLE HAPPENED HERE, MILLIONS YEARS AGO...

...LIFE.

LIFE EVOLVES IN BABY STEPS, PIECE BY PIECE...BUT THIS PROCESS NEEDS TO START SOMEWHERE.

SOMEHOW, AMINO ACIDS MUST MAKE THAT ONE GIANT LEAP FROM LIFELESS CHEMICALS INTO ORGANIC PROTEINS.

PROTEINS THAT CAN COLLECT AND SUSTAIN THEMSELVES, PROTEINS THAT CAN RESPOND TO THEIR ENVIRONMENT, THAT CAN GROW AND CHANGE AND REPRODUCE.

WE DON'T KNOW HOW THIS FIRST LEAP--THIS FIRST MIRACLE--HAPPENED. WE CAN'T MAKE IT HAPPEN AGAIN, EVEN WHEN WE WANT IT TO. BUT LIFE BEGETS LIFE, AND ONCE IT'S THERE, IT TENDS TO STICK AROUND.

THIS WAS THE FIRST MIRACLE ON EARTH.

KRAAACK

THE SECOND MIRACLE HAPPENED LATER. LIKE THE FIRST, WE DON'T KNOW HOW IT HAPPENED, WE DON'T KNOW HOW TO MAKE IT HAPPEN AGAIN, AND WE'RE STILL DEALING WITH THE CONSEQUENCES.

POP

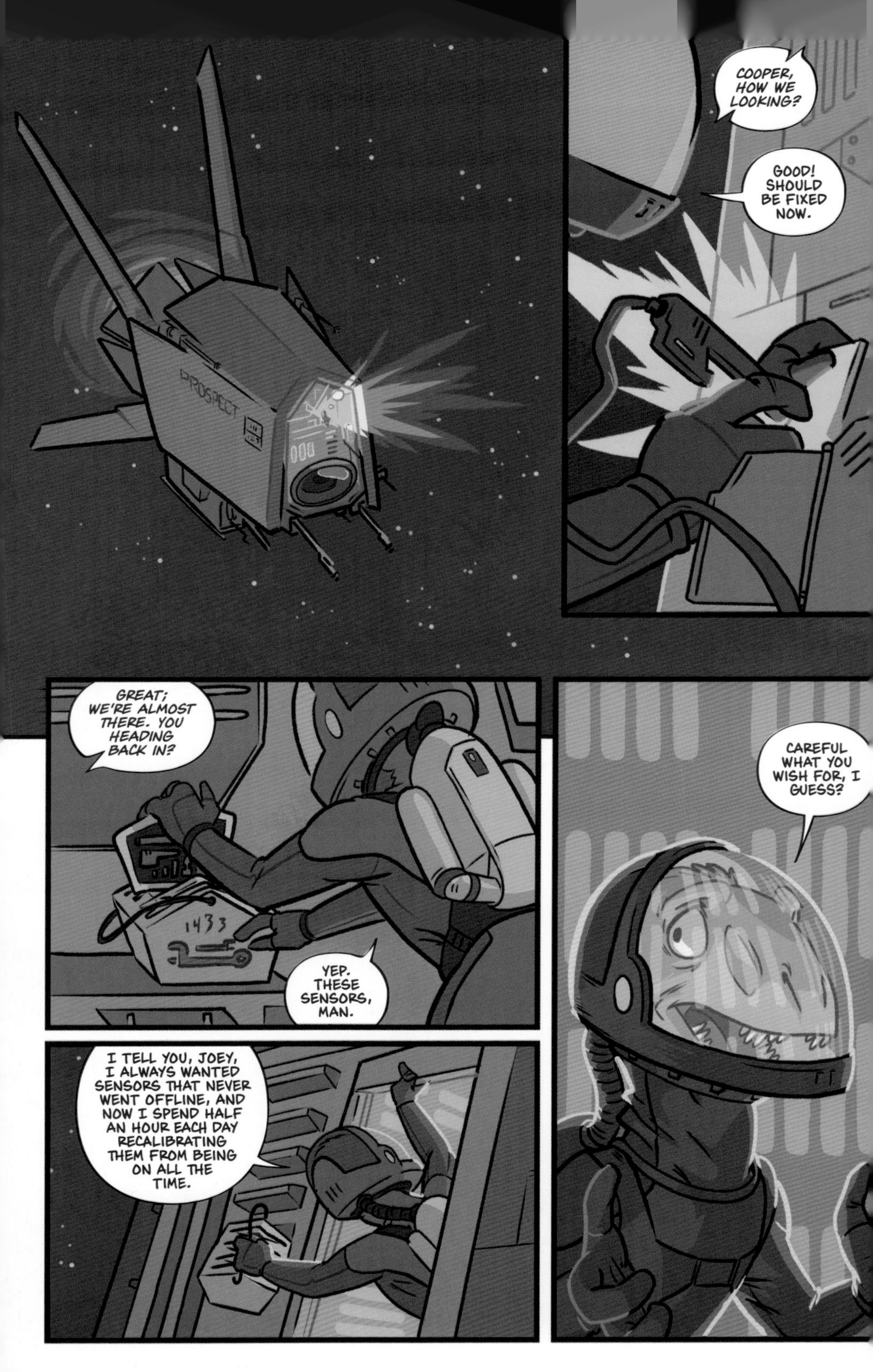
PROSPECT
COOPER, HOW WE LOOKING?
GOOD! SHOULD BE FIXED NOW.
GREAT; WE'RE ALMOST THERE. YOU HEADING BACK IN?
1433
YEP. THESE SENSORS, MAN.
I TELL YOU, JOEY, I ALWAYS WANTED SENSORS THAT NEVER WENT OFFLINE, AND NOW I SPEND HALF AN HOUR EACH DAY RECALIBRATING THEM FROM BEING ON ALL THE TIME.
CAREFUL WHAT YOU WISH FOR, I GUESS?

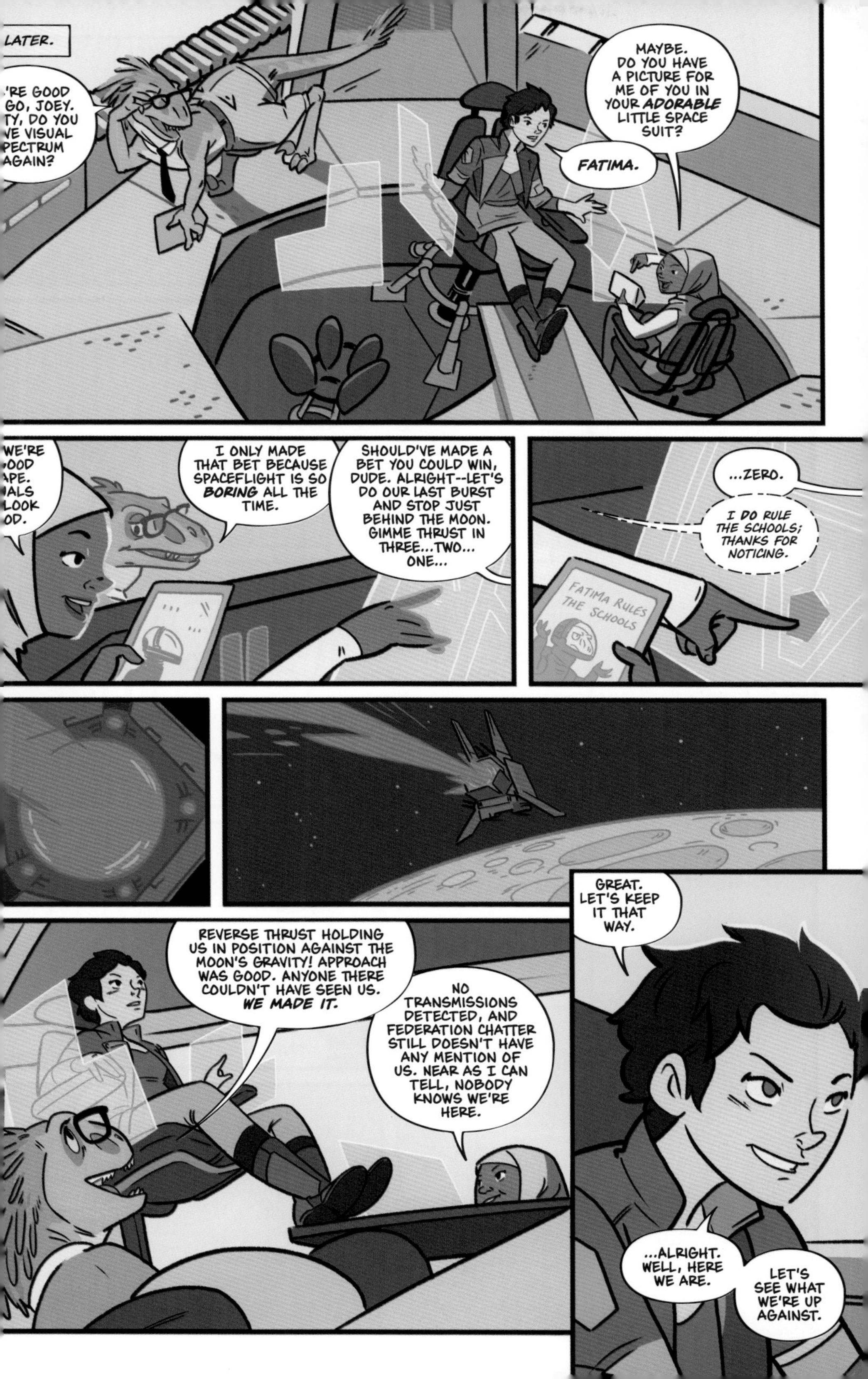

LATER.
'RE GOOD GO, JOEY. TY, DO YOU VE VISUAL PECTRUM AGAIN?
MAYBE. DO YOU HAVE A PICTURE FOR ME OF YOU IN YOUR ADORABLE LITTLE SPACE SUIT?
FATIMA.
WE'RE OOD APE. ALS LOOK OD.
I ONLY MADE THAT BET BECAUSE SPACEFLIGHT IS SO BORING ALL THE TIME.
SHOULD'VE MADE A BET YOU COULD WIN, DUDE. ALRIGHT--LET'S DO OUR LAST BURST AND STOP JUST BEHIND THE MOON. GIMME THRUST IN THREE...TWO... ONE...
...ZERO.
I DO RULE THE SCHOOLS; THANKS FOR NOTICING.
FATIMA RULES THE SCHOOLS
REVERSE THRUST HOLDING US IN POSITION AGAINST THE MOON'S GRAVITY! APPROACH WAS GOOD. ANYONE THERE COULDN'T HAVE SEEN US. WE MADE IT.
NO TRANSMISSIONS DETECTED, AND FEDERATION CHATTER STILL DOESN'T HAVE ANY MENTION OF US. NEAR AS I CAN TELL, NOBODY KNOWS WE'RE HERE.
GREAT. LET'S KEEP IT THAT WAY.
...ALRIGHT. WELL, HERE WE ARE.
LET'S SEE WHAT WE'RE UP AGAINST.

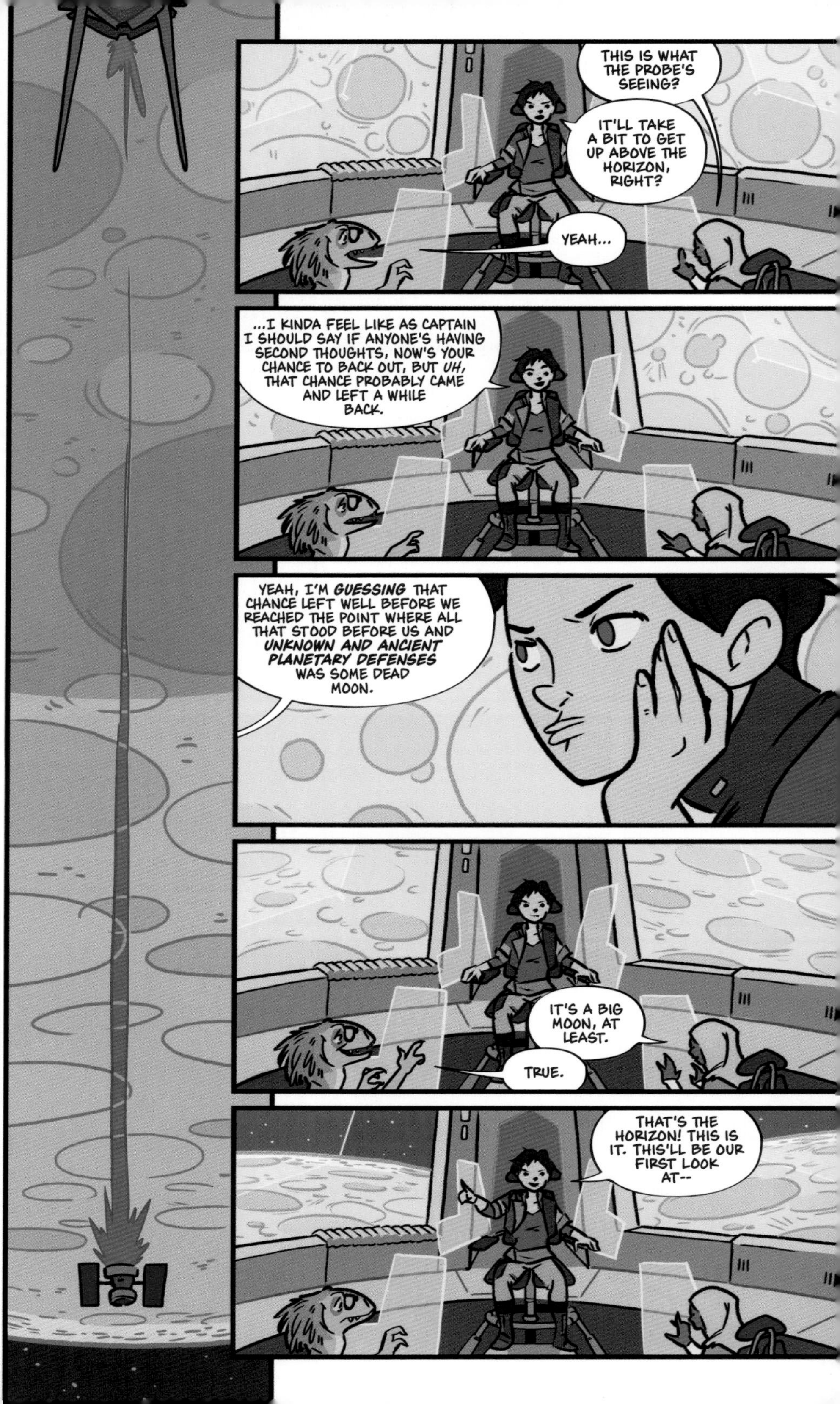
THIS IS WHAT THE PROBE'S SEEING?
IT'LL TAKE A BIT TO GET UP ABOVE THE HORIZON, RIGHT?
YEAH...
...I KINDA FEEL LIKE AS CAPTAIN I SHOULD SAY IF ANYONE'S HAVING SECOND THOUGHTS, NOW'S YOUR CHANCE TO BACK OUT, BUT UH, THAT CHANCE PROBABLY CAME AND LEFT A WHILE BACK.
YEAH, I'M GUESSING THAT CHANCE LEFT WELL BEFORE WE REACHED THE POINT WHERE ALL THAT STOOD BEFORE US AND UNKNOWN AND ANCIENT PLANETARY DEFENSES WAS SOME DEAD MOON.
IT'S A BIG MOON, AT LEAST.
TRUE.
THAT'S THE HORIZON! THIS IS IT. THIS'LL BE OUR FIRST LOOK AT--

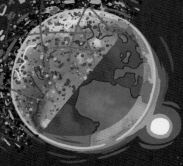

--YOU KNOW, WHATEVER THIS PLANET IS CALLED.

EARTH.

1,693,710 DAYS AFTER THE SECOND MIRACLE.

EARTH.

10 DAYS BEFORE THE SECOND MIRACLE.

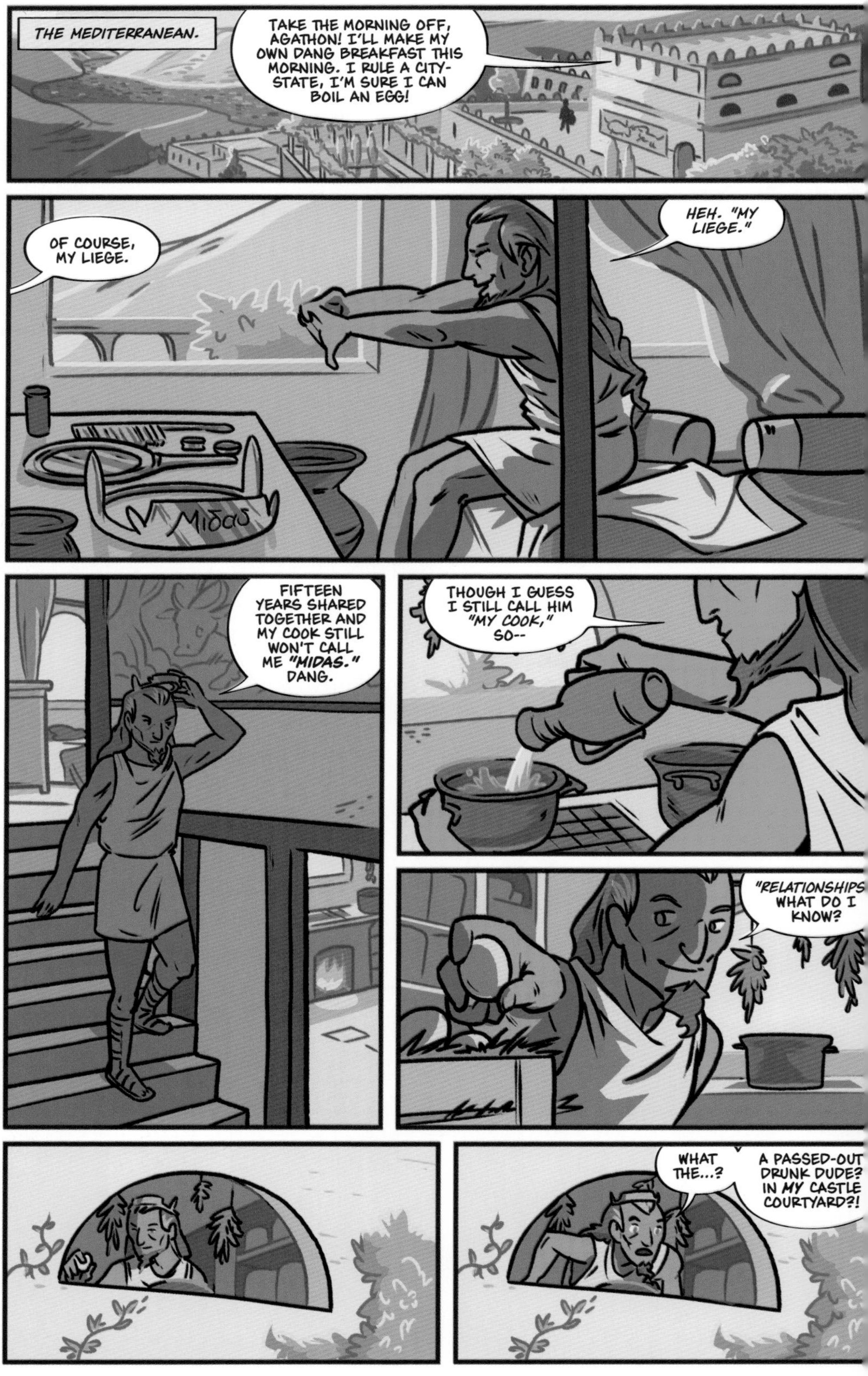
THE MEDITERRANEAN.
TAKE THE MORNING OFF, AGATHON! I'LL MAKE MY OWN DANG BREAKFAST THIS MORNING. I RULE A CITY-STATE, I'M SURE I CAN BOIL AN EGG!
OF COURSE, MY LIEGE.
HEH. "MY LIEGE."
Μιδας
FIFTEEN YEARS SHARED TOGETHER AND MY COOK STILL WON'T CALL ME "MIDAS." DANG.
THOUGH I GUESS I STILL CALL HIM "MY COOK," SO--
"RELATIONSHIPS." WHAT DO I KNOW?
WHAT THE...?
A PASSED-OUT DRUNK DUDE? IN MY CASTLE COURTYARD?!

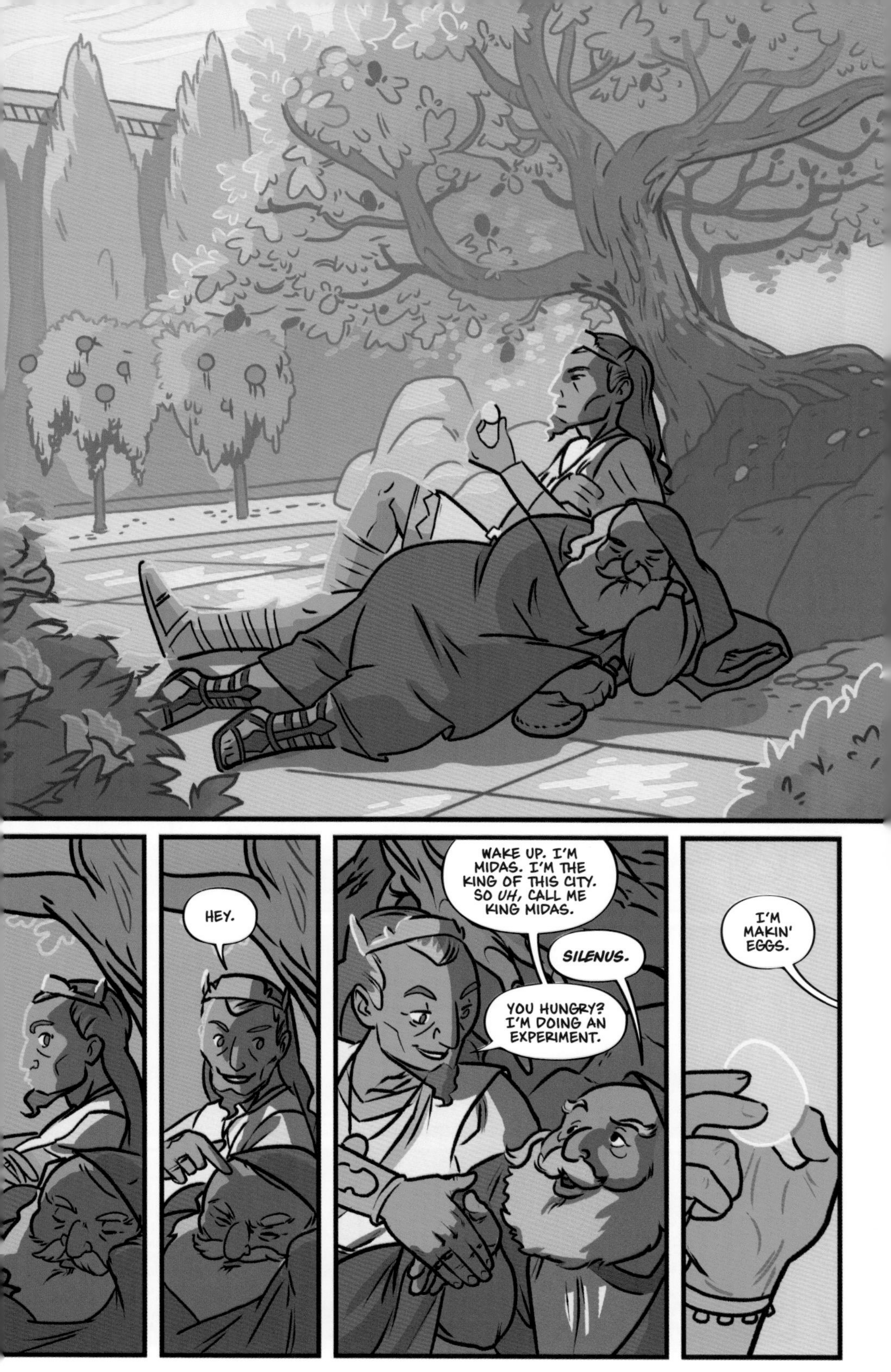
HEY.
WAKE UP. I'M MIDAS. I'M THE KING OF THIS CITY. SO *UH*, CALL ME KING MIDAS.
SILENUS.
YOU HUNGRY? I'M DOING AN EXPERIMENT.
I'M MAKIN' EGGS.

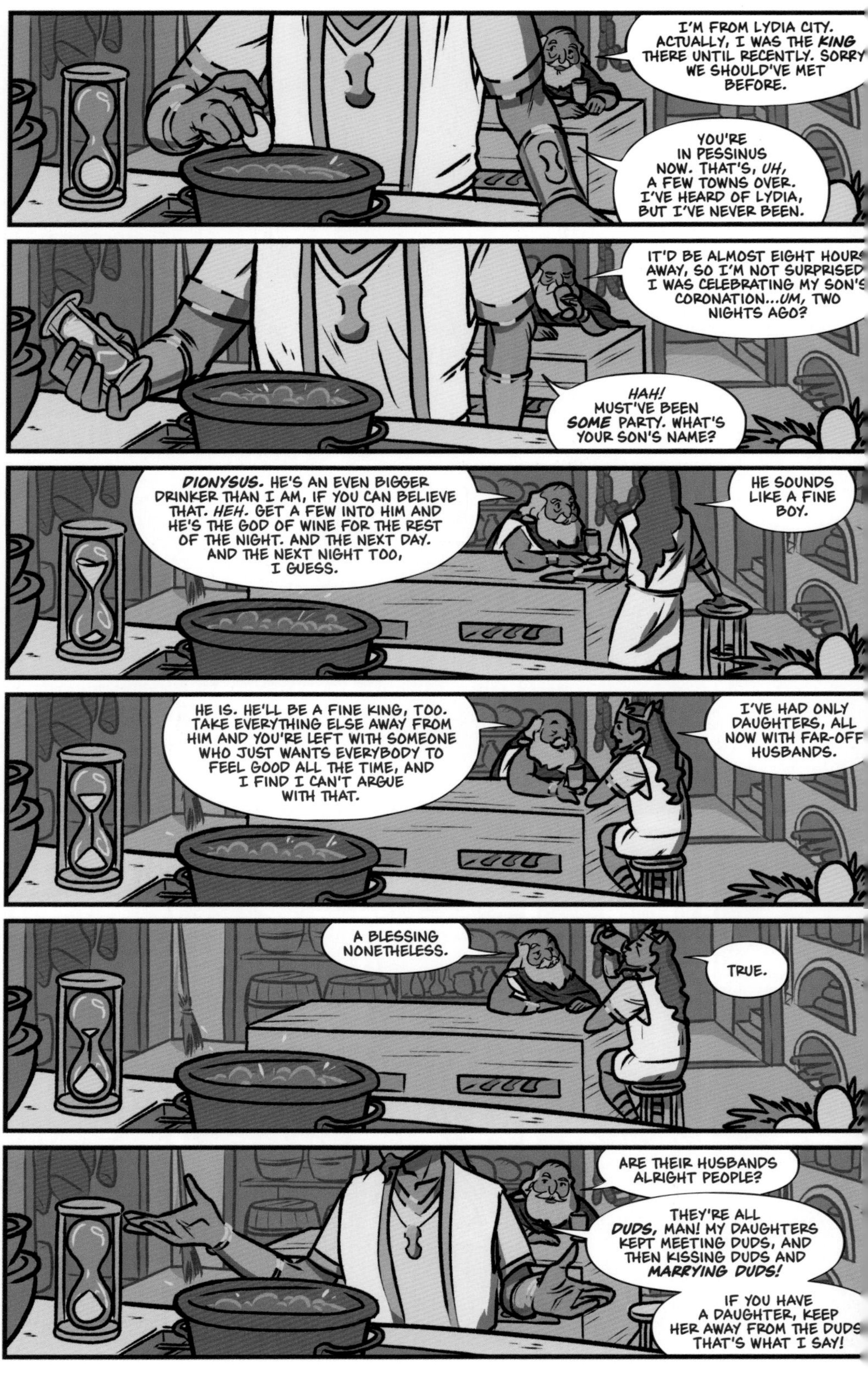
I'M FROM LYDIA CITY. ACTUALLY, I WAS THE *KING* THERE UNTIL RECENTLY. SORRY WE SHOULD'VE MET BEFORE.
YOU'RE IN PESSINUS NOW. THAT'S, *UH*, A FEW TOWNS OVER. I'VE HEARD OF LYDIA, BUT I'VE NEVER BEEN.
IT'D BE ALMOST EIGHT HOURS AWAY, SO I'M NOT SURPRISED. I WAS CELEBRATING MY SON'S CORONATION... *UM*, TWO NIGHTS AGO?
HAH! MUST'VE BEEN **SOME** PARTY. WHAT'S YOUR SON'S NAME?
DIONYSUS. HE'S AN EVEN BIGGER DRINKER THAN I AM, IF YOU CAN BELIEVE THAT. *HEH.* GET A FEW INTO HIM AND HE'S THE GOD OF WINE FOR THE REST OF THE NIGHT. AND THE NEXT DAY. AND THE NEXT NIGHT TOO, I GUESS.
HE SOUNDS LIKE A FINE BOY.
HE IS. HE'LL BE A FINE KING, TOO. TAKE EVERYTHING ELSE AWAY FROM HIM AND YOU'RE LEFT WITH SOMEONE WHO JUST WANTS EVERYBODY TO FEEL GOOD ALL THE TIME, AND I FIND I CAN'T ARGUE WITH THAT.
I'VE HAD ONLY DAUGHTERS, ALL NOW WITH FAR-OFF HUSBANDS.
A BLESSING NONETHELESS.
TRUE.
ARE THEIR HUSBANDS ALRIGHT PEOPLE?
THEY'RE ALL ***DUDS,*** MAN! MY DAUGHTERS KEPT MEETING DUDS, AND THEN KISSING DUDS AND ***MARRYING DUDS!***
IF YOU HAVE A DAUGHTER, KEEP HER AWAY FROM THE DUDS. THAT'S WHAT I SAY!

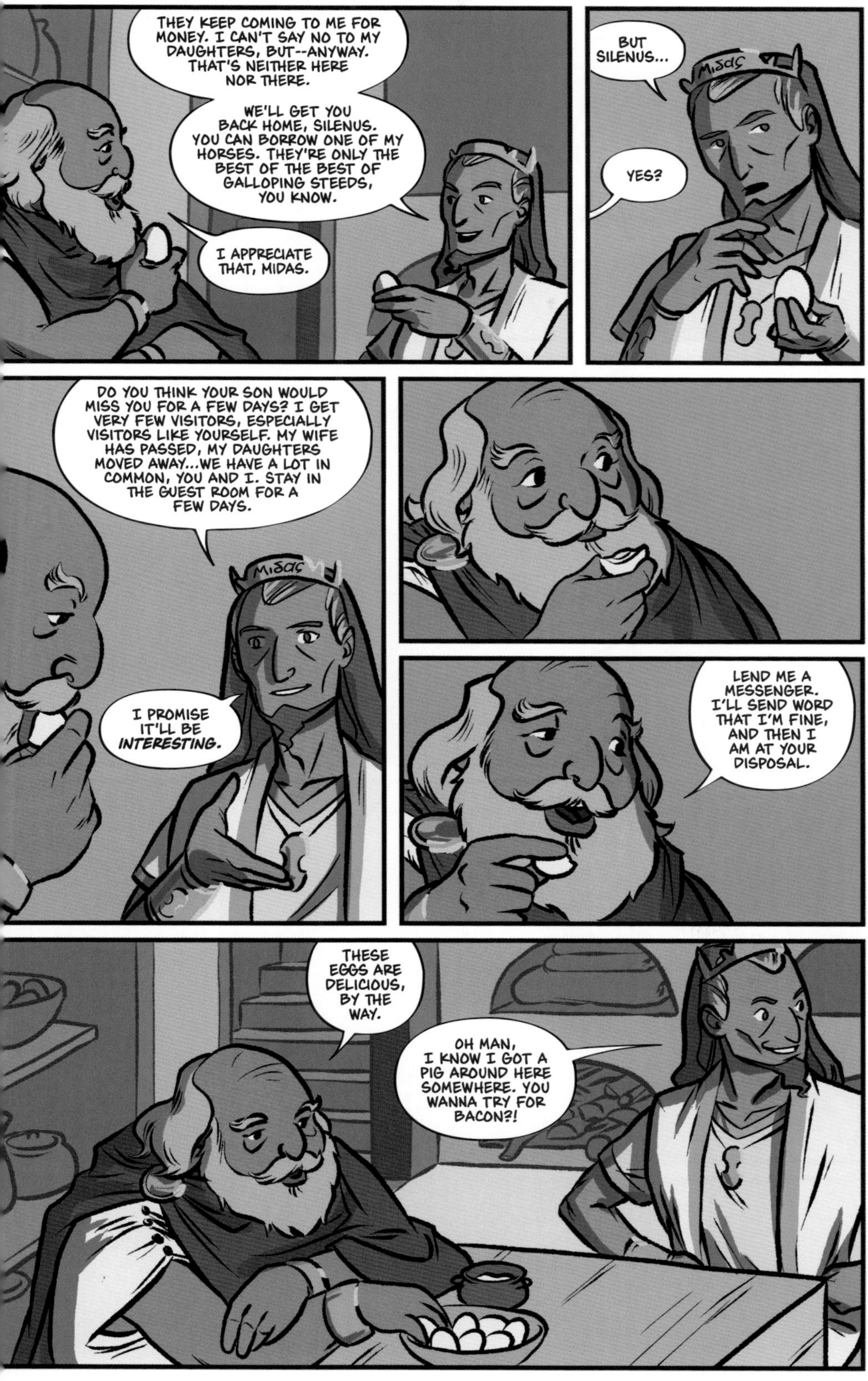
THEY KEEP COMING TO ME FOR MONEY. I CAN'T SAY NO TO MY DAUGHTERS, BUT--ANYWAY. THAT'S NEITHER HERE NOR THERE.
WE'LL GET YOU BACK HOME, SILENUS. YOU CAN BORROW ONE OF MY HORSES. THEY'RE ONLY THE BEST OF THE BEST OF GALLOPING STEEDS, YOU KNOW.
I APPRECIATE THAT, MIDAS.
BUT SILENUS...
Μιδας
YES?
DO YOU THINK YOUR SON WOULD MISS YOU FOR A FEW DAYS? I GET VERY FEW VISITORS, ESPECIALLY VISITORS LIKE YOURSELF. MY WIFE HAS PASSED, MY DAUGHTERS MOVED AWAY...WE HAVE A LOT IN COMMON, YOU AND I. STAY IN THE GUEST ROOM FOR A FEW DAYS.
Μιδας
I PROMISE IT'LL BE *INTERESTING*.
LEND ME A MESSENGER. I'LL SEND WORD THAT I'M FINE, AND THEN I AM AT YOUR DISPOSAL.
THESE EGGS ARE DELICIOUS, BY THE WAY.
OH MAN, I KNOW I GOT A PIG AROUND HERE SOMEWHERE. YOU WANNA TRY FOR BACON?!

NOW.

OKAY, IT'S JUST LIKE WE THOUGHT. I'VE NEVER SEEN SATELLITES LIKE THIS BEFORE, BUT IT'S OBVIOUSLY *FEDERATION TECHNOLOGY*, AND FROM THE LOOKS OF IT, SO ANCIENT IT SHOULD BE IN A MUSEUM.

AND *THAT* MEANS WE CAN REASONABLY EXPECT US TO SURVIVE AN ENGAGEMENT WITH IT, GIVEN ALL THE MONEY WE PUT INTO THIS SHIP'S DEFENSE. AGREED?

I WISH THE FEDERATION WAS STILL USING STUFF LIKE THIS. PEOPLE LIKE US MIGHT'VE HAD A CHANCE, YOU KNOW? MAYBE THE *DOMINATION WARS* COULD'VE BEEN AVOIDED.

OR WON.

WELL...I MEAN, THAT'S *KINDA* WHAT WE'RE HERE TO DO. WE'RE READY. ARE WE READY?

WE'RE READY.

YEAH WE ARE.

TAKE US IN, FATTY.

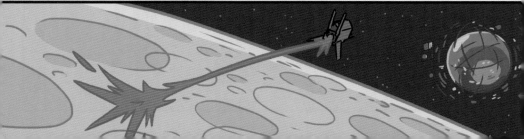

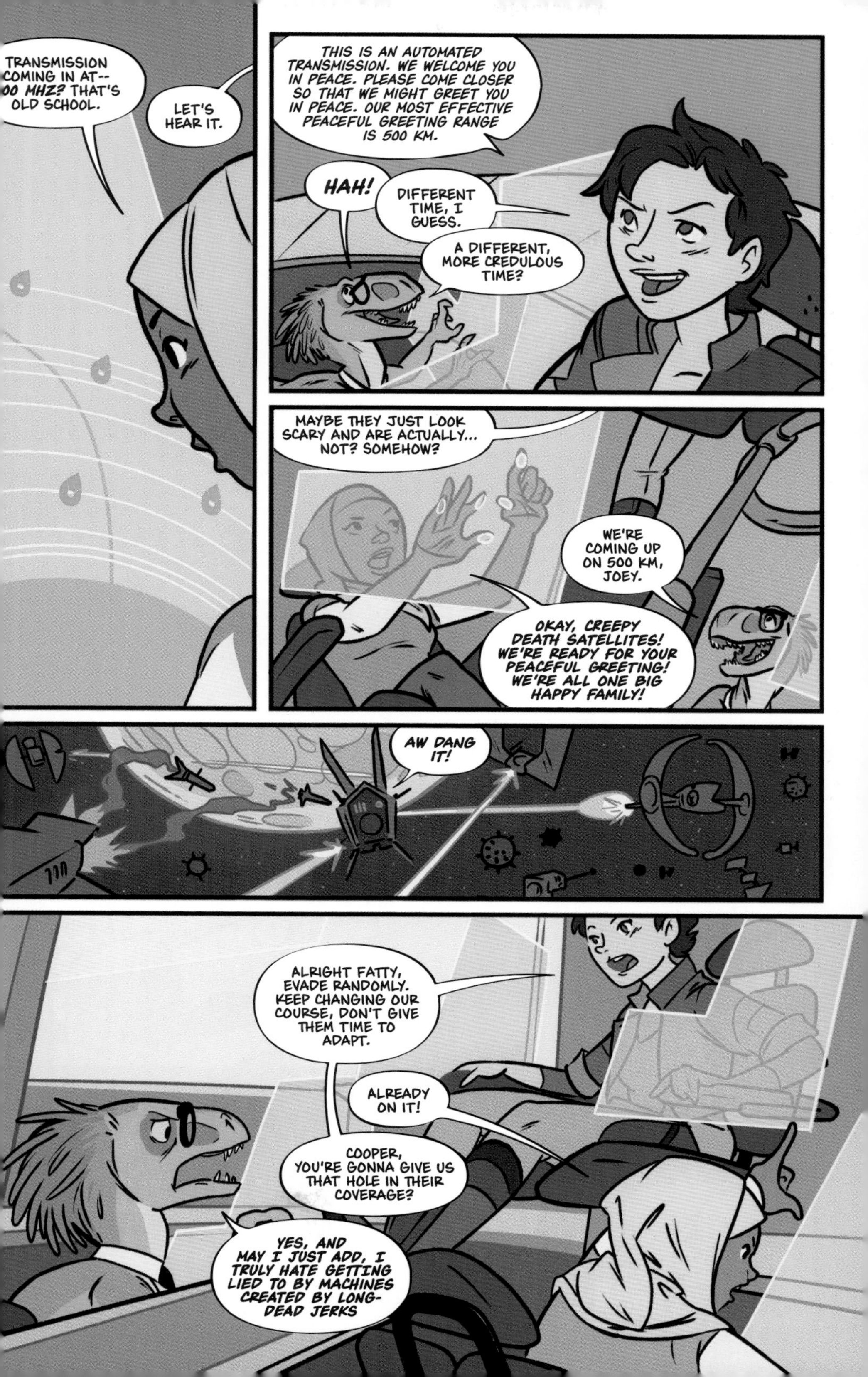
TRANSMISSION COMING IN AT-- 00 MHZ? THAT'S OLD SCHOOL.
LET'S HEAR IT.
THIS IS AN AUTOMATED TRANSMISSION. WE WELCOME YOU IN PEACE. PLEASE COME CLOSER SO THAT WE MIGHT GREET YOU IN PEACE. OUR MOST EFFECTIVE PEACEFUL GREETING RANGE IS 500 KM.
HAH!
DIFFERENT TIME, I GUESS.
A DIFFERENT, MORE CREDULOUS TIME?
MAYBE THEY JUST LOOK SCARY AND ARE ACTUALLY... NOT? SOMEHOW?
WE'RE COMING UP ON 500 KM, JOEY.
OKAY, CREEPY DEATH SATELLITES! WE'RE READY FOR YOUR PEACEFUL GREETING! WE'RE ALL ONE BIG HAPPY FAMILY!
AW DANG IT!
ALRIGHT FATTY, EVADE RANDOMLY. KEEP CHANGING OUR COURSE, DON'T GIVE THEM TIME TO ADAPT.
ALREADY ON IT!
COOPER, YOU'RE GONNA GIVE US THAT HOLE IN THEIR COVERAGE?
YES, AND MAY I JUST ADD, I TRULY HATE GETTING LIED TO BY MACHINES CREATED BY LONG-DEAD JERKS

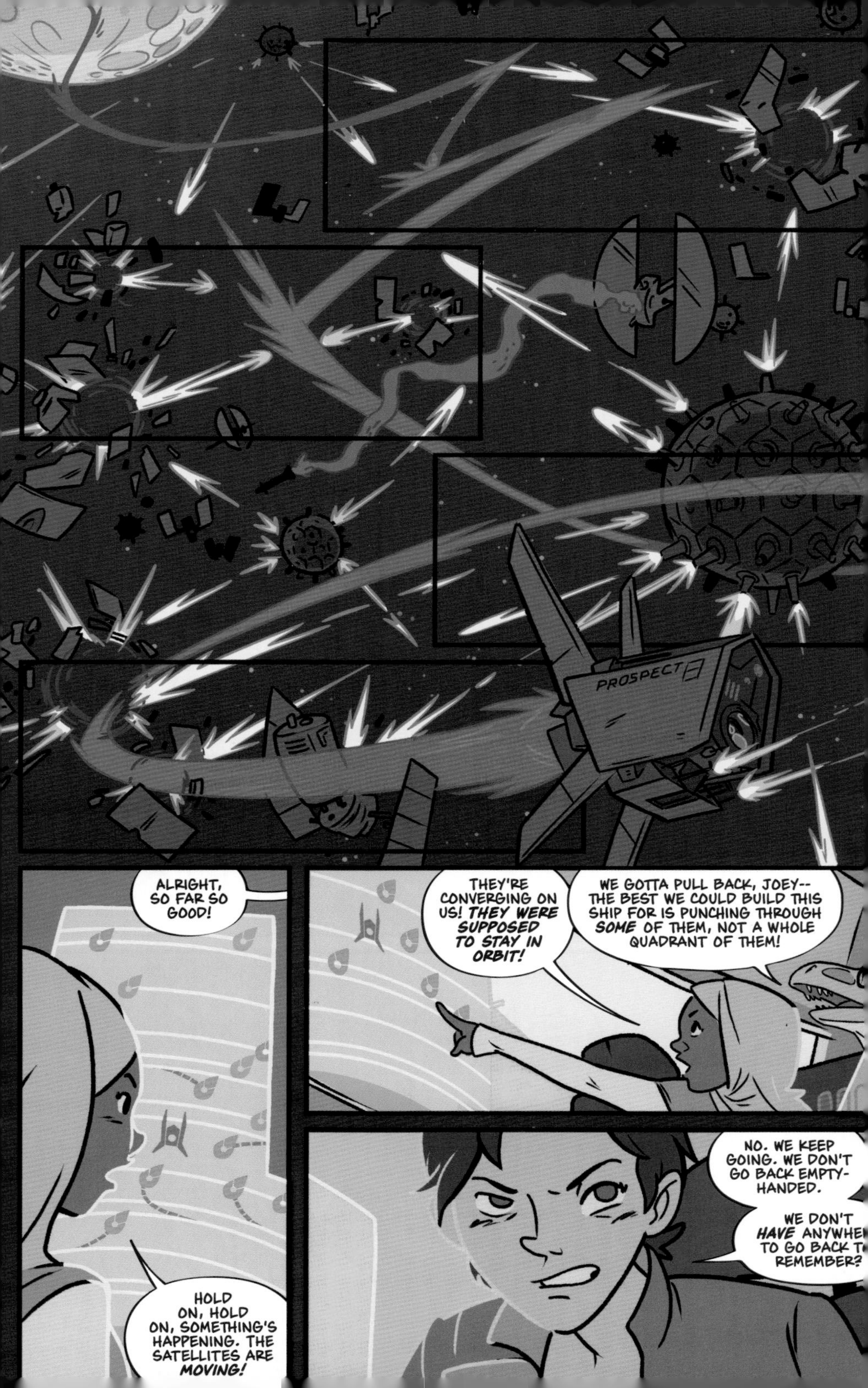
PROSPECT
ALRIGHT, SO FAR SO GOOD!
HOLD ON, HOLD ON, SOMETHING'S HAPPENING. THE SATELLITES ARE MOVING!
THEY'RE CONVERGING ON US! THEY WERE SUPPOSED TO STAY IN ORBIT!
WE GOTTA PULL BACK, JOEY-- THE BEST WE COULD BUILD THIS SHIP FOR IS PUNCHING THROUGH SOME OF THEM, NOT A WHOLE QUADRANT OF THEM!
NO. WE KEEP GOING. WE DON'T GO BACK EMPTY-HANDED.
WE DON'T HAVE ANYWHE TO GO BACK T REMEMBER?

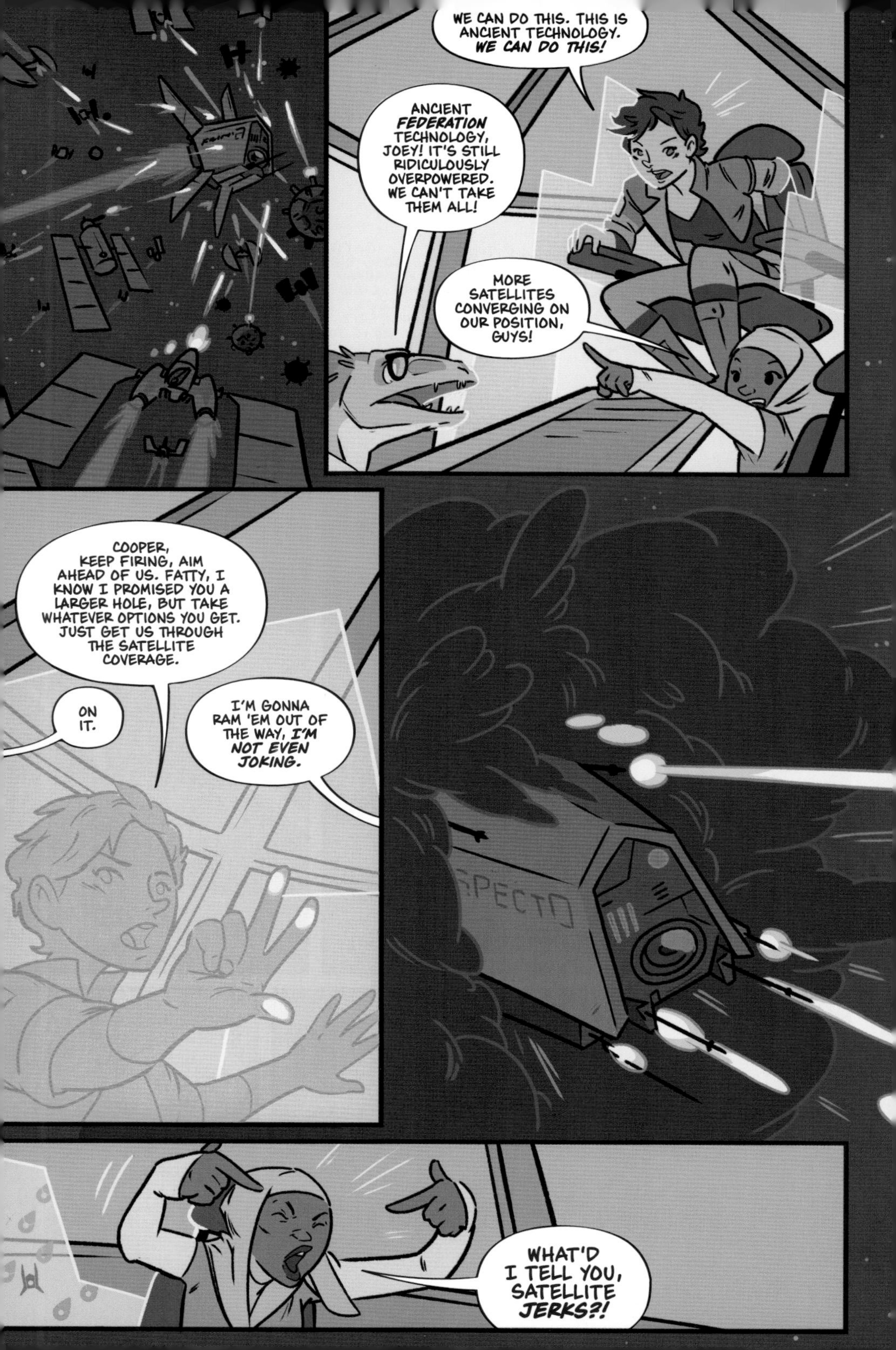
WE CAN DO THIS. THIS IS ANCIENT TECHNOLOGY. *WE CAN DO THIS!*
ANCIENT ***FEDERATION*** TECHNOLOGY, JOEY! IT'S STILL RIDICULOUSLY OVERPOWERED. WE CAN'T TAKE THEM ALL!
MORE SATELLITES CONVERGING ON OUR POSITION, GUYS!
COOPER, KEEP FIRING, AIM AHEAD OF US. FATTY, I KNOW I PROMISED YOU A LARGER HOLE, BUT TAKE WHATEVER OPTIONS YOU GET. JUST GET US THROUGH THE SATELLITE COVERAGE.
ON IT.
I'M GONNA RAM 'EM OUT OF THE WAY, ***I'M NOT EVEN JOKING.***
SPECTO
WHAT'D I TELL YOU, SATELLITE ***JERKS?!***

COOPER, THESE SATELLITES HAVE BEEN PREDICTING OUR MOVEMENT OUT. YOU AGREE?

I DO, FATTY.

SO HERE'S HOW WE'RE GONNA PLAY THIS...

YOU FIRE ALONG THE LINE I'VE MARKED. I MOVE US IN THE SAME DIRECTION, TOWARDS ANY SATELLITES WE'VE JUST TAKEN OUT.

OTHER SATS MOVE TO INTERCEPT. THIS OPENS A HOLE BENEATH 'EM BIG ENOUGH FOR US TO SLIP THROUGH: WE WAIT 'TIL THE LAST SECOND, AND--

--BAM! WE DIVE!

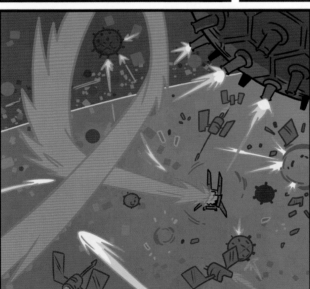

AND THAT'S HOW WE DO IT. PEACE.

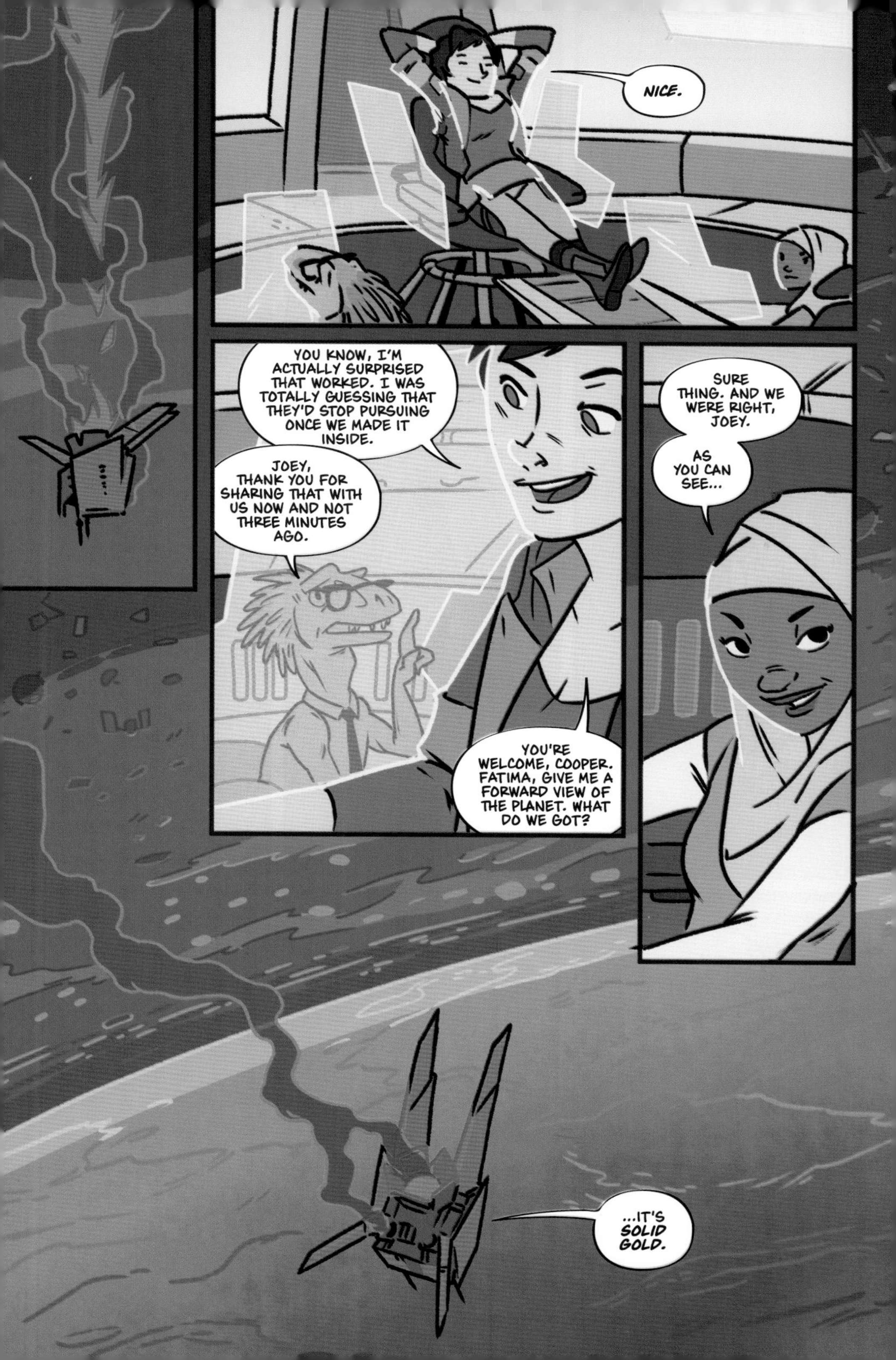
NICE.
YOU KNOW, I'M ACTUALLY SURPRISED THAT WORKED. I WAS TOTALLY GUESSING THAT THEY'D STOP PURSUING ONCE WE MADE IT INSIDE.
JOEY, THANK YOU FOR SHARING THAT WITH US NOW AND NOT THREE MINUTES AGO.
YOU'RE WELCOME, COOPER. FATIMA, GIVE ME A FORWARD VIEW OF THE PLANET. WHAT DO WE GOT?
SURE THING. AND WE WERE RIGHT, JOEY.
AS YOU CAN SEE...
...IT'S SOLID GOLD.

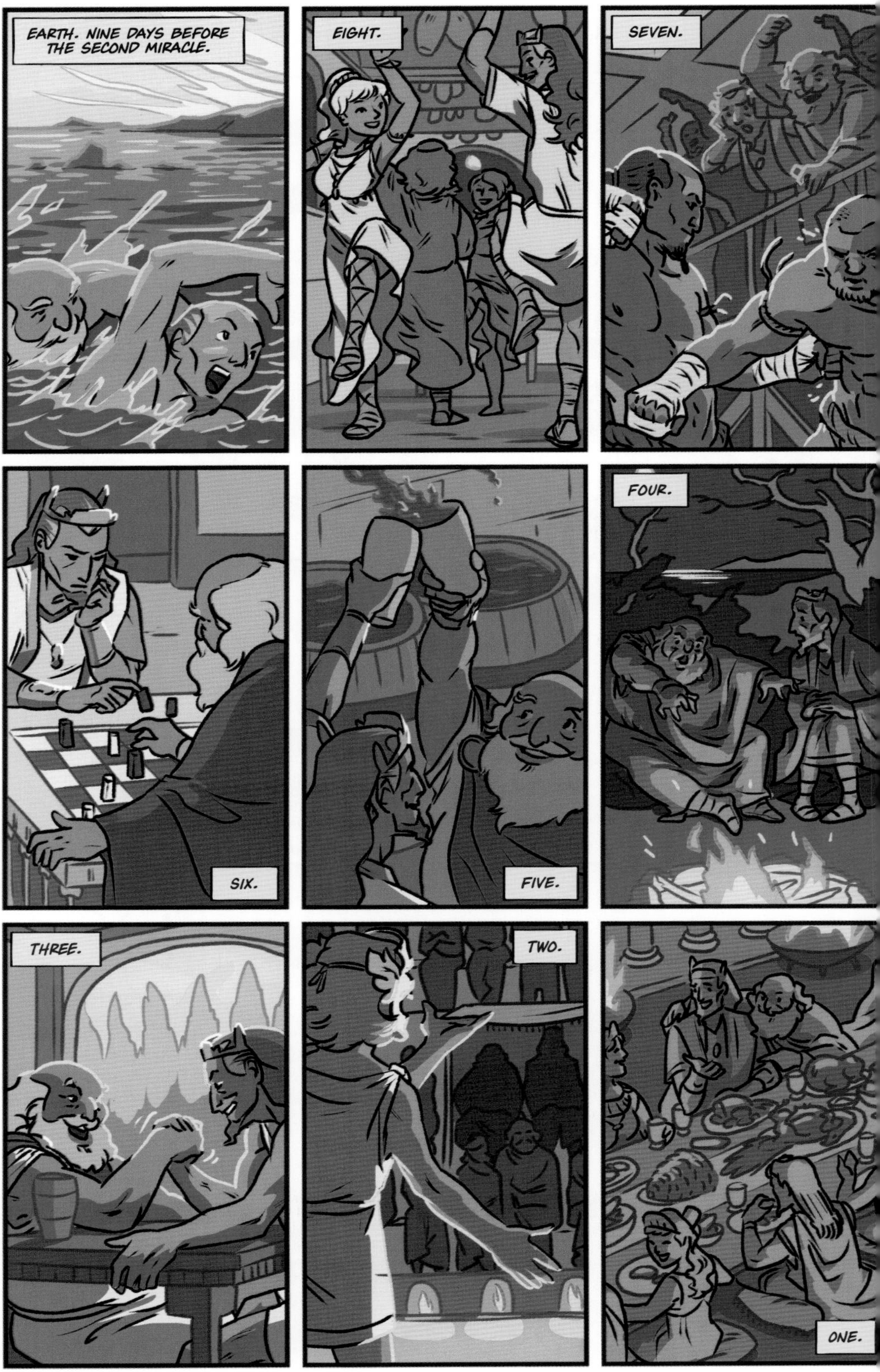
EARTH. NINE DAYS BEFORE THE SECOND MIRACLE.
EIGHT.
SEVEN.
SIX.
FIVE.
FOUR.
THREE.
TWO.
ONE.

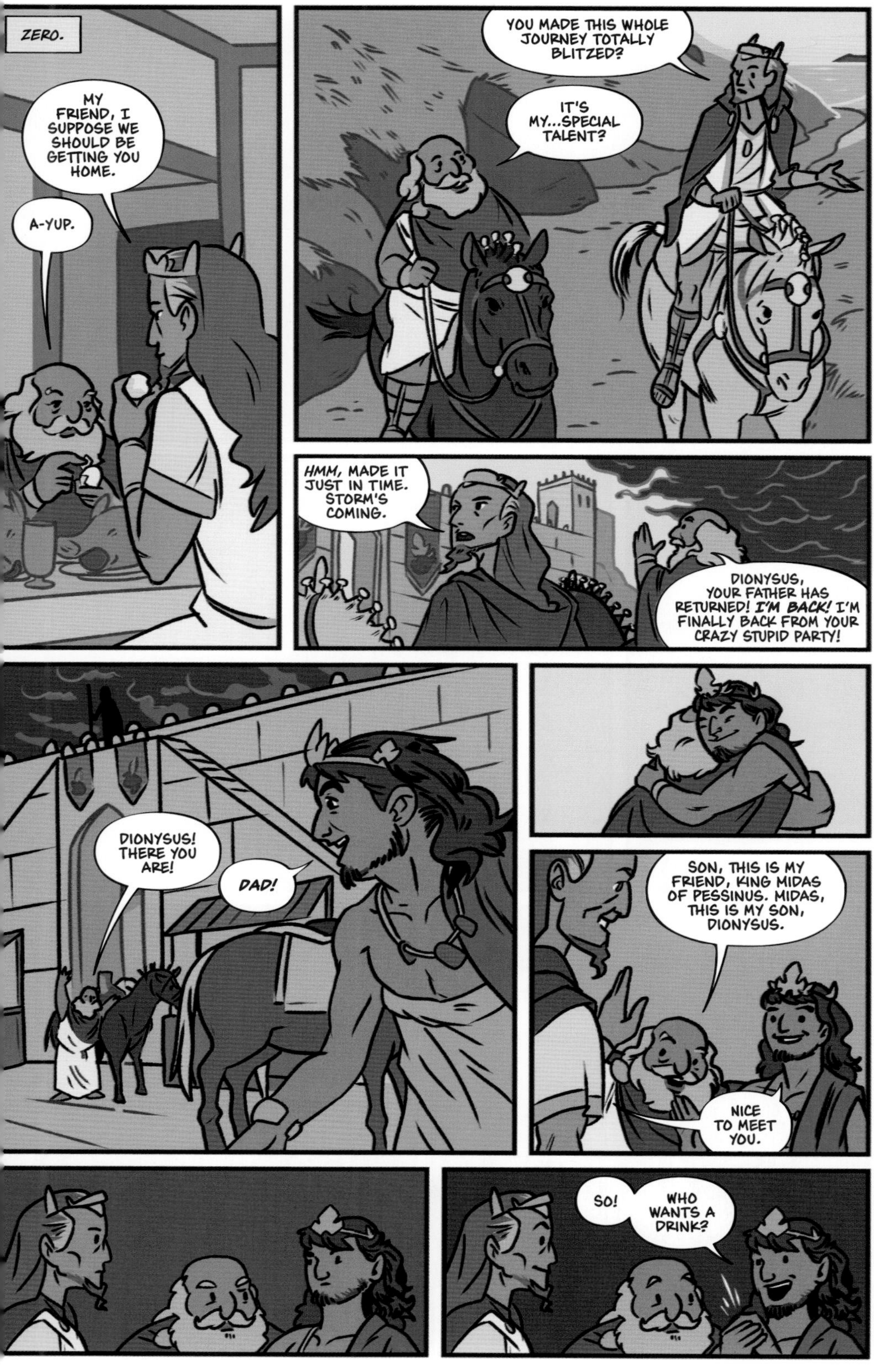
ZERO.
MY FRIEND, I SUPPOSE WE SHOULD BE GETTING YOU HOME.
A-YUP.
YOU MADE THIS WHOLE JOURNEY TOTALLY BLITZED?
IT'S MY...SPECIAL TALENT?
HMM, MADE IT JUST IN TIME. STORM'S COMING.
DIONYSUS, YOUR FATHER HAS RETURNED! I'M BACK! I'M FINALLY BACK FROM YOUR CRAZY STUPID PARTY!
DIONYSUS! THERE YOU ARE!
DAD!
SON, THIS IS MY FRIEND, KING MIDAS OF PESSINUS. MIDAS, THIS IS MY SON, DIONYSUS.
NICE TO MEET YOU.
SO!
WHO WANTS A DRINK?

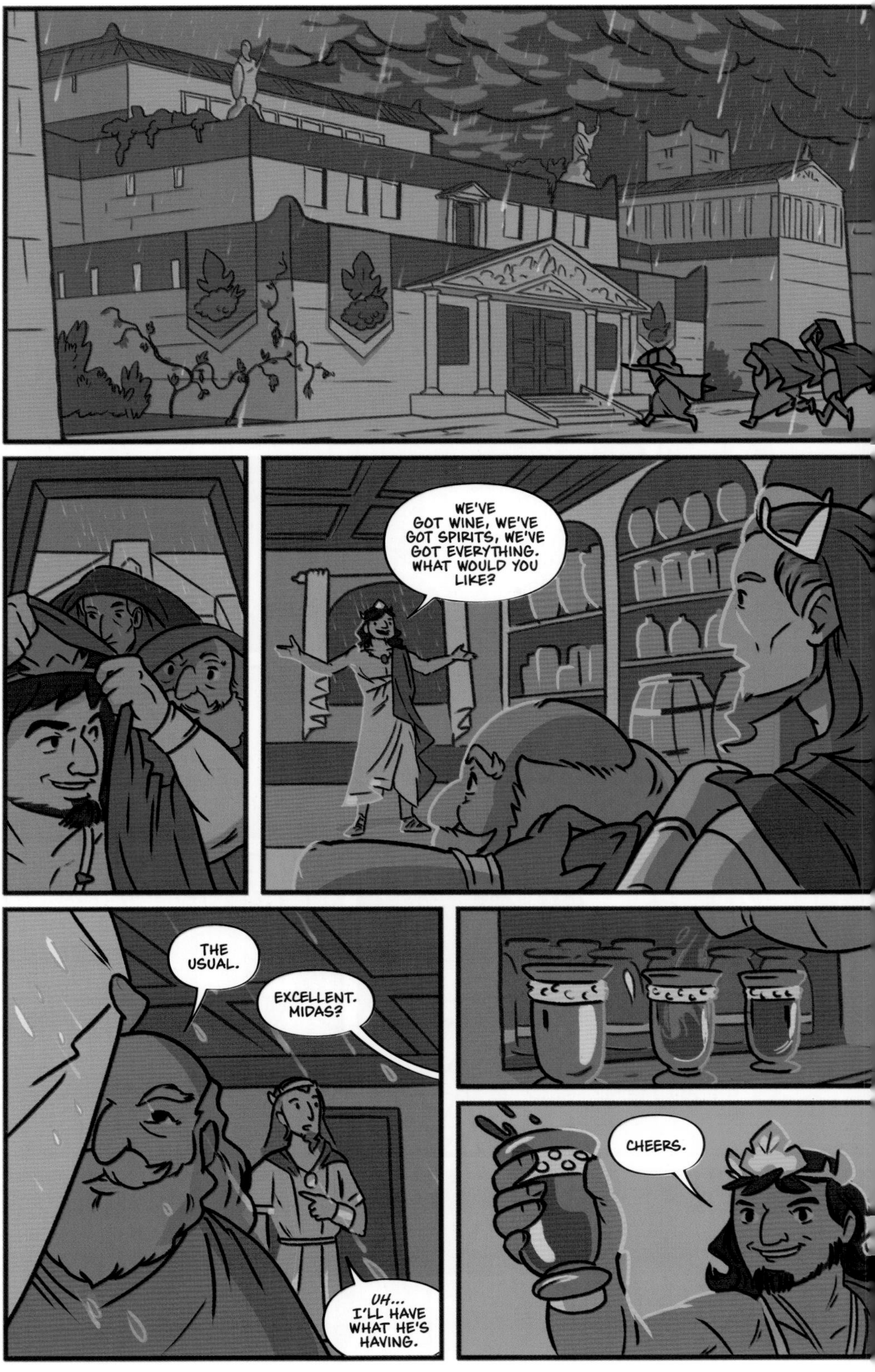
WE'VE GOT WINE, WE'VE GOT SPIRITS, WE'VE GOT EVERYTHING. WHAT WOULD YOU LIKE?
THE USUAL.
EXCELLENT. MIDAS?
UH... I'LL HAVE WHAT HE'S HAVING.
CHEERS.

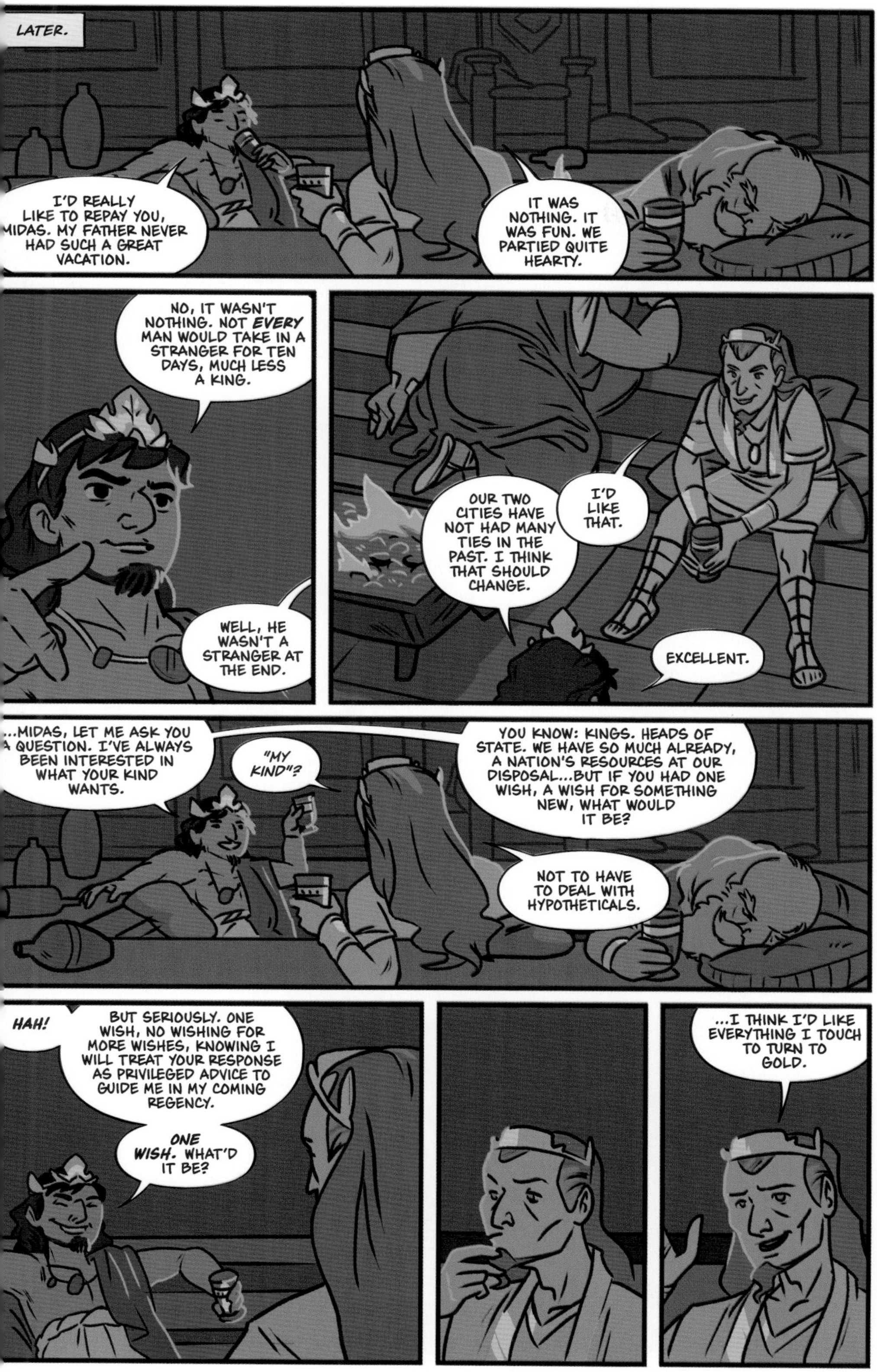

LATER.
I'D REALLY LIKE TO REPAY YOU, MIDAS. MY FATHER NEVER HAD SUCH A GREAT VACATION.
IT WAS NOTHING. IT WAS FUN. WE PARTIED QUITE HEARTY.
NO, IT WASN'T NOTHING. NOT *EVERY* MAN WOULD TAKE IN A STRANGER FOR TEN DAYS, MUCH LESS A KING.
WELL, HE WASN'T A STRANGER AT THE END.
OUR TWO CITIES HAVE NOT HAD MANY TIES IN THE PAST. I THINK THAT SHOULD CHANGE.
I'D LIKE THAT.
EXCELLENT.
...MIDAS, LET ME ASK YOU A QUESTION. I'VE ALWAYS BEEN INTERESTED IN WHAT YOUR KIND WANTS.
"MY KIND"?
YOU KNOW: KINGS. HEADS OF STATE. WE HAVE SO MUCH ALREADY, A NATION'S RESOURCES AT OUR DISPOSAL...BUT IF YOU HAD ONE WISH, A WISH FOR SOMETHING NEW, WHAT WOULD IT BE?
NOT TO HAVE TO DEAL WITH HYPOTHETICALS.
HAH!
BUT SERIOUSLY. ONE WISH, NO WISHING FOR MORE WISHES, KNOWING I WILL TREAT YOUR RESPONSE AS PRIVILEGED ADVICE TO GUIDE ME IN MY COMING REGENCY.
ONE WISH. WHAT'D IT BE?
...I THINK I'D LIKE EVERYTHING I TOUCH TO TURN TO GOLD.

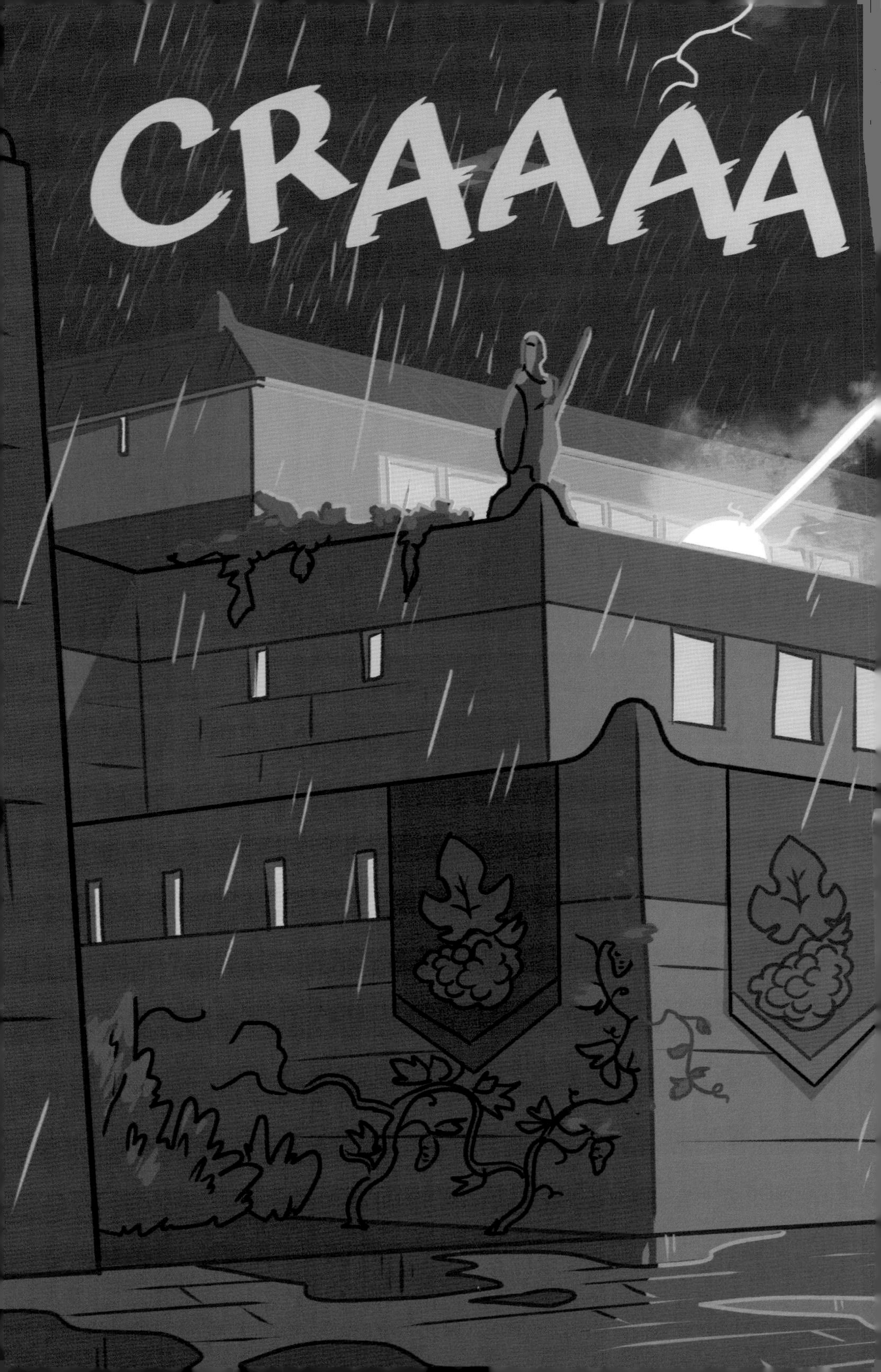
CRAAAA

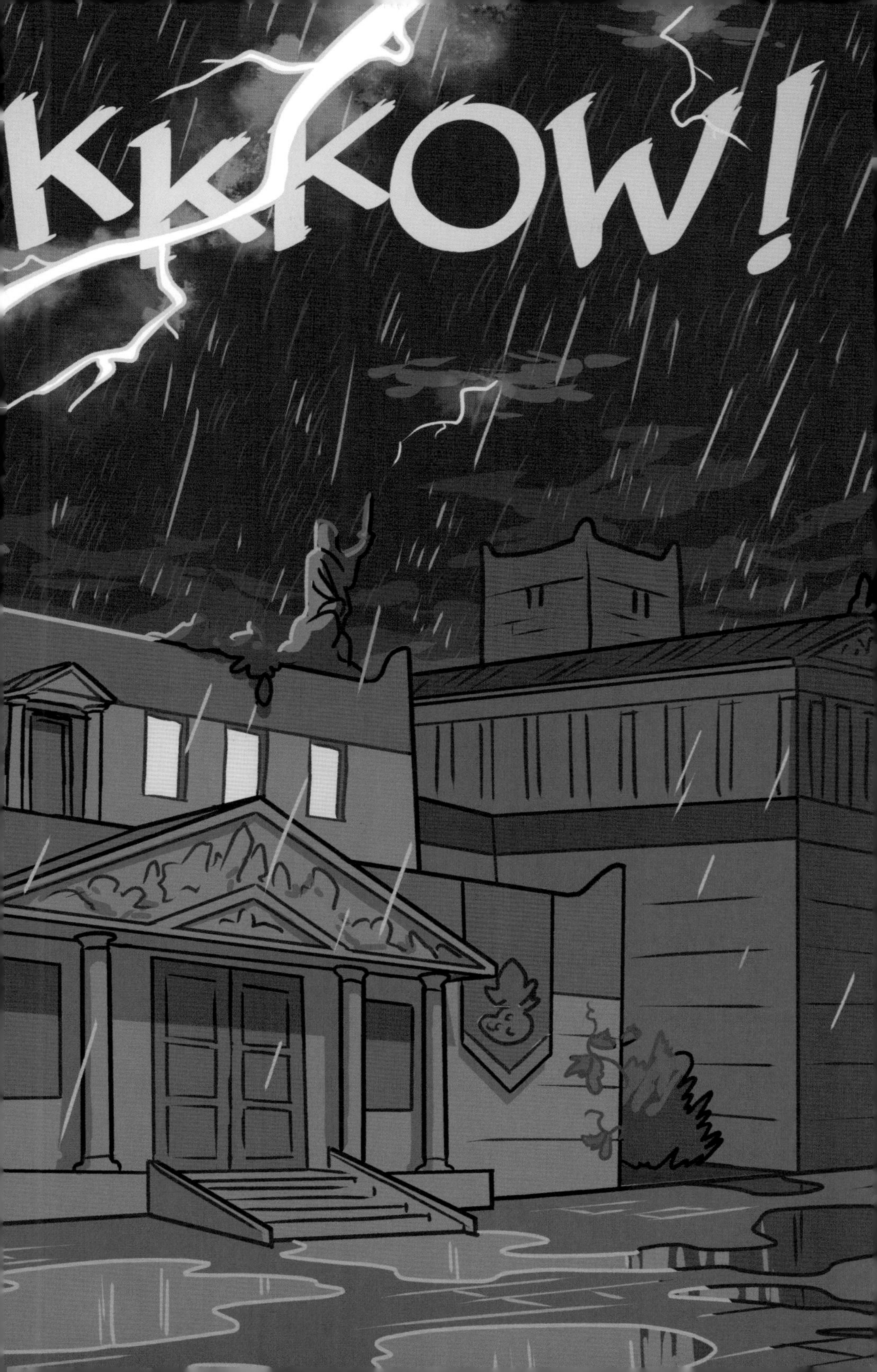
KKKOW!

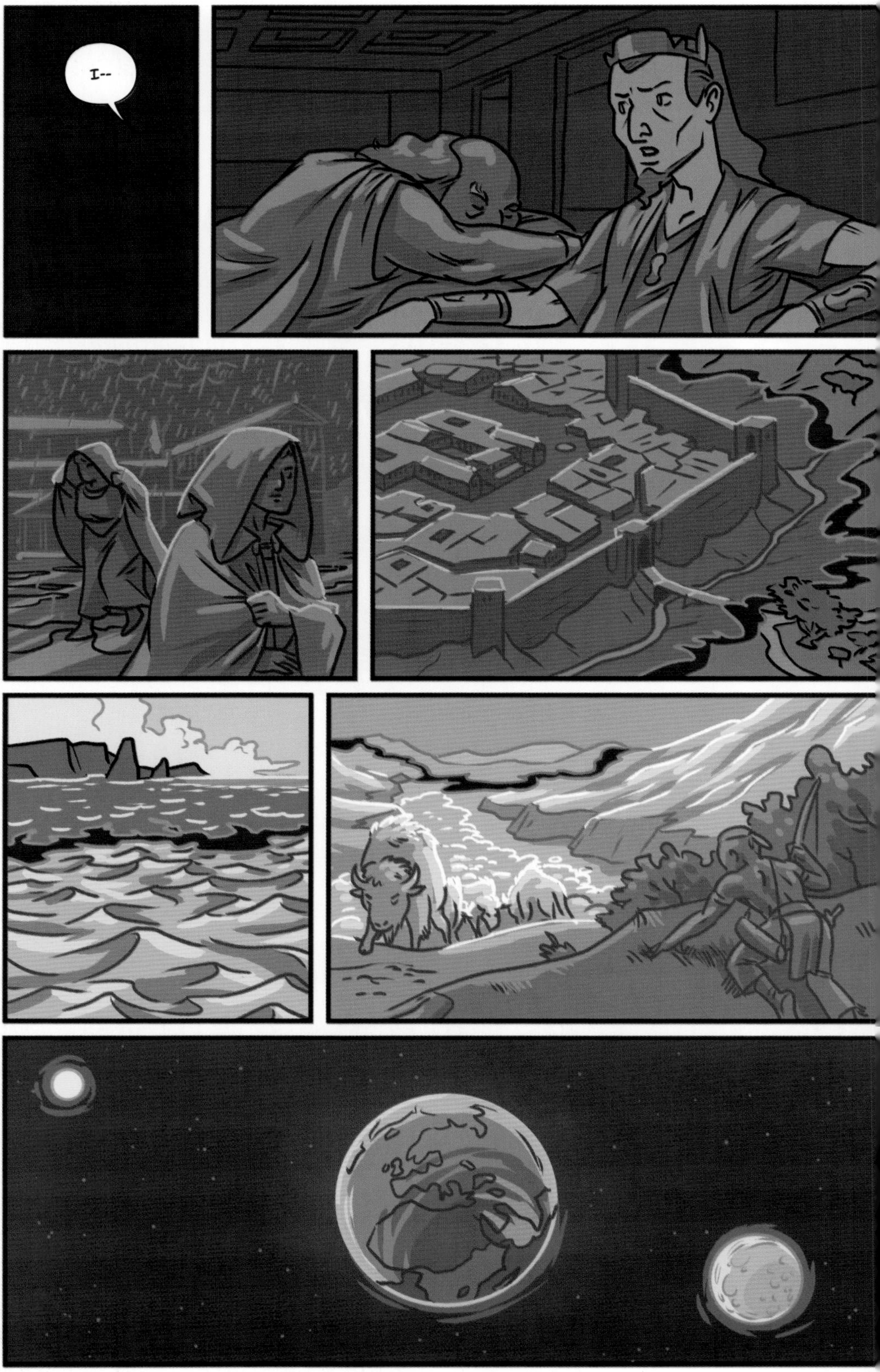
I--

THE SECOND MIRACLE: MIDAS'S WISH CAME TRUE. EVERYTHING HE TOUCHED TURNED TO GOLD.

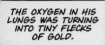

AHGHH...

IF HE WAS IN CONTACT WITH IT, IT WAS GOLD. IF HE WAS IN CONTACT WITH SOMETHING ELSE THAT WAS IN CONTACT WITH IT, IT WAS GOLD.

AS HIS PLANET DIED ABOUT HIM, MIDAS EXPERIENCED THE TERRIBLE SENSATION OF DROWNING ON DRY LAND.

THE OXYGEN IN HIS LUNGS WAS TURNING INTO TINY FLECKS OF GOLD.

AIR TOUCHING THE SURFACE OF THE PLANET CONTINUED TO TRANSMUTE. IN A FEW HOURS, EVERYTHING ON THE SURFACE WILL BE COVERED WITH A FINE LAYER OF GOLD ASH.

IT WILL BE ALL THAT REMAINS OF THE ATMOSPHERE.

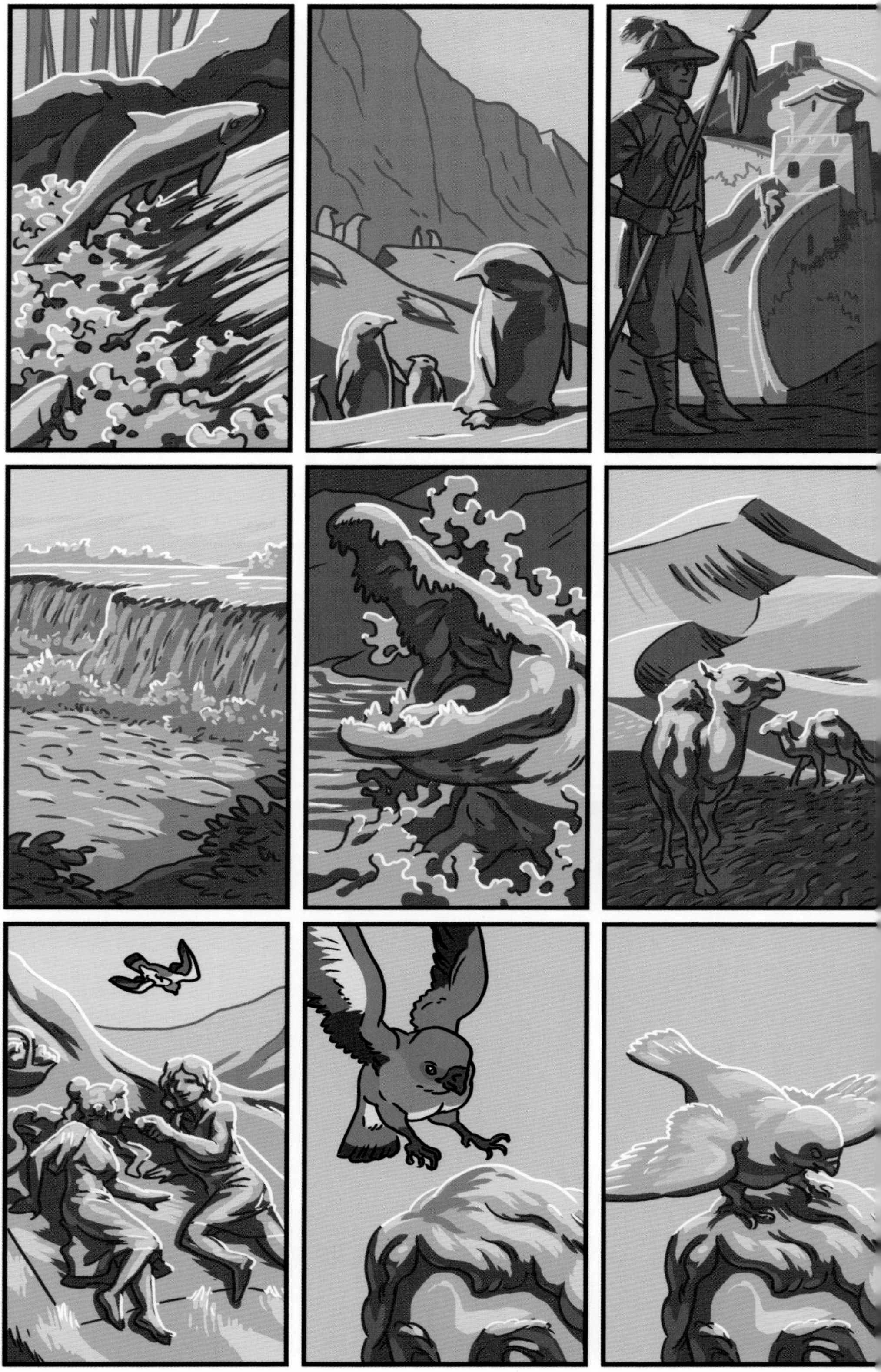

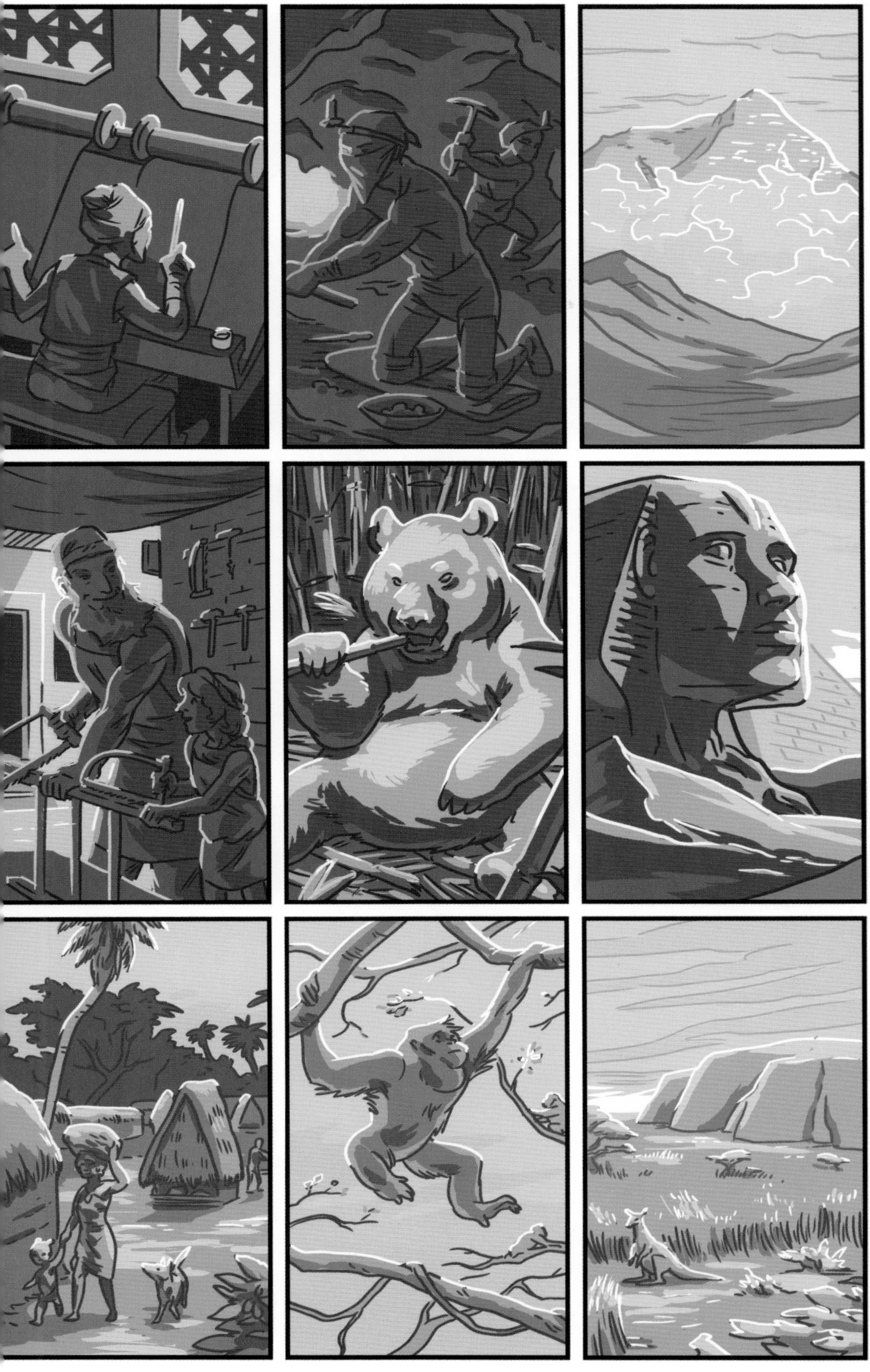

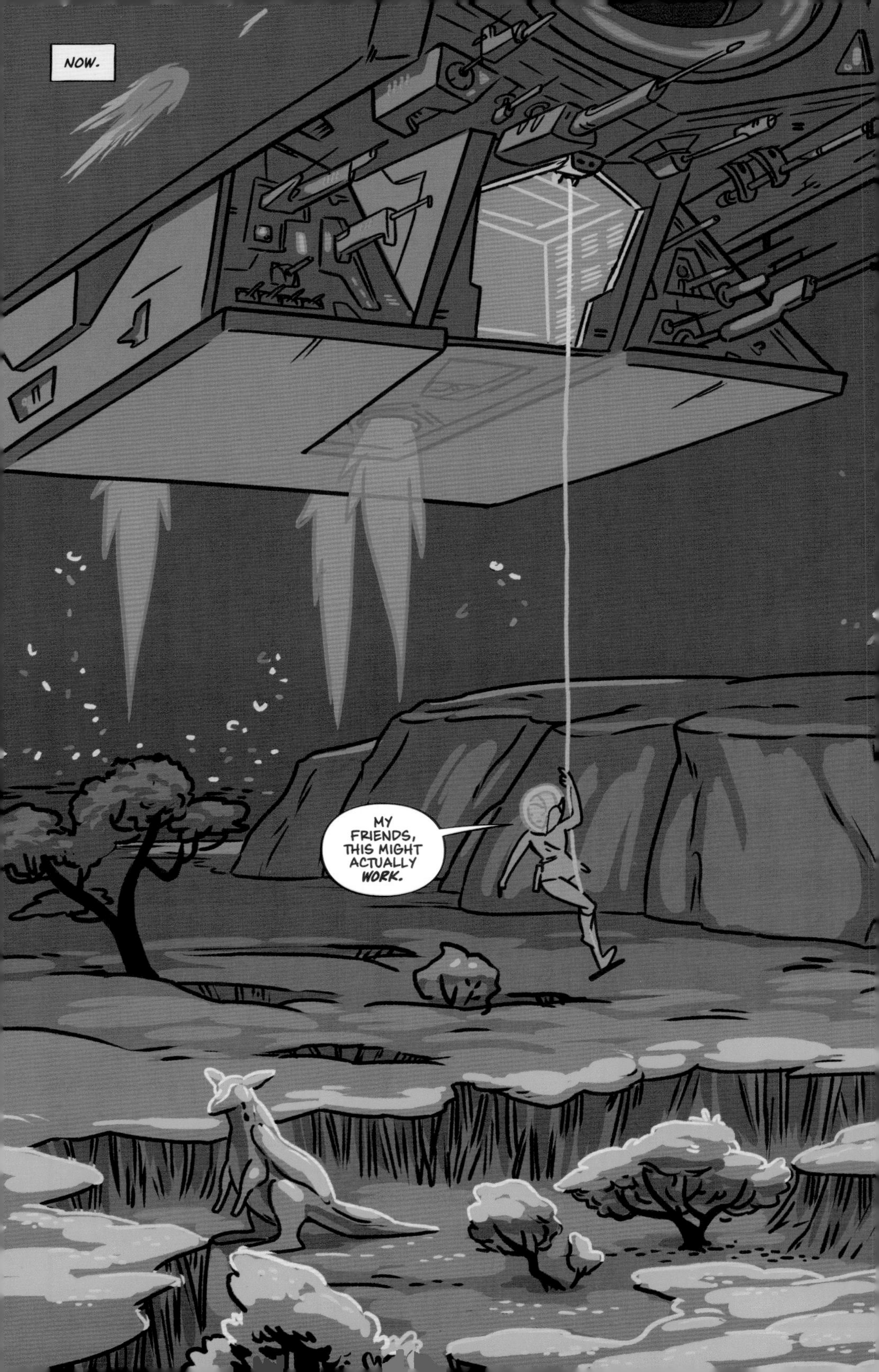
NOW.
MY FRIENDS, THIS MIGHT ACTUALLY WORK.

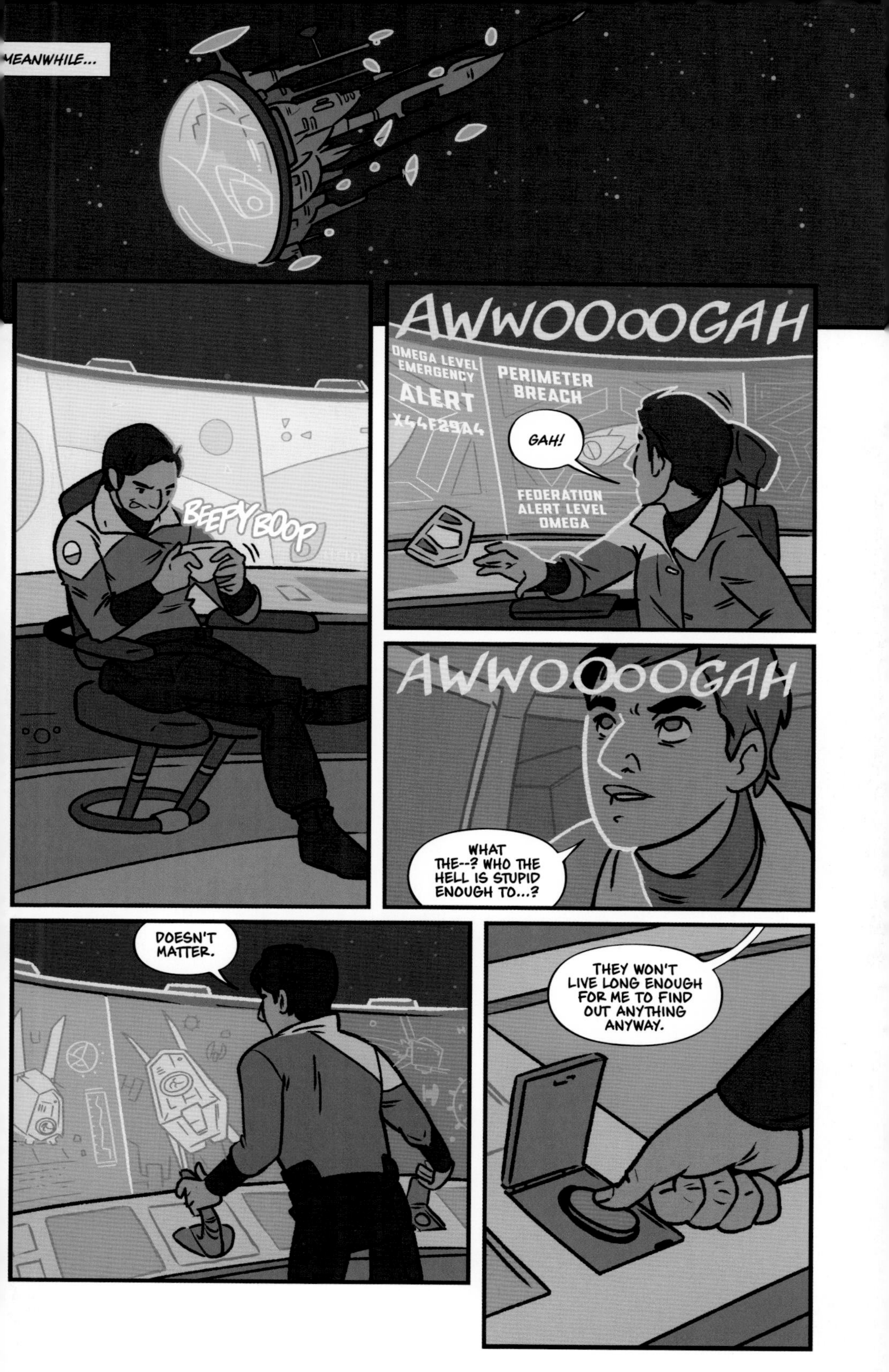
MEANWHILE...
BEEPY BOOP
AWWOOOOOGAH
OMEGA LEVEL EMERGENCY
ALERT
X44F29A4
PERIMETER BREACH
FEDERATION ALERT LEVEL OMEGA
GAH!
AWWOOOOOGAH
WHAT THE--? WHO THE HELL IS STUPID ENOUGH TO...?
DOESN'T MATTER.
THEY WON'T LIVE LONG ENOUGH FOR ME TO FIND OUT ANYTHING ANYWAY.

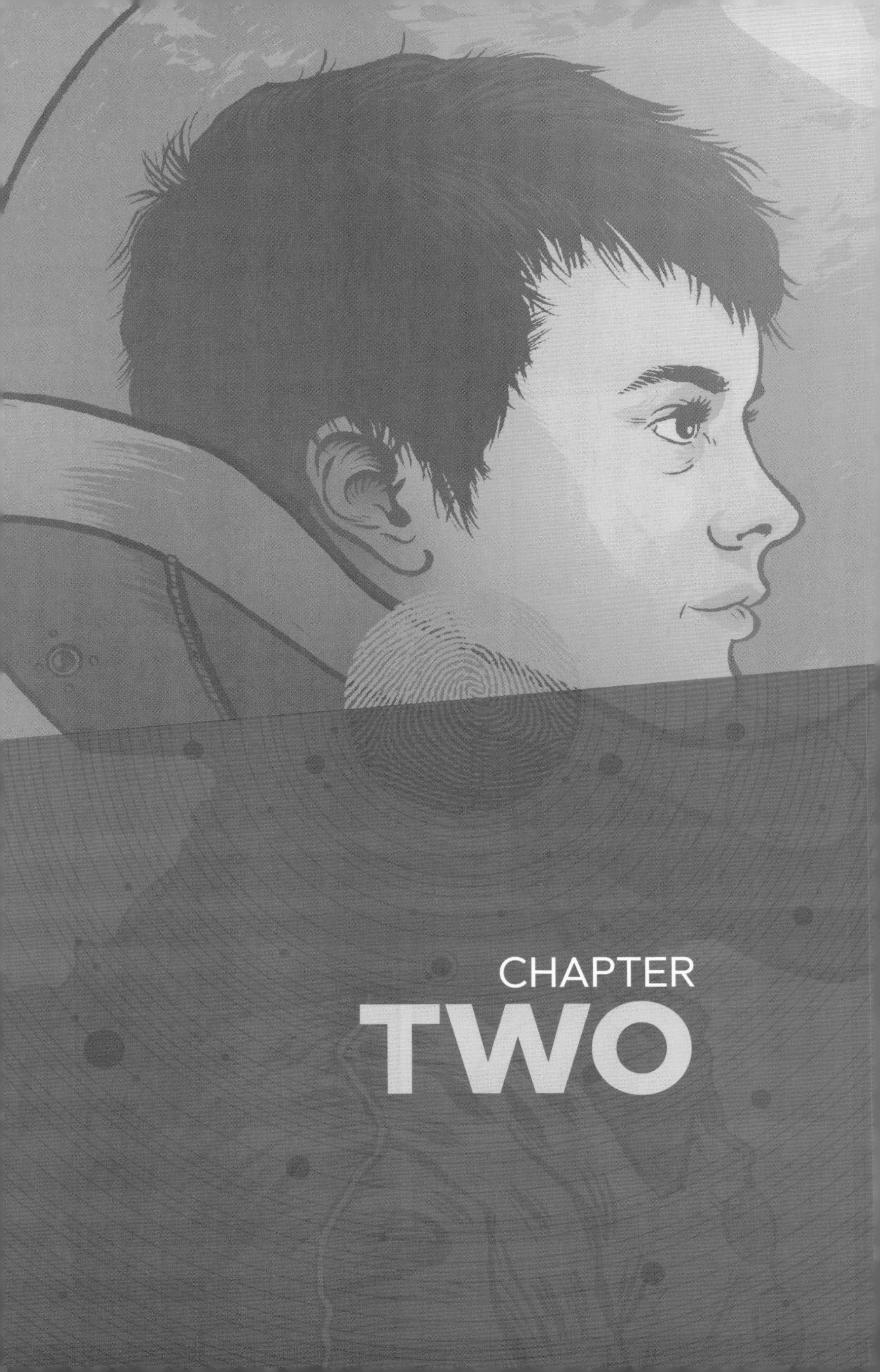

CHAPTER TWO

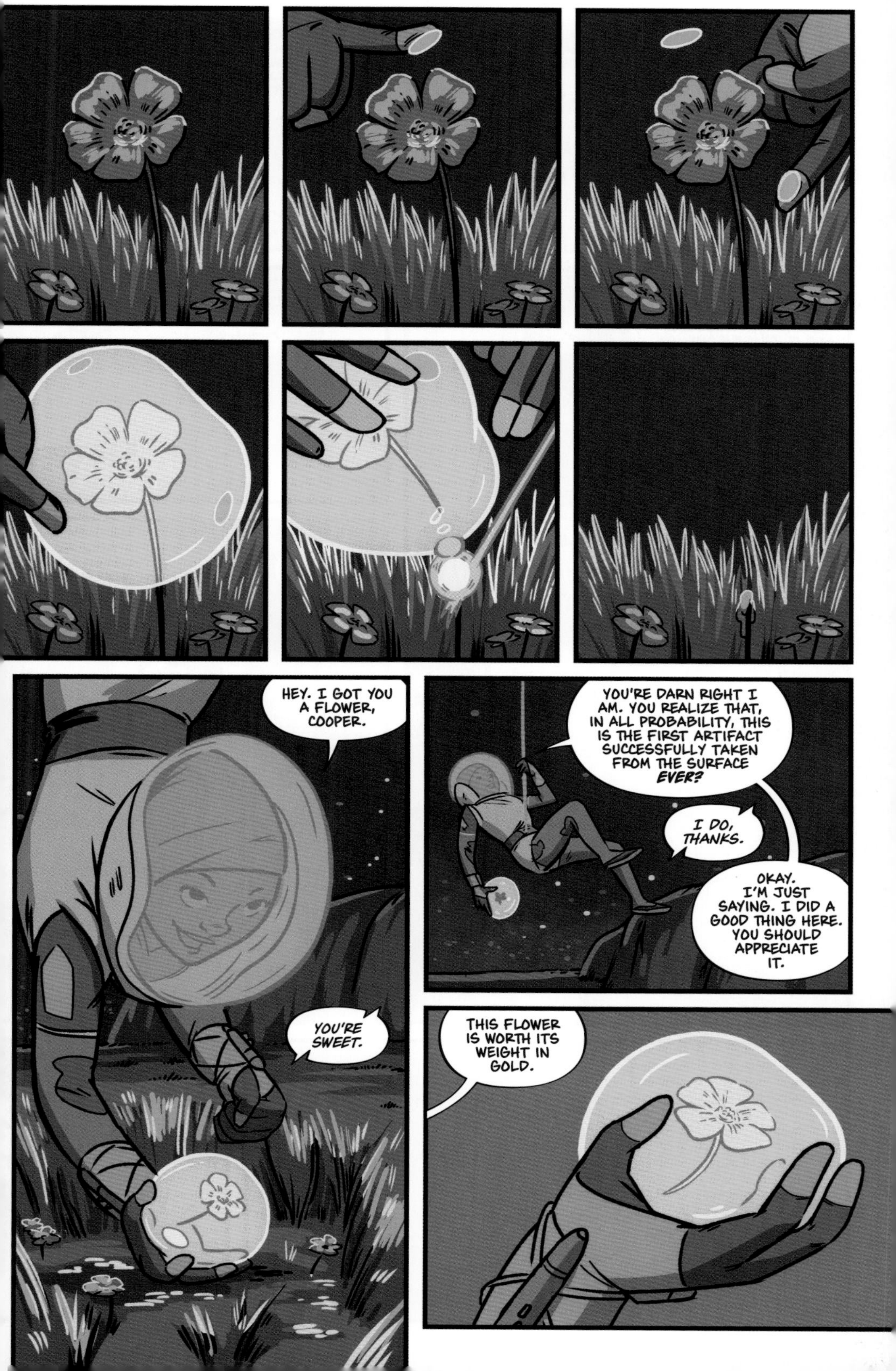
HEY. I GOT YOU A FLOWER, COOPER.
YOU'RE SWEET.
YOU'RE DARN RIGHT I AM. YOU REALIZE THAT, IN ALL PROBABILITY, THIS IS THE FIRST ARTIFACT SUCCESSFULLY TAKEN FROM THE SURFACE *EVER?*
I DO, THANKS.
OKAY. I'M JUST SAYING. I DID A GOOD THING HERE. YOU SHOULD APPRECIATE IT.
THIS FLOWER IS WORTH ITS WEIGHT IN GOLD.

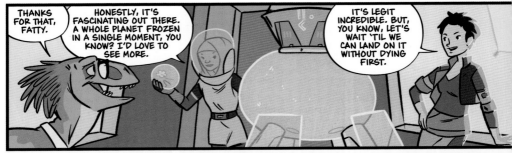

THANKS FOR THAT, FATTY.

HONESTLY, IT'S FASCINATING OUT THERE. A WHOLE PLANET FROZEN IN A SINGLE MOMENT, YOU KNOW? I'D LOVE TO SEE MORE.

IT'S LEGIT INCREDIBLE. BUT, YOU KNOW, LET'S WAIT 'TIL WE CAN LAND ON IT WITHOUT DYING FIRST.

ALL RIGHT, WE'VE GOT ALL FOUR STASIS FIELD EMITTERS RUNNING IN REDUNDANT PARALLEL, AND IF *THOSE* SOMEHOW ALL FAIL, THE ADAPTIVE COMPRESSED AIR IS ON A SEPARATE POWER SYSTEM...THAT'LL KEEP WHATEVER'S INSIDE THE CHAMBER AIRBORNE FOR ABOUT THIRTY MINUTES.

UM, GIVE OR TAKE.

PUT 'ER IN.

THRUMMMM

WE'RE STABLE.

HEY. YOU WERE RAD OUT THERE.

AND MOM SAID MY DEGREE IN MUSEUM STUDIES WOULD NEVER COME IN USEFUL.

IT... BARELY WAS?

LISTEN, ARE WE READY?

AS WE'LL EVER BE.

LET'S DO IT, COOPER. *ENGAGE.*

CHOO

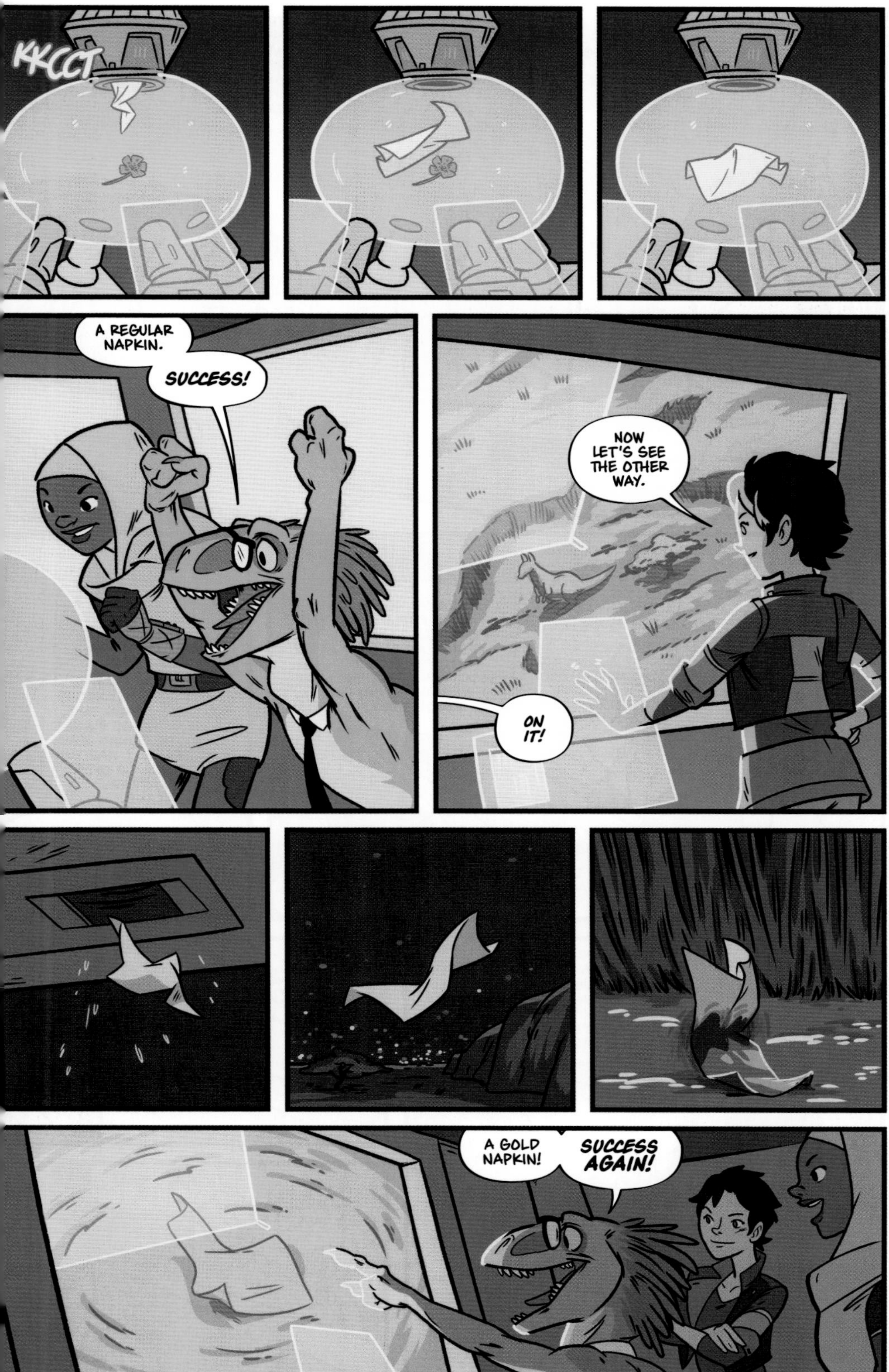
KKCCT
A REGULAR NAPKIN.
SUCCESS!
NOW LET'S SEE THE OTHER WAY.
ON IT!
A GOLD NAPKIN!
SUCCESS AGAIN!

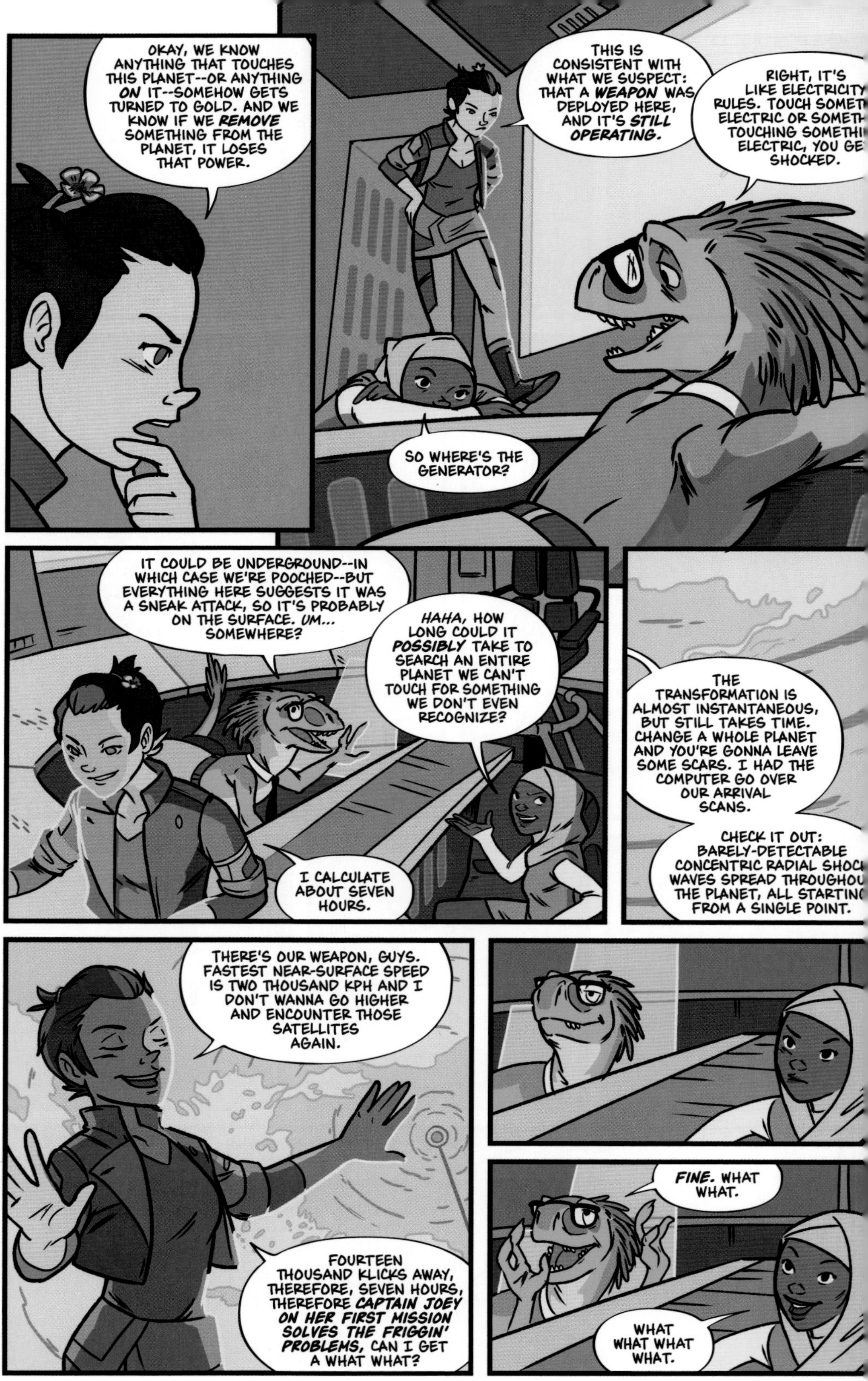
OKAY, WE KNOW ANYTHING THAT TOUCHES THIS PLANET--OR ANYTHING *ON* IT--SOMEHOW GETS TURNED TO GOLD. AND WE KNOW IF WE *REMOVE* SOMETHING FROM THE PLANET, IT LOSES THAT POWER.
THIS IS CONSISTENT WITH WHAT WE SUSPECT: THAT A *WEAPON* WAS DEPLOYED HERE, AND IT'S *STILL OPERATING.*
RIGHT, IT'S LIKE ELECTRICITY RULES. TOUCH SOMETH ELECTRIC OR SOMETH TOUCHING SOMETHI ELECTRIC, YOU GE SHOCKED.
SO WHERE'S THE GENERATOR?
IT COULD BE UNDERGROUND--IN WHICH CASE WE'RE POOCHED--BUT EVERYTHING HERE SUGGESTS IT WAS A SNEAK ATTACK, SO IT'S PROBABLY ON THE SURFACE. *UM...* SOMEWHERE?
HAHA, HOW LONG COULD IT *POSSIBLY* TAKE TO SEARCH AN ENTIRE PLANET WE CAN'T TOUCH FOR SOMETHING WE DON'T EVEN RECOGNIZE?
I CALCULATE ABOUT SEVEN HOURS.
THE TRANSFORMATION IS ALMOST INSTANTANEOUS, BUT STILL TAKES TIME. CHANGE A WHOLE PLANET AND YOU'RE GONNA LEAVE SOME SCARS. I HAD THE COMPUTER GO OVER OUR ARRIVAL SCANS.
CHECK IT OUT: BARELY-DETECTABLE CONCENTRIC RADIAL SHOCK WAVES SPREAD THROUGHOU THE PLANET, ALL STARTING FROM A SINGLE POINT.
THERE'S OUR WEAPON, GUYS. FASTEST NEAR-SURFACE SPEED IS TWO THOUSAND KPH AND I DON'T WANNA GO HIGHER AND ENCOUNTER THOSE SATELLITES AGAIN.
FOURTEEN THOUSAND KLICKS AWAY, THEREFORE, SEVEN HOURS, THEREFORE ***CAPTAIN JOEY ON HER FIRST MISSION SOLVES THE FRIGGIN' PROBLEMS,*** CAN I GET A WHAT WHAT?
FINE. WHAT WHAT.
WHAT WHAT WHAT WHAT.

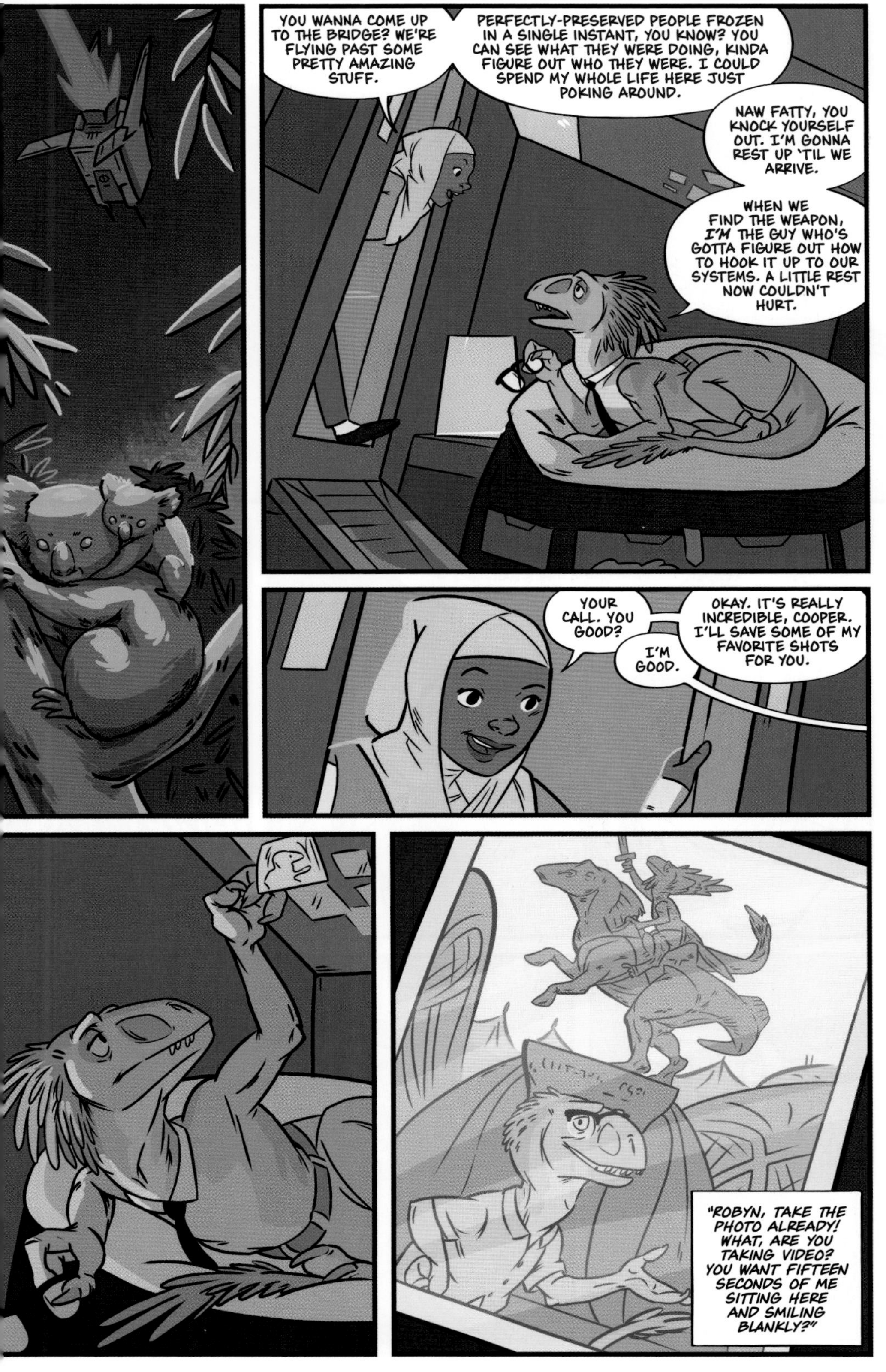
YOU WANNA COME UP TO THE BRIDGE? WE'RE FLYING PAST SOME PRETTY AMAZING STUFF.
PERFECTLY-PRESERVED PEOPLE FROZEN IN A SINGLE INSTANT, YOU KNOW? YOU CAN SEE WHAT THEY WERE DOING, KINDA FIGURE OUT WHO THEY WERE. I COULD SPEND MY WHOLE LIFE HERE JUST POKING AROUND.
NAW FATTY, YOU KNOCK YOURSELF OUT. I'M GONNA REST UP 'TIL WE ARRIVE.
WHEN WE FIND THE WEAPON, *I'M* THE GUY WHO'S GOTTA FIGURE OUT HOW TO HOOK IT UP TO OUR SYSTEMS. A LITTLE REST NOW COULDN'T HURT.
YOUR CALL. YOU GOOD?
I'M GOOD.
OKAY. IT'S REALLY INCREDIBLE, COOPER. I'LL SAVE SOME OF MY FAVORITE SHOTS FOR YOU.
"ROBYN, TAKE THE PHOTO ALREADY! WHAT, ARE YOU TAKING VIDEO? YOU WANT FIFTEEN SECONDS OF ME SITTING HERE AND SMILING BLANKLY?"

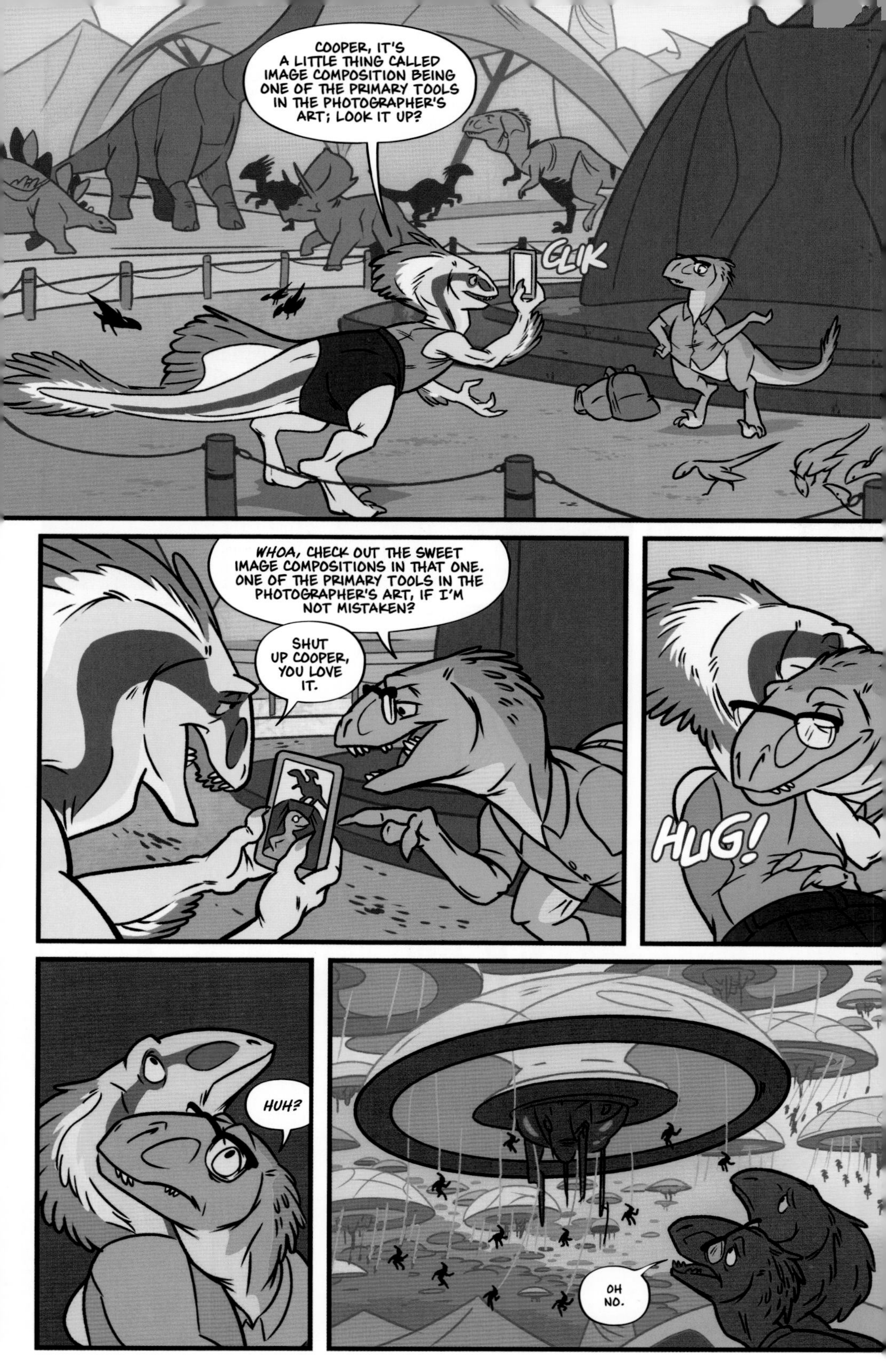
COOPER, IT'S A LITTLE THING CALLED IMAGE COMPOSITION BEING ONE OF THE PRIMARY TOOLS IN THE PHOTOGRAPHER'S ART; LOOK IT UP?
CLIK
WHOA, CHECK OUT THE SWEET IMAGE COMPOSITIONS IN THAT ONE. ONE OF THE PRIMARY TOOLS IN THE PHOTOGRAPHER'S ART, IF I'M NOT MISTAKEN?
SHUT UP COOPER, YOU LOVE IT.
HUG!
HUH?
OH NO.

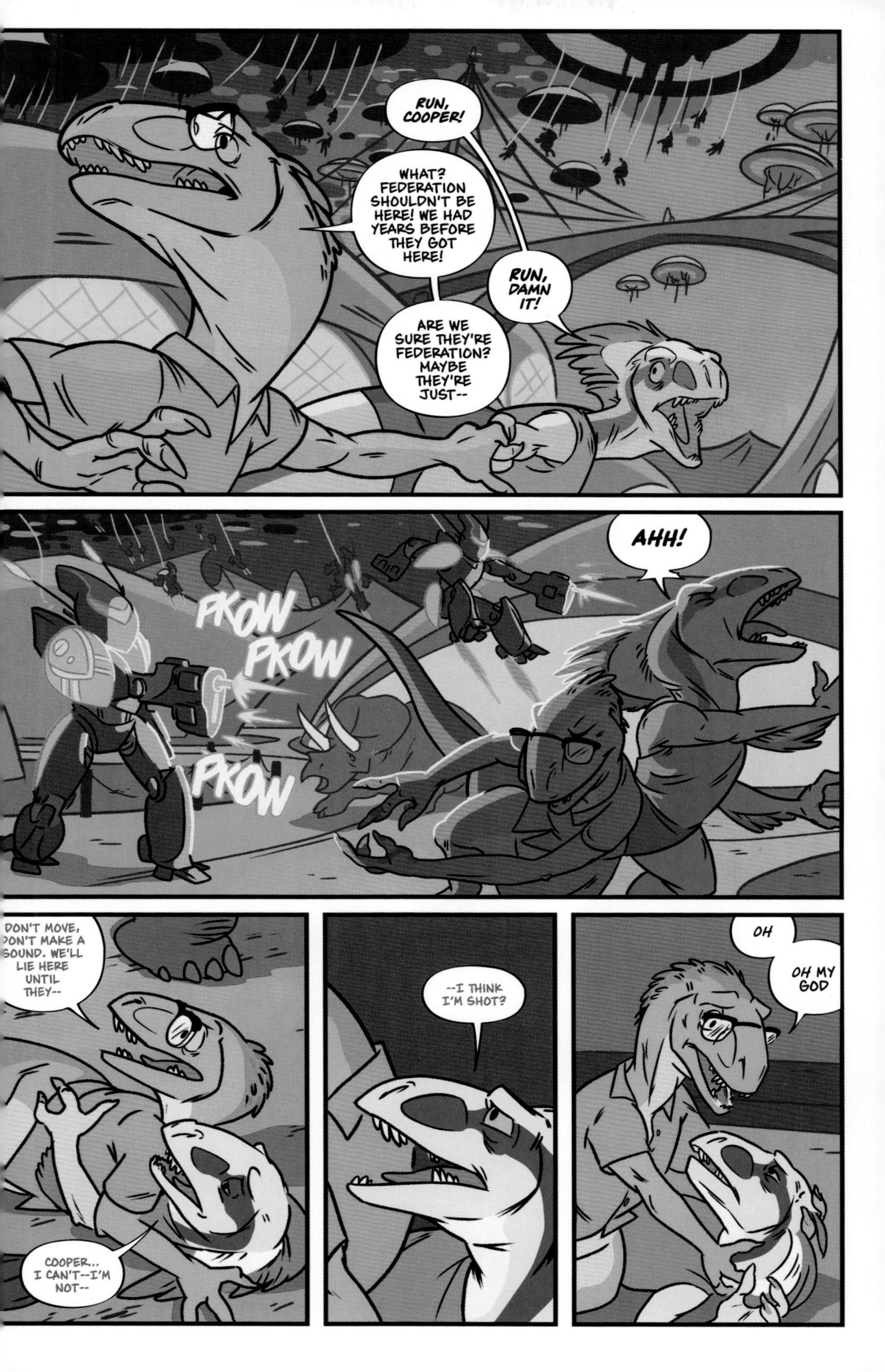
RUN, COOPER!
WHAT? FEDERATION SHOULDN'T BE HERE! WE HAD YEARS BEFORE THEY GOT HERE!
RUN, DAMN IT!
ARE WE SURE THEY'RE FEDERATION? MAYBE THEY'RE JUST--
AHH!
PKOW
PKOW
PKOW
DON'T MOVE, DON'T MAKE A SOUND. WE'LL LIE HERE UNTIL THEY--
COOPER... I CAN'T--I'M NOT--
--I THINK I'M SHOT?
OH
OH MY GOD

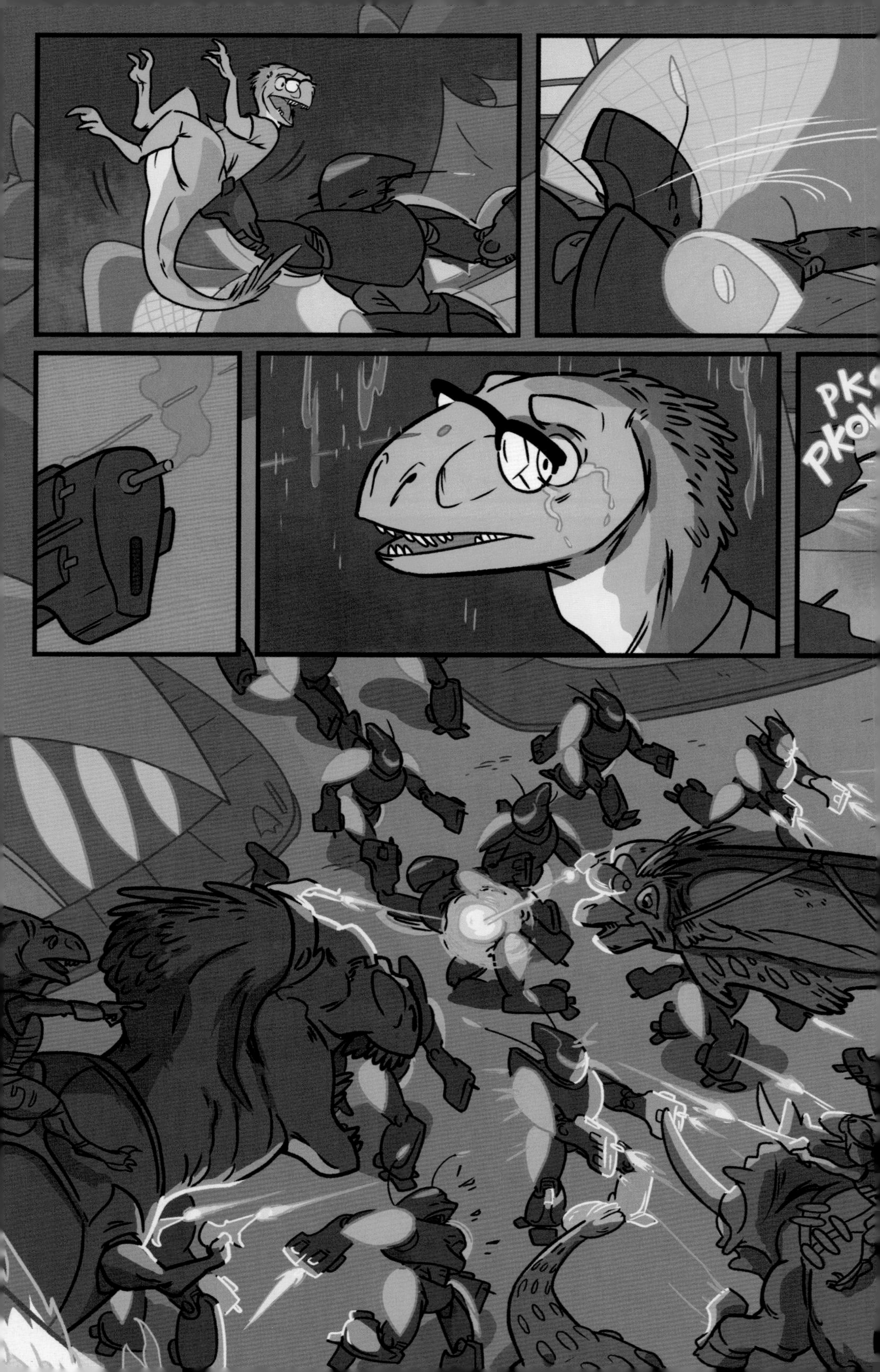
PK
PKO

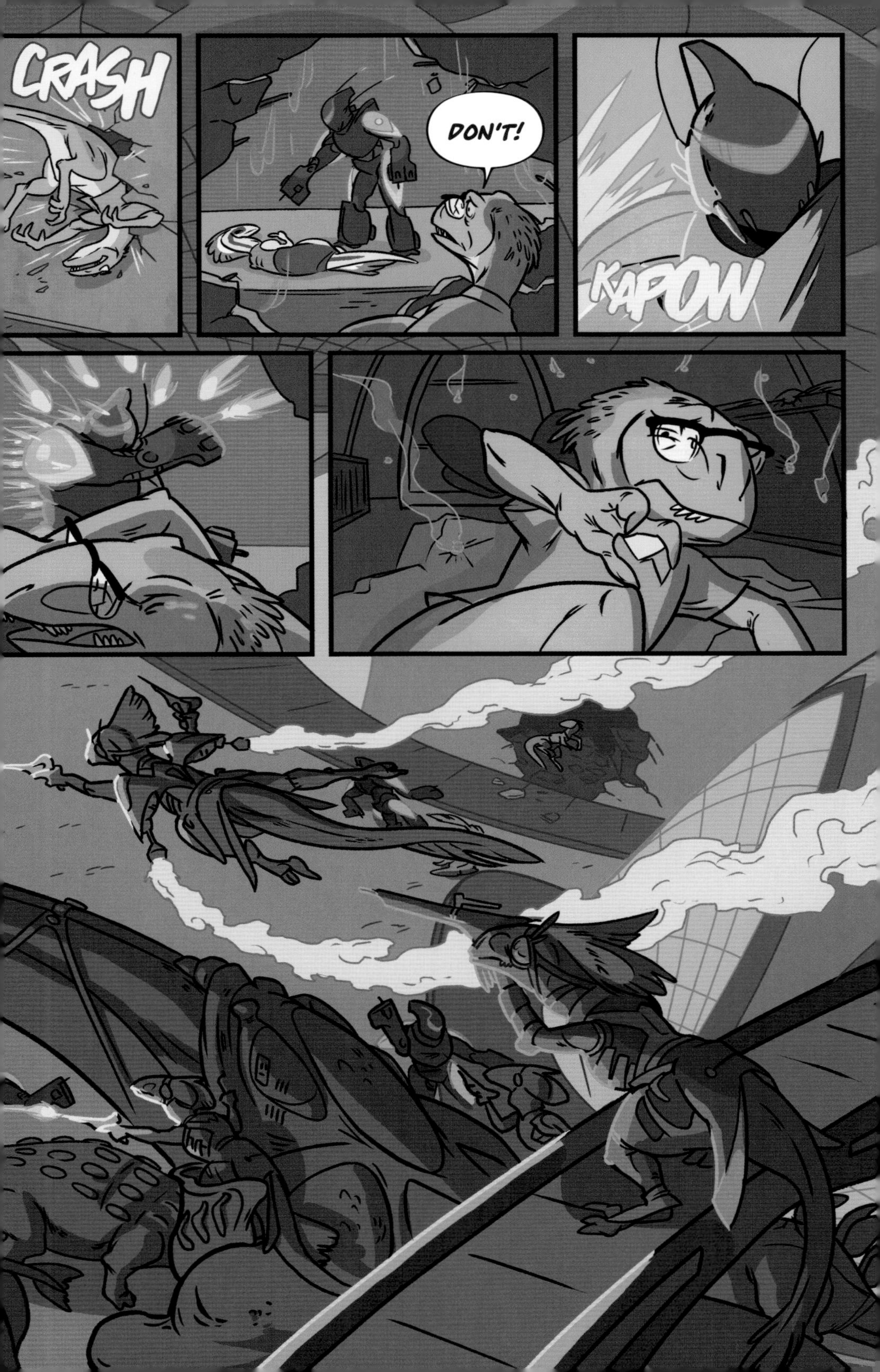
CRASH
DON'T!
KAPOW

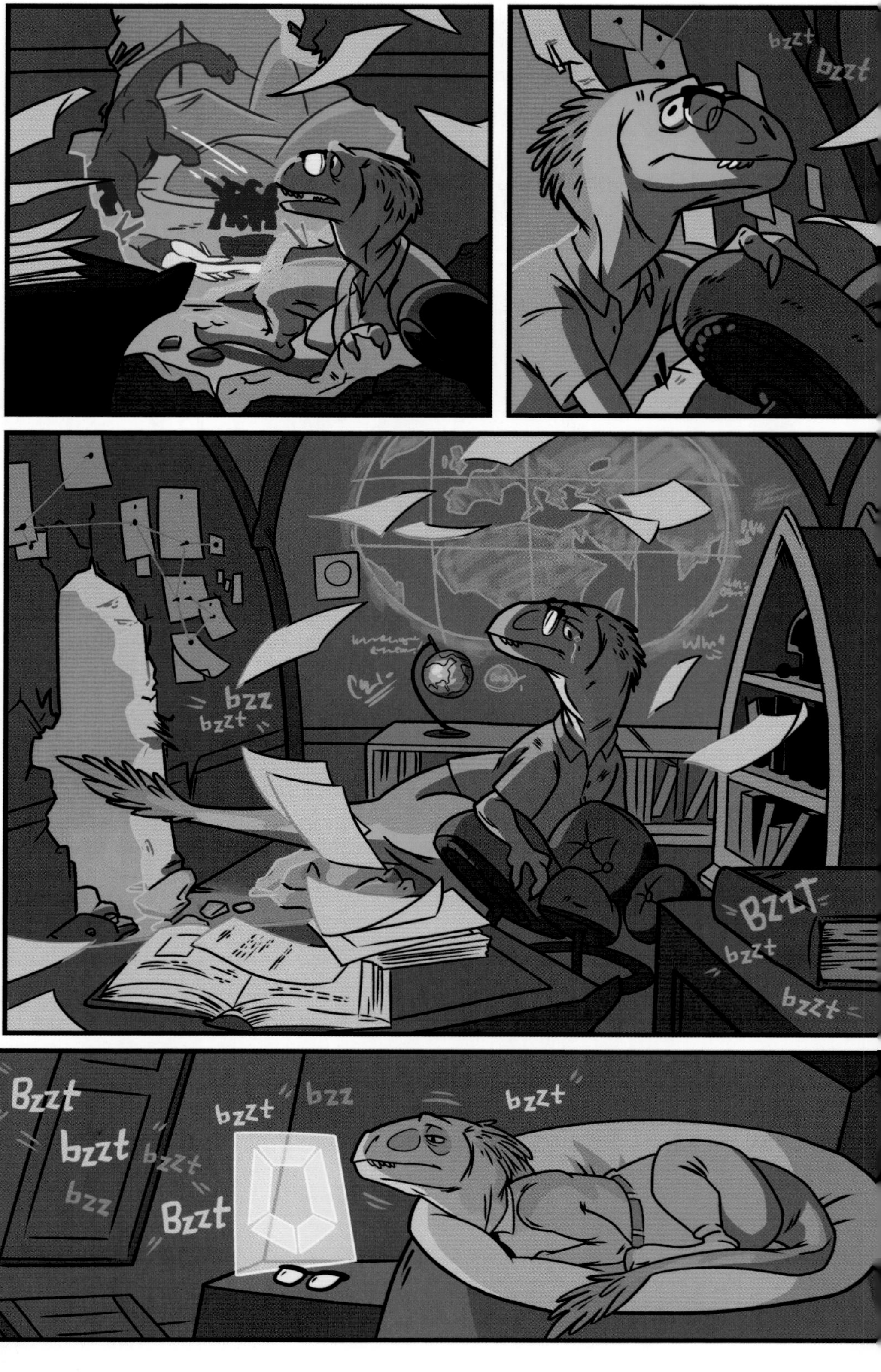
bzzt
bzzt
bzz
bzzt
BZZT
bzzt
bzzt
Bzzt
bzzt
bzzt
bzz
Bzzt
bzzt
bzz
bzzt

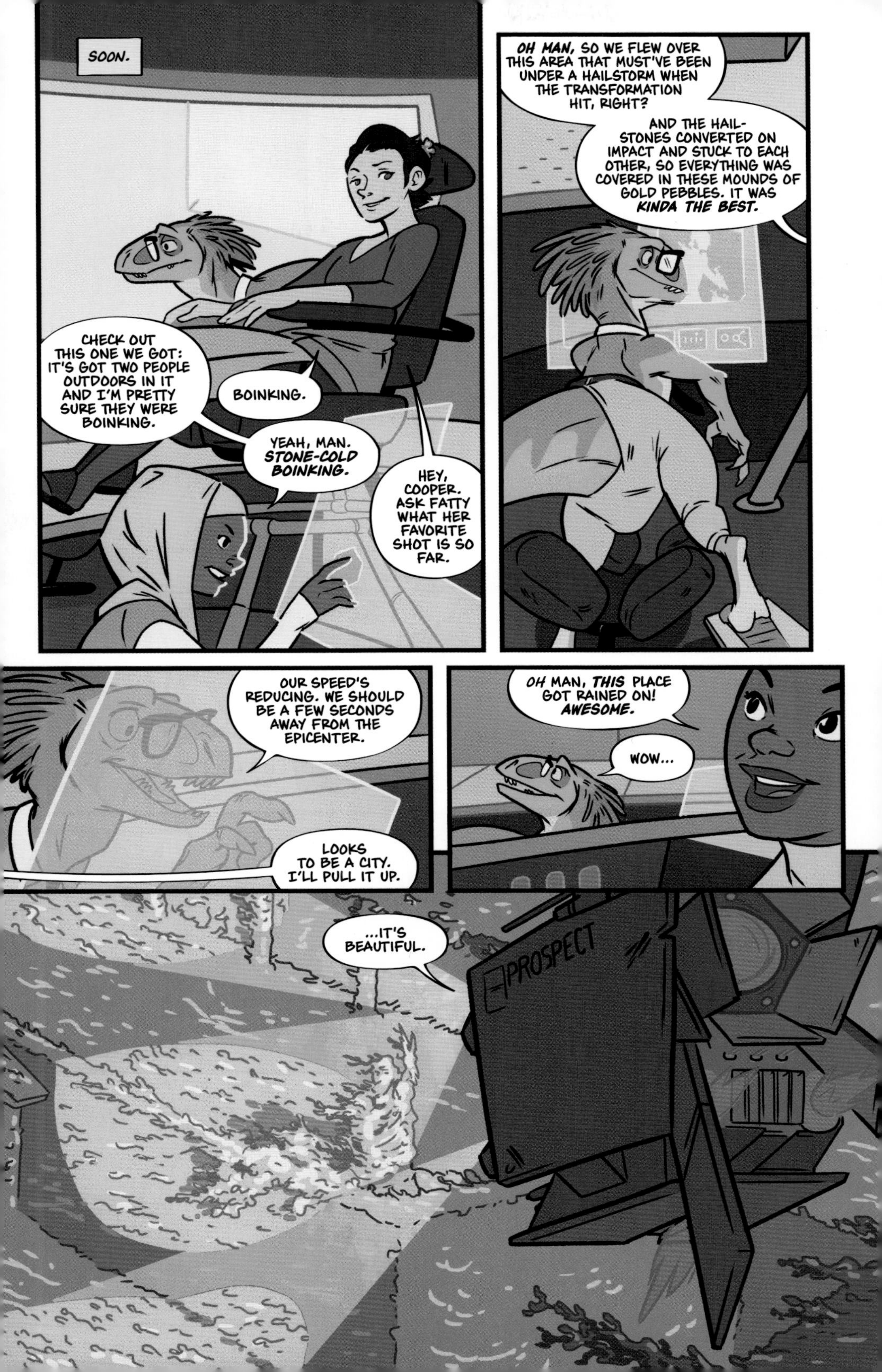
SOON.
CHECK OUT THIS ONE WE GOT: IT'S GOT TWO PEOPLE OUTDOORS IN IT AND I'M PRETTY SURE THEY WERE BOINKING.
BOINKING.
YEAH, MAN. STONE-COLD BOINKING.
HEY, COOPER. ASK FATTY WHAT HER FAVORITE SHOT IS SO FAR.
OH MAN, SO WE FLEW OVER THIS AREA THAT MUST'VE BEEN UNDER A HAILSTORM WHEN THE TRANSFORMATION HIT, RIGHT?
AND THE HAIL-STONES CONVERTED ON IMPACT AND STUCK TO EACH OTHER, SO EVERYTHING WAS COVERED IN THESE MOUNDS OF GOLD PEBBLES. IT WAS KINDA THE BEST.
OUR SPEED'S REDUCING. WE SHOULD BE A FEW SECONDS AWAY FROM THE EPICENTER.
LOOKS TO BE A CITY. I'LL PULL IT UP.
OH MAN, THIS PLACE GOT RAINED ON! AWESOME.
WOW...
...IT'S BEAUTIFUL.
PROSPECT

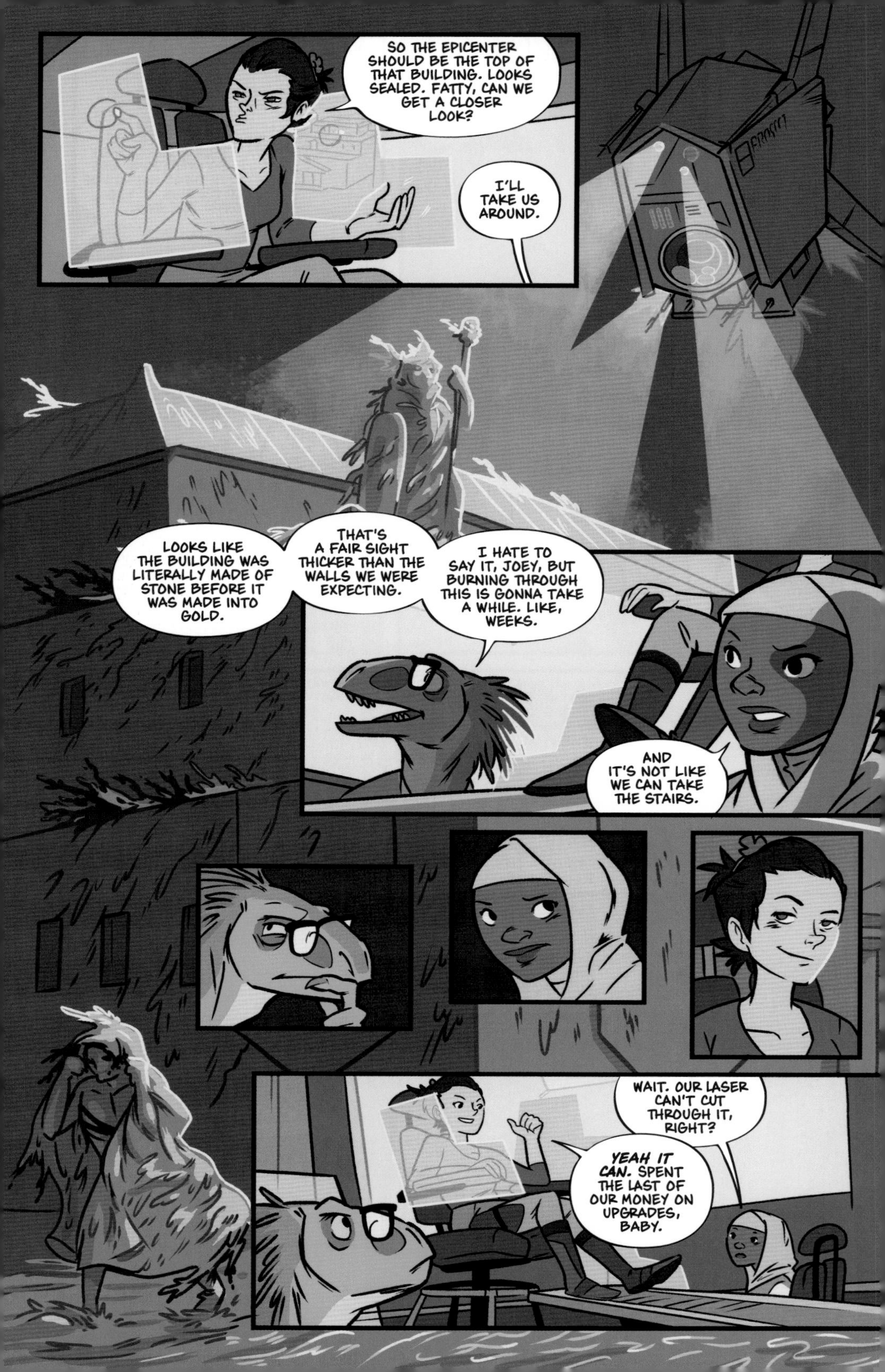
SO THE EPICENTER SHOULD BE THE TOP OF THAT BUILDING. LOOKS SEALED. FATTY, CAN WE GET A CLOSER LOOK?
I'LL TAKE US AROUND.
LOOKS LIKE THE BUILDING WAS LITERALLY MADE OF STONE BEFORE IT WAS MADE INTO GOLD.
THAT'S A FAIR SIGHT THICKER THAN THE WALLS WE WERE EXPECTING.
I HATE TO SAY IT, JOEY, BUT BURNING THROUGH THIS IS GONNA TAKE A WHILE. LIKE, WEEKS.
AND IT'S NOT LIKE WE CAN TAKE THE STAIRS.
WAIT. OUR LASER CAN'T CUT THROUGH IT, RIGHT?
YEAH IT CAN. SPENT THE LAST OF OUR MONEY ON UPGRADES, BABY.

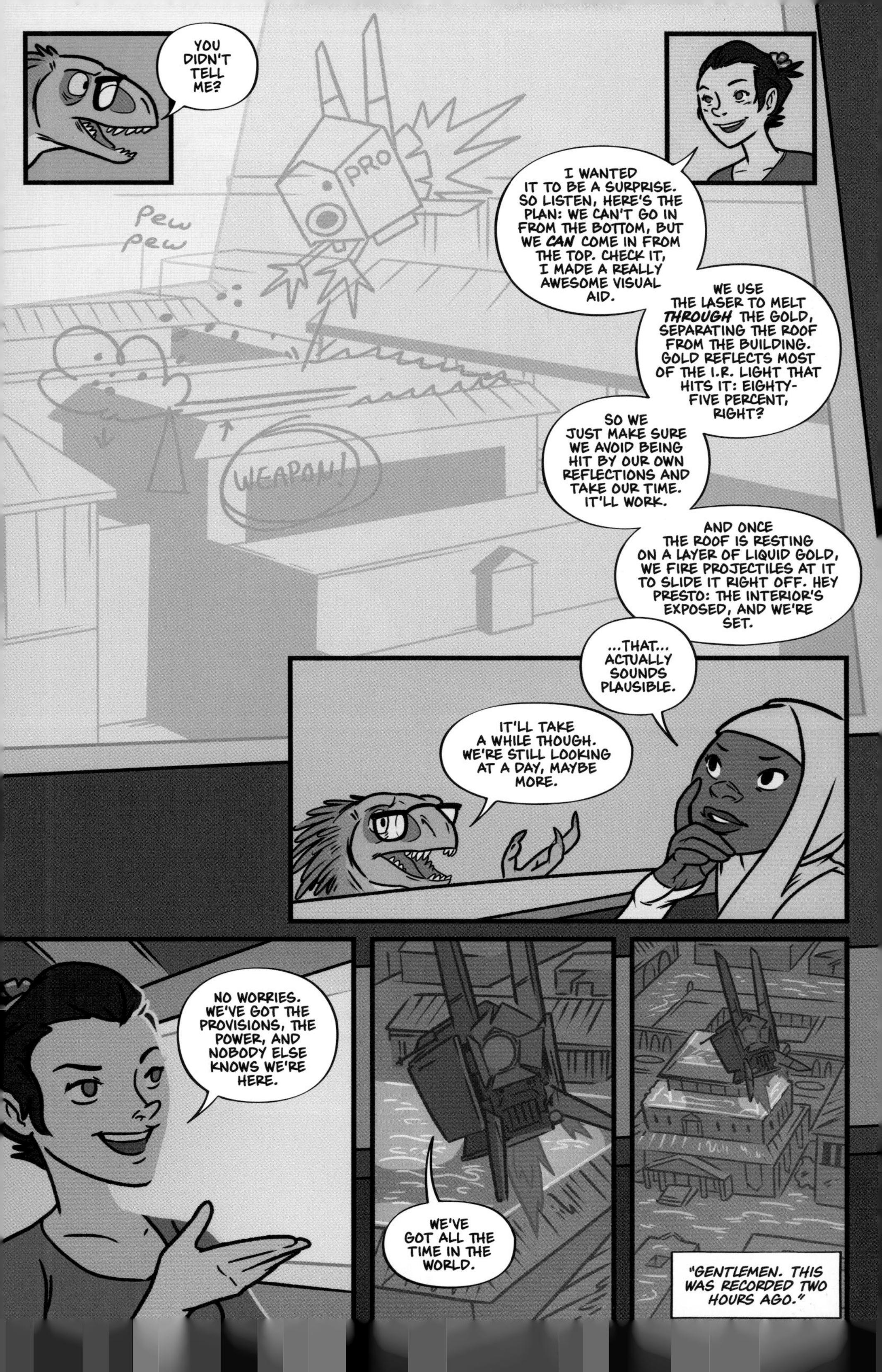

YOU DIDN'T TELL ME?
I WANTED IT TO BE A SURPRISE. SO LISTEN, HERE'S THE PLAN: WE CAN'T GO IN FROM THE BOTTOM, BUT WE *CAN* COME IN FROM THE TOP. CHECK IT, I MADE A REALLY AWESOME VISUAL AID.
PRO
Pew pew
WEAPON!
WE USE THE LASER TO MELT *THROUGH* THE GOLD, SEPARATING THE ROOF FROM THE BUILDING. GOLD REFLECTS MOST OF THE I.R. LIGHT THAT HITS IT: EIGHTY-FIVE PERCENT, RIGHT?
SO WE JUST MAKE SURE WE AVOID BEING HIT BY OUR OWN REFLECTIONS AND TAKE OUR TIME. IT'LL WORK.
AND ONCE THE ROOF IS RESTING ON A LAYER OF LIQUID GOLD, WE FIRE PROJECTILES AT IT TO SLIDE IT RIGHT OFF. HEY PRESTO: THE INTERIOR'S EXPOSED, AND WE'RE SET.
...THAT... ACTUALLY SOUNDS PLAUSIBLE.
IT'LL TAKE A WHILE THOUGH. WE'RE STILL LOOKING AT A DAY, MAYBE MORE.
NO WORRIES. WE'VE GOT THE PROVISIONS, THE POWER, AND NOBODY ELSE KNOWS WE'RE HERE.
WE'VE GOT ALL THE TIME IN THE WORLD.
"GENTLEMEN. THIS WAS RECORDED TWO HOURS AGO."

ELEVEN HOURS BEFORE THAT, WE RECEIVED AN ALARM FROM AN AUTOMATED SYSTEM SO OLD WE COULDN'T UNDERSTAND IT AT FIRST.

TOOK US SIX HOURS JUST TO DECODE WHAT THE ALERT WAS ABOUT--OBSOLETE PROTOCOL WITHOUT ANY EXTANT DOCUMENTATION--AND SEVERAL MORE TO VERIFY WHAT IT WAS SAYING. THAT LED US TO SOME FORGOTTEN AND ENCRYPTED ARCHIVES, WHERE WE HAD TO BREAK INTO OUR OWN DAMN FILES.

WHAT YOU ARE ABOUT TO BRIEFED ON ARE THE FRUITS OF THAT EFFORT. I REMIND YOU THIS COMMUNICATION IS CLASSIFIED.

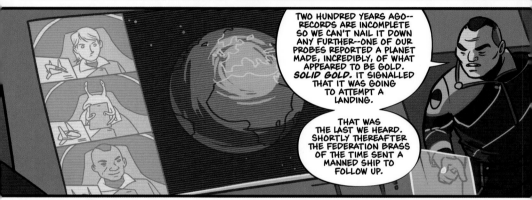

TWO HUNDRED YEARS AGO-- RECORDS ARE INCOMPLETE SO WE CAN'T NAIL IT DOWN ANY FURTHER--ONE OF OUR PROBES REPORTED A PLANET MADE, INCREDIBLY, OF WHAT APPEARED TO BE GOLD. SOLID GOLD. IT SIGNALLED THAT IT WAS GOING TO ATTEMPT A LANDING.

THAT WAS THE LAST WE HEARD. SHORTLY THEREAFTER THE FEDERATION BRASS OF THE TIME SENT A MANNED SHIP TO FOLLOW UP.

"THEY NEVER MADE IT OUT THE DOOR."

CAM 02

"THAT GOT OUR ATTENTION. THIS TIME THE FEDERATION SENT FIVE MORE SHIPS WITH EXPLICIT ORDERS: TEST IT, OBSERVE IT, REPORT BACK. NO LANDINGS TO BE ATTEMPTED.

CAM 02

"THESE SHIPS DISCOVERED FOUR THINGS. ONE: THE PLANET WAS AS IT APPEARED: SOLID GOLD. TWO: THE PLANET HAD BEEN UNREMARKABLE UNTIL THIS TRANSFORMATION TOOK PLACE, WHICH APPEARED TO HAVE CAUGHT THE WORLD OFF-GUARD.

CAM 03

"THREE: ANY CONTACT WITH THE PLANET WOULD TURN THAT CONTACTING ENTITY, WHETHER ANIMAL, VEGETABLE, OR MINERAL, INTO GOLD ITSELF.

"AND FOUR: THERE WAS NO WAY TO CONTROL THAT INTERACTION."

CAM 02

THE FEDERATION HAD STUMBLED UPON A WORLD LEFT PERMANENTLY UNINHABITABLE BY AN UNKNOWN WEAPON-- LIKELY AN EXTREMELY STABLE POLYMORPH. IT OUTCLASSED OUR TECHNOLOGY IN EVERY WAY. WE DIDN'T EVEN KNOW HOW TO BEGIN PULLING OFF SOMETHING LIKE THIS.

HELL, WE *STILL* DON'T.

BUT SOMEONE OUT THERE DID, AND THEY'D ALREADY DEPLOYED IT AT LEAST ONCE. MAYBE THEY'D LEFT OUR GALAXY AND MAYBE THEY'D STUCK AROUND, BUT THERE WAS NO REASON TO ASSUME THEY WEREN'T HOSTILE.

WE NEEDED TO BE STRONGER.

"AND WE *BECAME* STRONGER. BUT IN THE BEGINNING, WHEN THE FEDERATION DETERMINED WE COULDN'T CONTROL, DUPLICATE--OR EVEN LOCATE--THE WEAPON, WE DID THE NEXT BEST THING. WE ENSURED THAT NOBODY ELSE COULD EITHER. WE ERASED THE PLANET.

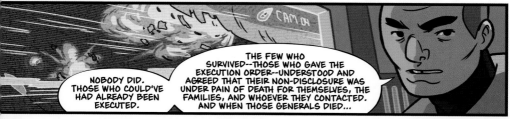

"WE COVERED THE PLANET IN LAYERS OF SELF-SUSTAINING SATELLITES, INVISIBLE AT LONG RANGE. WE MADE THE PLANET AS UNREMARKABLE AS POSSIBLE, AND THEN WE ERASED IT. ONE SYSTEM OUT OF BILLIONS: NOBODY WOULD NOTICE."

NOBODY DID. THOSE WHO COULD'VE HAD ALREADY BEEN EXECUTED.

THE FEW WHO SURVIVED--THOSE WHO GAVE THE EXECUTION ORDER--UNDERSTOOD AND AGREED THAT THEIR NON-DISCLOSURE WAS UNDER PAIN OF DEATH FOR THEMSELVES, THE FAMILIES, AND WHOEVER THEY CONTACTED. AND WHEN THOSE GENERALS DIED...

...THE SECRET WAS FORGOTTEN. WE'D ERASED IT TOO WELL. THE AUTOMATIC SYSTEMS AROUND THE PLANET RAN THEMSELVES WITHOUT INCIDENT UNTIL YESTERDAY, WHEN FOR THE FIRST TIME IN CENTURIES, THEY WERE ENCOUNTERED. THEY WERE ENGAGED.

AND THEY WERE *BREACHED.*

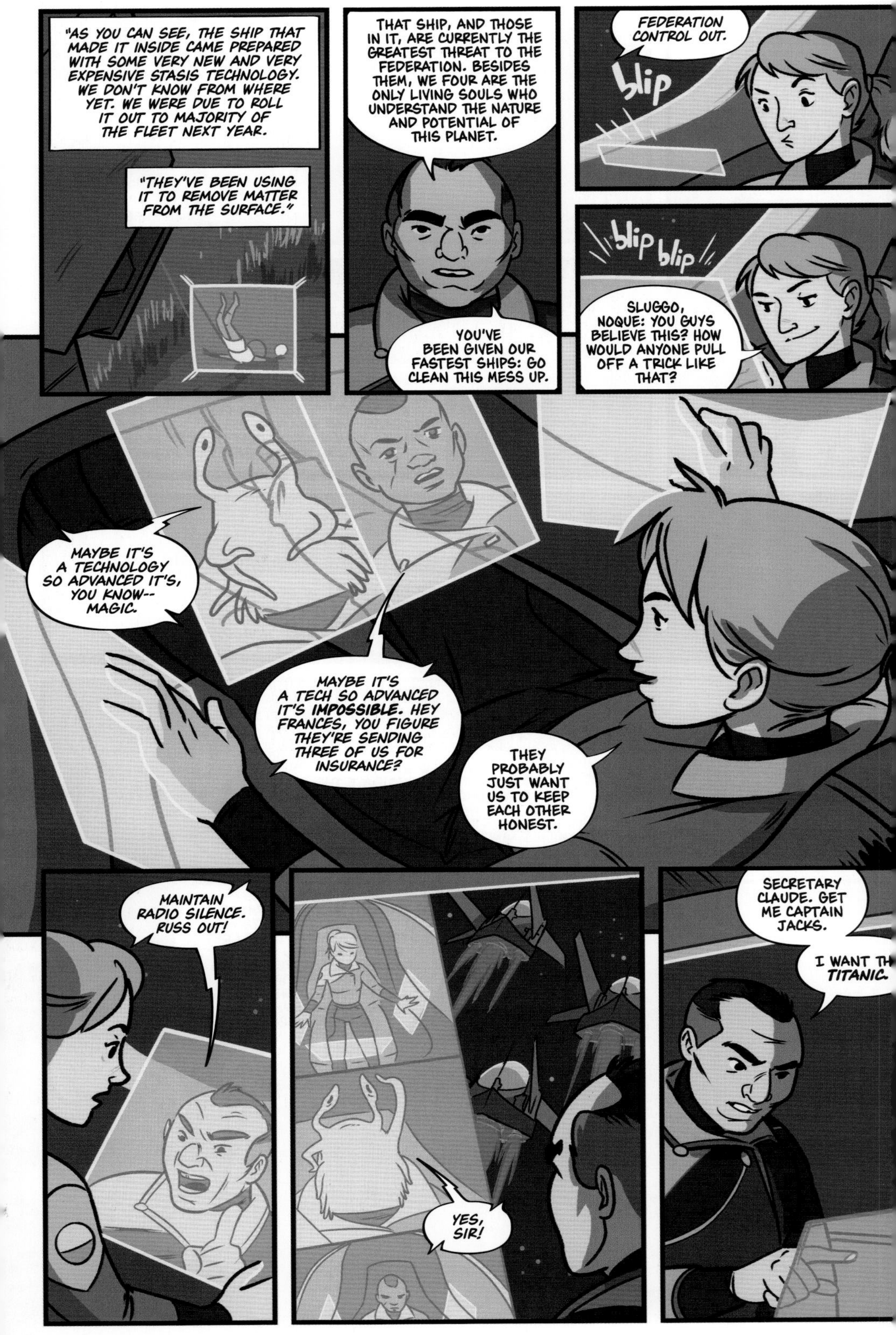
"AS YOU CAN SEE, THE SHIP THAT MADE IT INSIDE CAME PREPARED WITH SOME VERY NEW AND VERY EXPENSIVE STASIS TECHNOLOGY. WE DON'T KNOW FROM WHERE YET. WE WERE DUE TO ROLL IT OUT TO MAJORITY OF THE FLEET NEXT YEAR.
"THEY'VE BEEN USING IT TO REMOVE MATTER FROM THE SURFACE."
THAT SHIP, AND THOSE IN IT, ARE CURRENTLY THE GREATEST THREAT TO THE FEDERATION. BESIDES THEM, WE FOUR ARE THE ONLY LIVING SOULS WHO UNDERSTAND THE NATURE AND POTENTIAL OF THIS PLANET.
YOU'VE BEEN GIVEN OUR FASTEST SHIPS: GO CLEAN THIS MESS UP.
FEDERATION CONTROL OUT.
blip
blip blip
SLUGGO, NOQUE: YOU GUYS BELIEVE THIS? HOW WOULD ANYONE PULL OFF A TRICK LIKE THAT?
MAYBE IT'S A TECHNOLOGY SO ADVANCED IT'S, YOU KNOW-- MAGIC.
MAYBE IT'S A TECH SO ADVANCED IT'S IMPOSSIBLE. HEY FRANCES, YOU FIGURE THEY'RE SENDING THREE OF US FOR INSURANCE?
THEY PROBABLY JUST WANT US TO KEEP EACH OTHER HONEST.
MAINTAIN RADIO SILENCE. RUSS OUT!
YES, SIR!
SECRETARY CLAUDE. GET ME CAPTAIN JACKS.
I WANT TH
TITANIC.

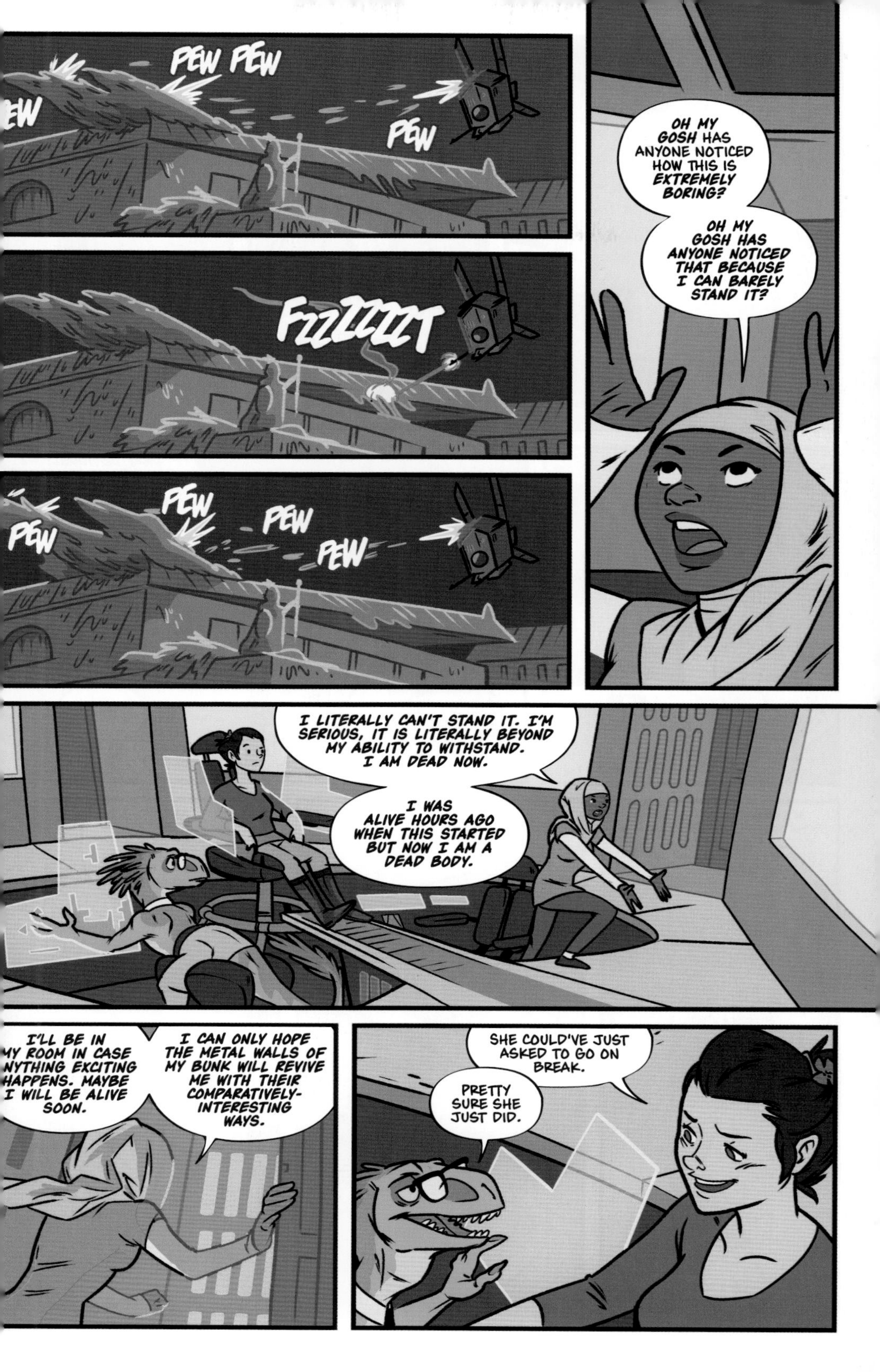

PEW PEW
EW
PEW
OH MY GOSH HAS ANYONE NOTICED HOW THIS IS EXTREMELY BORING?
OH MY GOSH HAS ANYONE NOTICED THAT BECAUSE I CAN BARELY STAND IT?
FzzZZZZZT
PEW
PEW
PEW
PEW
I LITERALLY CAN'T STAND IT. I'M SERIOUS, IT IS LITERALLY BEYOND MY ABILITY TO WITHSTAND. I AM DEAD NOW.
I WAS ALIVE HOURS AGO WHEN THIS STARTED BUT NOW I AM A DEAD BODY.
I'LL BE IN MY ROOM IN CASE NYTHING EXCITING HAPPENS. MAYBE I WILL BE ALIVE SOON.
I CAN ONLY HOPE THE METAL WALLS OF MY BUNK WILL REVIVE ME WITH THEIR COMPARATIVELY-INTERESTING WAYS.
SHE COULD'VE JUST ASKED TO GO ON BREAK.
PRETTY SURE SHE JUST DID.

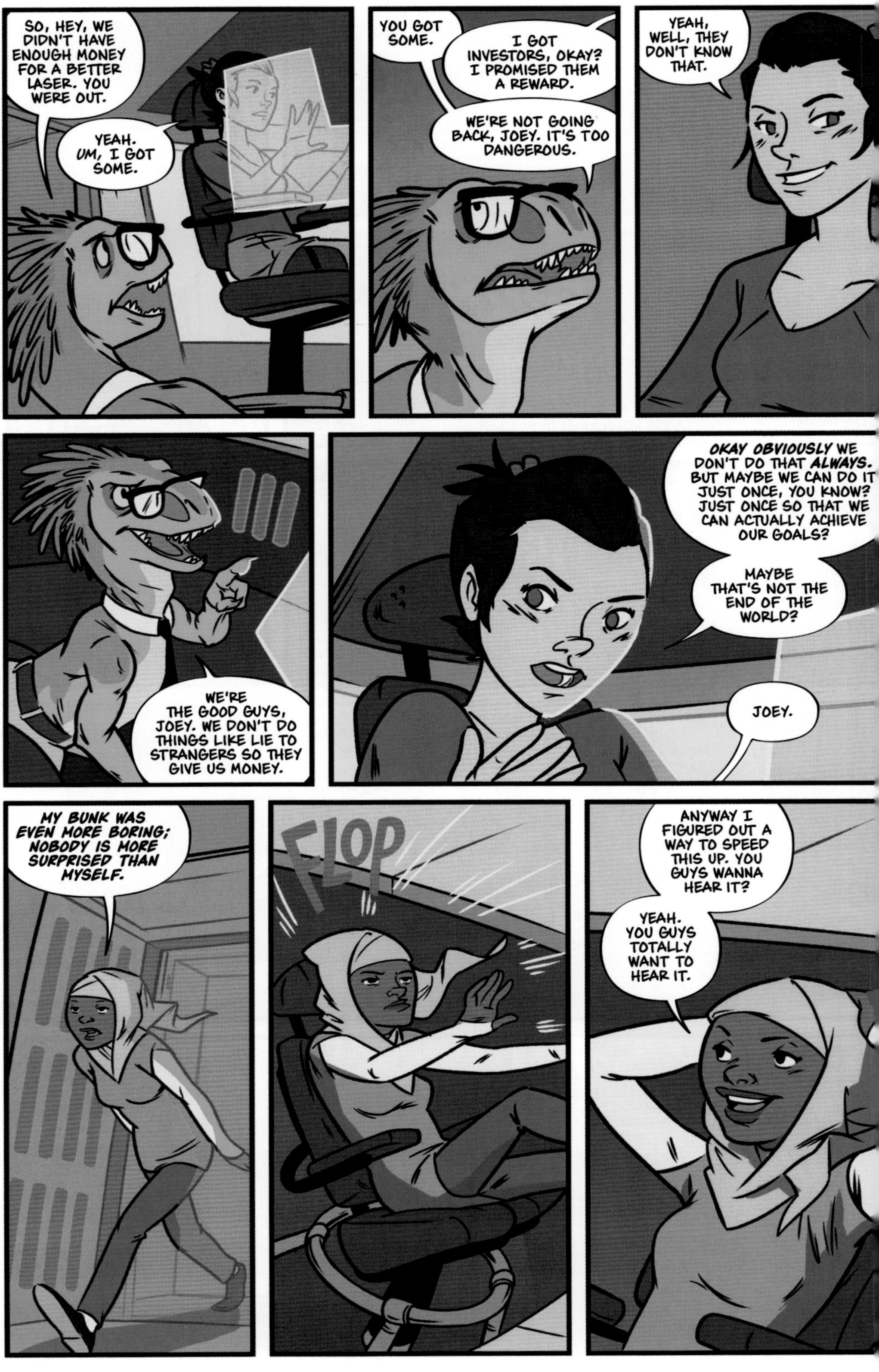
SO, HEY, WE DIDN'T HAVE ENOUGH MONEY FOR A BETTER LASER. YOU WERE OUT.
YEAH. UM, I GOT SOME.
YOU GOT SOME.
I GOT INVESTORS, OKAY? I PROMISED THEM A REWARD.
WE'RE NOT GOING BACK, JOEY. IT'S TOO DANGEROUS.
YEAH, WELL, THEY DON'T KNOW THAT.
WE'RE THE GOOD GUYS, JOEY. WE DON'T DO THINGS LIKE LIE TO STRANGERS SO THEY GIVE US MONEY.
OKAY OBVIOUSLY WE DON'T DO THAT *ALWAYS.* BUT MAYBE WE CAN DO IT JUST ONCE, YOU KNOW? JUST ONCE SO THAT WE CAN ACTUALLY ACHIEVE OUR GOALS?
MAYBE THAT'S NOT THE END OF THE WORLD?
JOEY.
MY BUNK WAS EVEN MORE BORING; NOBODY IS MORE SURPRISED THAN MYSELF.
FLOP
ANYWAY I FIGURED OUT A WAY TO SPEED THIS UP. YOU GUYS WANNA HEAR IT?
YEAH. YOU GUYS TOTALLY WANT TO HEAR IT.

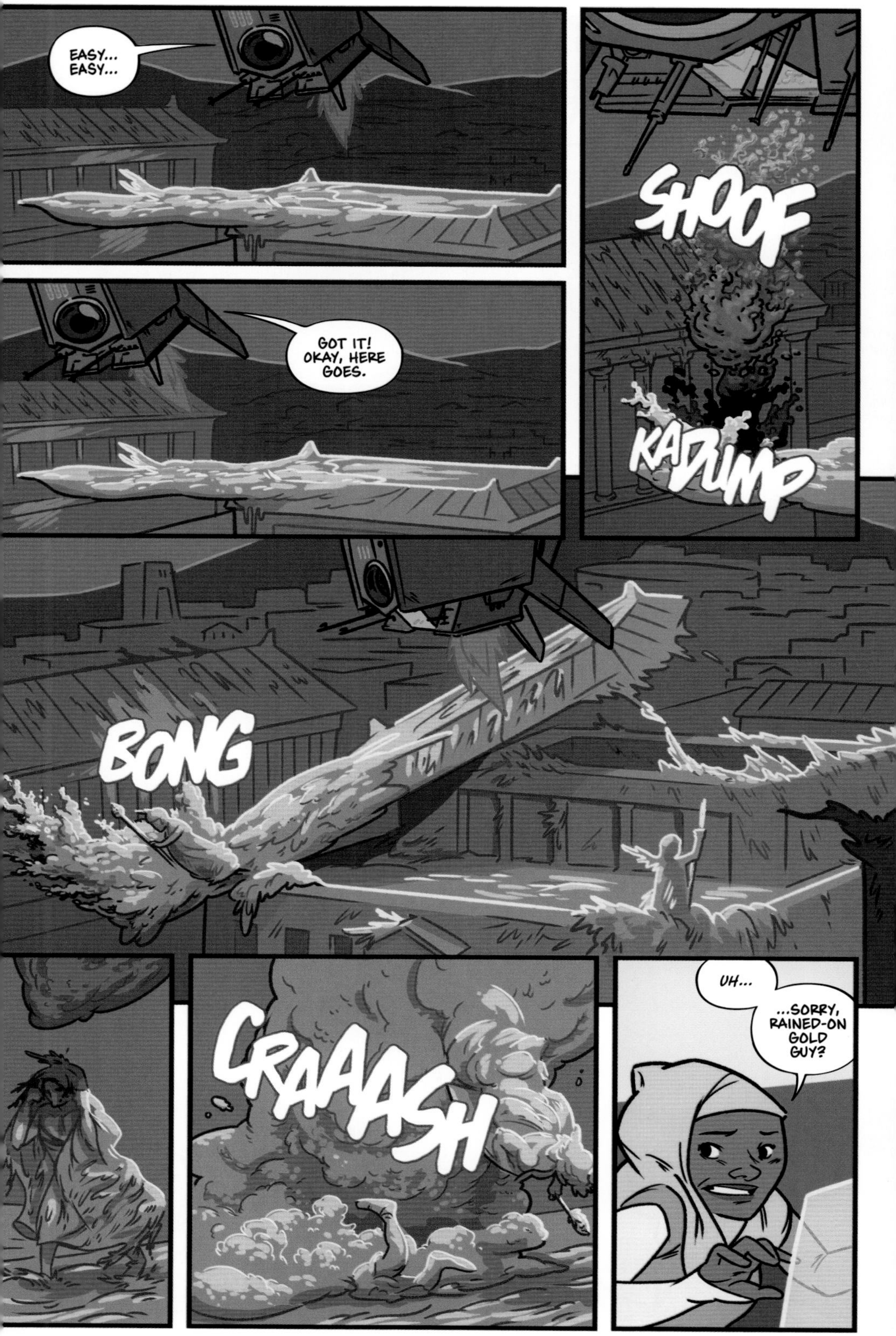
EASY... EASY...
SHOOF
GOT IT! OKAY, HERE GOES.
KADUMP
BONG
CRAAAASH
UH...
...SORRY, RAINED-ON GOLD GUY?

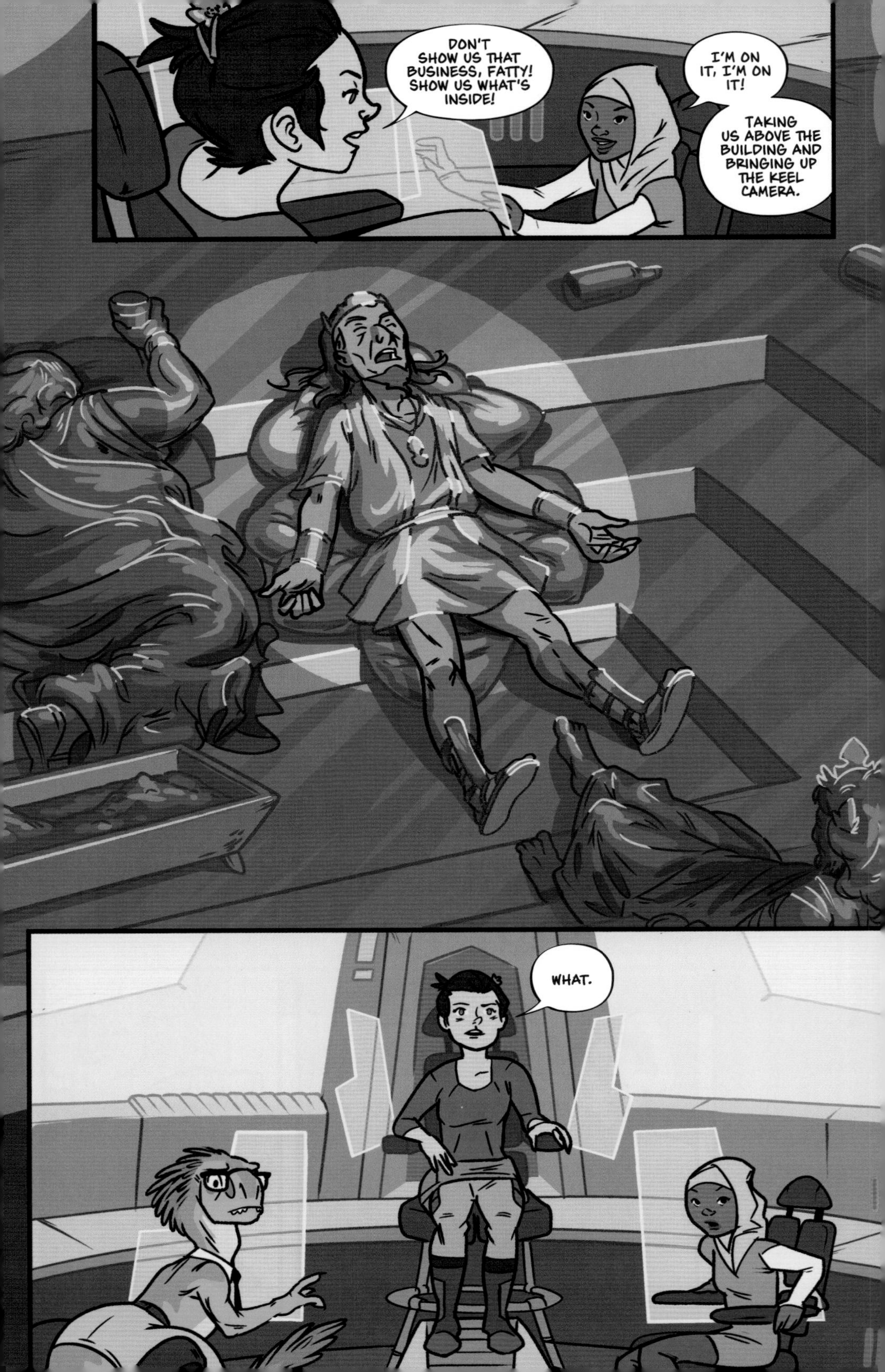
DON'T SHOW US THAT BUSINESS, FATTY! SHOW US WHAT'S INSIDE!
I'M ON IT, I'M ON IT!
TAKING US ABOVE THE BUILDING AND BRINGING UP THE KEEL CAMERA.
WHAT.

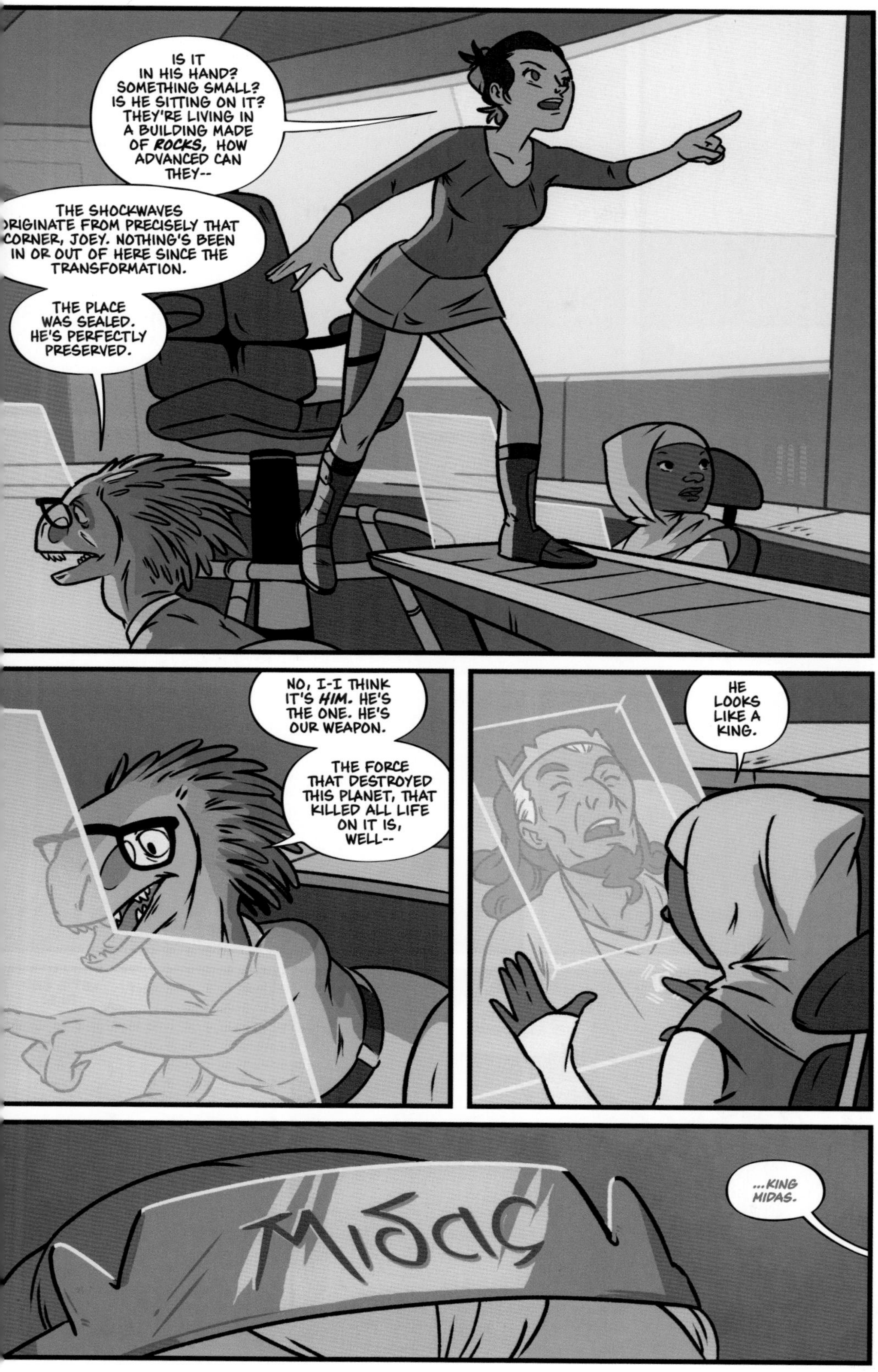
IS IT IN HIS HAND? SOMETHING SMALL? IS HE SITTING ON IT? THEY'RE LIVING IN A BUILDING MADE OF *ROCKS*, HOW ADVANCED CAN THEY--
THE SHOCKWAVES ORIGINATE FROM PRECISELY THAT CORNER, JOEY. NOTHING'S BEEN IN OR OUT OF HERE SINCE THE TRANSFORMATION.
THE PLACE WAS SEALED. HE'S PERFECTLY PRESERVED.
NO, I-I THINK IT'S *HIM*. HE'S THE ONE. HE'S OUR WEAPON.
THE FORCE THAT DESTROYED THIS PLANET, THAT KILLED ALL LIFE ON IT IS, WELL--
HE LOOKS LIKE A KING.
...KING MIDAS.

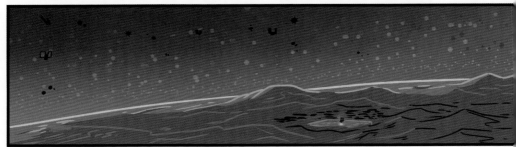

BRING 'EM
UP, EVERYONE.

ACKNOWLEDGED.
WEAPONS HOT.

TIME TO
CONTACT: TEN
MINUTES.

ALRIGHT.   LET'S END
THIS.

"A WHOLE PLANET **FROZEN** IN A SINGLE MOMENT..."

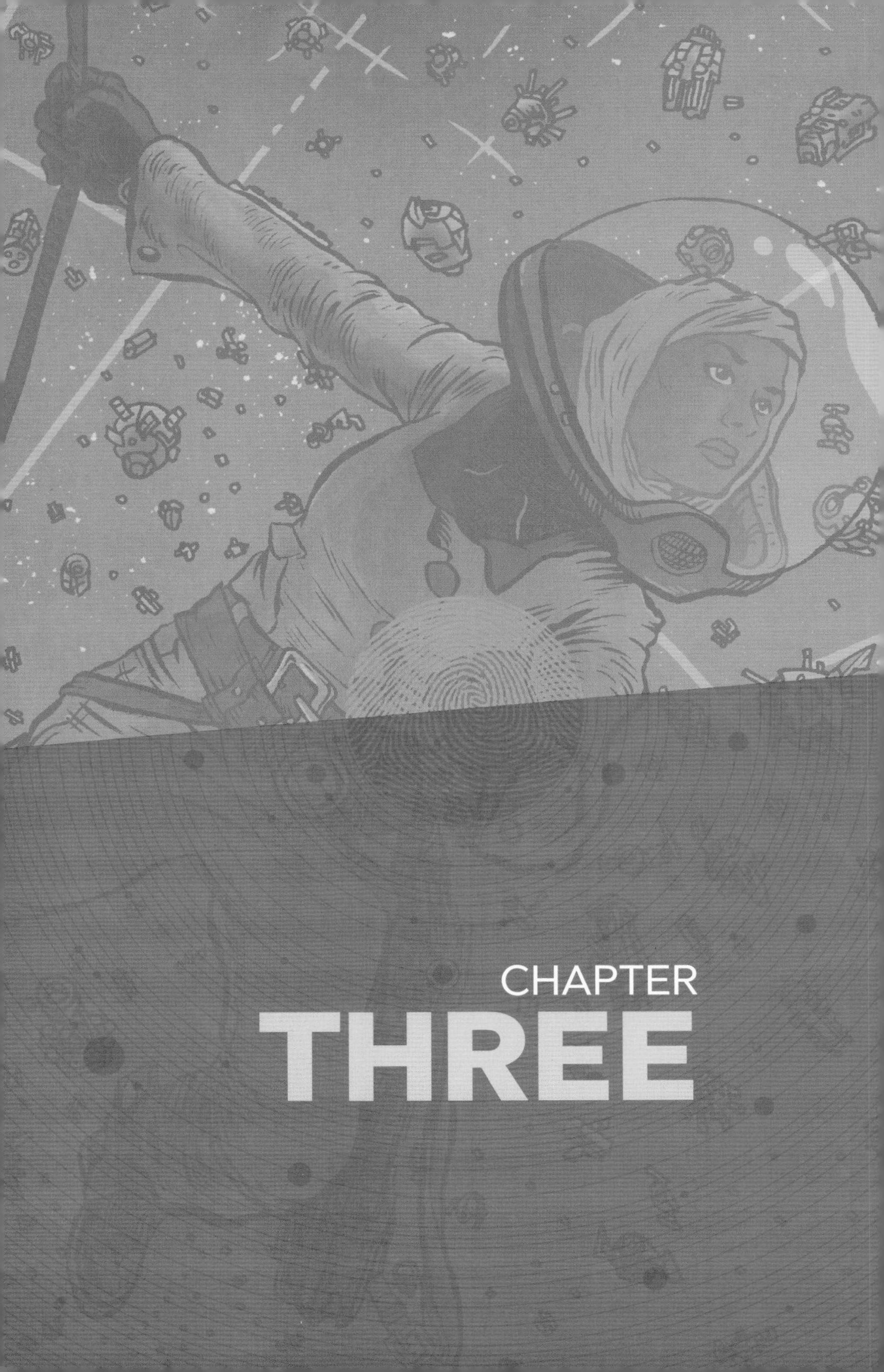

CHAPTER THREE

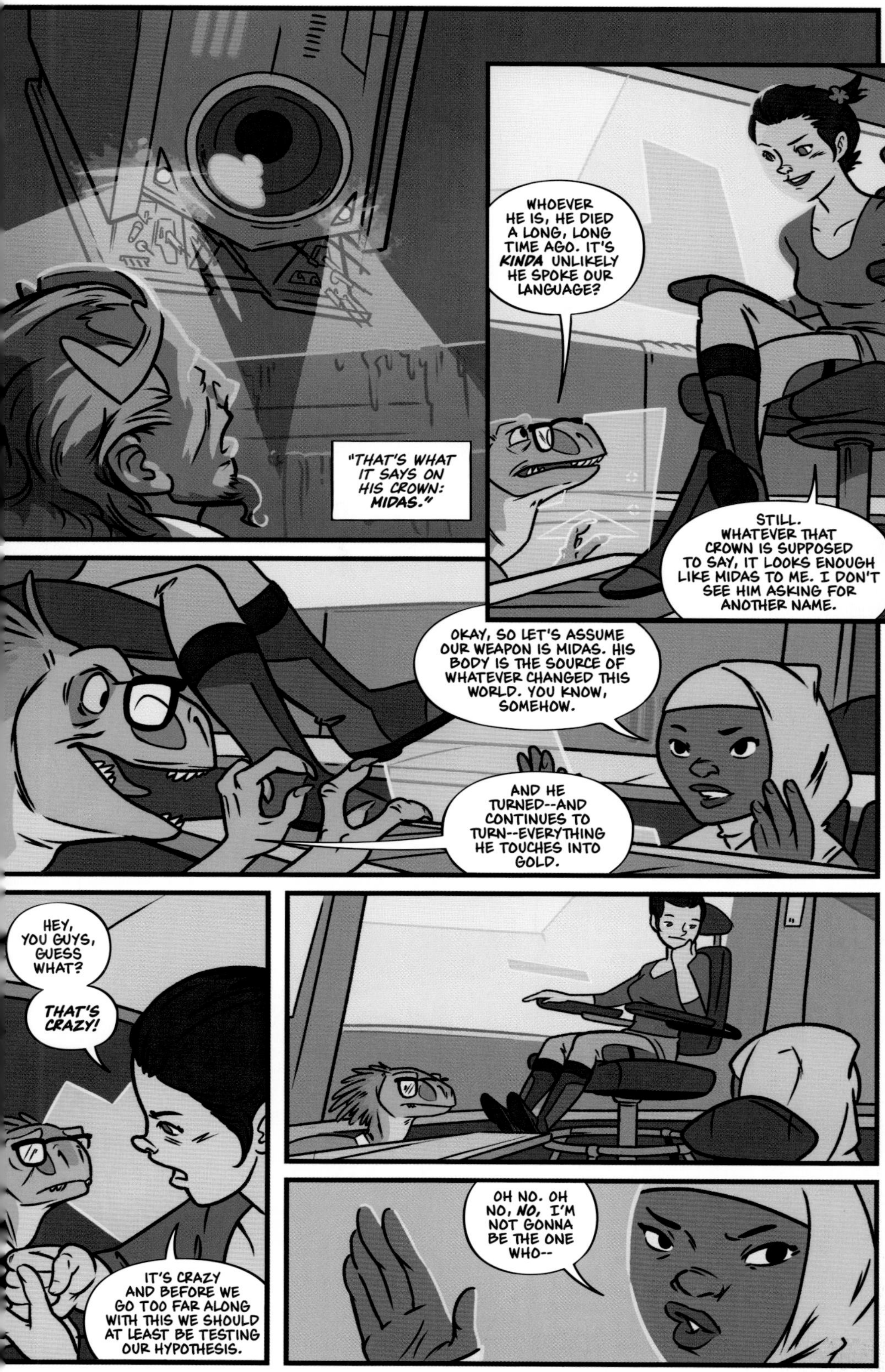
WHOEVER HE IS, HE DIED A LONG, LONG TIME AGO. IT'S *KINDA* UNLIKELY HE SPOKE OUR LANGUAGE?
"THAT'S WHAT IT SAYS ON HIS CROWN: *MIDAS*."
STILL. WHATEVER THAT CROWN IS SUPPOSED TO SAY, IT LOOKS ENOUGH LIKE MIDAS TO ME. I DON'T SEE HIM ASKING FOR ANOTHER NAME.
OKAY, SO LET'S ASSUME OUR WEAPON IS MIDAS. HIS BODY IS THE SOURCE OF WHATEVER CHANGED THIS WORLD. YOU KNOW, SOMEHOW.
AND HE TURNED--AND CONTINUES TO TURN--EVERYTHING HE TOUCHES INTO GOLD.
HEY, YOU GUYS, GUESS WHAT?
THAT'S CRAZY!
IT'S CRAZY AND BEFORE WE GO TOO FAR ALONG WITH THIS WE SHOULD AT LEAST BE TESTING OUR HYPOTHESIS.
OH NO. OH NO, *NO*, I'M NOT GONNA BE THE ONE WHO--

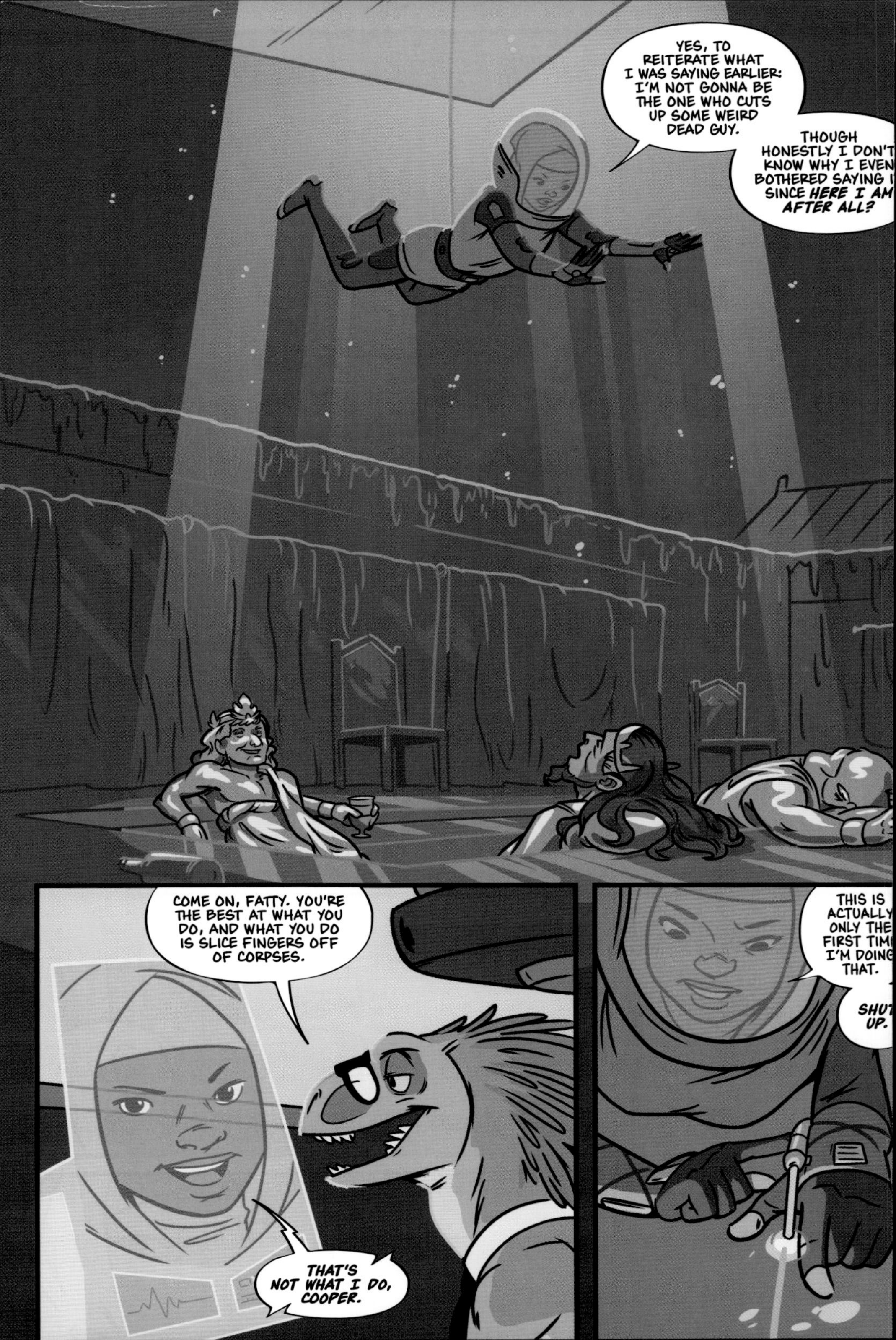
YES, TO REITERATE WHAT I WAS SAYING EARLIER: I'M NOT GONNA BE THE ONE WHO CUTS UP SOME WEIRD DEAD GUY.
THOUGH HONESTLY I DON'T KNOW WHY I EVEN BOTHERED SAYING I SINCE *HERE I AM AFTER ALL?*
COME ON, FATTY. YOU'RE THE BEST AT WHAT YOU DO, AND WHAT YOU DO IS SLICE FINGERS OFF OF CORPSES.
THAT'S NOT WHAT I DO, COOPER.
THIS IS ACTUALLY ONLY THE FIRST TIM I'M DOING THAT.
SHUT UP.

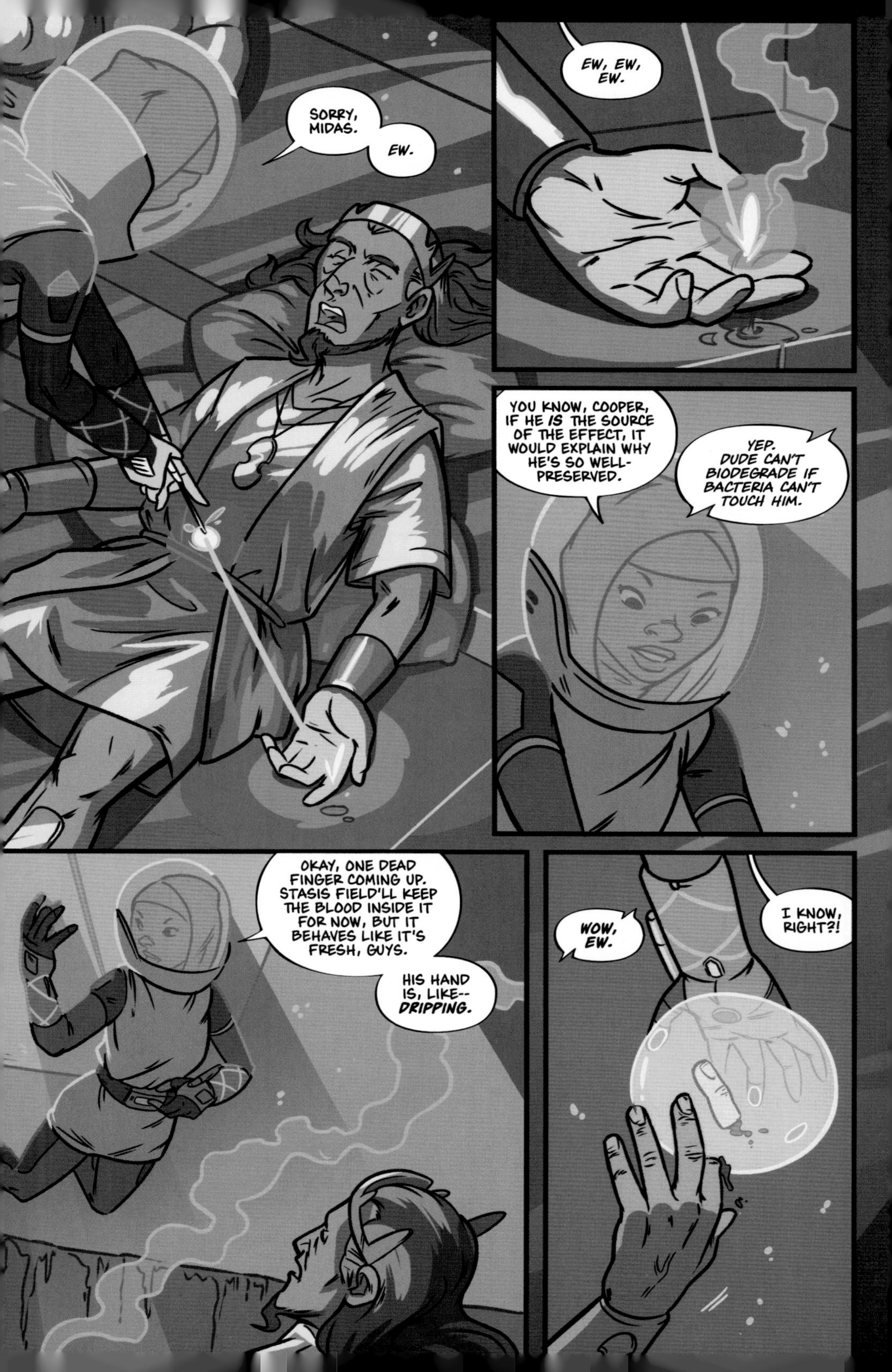
SORRY, MIDAS.
EW.
EW, EW, EW.
YOU KNOW, COOPER, IF HE IS THE SOURCE OF THE EFFECT, IT WOULD EXPLAIN WHY HE'S SO WELL-PRESERVED.
YEP. DUDE CAN'T BIODEGRADE IF BACTERIA CAN'T TOUCH HIM.
OKAY, ONE DEAD FINGER COMING UP. STASIS FIELD'LL KEEP THE BLOOD INSIDE IT FOR NOW, BUT IT BEHAVES LIKE IT'S FRESH, GUYS.
HIS HAND IS, LIKE-- DRIPPING.
WOW, EW.
I KNOW, RIGHT?!

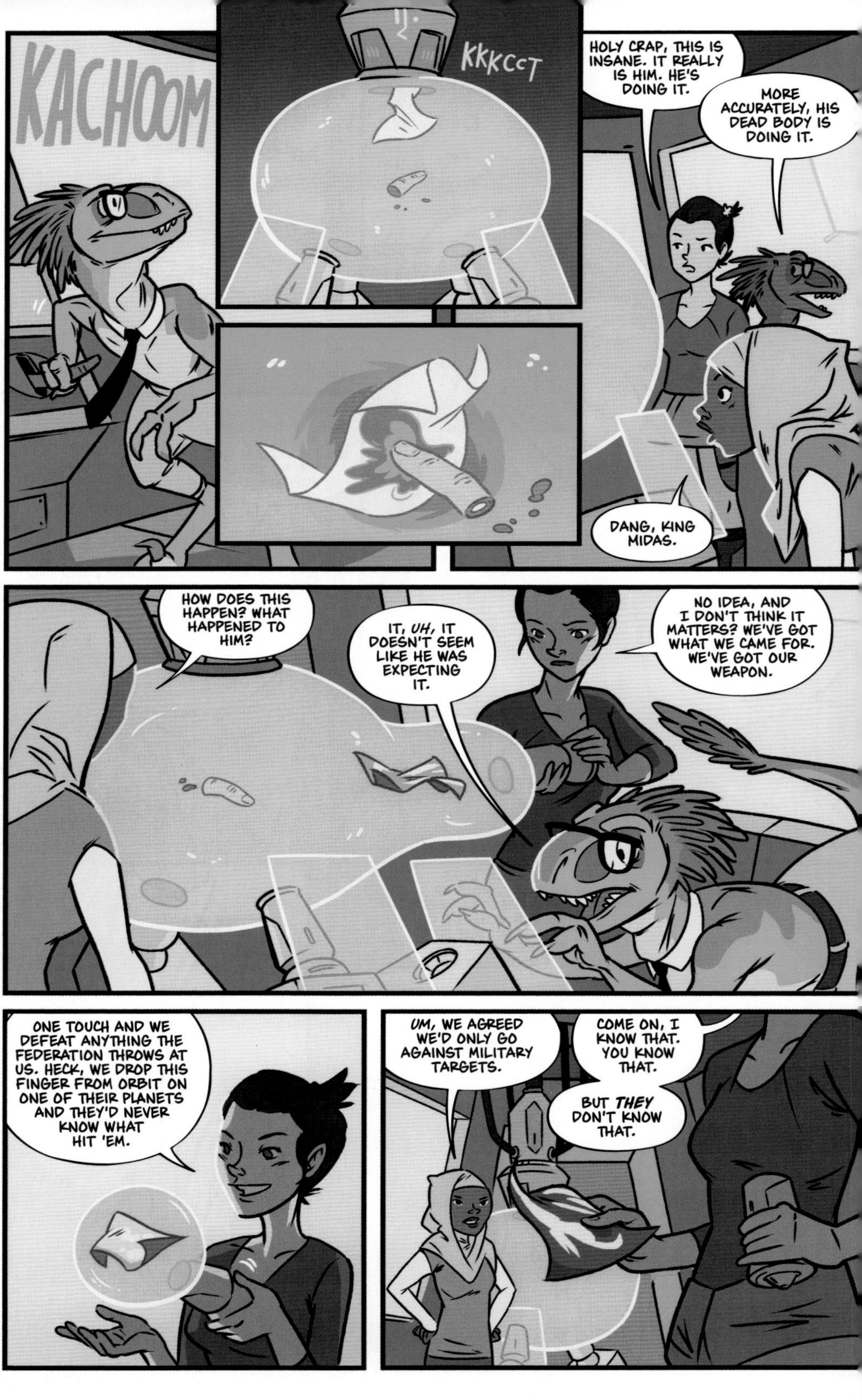
KACHOOM
KKKCCT
HOLY CRAP, THIS IS INSANE. IT REALLY IS HIM. HE'S DOING IT.
MORE ACCURATELY, HIS DEAD BODY IS DOING IT.
DANG, KING MIDAS.
HOW DOES THIS HAPPEN? WHAT HAPPENED TO HIM?
IT, UH, IT DOESN'T SEEM LIKE HE WAS EXPECTING IT.
NO IDEA, AND I DON'T THINK IT MATTERS? WE'VE GOT WHAT WE CAME FOR. WE'VE GOT OUR WEAPON.
ONE TOUCH AND WE DEFEAT ANYTHING THE FEDERATION THROWS AT US. HECK, WE DROP THIS FINGER FROM ORBIT ON ONE OF THEIR PLANETS AND THEY'D NEVER KNOW WHAT HIT 'EM.
UM, WE AGREED WE'D ONLY GO AGAINST MILITARY TARGETS.
COME ON, I KNOW THAT. YOU KNOW THAT.
BUT THEY DON'T KNOW THAT.

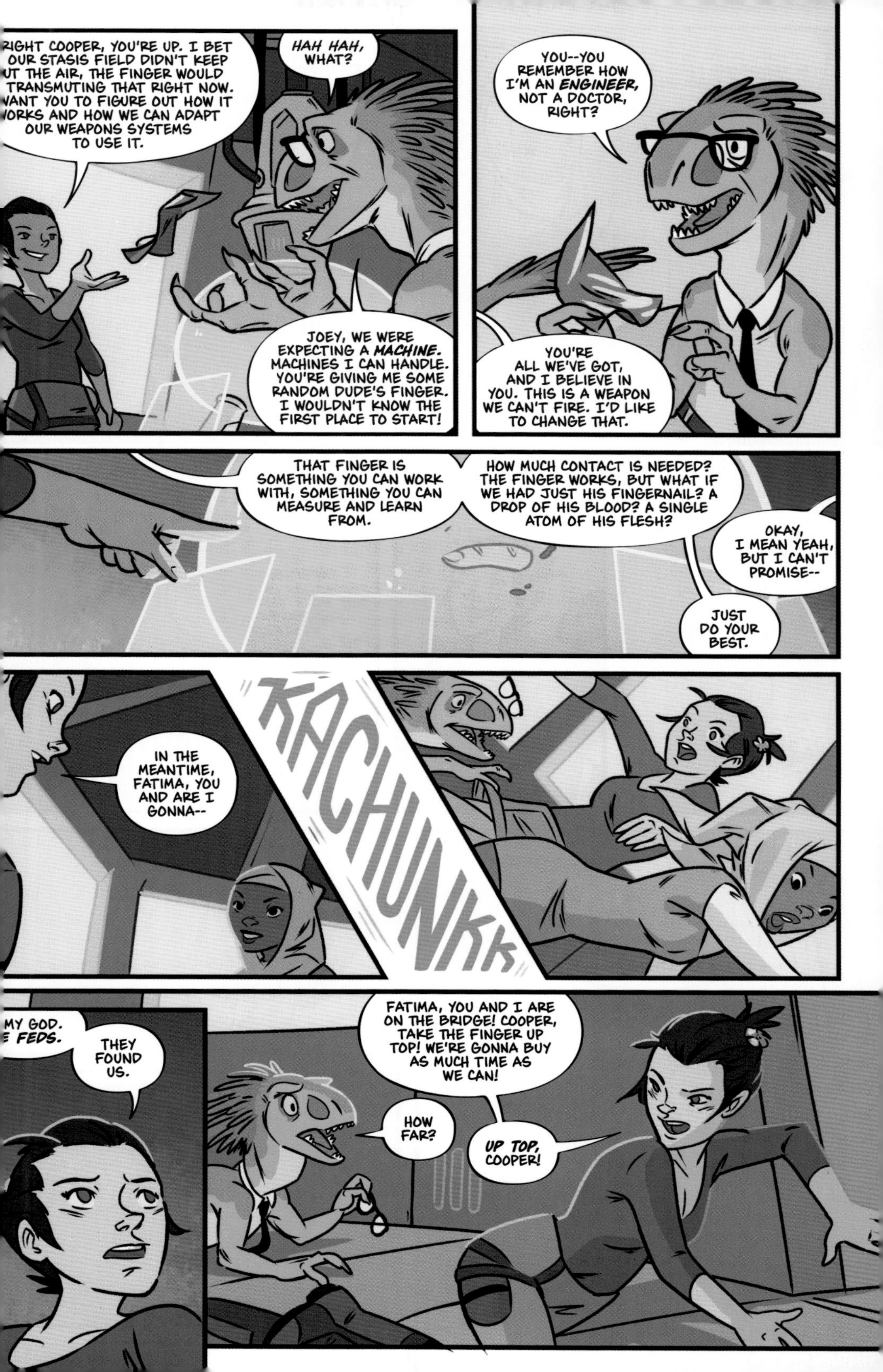
RIGHT COOPER, YOU'RE UP. I BET OUR STASIS FIELD DIDN'T KEEP UT THE AIR, THE FINGER WOULD TRANSMUTING THAT RIGHT NOW. VANT YOU TO FIGURE OUT HOW IT VORKS AND HOW WE CAN ADAPT OUR WEAPONS SYSTEMS TO USE IT.
HAH HAH, WHAT?
JOEY, WE WERE EXPECTING A MACHINE. MACHINES I CAN HANDLE. YOU'RE GIVING ME SOME RANDOM DUDE'S FINGER. I WOULDN'T KNOW THE FIRST PLACE TO START!
YOU--YOU REMEMBER HOW I'M AN ENGINEER, NOT A DOCTOR, RIGHT?
YOU'RE ALL WE'VE GOT, AND I BELIEVE IN YOU. THIS IS A WEAPON WE CAN'T FIRE. I'D LIKE TO CHANGE THAT.
THAT FINGER IS SOMETHING YOU CAN WORK WITH, SOMETHING YOU CAN MEASURE AND LEARN FROM.
HOW MUCH CONTACT IS NEEDED? THE FINGER WORKS, BUT WHAT IF WE HAD JUST HIS FINGERNAIL? A DROP OF HIS BLOOD? A SINGLE ATOM OF HIS FLESH?
OKAY, I MEAN YEAH, BUT I CAN'T PROMISE--
JUST DO YOUR BEST.
IN THE MEANTIME, FATIMA, YOU AND ARE I GONNA--
KACHUNKK
MY GOD. E FEDS.
THEY FOUND US.
FATIMA, YOU AND I ARE ON THE BRIDGE! COOPER, TAKE THE FINGER UP TOP! WE'RE GONNA BUY AS MUCH TIME AS WE CAN!
HOW FAR?
UP TOP, COOPER!

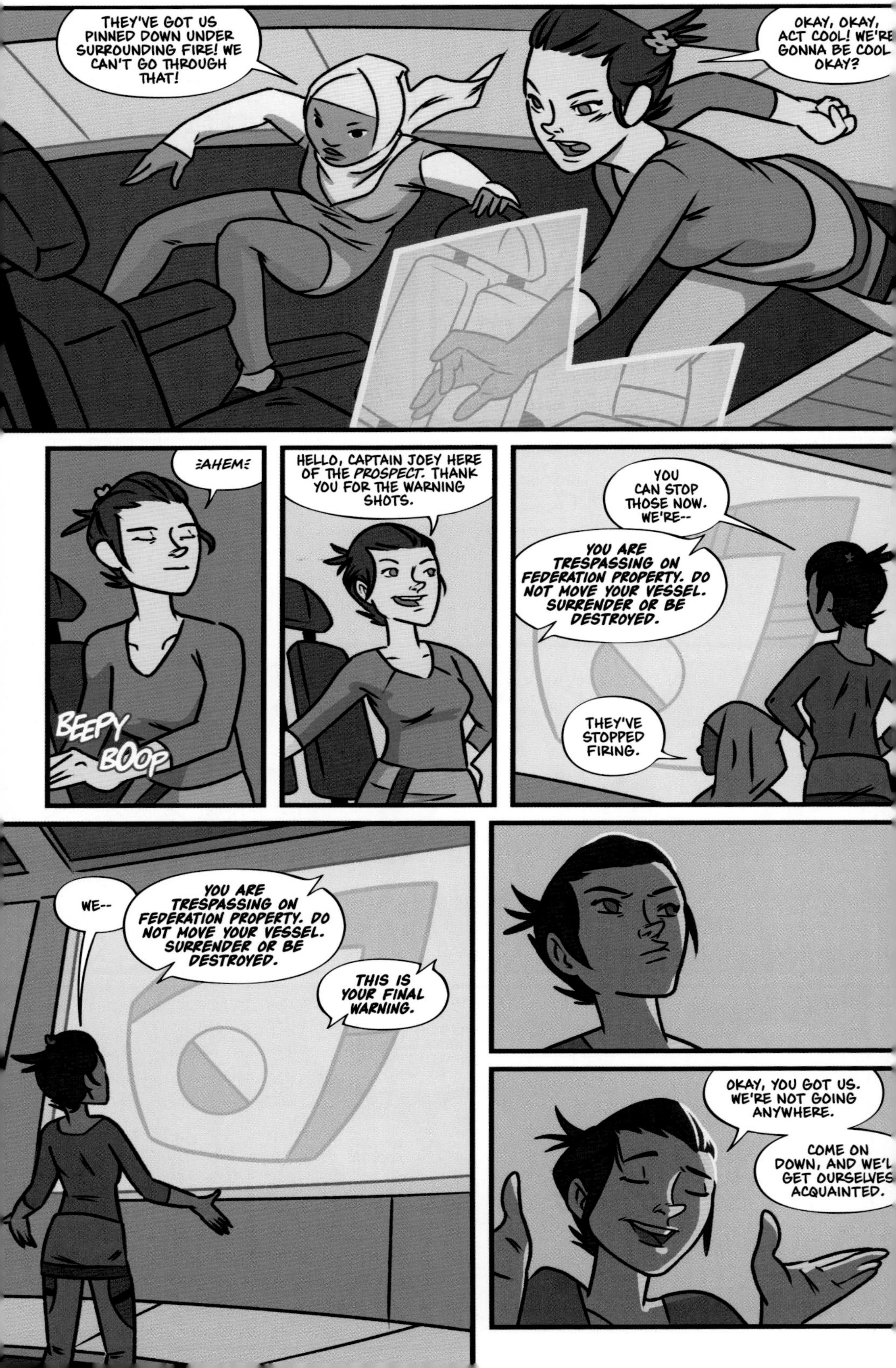
THEY'VE GOT US PINNED DOWN UNDER SURROUNDING FIRE! WE CAN'T GO THROUGH THAT!
OKAY, OKAY, ACT COOL! WE'RE GONNA BE COOL OKAY?
AHEM
BEEPY BOOP
HELLO, CAPTAIN JOEY HERE OF THE *PROSPECT*. THANK YOU FOR THE WARNING SHOTS.
YOU CAN STOP THOSE NOW. WE'RE--
YOU ARE TRESPASSING ON FEDERATION PROPERTY. DO NOT MOVE YOUR VESSEL. SURRENDER OR BE DESTROYED.
THEY'VE STOPPED FIRING.
WE--
YOU ARE TRESPASSING ON FEDERATION PROPERTY. DO NOT MOVE YOUR VESSEL. SURRENDER OR BE DESTROYED.
THIS IS YOUR FINAL WARNING.
OKAY, YOU GOT US. WE'RE NOT GOING ANYWHERE.
COME ON DOWN, AND WE'LL GET OURSELVES ACQUAINTED.

ALRIGHT JERKS, LET'S SEE HOW YOU DEAL WITH *THIS!*

UP OP!

AW DANG!

AW DANG
AW DANG
AW DANG

AW DANG THAT WAS SO CLOSE.

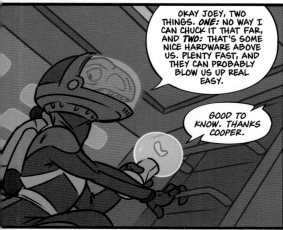

OKAY JOEY, TWO THINGS. *ONE:* NO WAY I CAN CHUCK IT THAT FAR, AND *TWO:* THAT'S SOME NICE HARDWARE ABOVE US. PLENTY FAST, AND THEY CAN PROBABLY BLOW US UP REAL EASY.

GOOD TO KNOW. THANKS COOPER.

NO PROBLEM. SORRY, JOEY.

SO UM-- RIGHT.

WE WERE TALKING ABOUT GIVING OURSELVES UP?

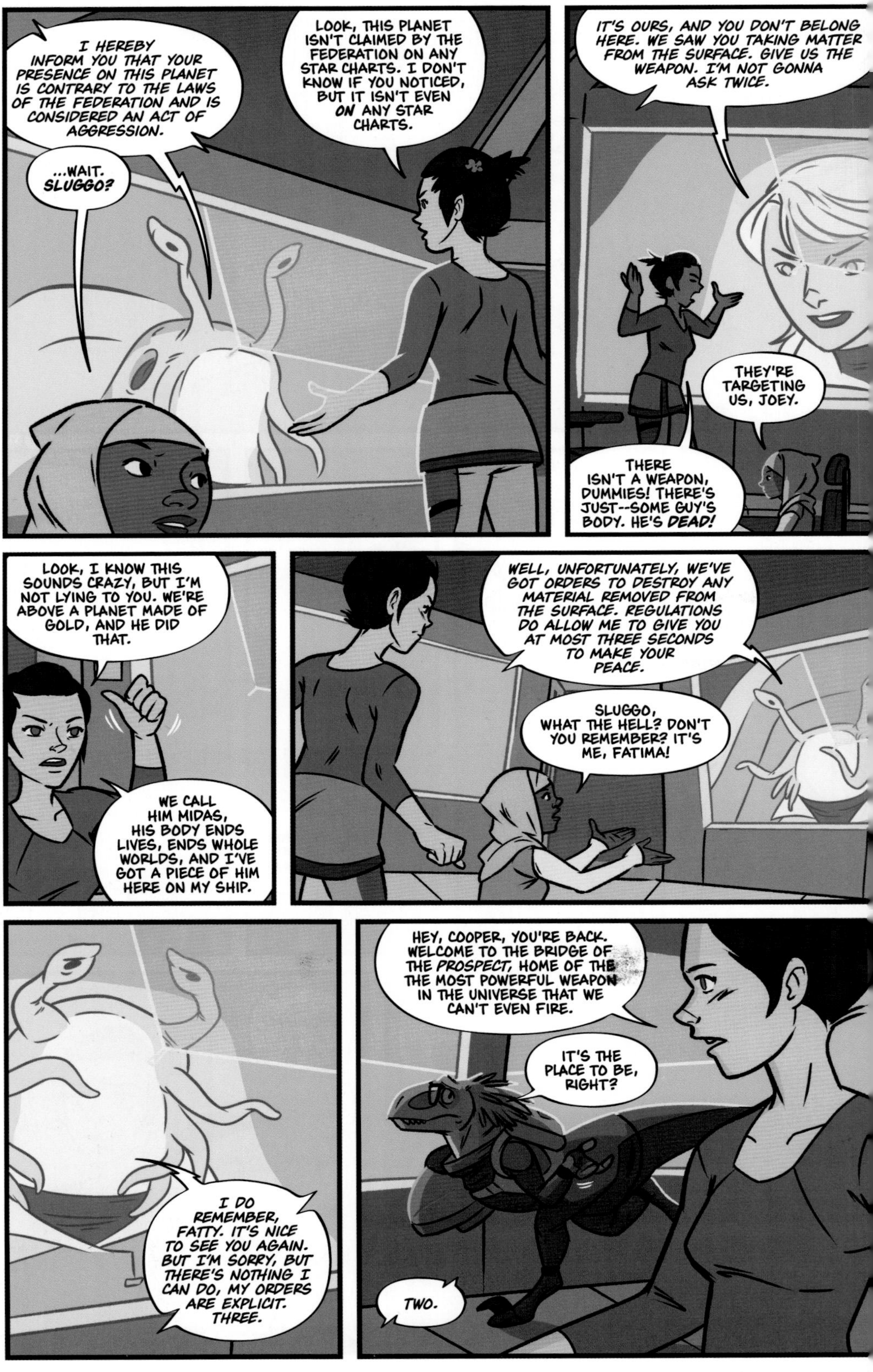
I HEREBY INFORM YOU THAT YOUR PRESENCE ON THIS PLANET IS CONTRARY TO THE LAWS OF THE FEDERATION AND IS CONSIDERED AN ACT OF AGGRESSION.
LOOK, THIS PLANET ISN'T CLAIMED BY THE FEDERATION ON ANY STAR CHARTS. I DON'T KNOW IF YOU NOTICED, BUT IT ISN'T EVEN ON ANY STAR CHARTS.
...WAIT. SLUGGO?
IT'S OURS, AND YOU DON'T BELONG HERE. WE SAW YOU TAKING MATTER FROM THE SURFACE. GIVE US THE WEAPON. I'M NOT GONNA ASK TWICE.
THEY'RE TARGETING US, JOEY.
THERE ISN'T A WEAPON, DUMMIES! THERE'S JUST--SOME GUY'S BODY. HE'S DEAD!
LOOK, I KNOW THIS SOUNDS CRAZY, BUT I'M NOT LYING TO YOU. WE'RE ABOVE A PLANET MADE OF GOLD, AND HE DID THAT.
WE CALL HIM MIDAS, HIS BODY ENDS LIVES, ENDS WHOLE WORLDS, AND I'VE GOT A PIECE OF HIM HERE ON MY SHIP.
WELL, UNFORTUNATELY, WE'VE GOT ORDERS TO DESTROY ANY MATERIAL REMOVED FROM THE SURFACE. REGULATIONS DO ALLOW ME TO GIVE YOU AT MOST THREE SECONDS TO MAKE YOUR PEACE.
SLUGGO, WHAT THE HELL? DON'T YOU REMEMBER? IT'S ME, FATIMA!
I DO REMEMBER, FATTY. IT'S NICE TO SEE YOU AGAIN. BUT I'M SORRY, BUT THERE'S NOTHING I CAN DO, MY ORDERS ARE EXPLICIT. THREE.
HEY, COOPER, YOU'RE BACK. WELCOME TO THE BRIDGE OF THE *PROSPECT*, HOME OF THE THE MOST POWERFUL WEAPON IN THE UNIVERSE THAT WE CAN'T EVEN FIRE.
IT'S THE PLACE TO BE, RIGHT?
TWO.

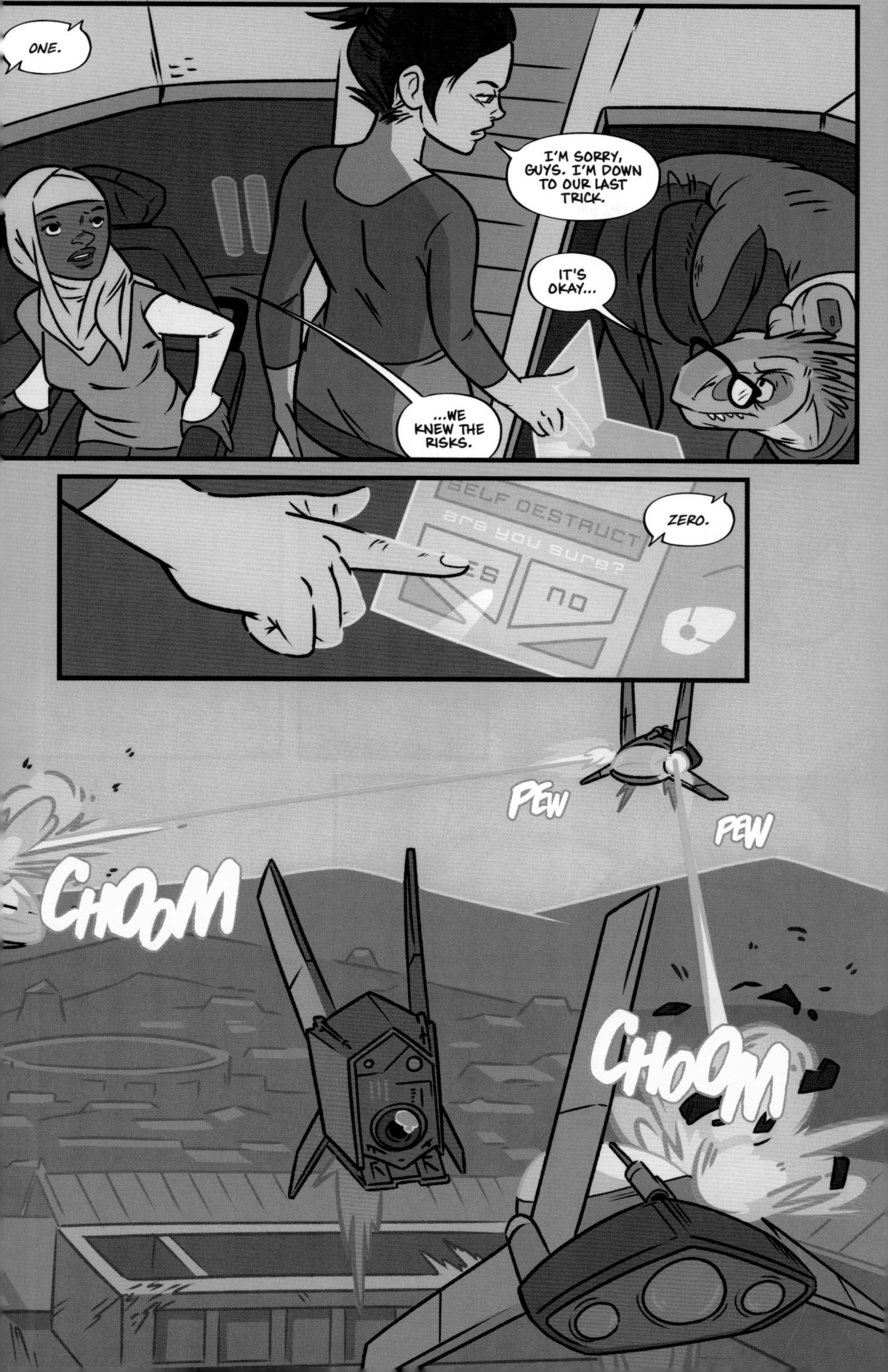
ONE.
I'M SORRY, GUYS. I'M DOWN TO OUR LAST TRICK.
IT'S OKAY...
...WE KNEW THE RISKS.
SELF DESTRUCT
are you sure?
NO
ZERO.
PEW
PEW
CHOOM
CHOOM

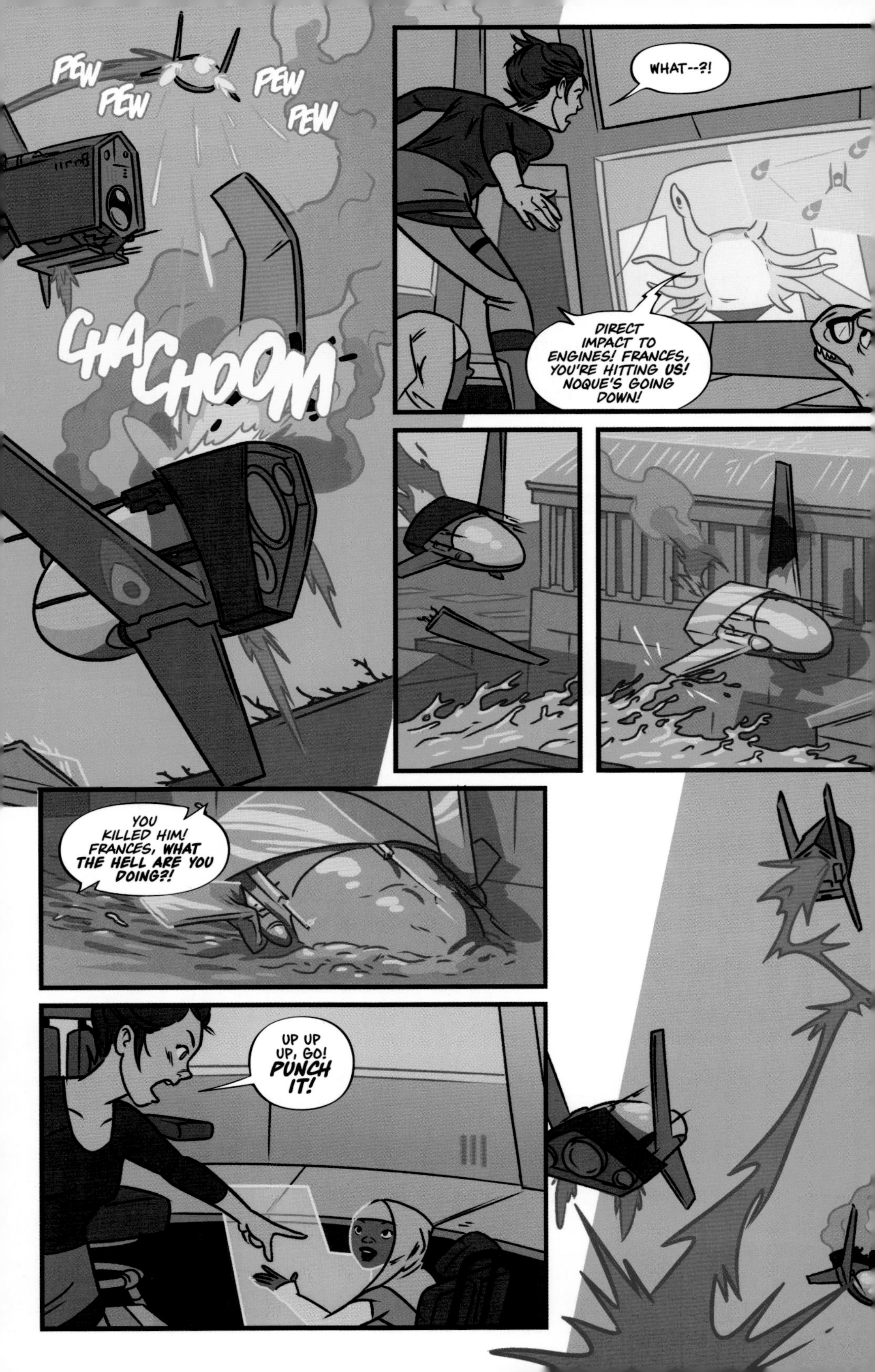
PEW
PEW
PEW
PEW
CHACHOOM
WHAT--?!
DIRECT IMPACT TO ENGINES! FRANCES, YOU'RE HITTING US! NOQUE'S GOING DOWN!
YOU KILLED HIM! FRANCES, WHAT THE HELL ARE YOU DOING?!
UP UP UP, GO! PUNCH IT!

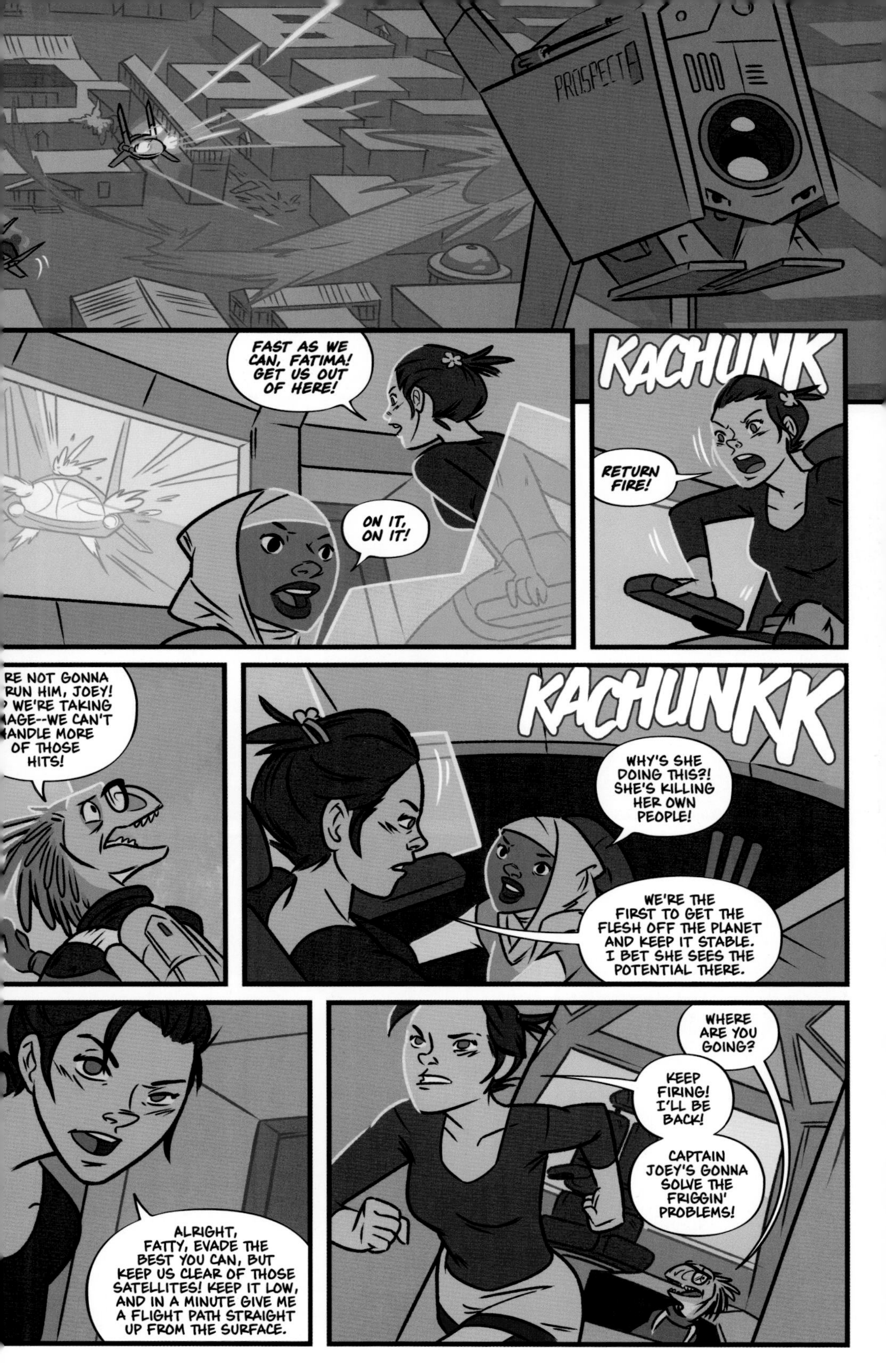
PROSPECT A
FAST AS WE CAN, FATIMA! GET US OUT OF HERE!
ON IT, ON IT!
KACHUNK
RETURN FIRE!
RE NOT GONNA RUN HIM, JOEY! WE'RE TAKING MAGE--WE CAN'T HANDLE MORE OF THOSE HITS!
KACHUNKK
WHY'S SHE DOING THIS?! SHE'S KILLING HER OWN PEOPLE!
WE'RE THE FIRST TO GET THE FLESH OFF THE PLANET AND KEEP IT STABLE. I BET SHE SEES THE POTENTIAL THERE.
ALRIGHT, FATTY, EVADE THE BEST YOU CAN, BUT KEEP US CLEAR OF THOSE SATELLITES! KEEP IT LOW, AND IN A MINUTE GIVE ME A FLIGHT PATH STRAIGHT UP FROM THE SURFACE.
WHERE ARE YOU GOING?
KEEP FIRING! I'LL BE BACK!
CAPTAIN JOEY'S GONNA SOLVE THE FRIGGIN' PROBLEMS!

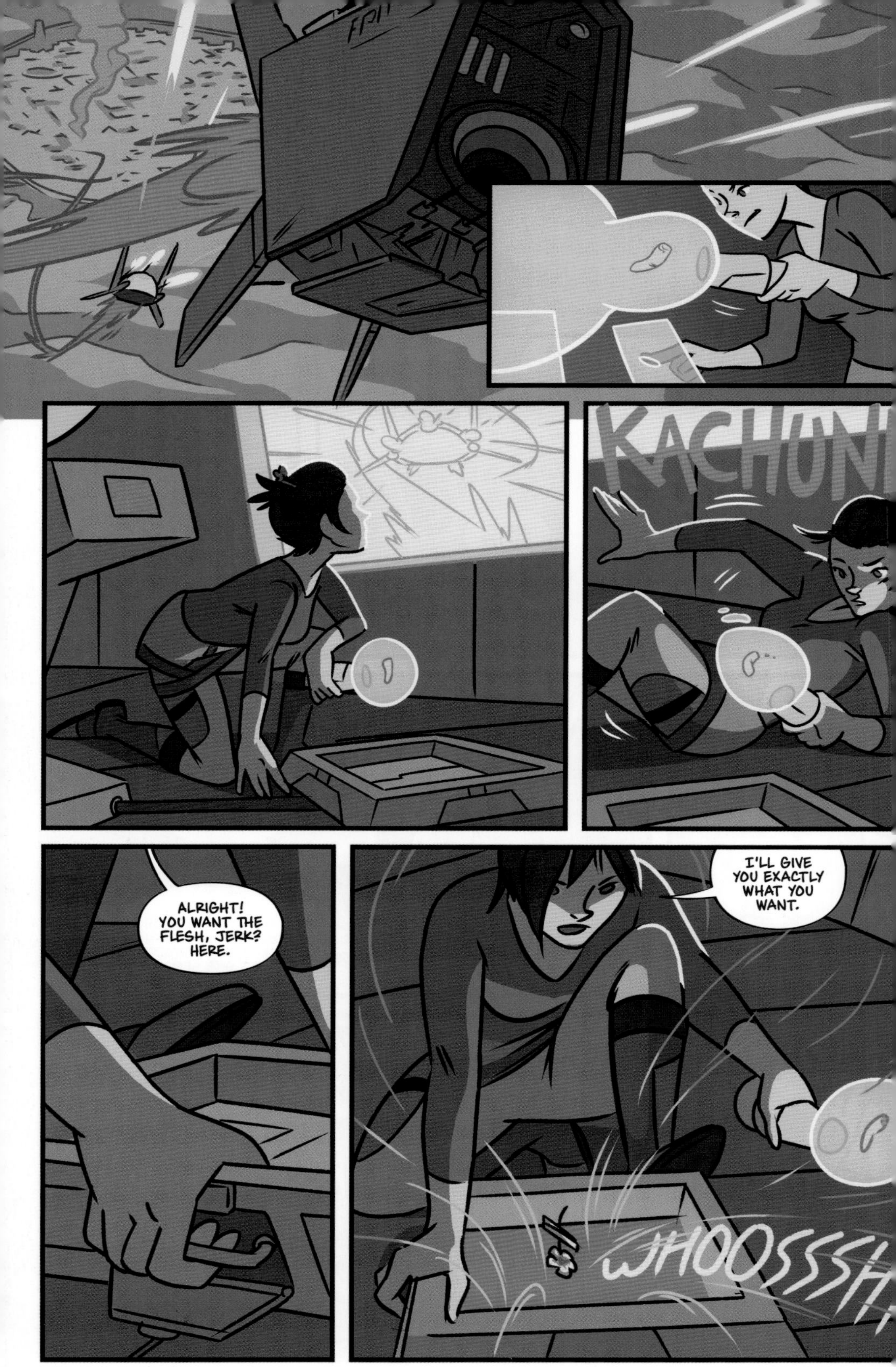
KACHUNK
ALRIGHT! YOU WANT THE FLESH, JERK? HERE.
I'LL GIVE YOU EXACTLY WHAT YOU WANT.
WHOOSSSH

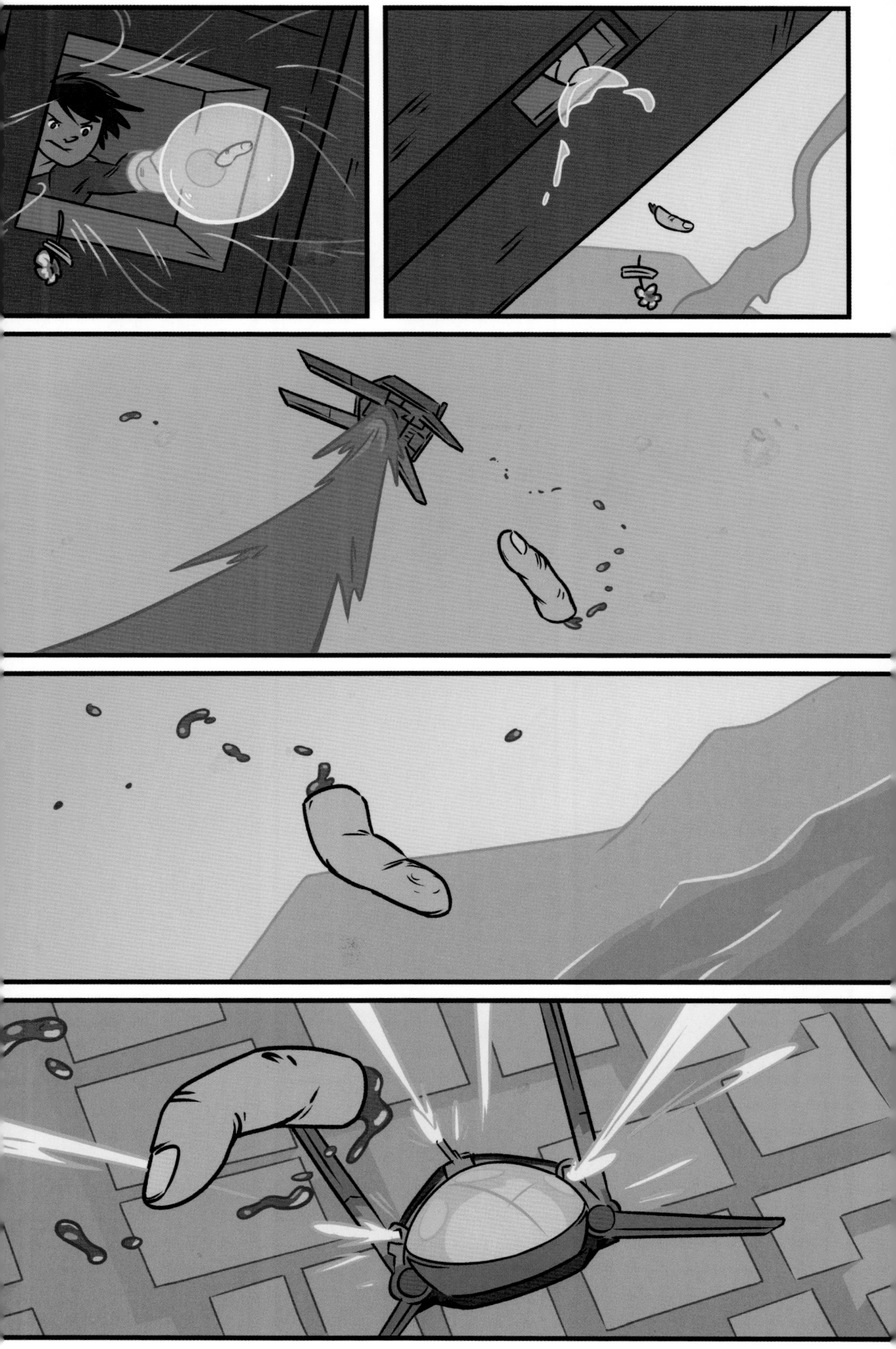

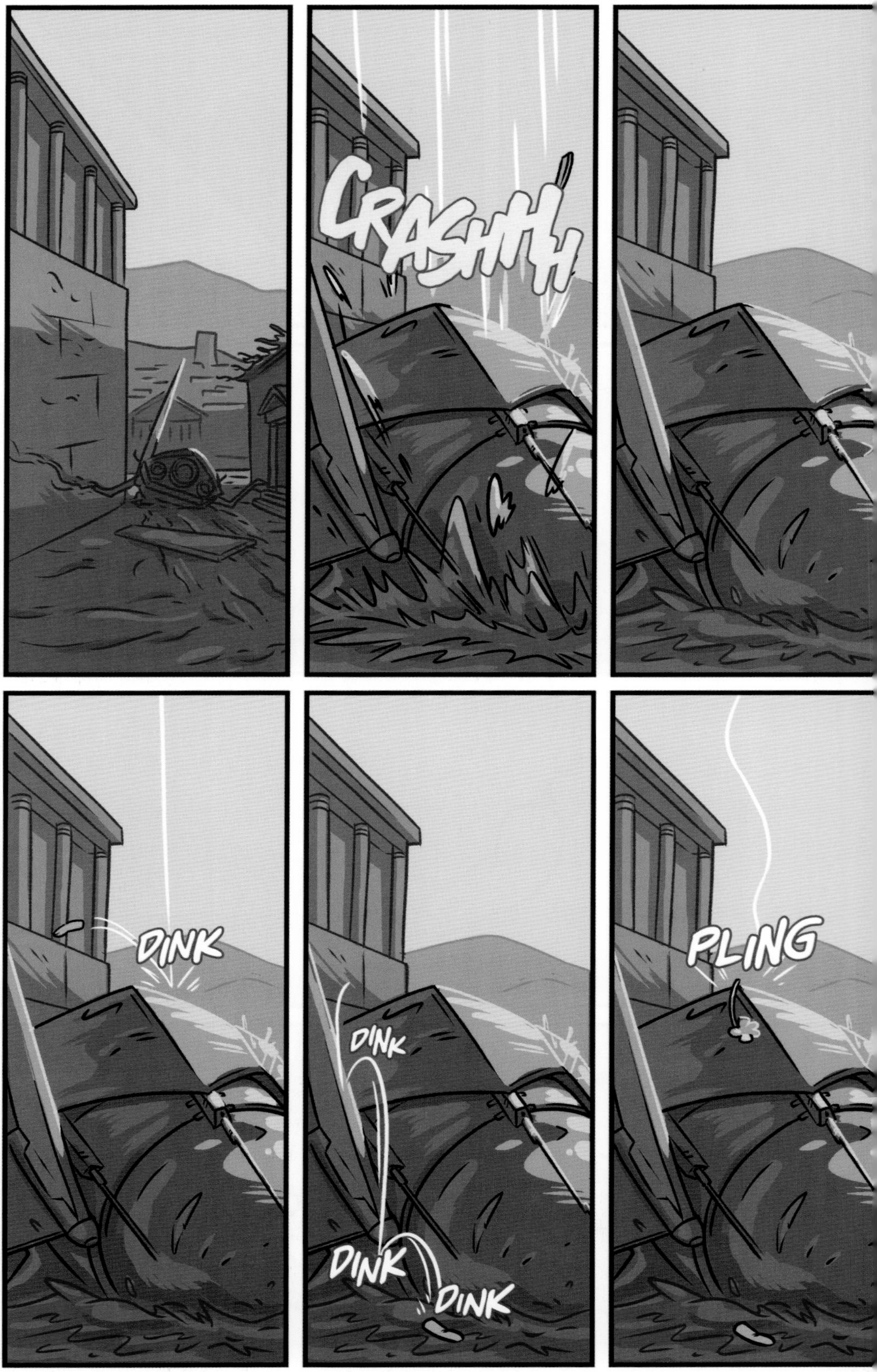
CRASHHH
DINK
DINK
DINK
DINK
PLING

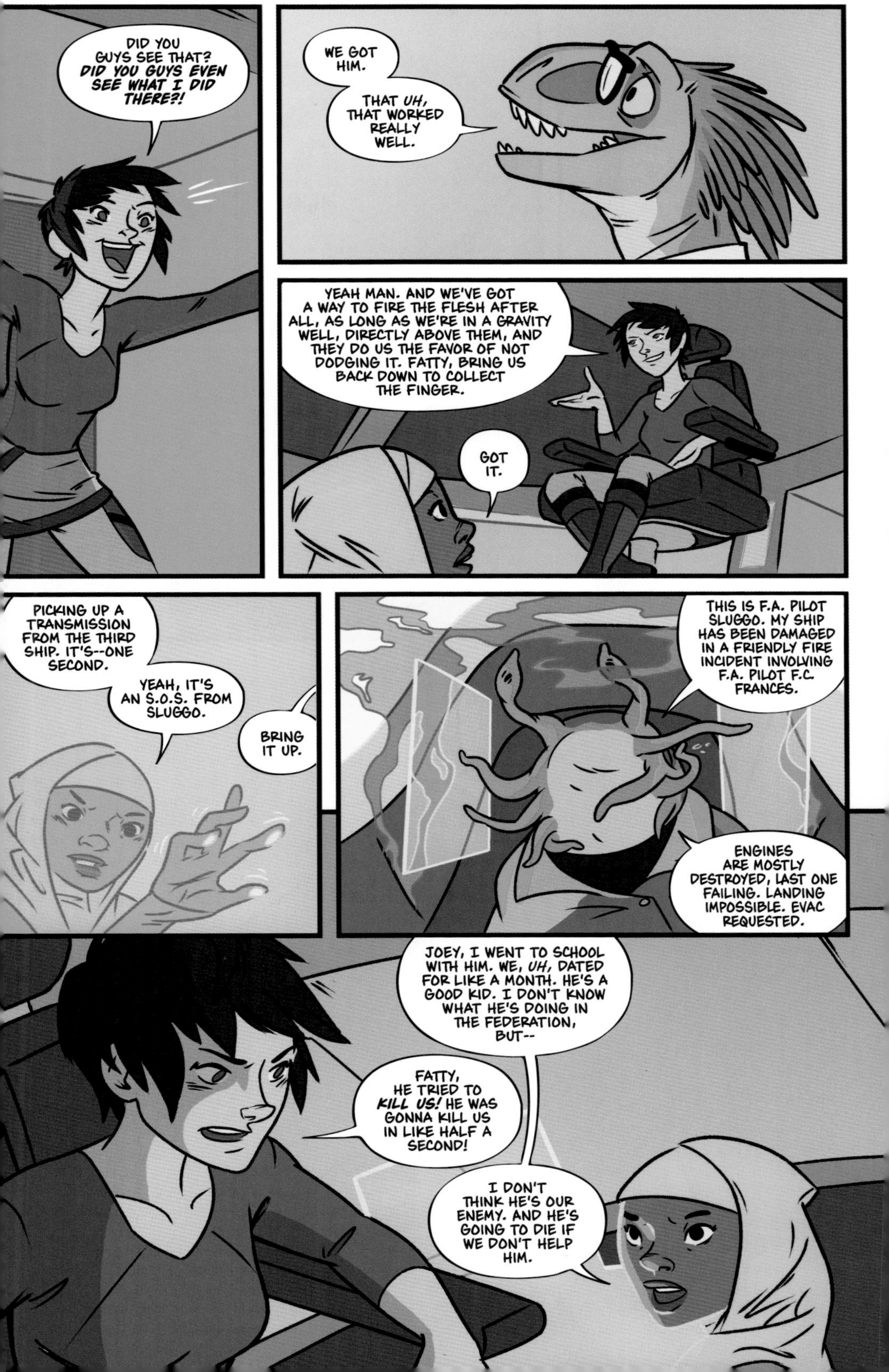

DID YOU GUYS SEE THAT? DID YOU GUYS EVEN SEE WHAT I DID THERE?!
WE GOT HIM.
THAT UH, THAT WORKED REALLY WELL.
YEAH MAN. AND WE'VE GOT A WAY TO FIRE THE FLESH AFTER ALL, AS LONG AS WE'RE IN A GRAVITY WELL, DIRECTLY ABOVE THEM, AND THEY DO US THE FAVOR OF NOT DODGING IT. FATTY, BRING US BACK DOWN TO COLLECT THE FINGER.
GOT IT.
PICKING UP A TRANSMISSION FROM THE THIRD SHIP. IT'S--ONE SECOND.
YEAH, IT'S AN S.O.S. FROM SLUGGO.
BRING IT UP.
THIS IS F.A. PILOT SLUGGO. MY SHIP HAS BEEN DAMAGED IN A FRIENDLY FIRE INCIDENT INVOLVING F.A. PILOT F.C. FRANCES.
ENGINES ARE MOSTLY DESTROYED, LAST ONE FAILING. LANDING IMPOSSIBLE. EVAC REQUESTED.
JOEY, I WENT TO SCHOOL WITH HIM. WE, UH, DATED FOR LIKE A MONTH. HE'S A GOOD KID. I DON'T KNOW WHAT HE'S DOING IN THE FEDERATION, BUT--
FATTY, HE TRIED TO KILL US! HE WAS GONNA KILL US IN LIKE HALF A SECOND!
I DON'T THINK HE'S OUR ENEMY. AND HE'S GOING TO DIE IF WE DON'T HELP HIM.

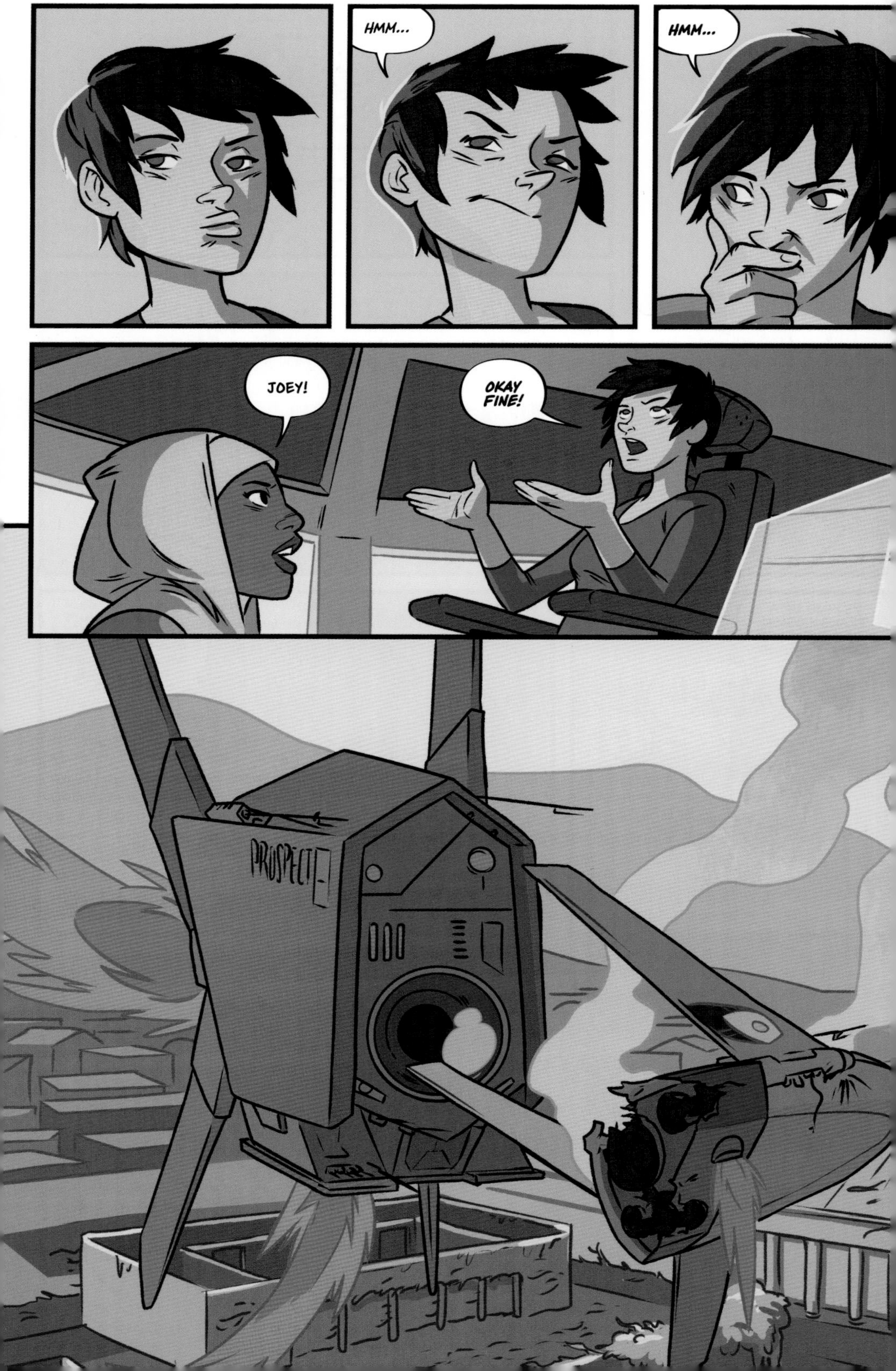
HMM...
HMM...
JOEY!
OKAY FINE!
PROSPECT

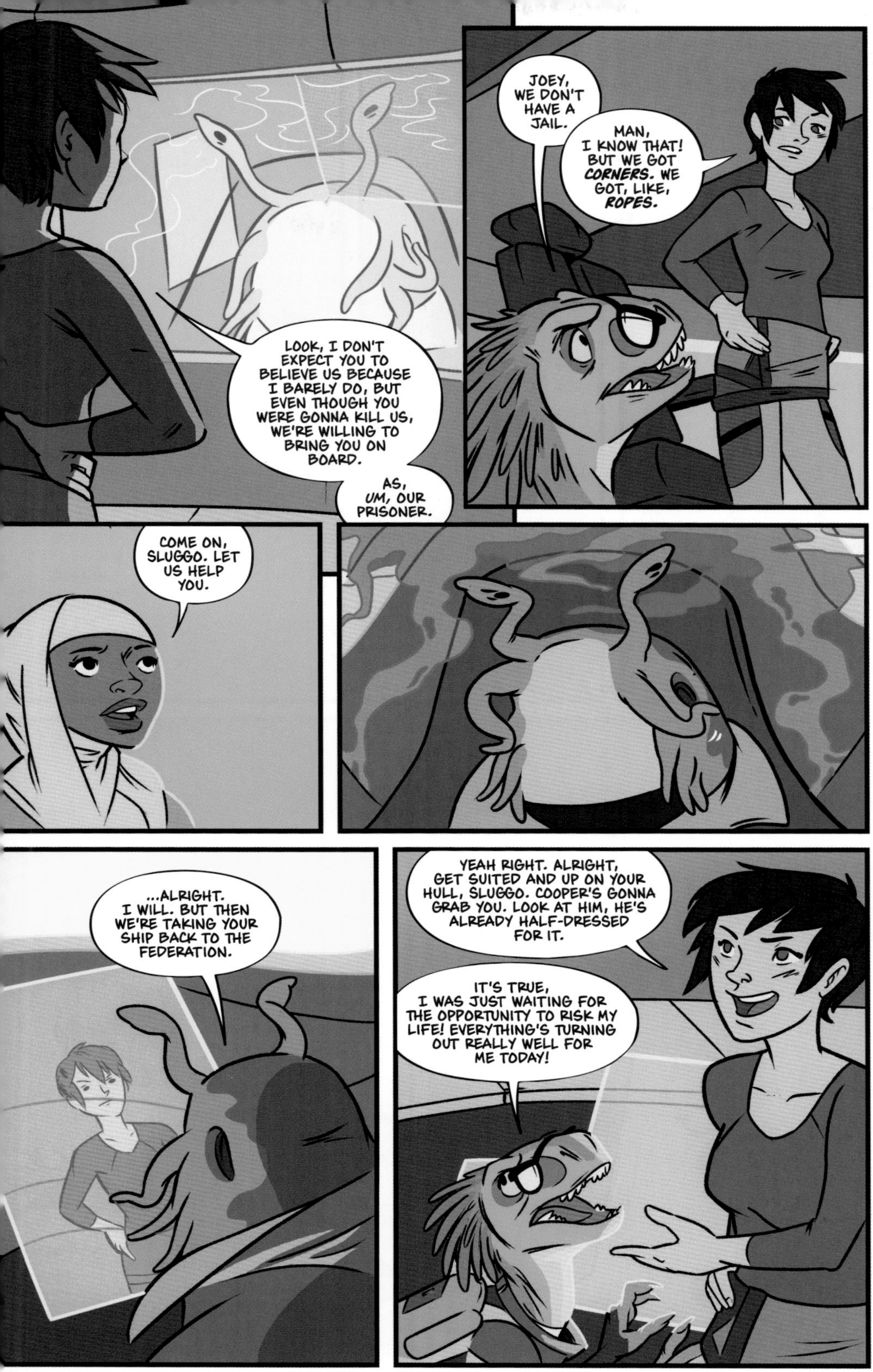
LOOK, I DON'T EXPECT YOU TO BELIEVE US BECAUSE I BARELY DO, BUT EVEN THOUGH YOU WERE GONNA KILL US, WE'RE WILLING TO BRING YOU ON BOARD.
AS, UM, OUR PRISONER.
JOEY, WE DON'T HAVE A JAIL.
MAN, I KNOW THAT! BUT WE GOT CORNERS. WE GOT, LIKE, ROPES.
COME ON, SLUGGO. LET US HELP YOU.
...ALRIGHT. I WILL. BUT THEN WE'RE TAKING YOUR SHIP BACK TO THE FEDERATION.
YEAH RIGHT. ALRIGHT, GET SUITED AND UP ON YOUR HULL, SLUGGO. COOPER'S GONNA GRAB YOU. LOOK AT HIM, HE'S ALREADY HALF-DRESSED FOR IT.
IT'S TRUE, I WAS JUST WAITING FOR THE OPPORTUNITY TO RISK MY LIFE! EVERYTHING'S TURNING OUT REALLY WELL FOR ME TODAY!

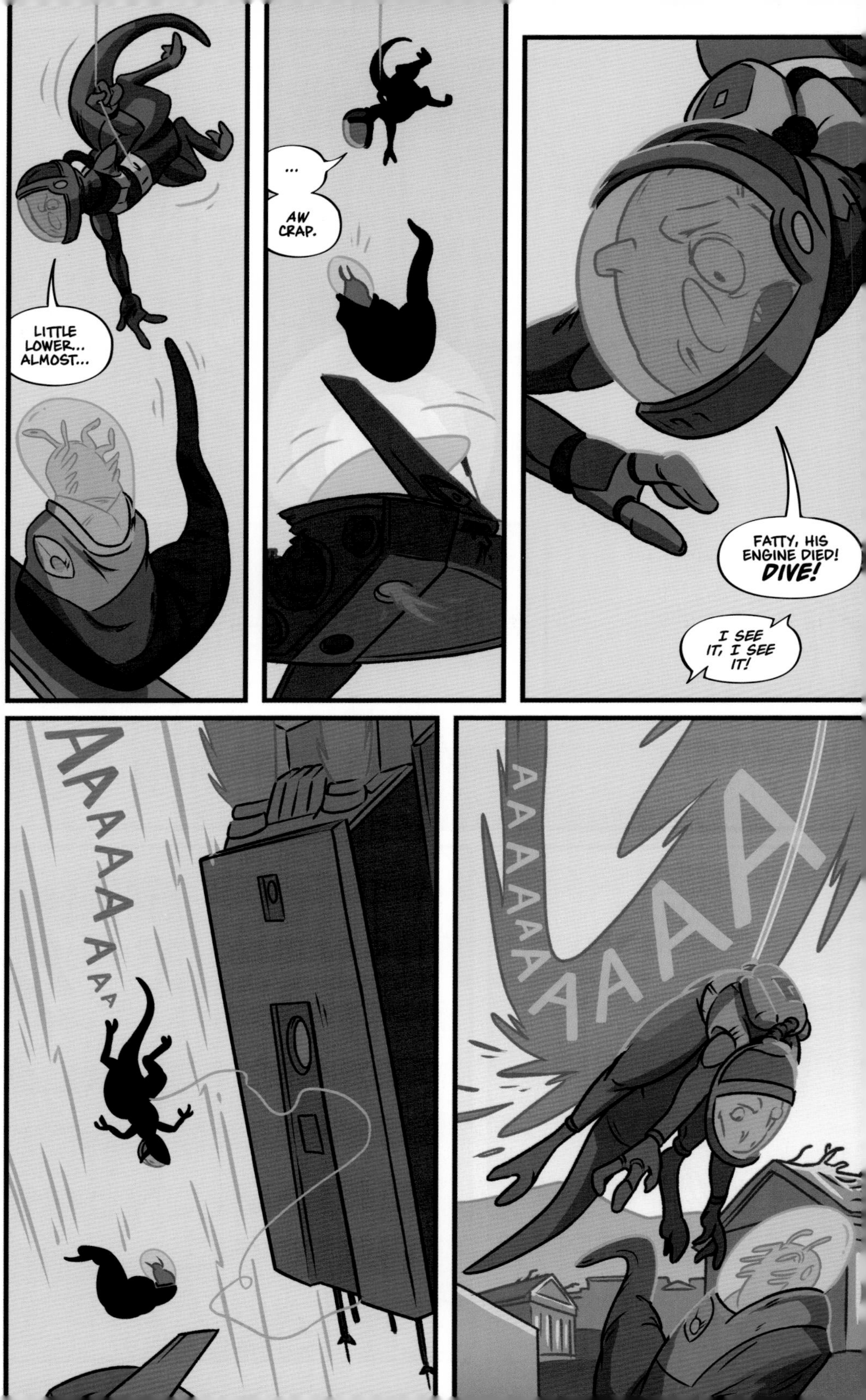
LITTLE LOWER... ALMOST...
...
AW CRAP.
FATTY, HIS ENGINE DIED! DIVE!
I SEE IT, I SEE IT!
AAAAAAAA
AAAAAAAAAA

AHHHHHHHHH YES THAT'S WHAT I'M TALKING ABOUT!

HI, SLUGGO, I'M COOPER. I'M THE DUDE WHO JUST SAVED YOUR LIFE.

COME ON. I WANNA INTRODUCE YOU TO MY FRIENDS.

SHORTLY.

WELCOME ABOARD. THIS IS *THE PROSPECT.*

GOOD TO BE BACK, FATTY. SLUGGO, THIS IS OUR CAPTAIN JOEY AND I BELIEVE YOU'VE MET FATIMA?

HELLO, CAPTAIN. HELLO, FATTY.

COOPER.

RIGHT.

I, UM, HAVE TO TIE YOU UP.

I'M SORRY ABOUT THIS, BUT THIS ISN'T EXACTLY GOING AS WE PLANNED. WE'RE NOT SET UP FOR PRISONERS, AND I'M NOT CONVINCED THAT YOU DON'T KNOW MORE ABOUT THE ATTACK ON US THAN YOU'VE SAID. SO I DON'T TRUST YOU.

SO YOU'RE GONNA STAY TIED UP FOR NOW.

I'M NOT GOING TO ATTACK YOU. I DON'T KNOW WHAT YOU KNOW ABOUT MY PEOPLE, BUT WE'RE NOT EXACTLY THE SPEEDIEST PICKLES IN THE JAR. AND EVEN IF I TRIED, YOU'VE GOT A *DINOSAUR* IN A TIE OVER THERE. I THINK HE CAN TAKE ME.

I LIKE HIM!

LOOK, SLUGGO, CARDS ON THE TABLE: *THE PROSPECT'S* A TOUGH SHIP. WE SURVIVED THE ATTACK THAT TOOK OUT TWO OF YOURS. BUT THAT UNEXPECTED FIGHT WITH YOUR FRIEND DAMAGED MOST OF OUR DEFENSES AND MANY OF OUR OFFENSES. WE'RE HURT. AND HONESTLY?

I DON'T THINK WE CAN MAKE IT OUT.

Tk Tk Tk

WE'LL BE DESTROYED BY THOSE SATELLITES IF WE TRY TO LEAVE, WE CAN'T STAY HERE ON A PLANET THAT'LL KILL US IF WE TOUCH IT, AND WE CAN'T USE OUR WEAPON UNLESS SOMEONE GETS DIRECTLY BENEATH US. CAN YOU HELP US ESCAPE?

...MAYBE.

I WON'T HELP WITH THE WEAPON, BUT I CAN GET YOU OUT. AND WHEN WE'RE OUT, WE'RE GONNA HAVE A CONVERSATION ABOUT TURNING YOURSELVES INTO THE FEDERATION.

YEAH, WE'RE NOT GONNA DO THAT.

HERE'S *MY* CARDS ON THE TABLE: YOU'RE DEAD IF YOU DON'T. IT'S NOT LIKE THE FEDERATION IS JUST GOING TO FORGET YOU WERE HERE STEALING FROM THEM.

LOOK, I DON'T THINK I HAVE MUCH OF A CHOICE. I'LL HELP YOU LEAVE. THERE'S AN OVERRIDE SIGNAL WE USED TO GET IN THAT I CAN SEND TO THE SATELLITES, AND I'LL SEND IT, ON ONE CONDITION:

YOU HAVE TO UNTIE ME.

...

COME ON! IT'S LIKE--I DON'T KNOW ABOUT YOU GUYS, BUT I CAN'T TYPE WITH BOTH ARMS TIED BEHIND MY BACK?

LATER.
FINGER'S PICKED UP AND BACK IN STASIS, JOEY. AND HERE'S YOUR FLOWER.
IF YOU WERE THE GOOD GUYS, SLUGGO, THEN I DOUBT YOUR FRIEND WOULD'VE HAD ORDERS TO KILL EVERYONE, *INCLUDING YOU.* CLASSIC FEDERATION: FEWER WITNESSES, EASIER CLEANUP.
THEY WOULDN'T GIVE ORDERS LIKE THAT! FRANCES WENT *ROGUE.* BESIDES, YOU'RE THE ONE WHO CAME HERE SEEKING A WEAPON TO DESTROY THE FEDERATION! *YOU'RE* THE TERRORISTS IN THIS SCENARIO!
THAT'S RICH.
FATTY, BRING US ABOUT...
...AND LET'S DO WHAT WE CAME HERE FOR.
ALRIGHT, WE'RE THROUGH. *NOW* CAN WE TALK ABOUT OUR NEXT DESTINATION? IF I SIGNAL FOR AN ESCORT TO TAKE US TO FEDERATION SPACE, I THINK I CAN GUARANTEE--
WAIT.
WAIT, SOMETHING'S WRONG. THERE'S SOMETHING OUT HERE.
SOMETHING BIG. GUYS--

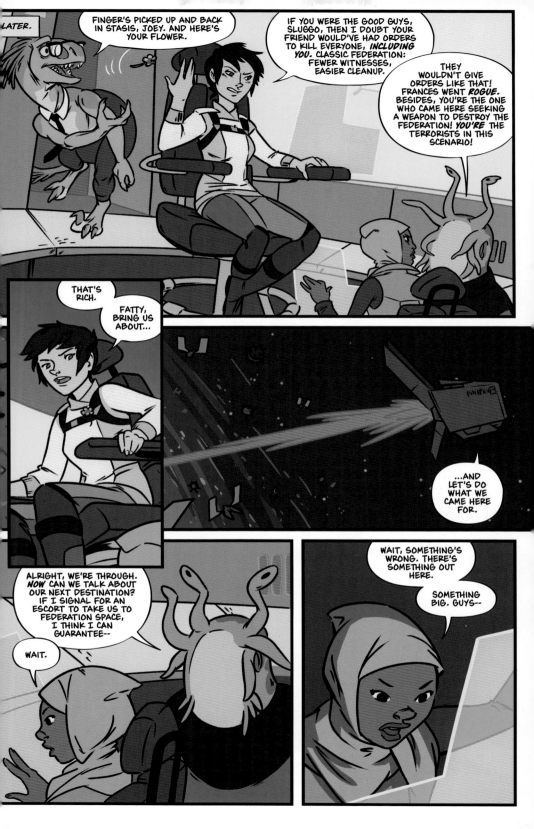

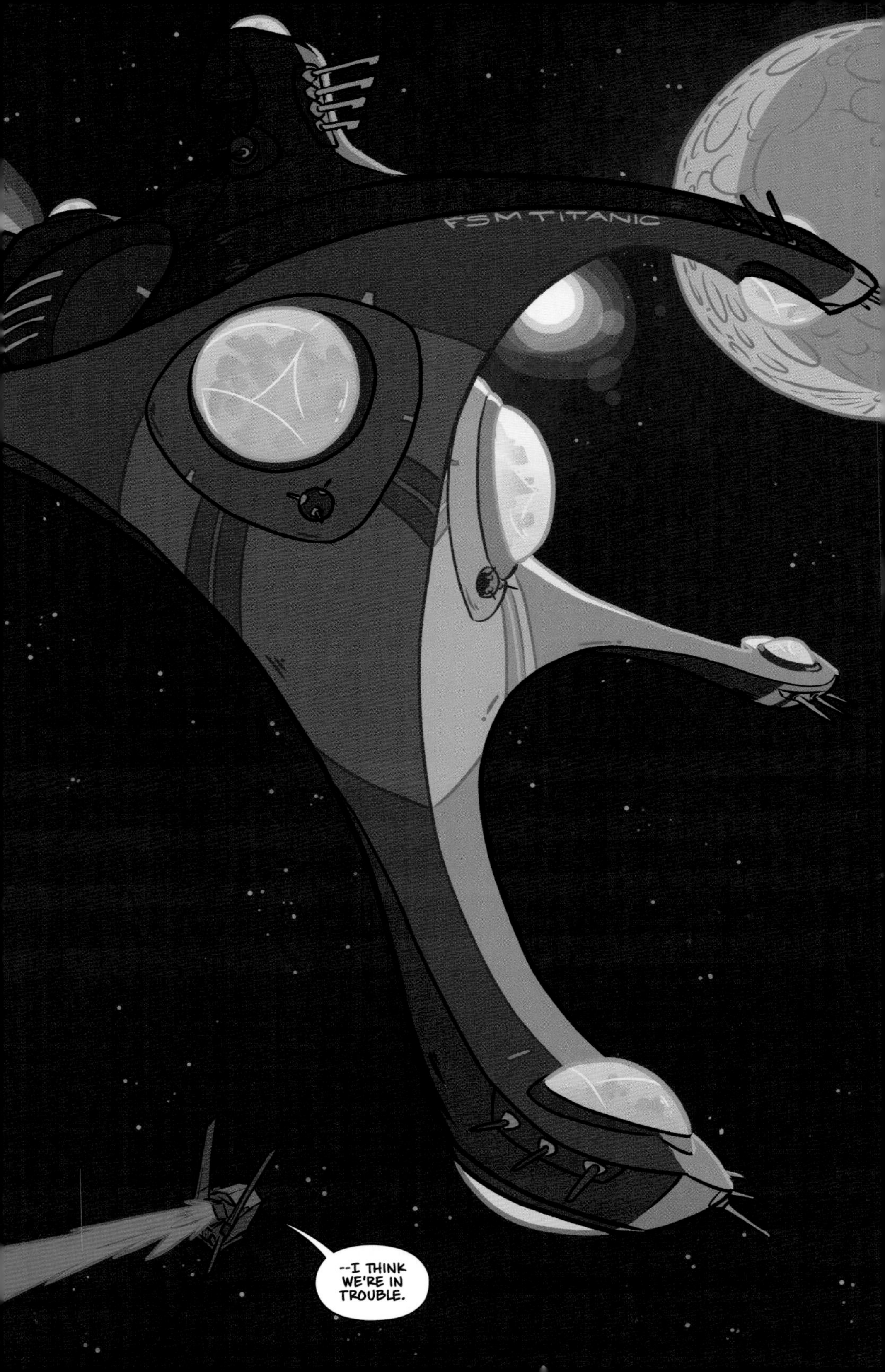
FSM TITANIC
--I THINK WE'RE IN TROUBLE.

"DAN
KIN
MIDA

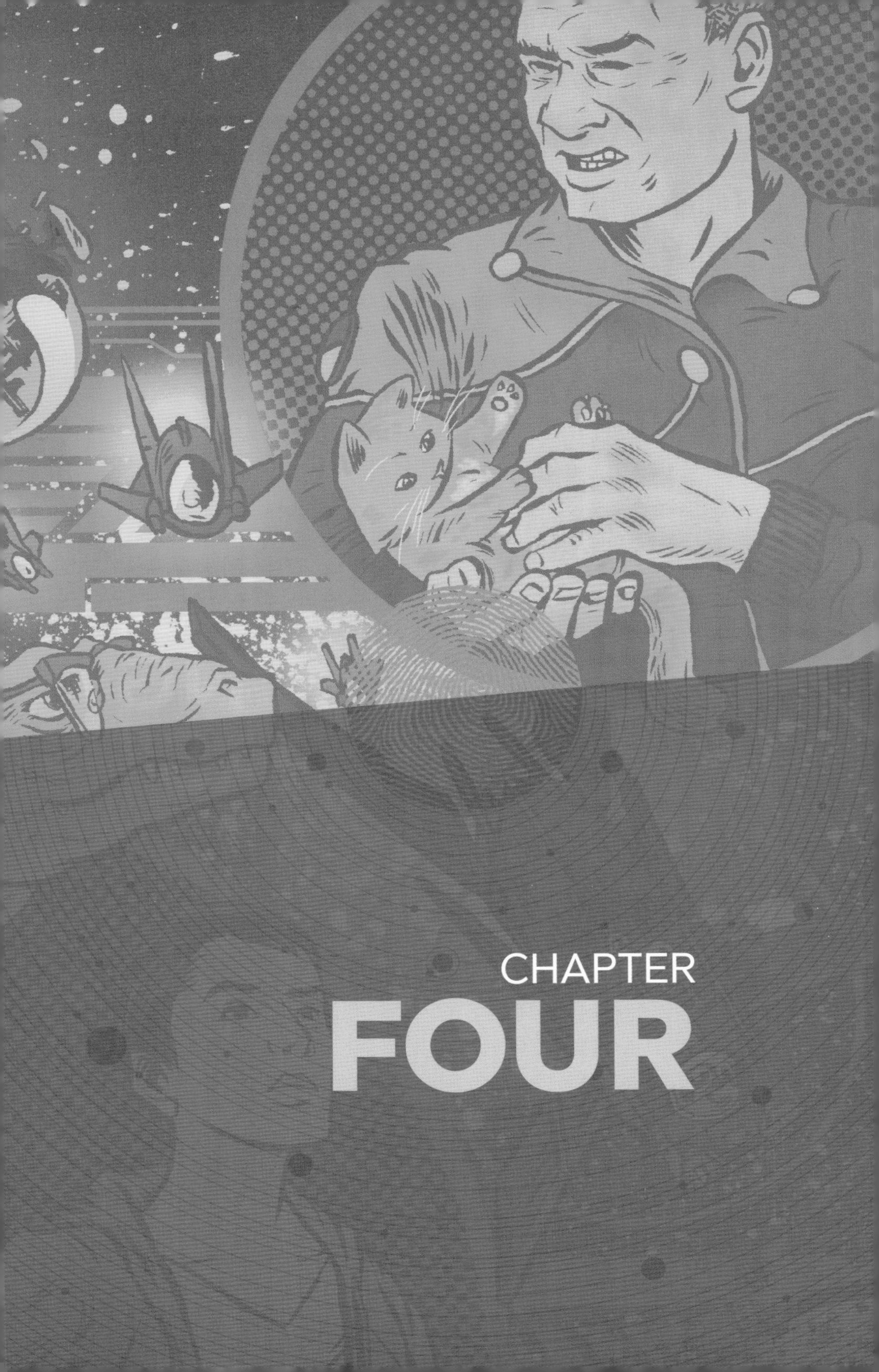

CHAPTER FOUR

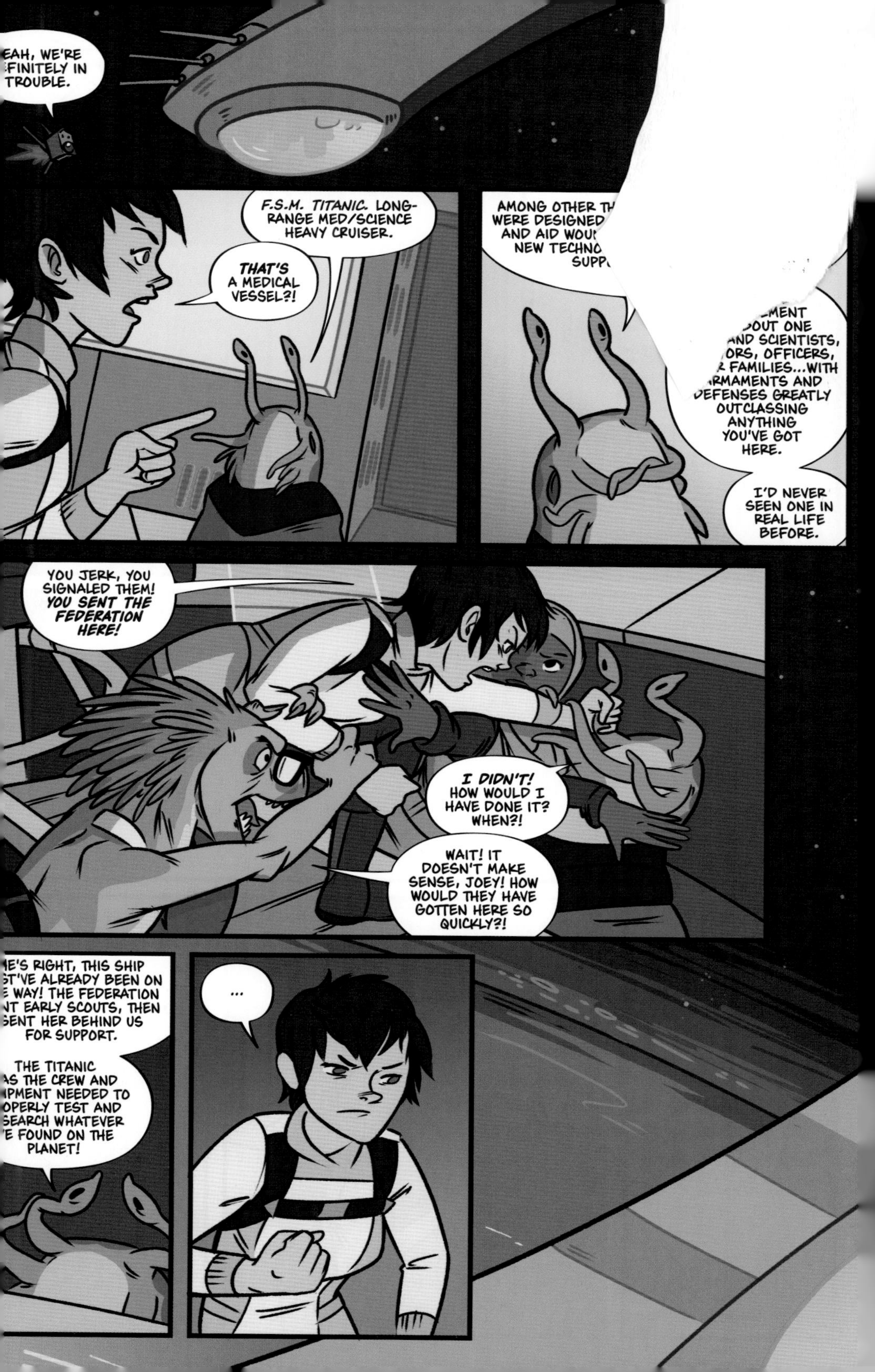

EAH, WE'RE
EFINITELY IN
TROUBLE.
F.S.M. TITANIC. LONG-RANGE MED/SCIENCE HEAVY CRUISER.
THAT'S A MEDICAL VESSEL?!
AMONG OTHER TH
WERE DESIGNED
AND AID WOU
NEW TECHNO
SUPP
EMENT
OUT ONE
AND SCIENTISTS,
TORS, OFFICERS,
R FAMILIES...WITH
RMAMENTS AND
DEFENSES GREATLY OUTCLASSING ANYTHING YOU'VE GOT HERE.
I'D NEVER SEEN ONE IN REAL LIFE BEFORE.
YOU JERK, YOU SIGNALED THEM! YOU SENT THE FEDERATION HERE!
I DIDN'T! HOW WOULD I HAVE DONE IT? WHEN?!
WAIT! IT DOESN'T MAKE SENSE, JOEY! HOW WOULD THEY HAVE GOTTEN HERE SO QUICKLY?!
E'S RIGHT, THIS SHIP
ST'VE ALREADY BEEN ON
WAY! THE FEDERATION
NT EARLY SCOUTS, THEN
SENT HER BEHIND US
FOR SUPPORT.
THE TITANIC
AS THE CREW AND
IPMENT NEEDED TO
OPERLY TEST AND
SEARCH WHATEVER
'E FOUND ON THE
PLANET!
...

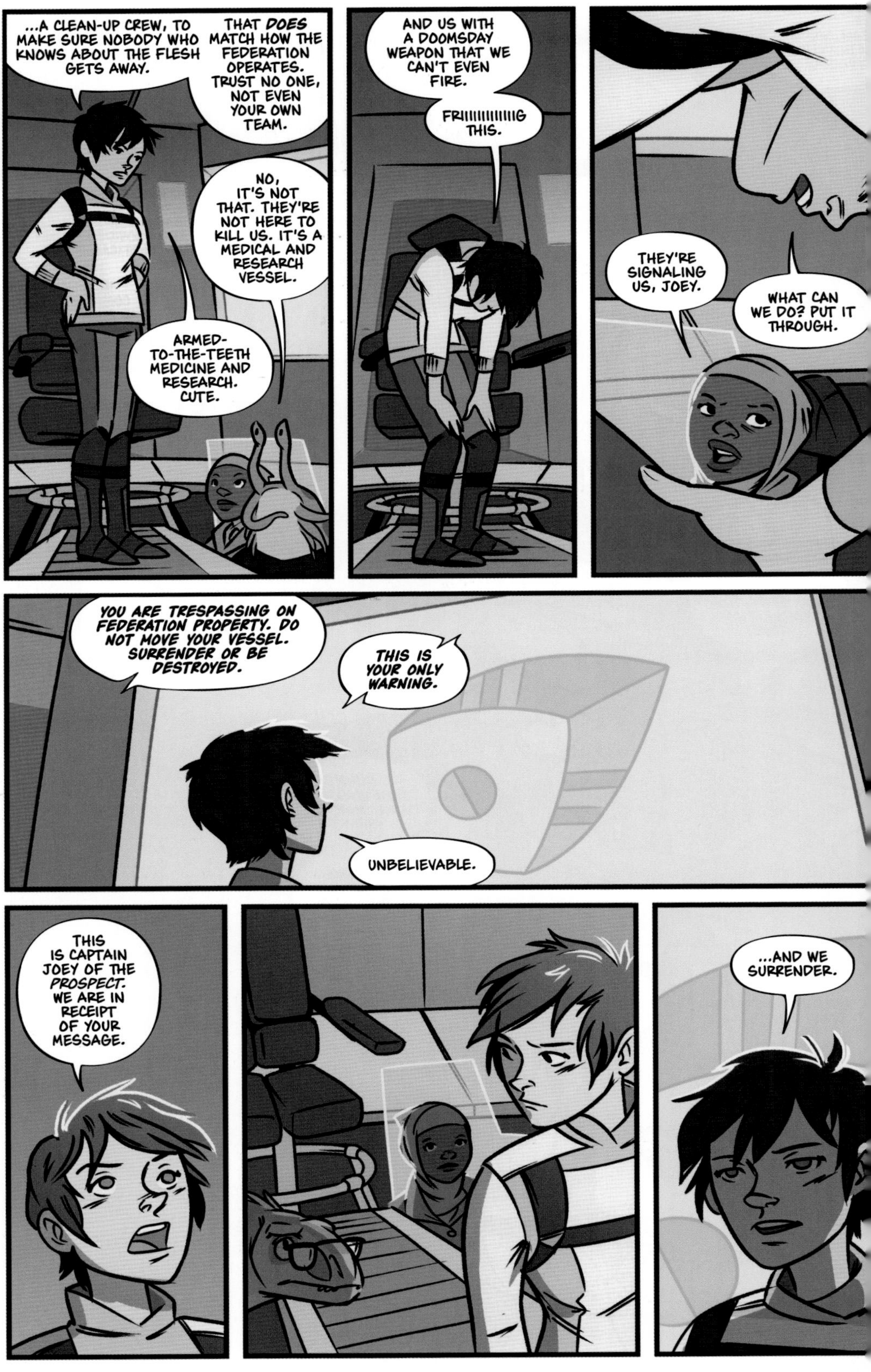
...A CLEAN-UP CREW, TO MAKE SURE NOBODY WHO KNOWS ABOUT THE FLESH GETS AWAY.
THAT *DOES* MATCH HOW THE FEDERATION OPERATES. TRUST NO ONE, NOT EVEN YOUR OWN TEAM.
NO, IT'S NOT THAT. THEY'RE NOT HERE TO KILL US. IT'S A MEDICAL AND RESEARCH VESSEL.
ARMED-TO-THE-TEETH MEDICINE AND RESEARCH. CUTE.
AND US WITH A DOOMSDAY WEAPON THAT WE CAN'T EVEN FIRE.
FRIIIIIIIIIIIIG THIS.
THEY'RE SIGNALING US, JOEY.
WHAT CAN WE DO? PUT IT THROUGH.
YOU ARE TRESPASSING ON FEDERATION PROPERTY. DO NOT MOVE YOUR VESSEL. SURRENDER OR BE DESTROYED.
THIS IS YOUR ONLY WARNING.
UNBELIEVABLE.
THIS IS CAPTAIN JOEY OF THE *PROSPECT*. WE ARE IN RECEIPT OF YOUR MESSAGE.
...AND WE SURRENDER.

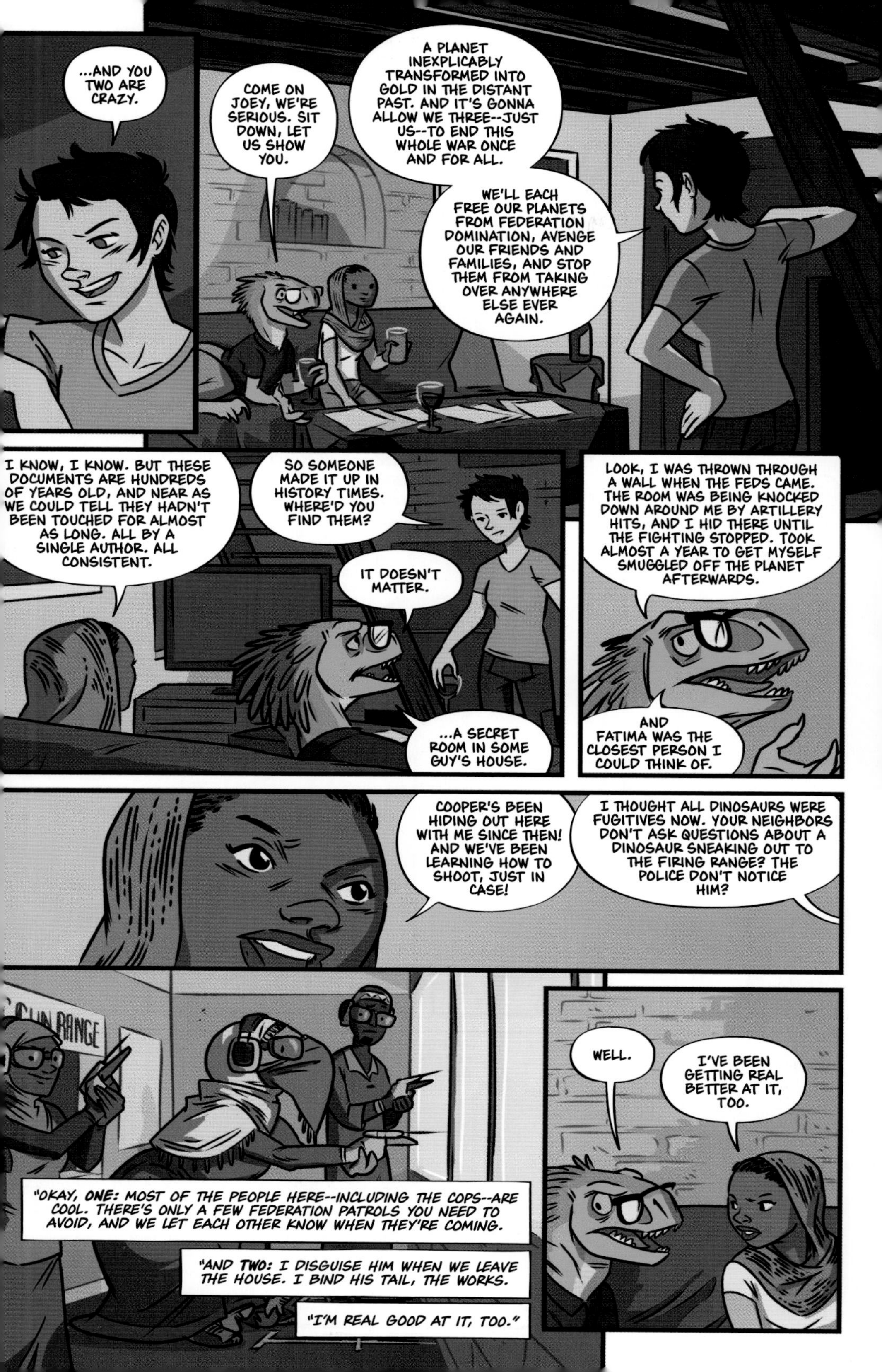
...AND YOU TWO ARE CRAZY.
COME ON JOEY, WE'RE SERIOUS. SIT DOWN, LET US SHOW YOU.
A PLANET INEXPLICABLY TRANSFORMED INTO GOLD IN THE DISTANT PAST. AND IT'S GONNA ALLOW WE THREE--JUST US--TO END THIS WHOLE WAR ONCE AND FOR ALL.
WE'LL EACH FREE OUR PLANETS FROM FEDERATION DOMINATION, AVENGE OUR FRIENDS AND FAMILIES, AND STOP THEM FROM TAKING OVER ANYWHERE ELSE EVER AGAIN.
I KNOW, I KNOW. BUT THESE DOCUMENTS ARE HUNDREDS OF YEARS OLD, AND NEAR AS WE COULD TELL THEY HADN'T BEEN TOUCHED FOR ALMOST AS LONG. ALL BY A SINGLE AUTHOR. ALL CONSISTENT.
SO SOMEONE MADE IT UP IN HISTORY TIMES. WHERE'D YOU FIND THEM?
IT DOESN'T MATTER.
...A SECRET ROOM IN SOME GUY'S HOUSE.
LOOK, I WAS THROWN THROUGH A WALL WHEN THE FEDS CAME. THE ROOM WAS BEING KNOCKED DOWN AROUND ME BY ARTILLERY HITS, AND I HID THERE UNTIL THE FIGHTING STOPPED. TOOK ALMOST A YEAR TO GET MYSELF SMUGGLED OFF THE PLANET AFTERWARDS.
AND FATIMA WAS THE CLOSEST PERSON I COULD THINK OF.
COOPER'S BEEN HIDING OUT HERE WITH ME SINCE THEN! AND WE'VE BEEN LEARNING HOW TO SHOOT, JUST IN CASE!
I THOUGHT ALL DINOSAURS WERE FUGITIVES NOW. YOUR NEIGHBORS DON'T ASK QUESTIONS ABOUT A DINOSAUR SNEAKING OUT TO THE FIRING RANGE? THE POLICE DON'T NOTICE HIM?
GUN RANGE
"OKAY, ONE: MOST OF THE PEOPLE HERE--INCLUDING THE COPS--ARE COOL. THERE'S ONLY A FEW FEDERATION PATROLS YOU NEED TO AVOID, AND WE LET EACH OTHER KNOW WHEN THEY'RE COMING.
"AND TWO: I DISGUISE HIM WHEN WE LEAVE THE HOUSE. I BIND HIS TAIL, THE WORKS.
"I'M REAL GOOD AT IT, TOO."
WELL.
I'VE BEEN GETTING REAL BETTER AT IT, TOO.

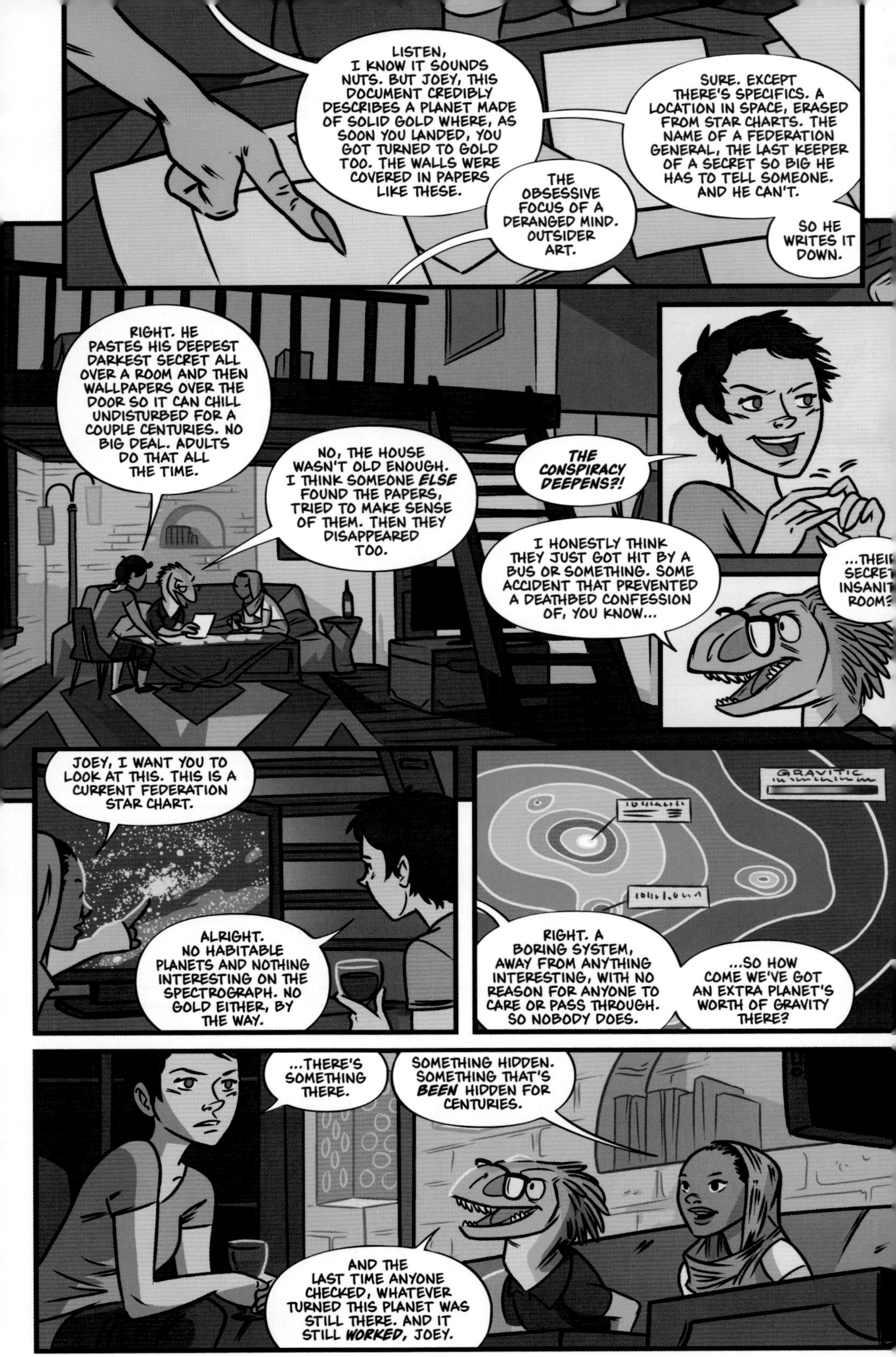
LISTEN, I KNOW IT SOUNDS NUTS. BUT JOEY, THIS DOCUMENT CREDIBLY DESCRIBES A PLANET MADE OF SOLID GOLD WHERE, AS SOON YOU LANDED, YOU GOT TURNED TO GOLD TOO. THE WALLS WERE COVERED IN PAPERS LIKE THESE.
THE OBSESSIVE FOCUS OF A DERANGED MIND. OUTSIDER ART.
SURE. EXCEPT THERE'S SPECIFICS. A LOCATION IN SPACE, ERASED FROM STAR CHARTS. THE NAME OF A FEDERATION GENERAL, THE LAST KEEPER OF A SECRET SO BIG HE HAS TO TELL SOMEONE. AND HE CAN'T.
SO HE WRITES IT DOWN.
RIGHT. HE PASTES HIS DEEPEST DARKEST SECRET ALL OVER A ROOM AND THEN WALLPAPERS OVER THE DOOR SO IT CAN CHILL UNDISTURBED FOR A COUPLE CENTURIES. NO BIG DEAL. ADULTS DO THAT ALL THE TIME.
NO, THE HOUSE WASN'T OLD ENOUGH. I THINK SOMEONE *ELSE* FOUND THE PAPERS, TRIED TO MAKE SENSE OF THEM. THEN THEY DISAPPEARED TOO.
THE CONSPIRACY DEEPENS?!
I HONESTLY THINK THEY JUST GOT HIT BY A BUS OR SOMETHING. SOME ACCIDENT THAT PREVENTED A DEATHBED CONFESSION OF, YOU KNOW...
...THEIR SECRET INSANITY ROOM?
JOEY, I WANT YOU TO LOOK AT THIS. THIS IS A CURRENT FEDERATION STAR CHART.
ALRIGHT. NO HABITABLE PLANETS AND NOTHING INTERESTING ON THE SPECTROGRAPH. NO GOLD EITHER, BY THE WAY.
GRAVITIC
RIGHT. A BORING SYSTEM, AWAY FROM ANYTHING INTERESTING, WITH NO REASON FOR ANYONE TO CARE OR PASS THROUGH. SO NOBODY DOES.
...SO HOW COME WE'VE GOT AN EXTRA PLANET'S WORTH OF GRAVITY THERE?
...THERE'S SOMETHING THERE.
SOMETHING HIDDEN. SOMETHING THAT'S *BEEN* HIDDEN FOR CENTURIES.
AND THE LAST TIME ANYONE CHECKED, WHATEVER TURNED THIS PLANET WAS STILL THERE. AND IT STILL *WORKED*, JOEY.

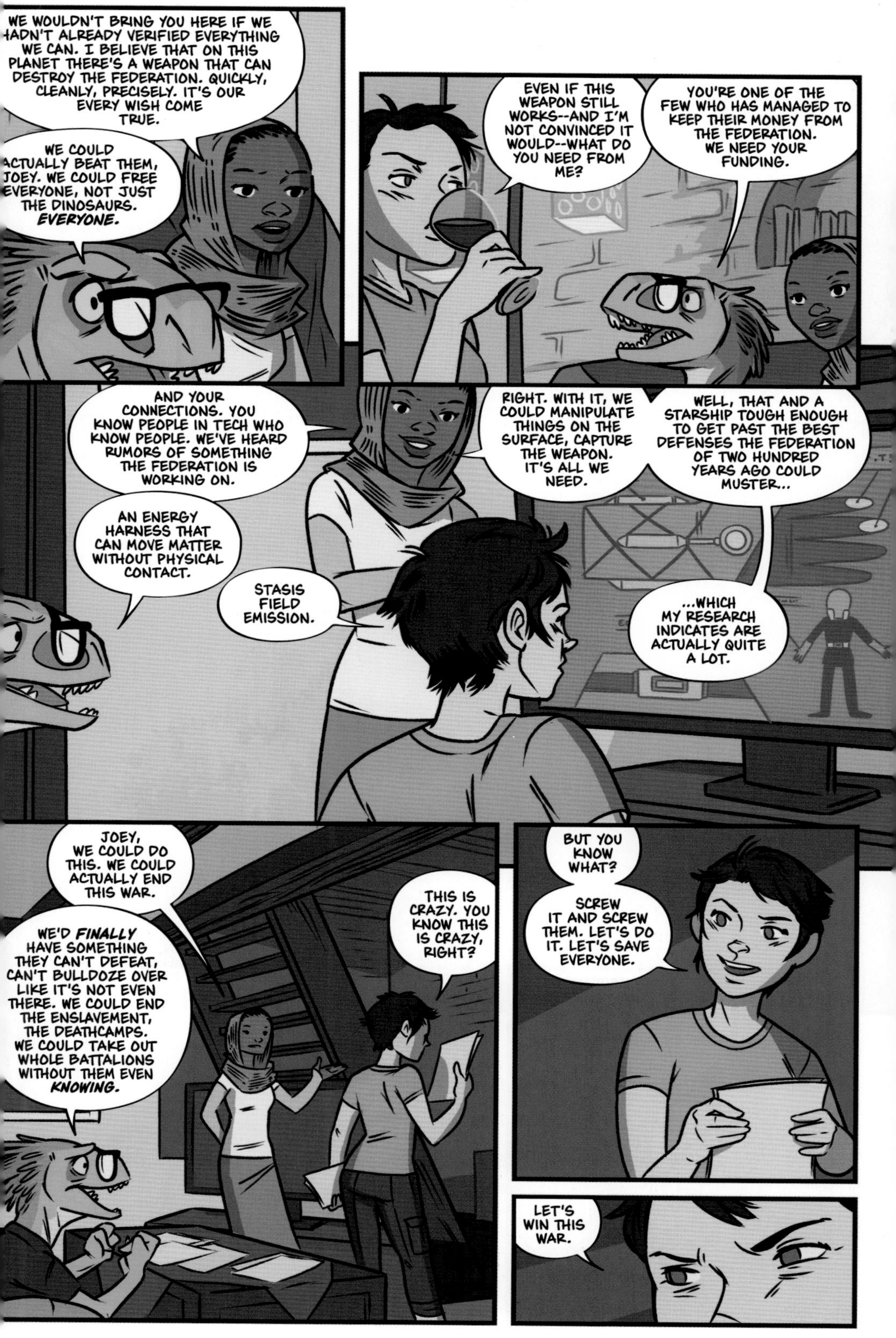

WE WOULDN'T BRING YOU HERE IF WE HADN'T ALREADY VERIFIED EVERYTHING WE CAN. I BELIEVE THAT ON THIS PLANET THERE'S A WEAPON THAT CAN DESTROY THE FEDERATION. QUICKLY, CLEANLY, PRECISELY. IT'S OUR EVERY WISH COME TRUE.
WE COULD ACTUALLY BEAT THEM, JOEY. WE COULD FREE EVERYONE, NOT JUST THE DINOSAURS. *EVERYONE.*
EVEN IF THIS WEAPON STILL WORKS--AND I'M NOT CONVINCED IT WOULD--WHAT DO YOU NEED FROM ME?
YOU'RE ONE OF THE FEW WHO HAS MANAGED TO KEEP THEIR MONEY FROM THE FEDERATION. WE NEED YOUR FUNDING.
AND YOUR CONNECTIONS. YOU KNOW PEOPLE IN TECH WHO KNOW PEOPLE. WE'VE HEARD RUMORS OF SOMETHING THE FEDERATION IS WORKING ON.
AN ENERGY HARNESS THAT CAN MOVE MATTER WITHOUT PHYSICAL CONTACT.
STASIS FIELD EMISSION.
RIGHT. WITH IT, WE COULD MANIPULATE THINGS ON THE SURFACE, CAPTURE THE WEAPON. IT'S ALL WE NEED.
WELL, THAT AND A STARSHIP TOUGH ENOUGH TO GET PAST THE BEST DEFENSES THE FEDERATION OF TWO HUNDRED YEARS AGO COULD MUSTER...
...WHICH MY RESEARCH INDICATES ARE ACTUALLY QUITE A LOT.
JOEY, WE COULD DO THIS. WE COULD ACTUALLY END THIS WAR.
WE'D *FINALLY* HAVE SOMETHING THEY CAN'T DEFEAT, CAN'T BULLDOZE OVER LIKE IT'S NOT EVEN THERE. WE COULD END THE ENSLAVEMENT, THE DEATHCAMPS. WE COULD TAKE OUT WHOLE BATTALIONS WITHOUT THEM EVEN *KNOWING.*
THIS IS CRAZY. YOU KNOW THIS IS CRAZY, RIGHT?
BUT YOU KNOW WHAT?
SCREW IT AND SCREW THEM. LET'S DO IT. LET'S SAVE EVERYONE.
LET'S WIN THIS WAR.

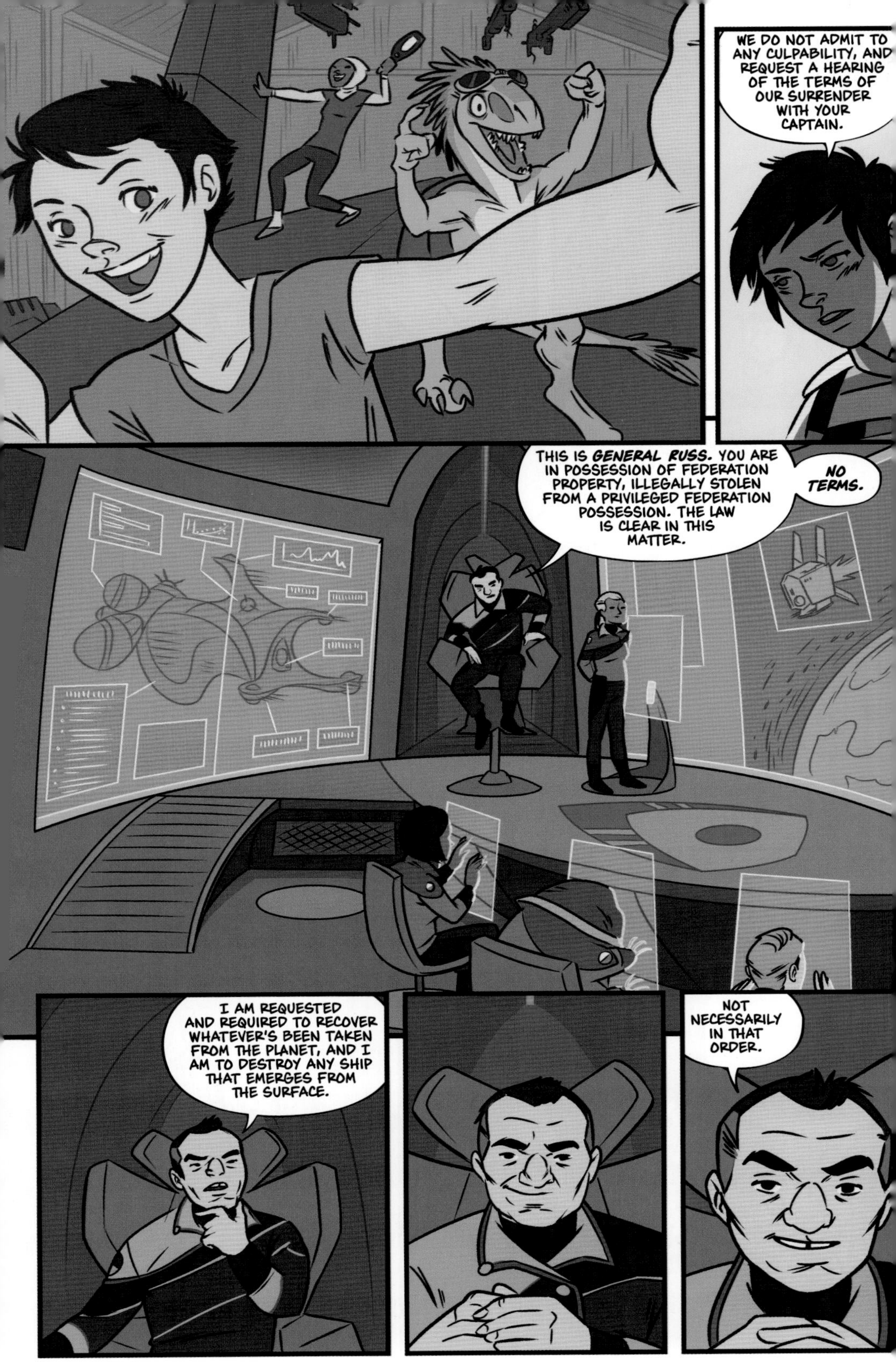

WE DO NOT ADMIT TO ANY CULPABILITY, AND REQUEST A HEARING OF THE TERMS OF OUR SURRENDER WITH YOUR CAPTAIN.
THIS IS GENERAL RUSS. YOU ARE IN POSSESSION OF FEDERATION PROPERTY, ILLEGALLY STOLEN FROM A PRIVILEGED FEDERATION POSSESSION. THE LAW IS CLEAR IN THIS MATTER.
NO TERMS.
I AM REQUESTED AND REQUIRED TO RECOVER WHATEVER'S BEEN TAKEN FROM THE PLANET, AND I AM TO DESTROY ANY SHIP THAT EMERGES FROM THE SURFACE.
NOT NECESSARILY IN THAT ORDER.

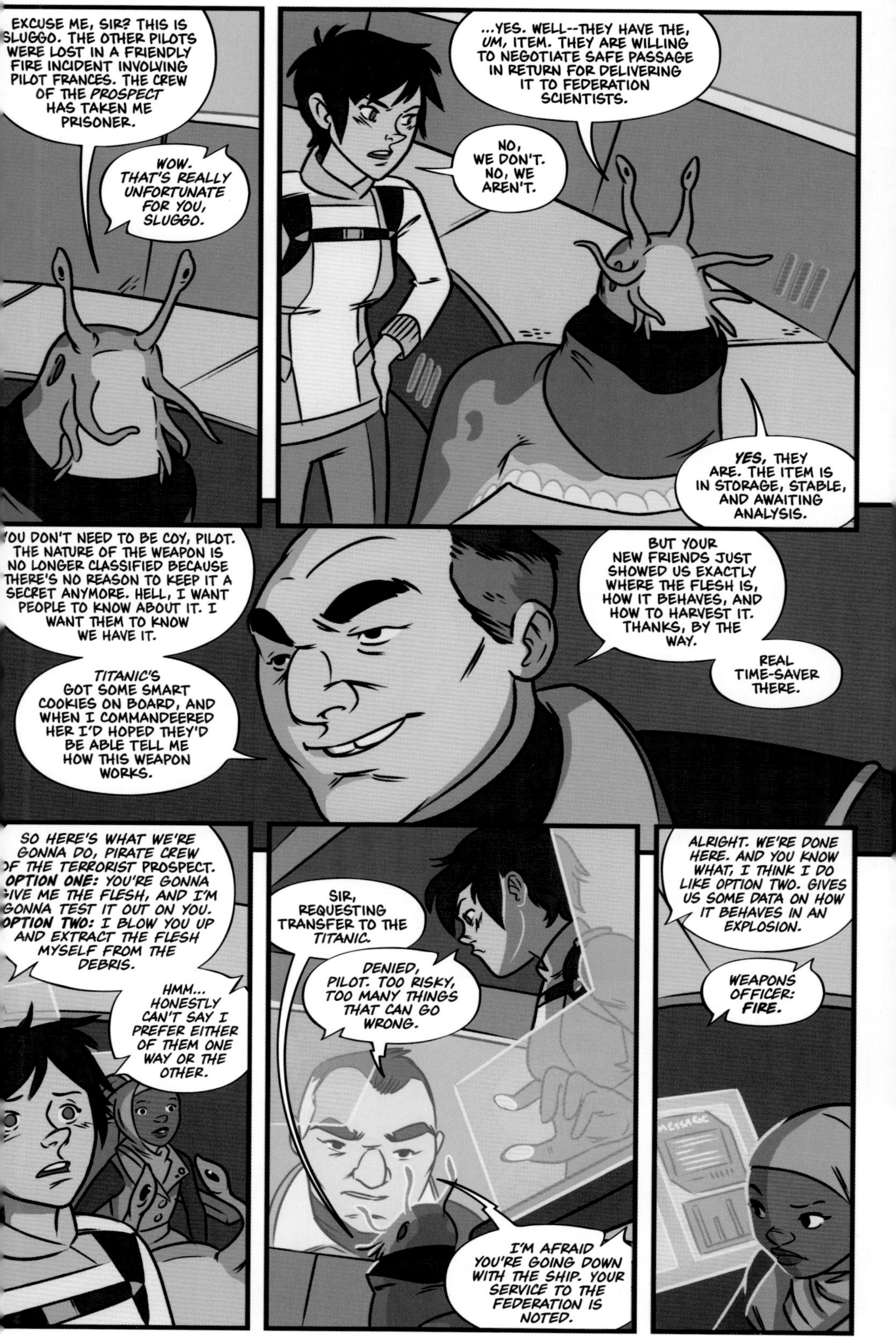
EXCUSE ME, SIR? THIS IS SLUGGO. THE OTHER PILOTS WERE LOST IN A FRIENDLY FIRE INCIDENT INVOLVING PILOT FRANCES. THE CREW OF THE PROSPECT HAS TAKEN ME PRISONER.
WOW. THAT'S REALLY UNFORTUNATE FOR YOU, SLUGGO.
...YES. WELL--THEY HAVE THE, UM, ITEM. THEY ARE WILLING TO NEGOTIATE SAFE PASSAGE IN RETURN FOR DELIVERING IT TO FEDERATION SCIENTISTS.
NO, WE DON'T. NO, WE AREN'T.
YES, THEY ARE. THE ITEM IS IN STORAGE, STABLE, AND AWAITING ANALYSIS.
YOU DON'T NEED TO BE COY, PILOT. THE NATURE OF THE WEAPON IS NO LONGER CLASSIFIED BECAUSE THERE'S NO REASON TO KEEP IT A SECRET ANYMORE. HELL, I WANT PEOPLE TO KNOW ABOUT IT. I WANT THEM TO KNOW WE HAVE IT.
TITANIC'S GOT SOME SMART COOKIES ON BOARD, AND WHEN I COMMANDEERED HER I'D HOPED THEY'D BE ABLE TELL ME HOW THIS WEAPON WORKS.
BUT YOUR NEW FRIENDS JUST SHOWED US EXACTLY WHERE THE FLESH IS, HOW IT BEHAVES, AND HOW TO HARVEST IT. THANKS, BY THE WAY.
REAL TIME-SAVER THERE.
SO HERE'S WHAT WE'RE GONNA DO, PIRATE CREW OF THE TERRORIST PROSPECT. OPTION ONE: YOU'RE GONNA GIVE ME THE FLESH, AND I'M GONNA TEST IT OUT ON YOU. OPTION TWO: I BLOW YOU UP AND EXTRACT THE FLESH MYSELF FROM THE DEBRIS.
HMM... HONESTLY CAN'T SAY I PREFER EITHER OF THEM ONE WAY OR THE OTHER.
SIR, REQUESTING TRANSFER TO THE TITANIC.
DENIED, PILOT. TOO RISKY, TOO MANY THINGS THAT CAN GO WRONG.
I'M AFRAID YOU'RE GOING DOWN WITH THE SHIP. YOUR SERVICE TO THE FEDERATION IS NOTED.
ALRIGHT. WE'RE DONE HERE. AND YOU KNOW WHAT, I THINK I DO LIKE OPTION TWO. GIVES US SOME DATA ON HOW IT BEHAVES IN AN EXPLOSION.
WEAPONS OFFICER: FIRE.
MESSAGE

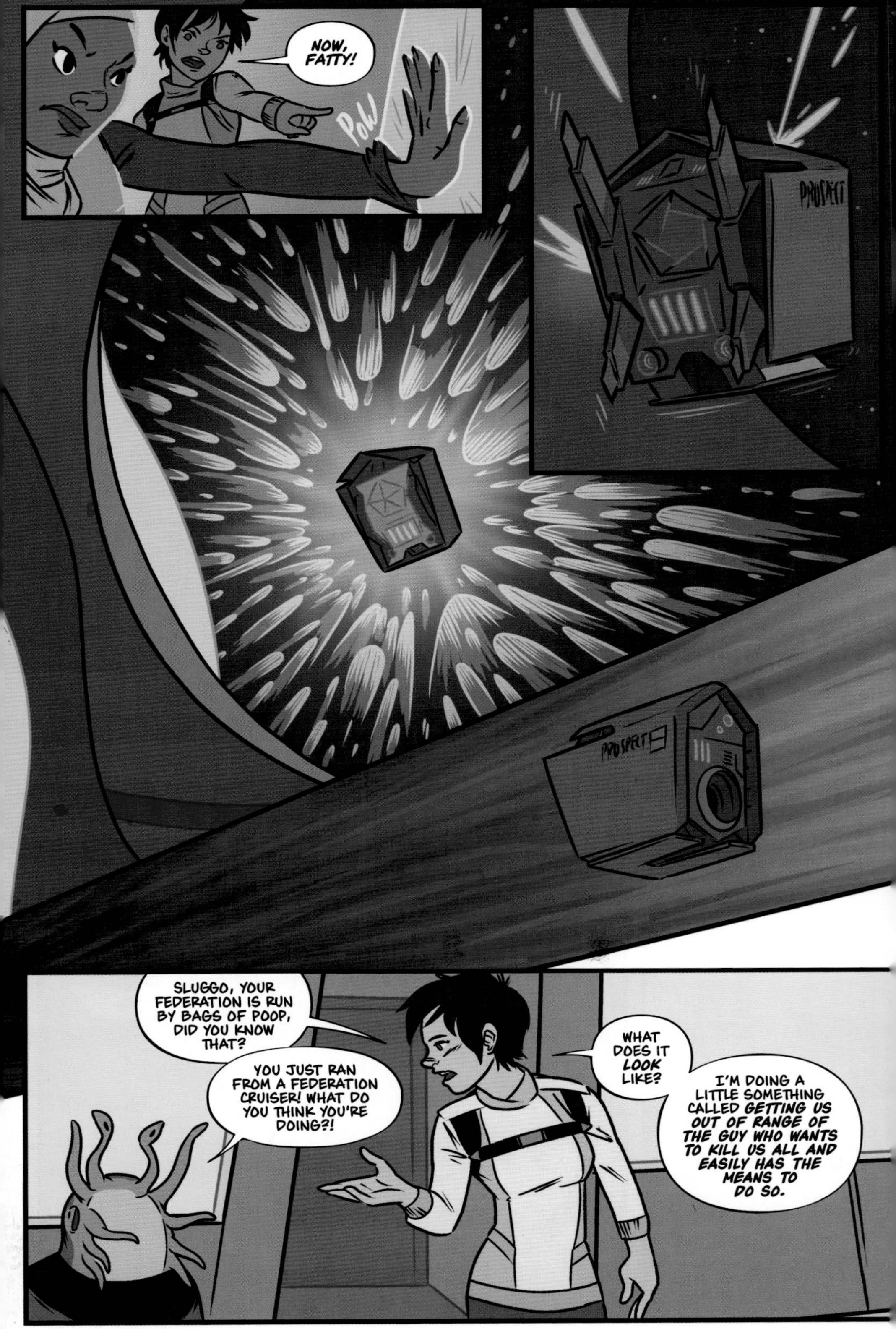
NOW, FATTY!
POW
PROSPECT
PROSPECT
SLUGGO, YOUR FEDERATION IS RUN BY BAGS OF POOP, DID YOU KNOW THAT?
YOU JUST RAN FROM A FEDERATION CRUISER! WHAT DO YOU THINK YOU'RE DOING?!
WHAT DOES IT LOOK LIKE?
I'M DOING A LITTLE SOMETHING CALLED GETTING US OUT OF RANGE OF THE GUY WHO WANTS TO KILL US ALL AND EASILY HAS THE MEANS TO DO SO.

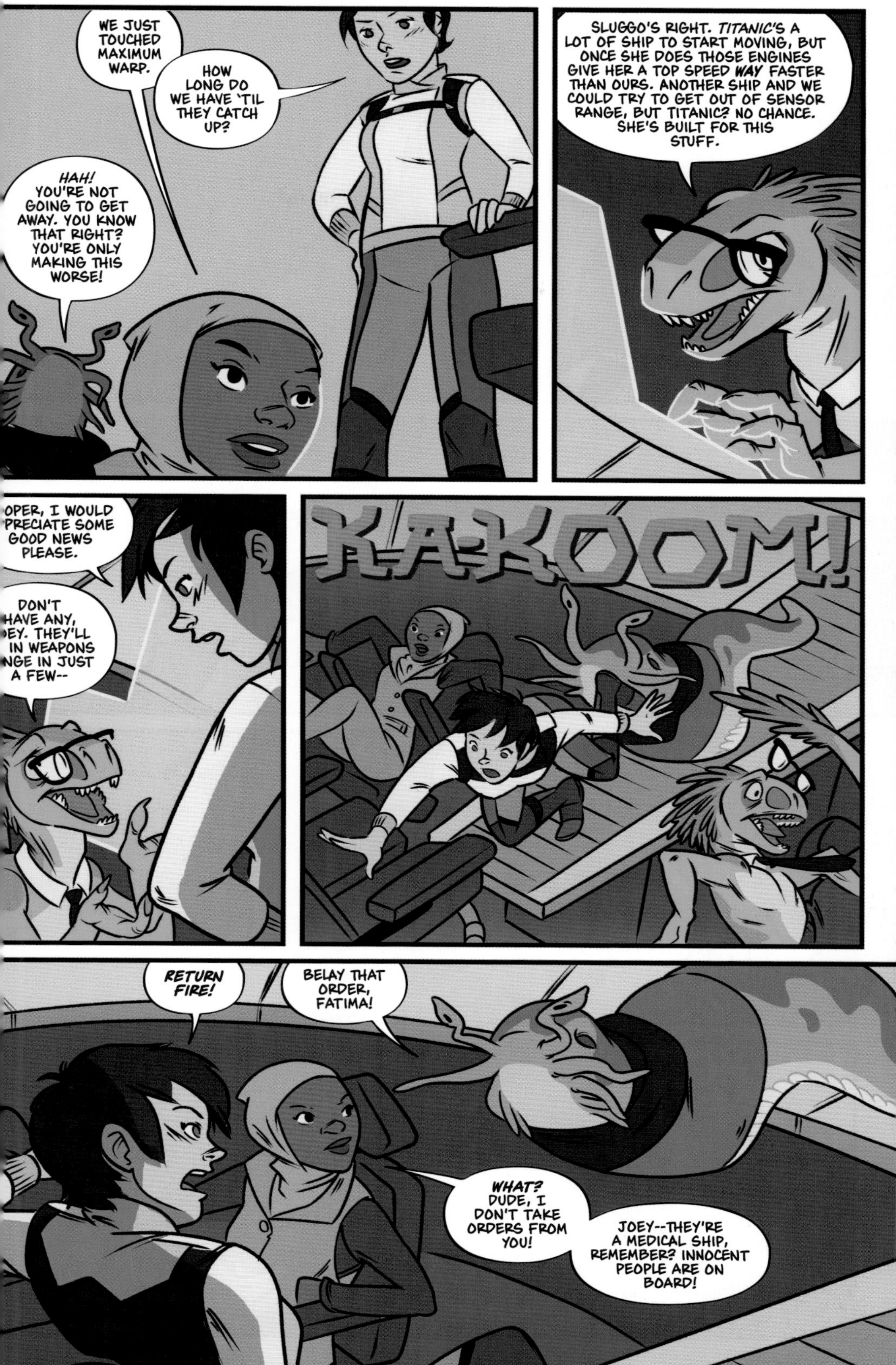
WE JUST TOUCHED MAXIMUM WARP.
HOW LONG DO WE HAVE 'TIL THEY CATCH UP?
HAH! YOU'RE NOT GOING TO GET AWAY. YOU KNOW THAT RIGHT? YOU'RE ONLY MAKING THIS WORSE!
SLUGGO'S RIGHT. TITANIC'S A LOT OF SHIP TO START MOVING, BUT ONCE SHE DOES THOSE ENGINES GIVE HER A TOP SPEED WAY FASTER THAN OURS. ANOTHER SHIP AND WE COULD TRY TO GET OUT OF SENSOR RANGE, BUT TITANIC? NO CHANCE. SHE'S BUILT FOR THIS STUFF.
OPER, I WOULD PRECIATE SOME GOOD NEWS PLEASE.
DON'T HAVE ANY, EY. THEY'LL IN WEAPONS NGE IN JUST A FEW--
KA-KOOM!
RETURN FIRE!
BELAY THAT ORDER, FATIMA!
WHAT? DUDE, I DON'T TAKE ORDERS FROM YOU!
JOEY--THEY'RE A MEDICAL SHIP, REMEMBER? INNOCENT PEOPLE ARE ON BOARD!

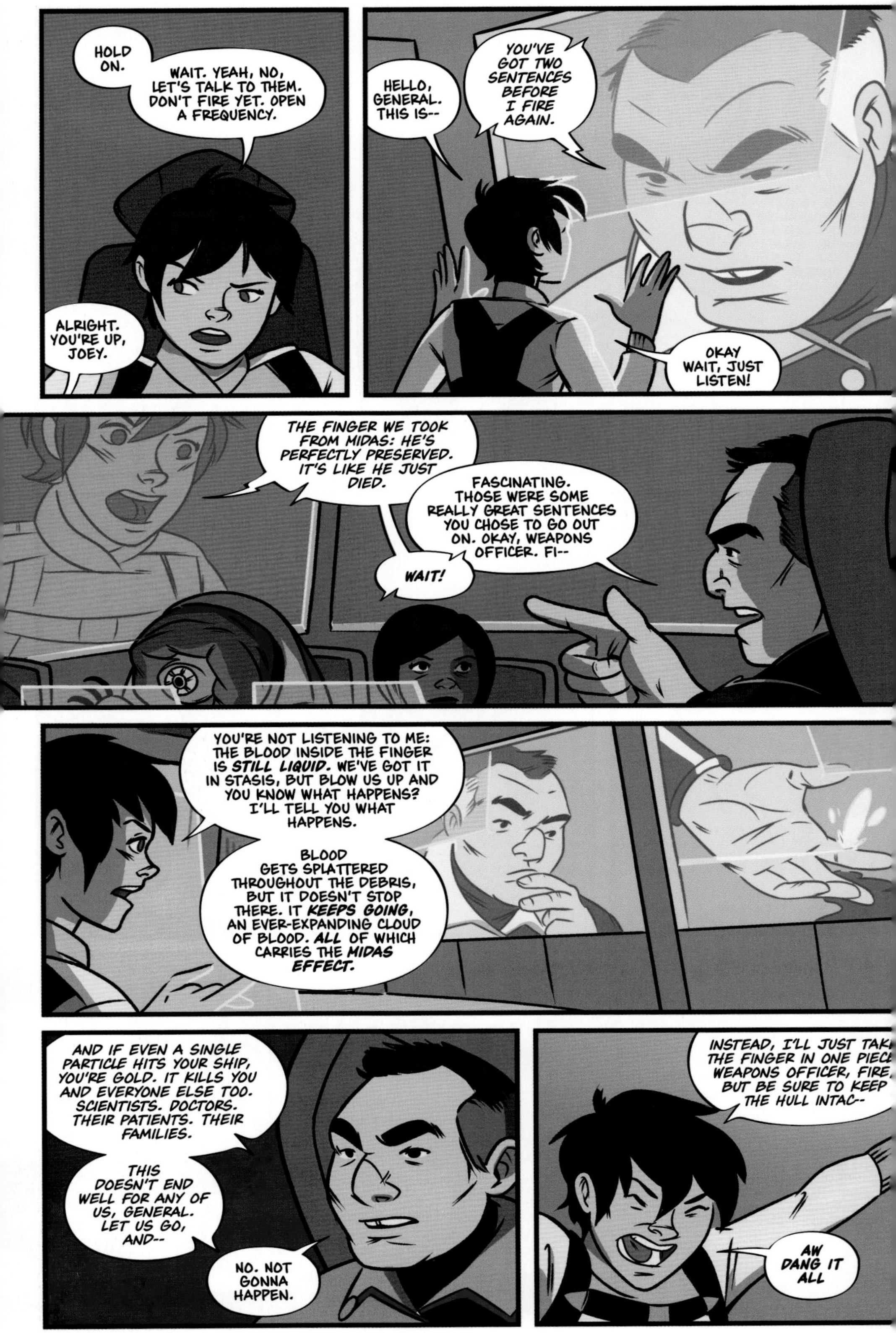
HOLD ON.
WAIT. YEAH, NO, LET'S TALK TO THEM. DON'T FIRE YET. OPEN A FREQUENCY.
ALRIGHT. YOU'RE UP, JOEY.
HELLO, GENERAL. THIS IS--
YOU'VE GOT TWO SENTENCES BEFORE I FIRE AGAIN.
OKAY WAIT, JUST LISTEN!
THE FINGER WE TOOK FROM MIDAS: HE'S PERFECTLY PRESERVED. IT'S LIKE HE JUST DIED.
FASCINATING. THOSE WERE SOME REALLY GREAT SENTENCES YOU CHOSE TO GO OUT ON. OKAY, WEAPONS OFFICER. FI--
WAIT!
YOU'RE NOT LISTENING TO ME: THE BLOOD INSIDE THE FINGER IS STILL LIQUID. WE'VE GOT IT IN STASIS, BUT BLOW US UP AND YOU KNOW WHAT HAPPENS? I'LL TELL YOU WHAT HAPPENS.
BLOOD GETS SPLATTERED THROUGHOUT THE DEBRIS, BUT IT DOESN'T STOP THERE. IT KEEPS GOING, AN EVER-EXPANDING CLOUD OF BLOOD. ALL OF WHICH CARRIES THE MIDAS EFFECT.
AND IF EVEN A SINGLE PARTICLE HITS YOUR SHIP, YOU'RE GOLD. IT KILLS YOU AND EVERYONE ELSE TOO. SCIENTISTS. DOCTORS. THEIR PATIENTS. THEIR FAMILIES.
THIS DOESN'T END WELL FOR ANY OF US, GENERAL. LET US GO, AND--
NO. NOT GONNA HAPPEN.
INSTEAD, I'LL JUST TAK THE FINGER IN ONE PIEC WEAPONS OFFICER, FIRE BUT BE SURE TO KEEP THE HULL INTAC--
AW DANG IT ALL

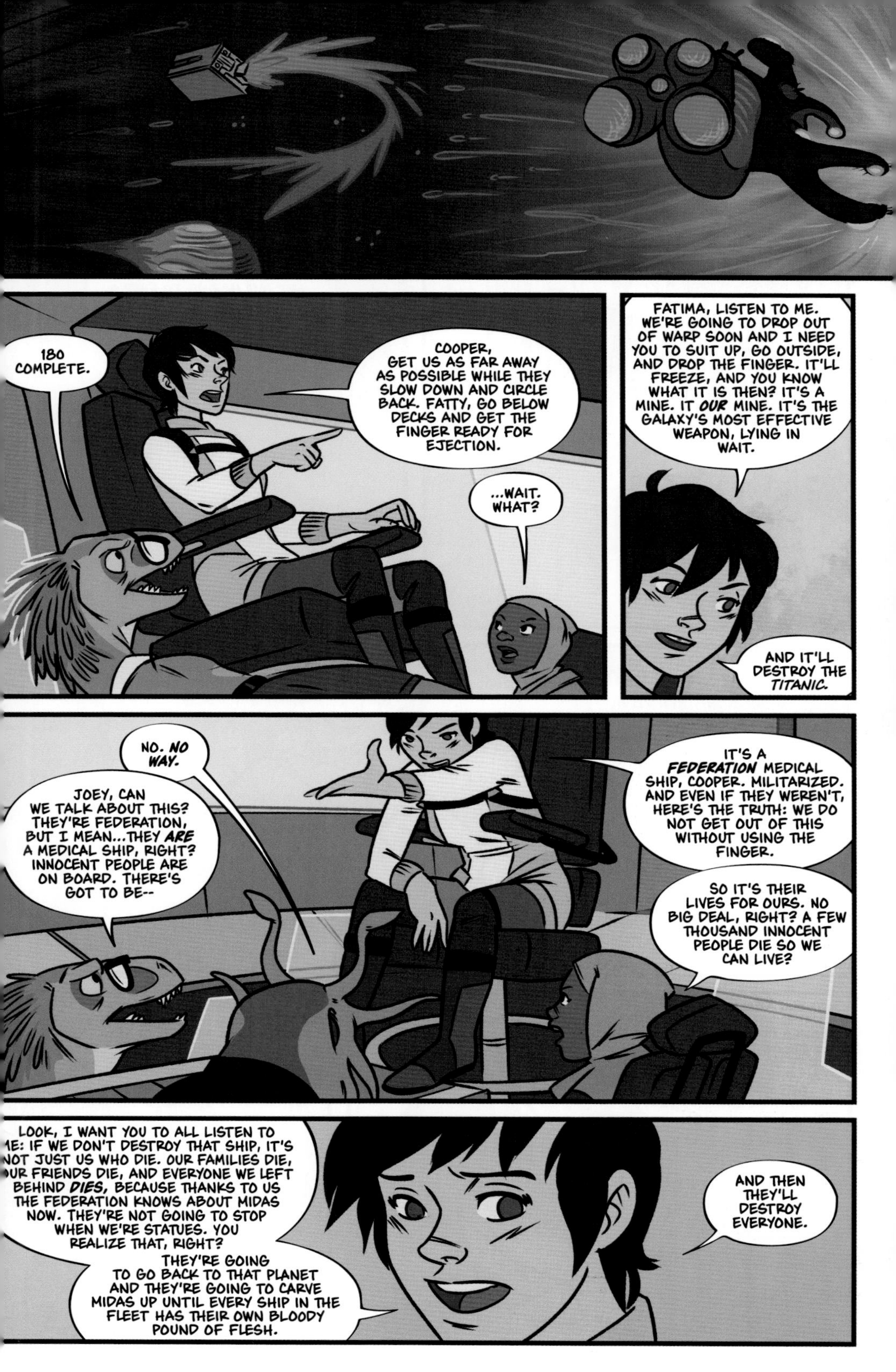
180 COMPLETE.
COOPER, GET US AS FAR AWAY AS POSSIBLE WHILE THEY SLOW DOWN AND CIRCLE BACK. FATTY, GO BELOW DECKS AND GET THE FINGER READY FOR EJECTION.
...WAIT. WHAT?
FATIMA, LISTEN TO ME. WE'RE GOING TO DROP OUT OF WARP SOON AND I NEED YOU TO SUIT UP, GO OUTSIDE, AND DROP THE FINGER. IT'LL FREEZE, AND YOU KNOW WHAT IT IS THEN? IT'S A MINE. IT OUR MINE. IT'S THE GALAXY'S MOST EFFECTIVE WEAPON, LYING IN WAIT.
AND IT'LL DESTROY THE TITANIC.
NO. NO WAY.
JOEY, CAN WE TALK ABOUT THIS? THEY'RE FEDERATION, BUT I MEAN...THEY ARE A MEDICAL SHIP, RIGHT? INNOCENT PEOPLE ARE ON BOARD. THERE'S GOT TO BE--
IT'S A FEDERATION MEDICAL SHIP, COOPER. MILITARIZED. AND EVEN IF THEY WEREN'T, HERE'S THE TRUTH: WE DO NOT GET OUT OF THIS WITHOUT USING THE FINGER.
SO IT'S THEIR LIVES FOR OURS. NO BIG DEAL, RIGHT? A FEW THOUSAND INNOCENT PEOPLE DIE SO WE CAN LIVE?
LOOK, I WANT YOU TO ALL LISTEN TO ME: IF WE DON'T DESTROY THAT SHIP, IT'S NOT JUST US WHO DIE. OUR FAMILIES DIE, OUR FRIENDS DIE, AND EVERYONE WE LEFT BEHIND DIES, BECAUSE THANKS TO US THE FEDERATION KNOWS ABOUT MIDAS NOW. THEY'RE NOT GOING TO STOP WHEN WE'RE STATUES. YOU REALIZE THAT, RIGHT?
THEY'RE GOING TO GO BACK TO THAT PLANET AND THEY'RE GOING TO CARVE MIDAS UP UNTIL EVERY SHIP IN THE FLEET HAS THEIR OWN BLOODY POUND OF FLESH.
AND THEN THEY'LL DESTROY EVERYONE.

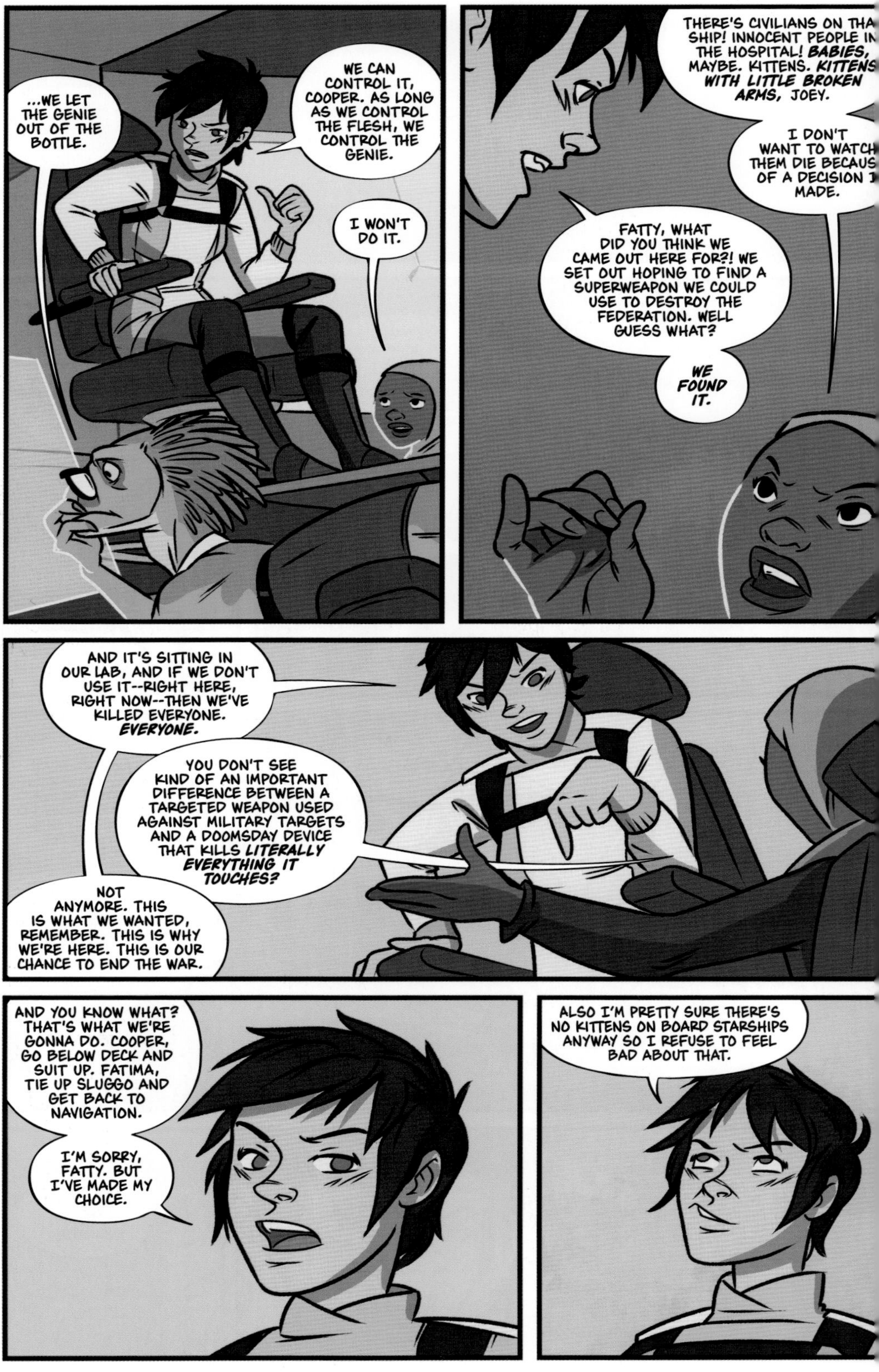
...WE LET THE GENIE OUT OF THE BOTTLE.
WE CAN CONTROL IT, COOPER. AS LONG AS WE CONTROL THE FLESH, WE CONTROL THE GENIE.
I WON'T DO IT.
THERE'S CIVILIANS ON THA SHIP! INNOCENT PEOPLE IN THE HOSPITAL! BABIES, MAYBE. KITTENS. KITTENS WITH LITTLE BROKEN ARMS, JOEY.
I DON'T WANT TO WATCH THEM DIE BECAUS OF A DECISION I MADE.
FATTY, WHAT DID YOU THINK WE CAME OUT HERE FOR?! WE SET OUT HOPING TO FIND A SUPERWEAPON WE COULD USE TO DESTROY THE FEDERATION. WELL GUESS WHAT?
WE FOUND IT.
AND IT'S SITTING IN OUR LAB, AND IF WE DON'T USE IT--RIGHT HERE, RIGHT NOW--THEN WE'VE KILLED EVERYONE. EVERYONE.
YOU DON'T SEE KIND OF AN IMPORTANT DIFFERENCE BETWEEN A TARGETED WEAPON USED AGAINST MILITARY TARGETS AND A DOOMSDAY DEVICE THAT KILLS LITERALLY EVERYTHING IT TOUCHES?
NOT ANYMORE. THIS IS WHAT WE WANTED, REMEMBER. THIS IS WHY WE'RE HERE. THIS IS OUR CHANCE TO END THE WAR.
AND YOU KNOW WHAT? THAT'S WHAT WE'RE GONNA DO. COOPER, GO BELOW DECK AND SUIT UP. FATIMA, TIE UP SLUGGO AND GET BACK TO NAVIGATION.
I'M SORRY, FATTY. BUT I'VE MADE MY CHOICE.
ALSO I'M PRETTY SURE THERE'S NO KITTENS ON BOARD STARSHIPS ANYWAY SO I REFUSE TO FEEL BAD ABOUT THAT.

INCOMING MESSAGE FROM FATIMA, TEXT ONLY.

WEIRDO. PATCH IT THROUGH AS AUDIO.

COOPER, DON'T DO THIS. YOU DON'T HAVE TO DO THIS.

I DO, FATTY. JOEY'S RIGHT.

I KNOW WE WERE HOPING FOR SOMETHING DIFFERENT, BUT WE'VE GOT OUR WEAPON. AND IF WE DON'T USE IT, THEY WILL.

SLUGGO SAYS HALF THE COMPLEMENT OF THAT SHIP ISN'T EVEN ENLISTED! THERE ARE PEOPLE ON THAT SHIP FROM A PLANETARY RESCUE MISSION. WE DIDN'T COME OUT HERE TO KILL INNOCENT PEOPLE.

...I KNOW I DIDN'T.

COME ON, I DIDN'T EITHER. BUT WE NEED TIME TO GET BACK TO THE PLANET AND RECOVER THE REST OF THE FLESH. AND WE CAN'T LET FEDERATION HANDS GET ON THAT FINGER.

IS THAT A PUN? ARE YOU PUNNING?

HEH. I DON'T THINK SO. THEY'RE JUST LIKE--RELATED WORDS?

COOPER... I THINK WE'RE MAKING A MISTAKE.

COME ON. IT'S OUR ONLY CHOICE.

...THAT DOESN'T MEAN IT'S NOT A MISTAKE.

KLIK!

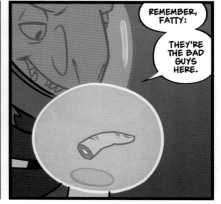

REMEMBER, FATTY:

THEY'RE THE BAD GUYS HERE.

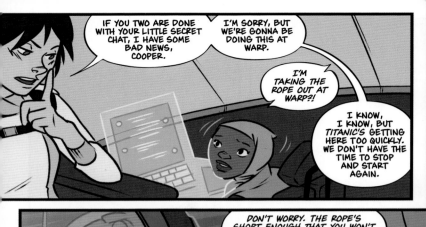

IF YOU TWO ARE DONE WITH YOUR LITTLE SECRET CHAT, I HAVE SOME BAD NEWS, COOPER.

I'M SORRY, BUT WE'RE GONNA BE DOING THIS AT WARP.

I'M TAKING THE ROPE OUT AT WARP?!

I KNOW, I KNOW, BUT TITANIC'S GETTING HERE TOO QUICKLY. WE DON'T HAVE THE TIME TO STOP AND START AGAIN.

DON'T WORRY. THE ROPE'S SHORT ENOUGH THAT YOU WON'T ACCIDENTALLY BE STICKING YOUR TAIL OUT OF THE WARP FIELD.

TERRIFIC.

JOEY, IF I DIE I WANT YOU TO KNOW THAT MY LAST WORDS WERE *"JOEY SCREWED ME ON THIS ONE."* I WANT YOU TO TELL EVERYONE, OKAY?

WOW.

...THIS IS REALLY DANGEROUS.

OKAY. WE'RE READY HERE.

PERFECT. WAIT FOR MY ORDER, COOPER. IF WE DROP IT TOO SOON THEY MIGHT STOP IN TIME.

GOT IT. LET'S NOT WAIT TOO LONG, OKAY? IT LOOKS LIKE THEY'RE ALMOST IN WEAPONS RAN--

THEY'VE OPENED FIRE!

ALRIGHT, COOPER, SO YOU MAY BE SEEING SOME FIRE COMING YOUR WAY. BUT THEY'RE FIRING AT *US,* NOT AT YOU. YOU SHOULD BE FINE, OKAY?

I, UM--

...OK

FATTY, RETURN FIRE! EVASIVE MANEUVERS!

...NO. I WON'T. I'M SORRY, JOEY. THIS ISN'T--

WHAT? "NO"? DID SHE JUST SAY "NO"?!

COOPER, HOLD TIGHT, OKAY?! I'M TAKING OVER NAVIGATION! EVERYTHING'S FINE! I'LL SORT THIS OUT!

blip blip!

blip!

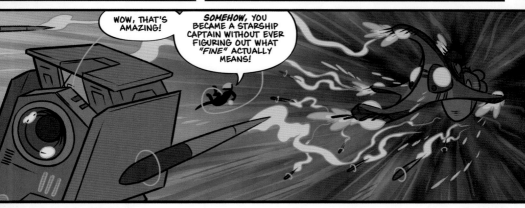

WOW, THAT'S AMAZING!

SOMEHOW, YOU BECAME A STARSHIP CAPTAIN WITHOUT EVER FIGURING OUT WHAT "FINE" ACTUALLY MEANS!

FATIMA, I GET WHAT YOU'RE TRYING TO SAY. I REALLY DO. BUT YOU'RE THE BEST PILOT I'VE EVER MET, AND I CAN'T DO WHAT YOU DO. I NEED YOU TO EVADE THIS FIRE FOR US.

I CAN'T HELP YOU, JOEY! I'M SORRY! I CAN'T.

IF THAT'S TRUE, WE'RE DEAD. AND THE FEDERATION GETS THE WEAPON.

FATIMA, LISTEN TO ME. COOPER'S LITERALLY HANGING FROM A ROPE IN SPACE, AND HE'S GOING TO GET SHOT AND DIE UNLESS YOU STOP BEHAVING LIKE A CHILD AND FLY THIS SHIP LIKE I KNOW YOU CAN.

DO WHAT NEEDS TO BE DONE. SAVE HIM. SAVE EVERYONE.

...

THIS IS IT. THIS IS ALL I'M DOING. WE GET OUT OF THIS AND I'M DONE.

THANK YOU.

FATIMA'S COMING BACK ON NAV, COOPER. YOU READY?

AHHH, GIVE ME A SECOND!

YOU DON'T HAVE A SECOND!

NOW, COOPER!

DONE.

FATTY, JUST KEEP US IN A STRAIGHT LINE. I WANT--

BEEPY BOOP

--HUH?

THIS IS SLUGGO ON PROSPECT, THE WEAPON HAS BEEN JETTISONED DIRECTLY BEHIND THIS SHIP! ANY CONTACT WILL TURN TITANIC TO GOLD! TAKE EVASIVE ACTION, SIR! IT'LL--

KAPOW

...THAT WENT OUT ON FULL POWER. ALL FREQUENCIES, JOEY.

THERE'S NO WAY THEY COULD'VE MISSED IT.

BROADBAND COMMUNICATION FROM THE PROSPECT.

LET'S HEAR IT.

--SPECT, THE WEAPON HAS BEEN JETTISONED DIRECTLY BEHIND THIS SHIP! ANY CONTACT WILL TURN TITANIC TO GOLD! TAKE EVASIVE ACTION, SIR! IT'LL--

NAVIGATION, FULL REVERSE! HARD TO STARBOARD, EMERGENCY DEEP! GET US OUT OF THEIR WAKE!

NOW, NAVIGATOR!

AYE! HARD OVER, DESCENDING, REVERSE THRUST!

RRRRRRRRRRRRRRRRRRR

OPS, FIND THAT FINGER!

SIR, IF IT'S WHERE THEY SAY IT IS, GENERAL, WE--WE MAY NOT BE ABLE TO AVOID A COLLISION.

THIS SHIP IS NOT GOING TO BE TAKEN DOWN BY A FINGER, NAVIGATOR. GET US CLEAR.

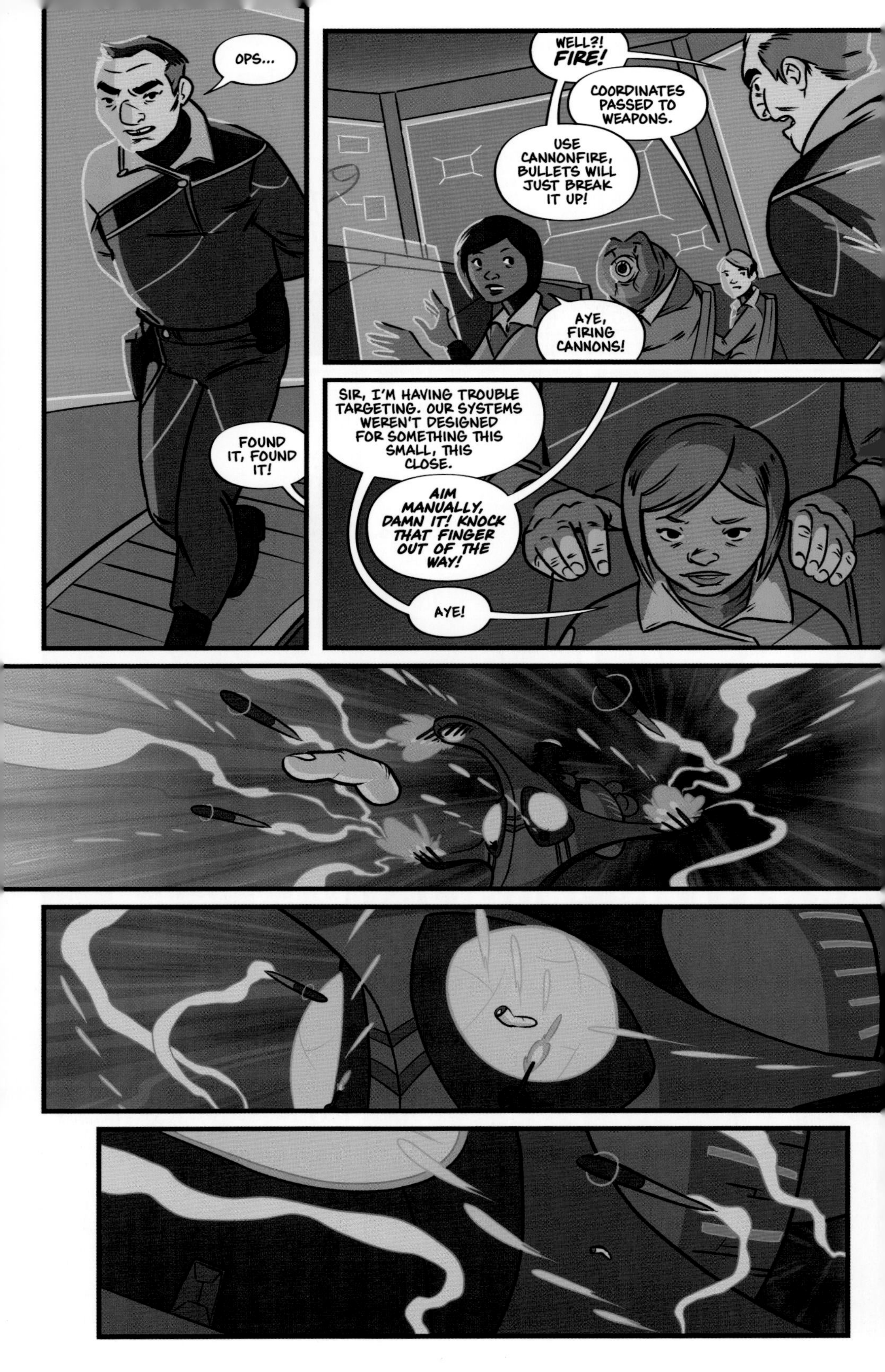
OPS...
FOUND IT, FOUND IT!
WELL?! FIRE!
COORDINATES PASSED TO WEAPONS.
USE CANNONFIRE, BULLETS WILL JUST BREAK IT UP!
AYE, FIRING CANNONS!
SIR, I'M HAVING TROUBLE TARGETING. OUR SYSTEMS WEREN'T DESIGNED FOR SOMETHING THIS SMALL, THIS CLOSE.
AIM MANUALLY, DAMN IT! KNOCK THAT FINGER OUT OF THE WAY!
AYE!

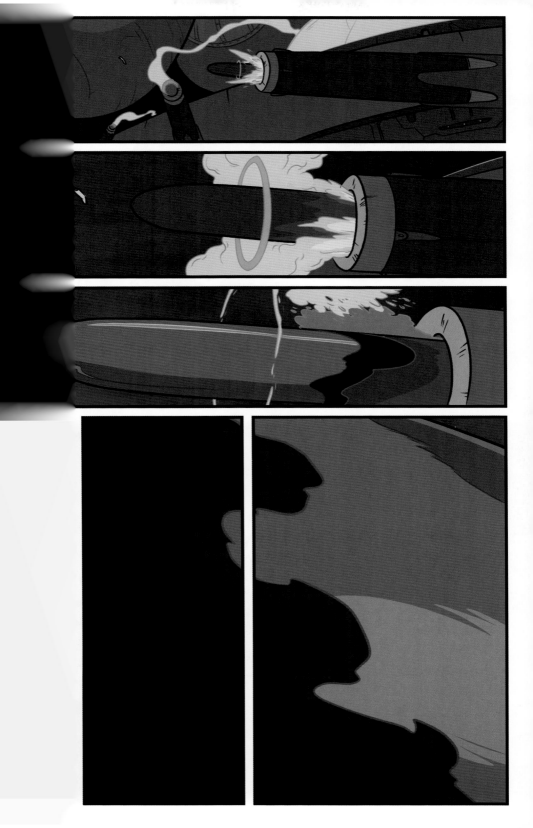

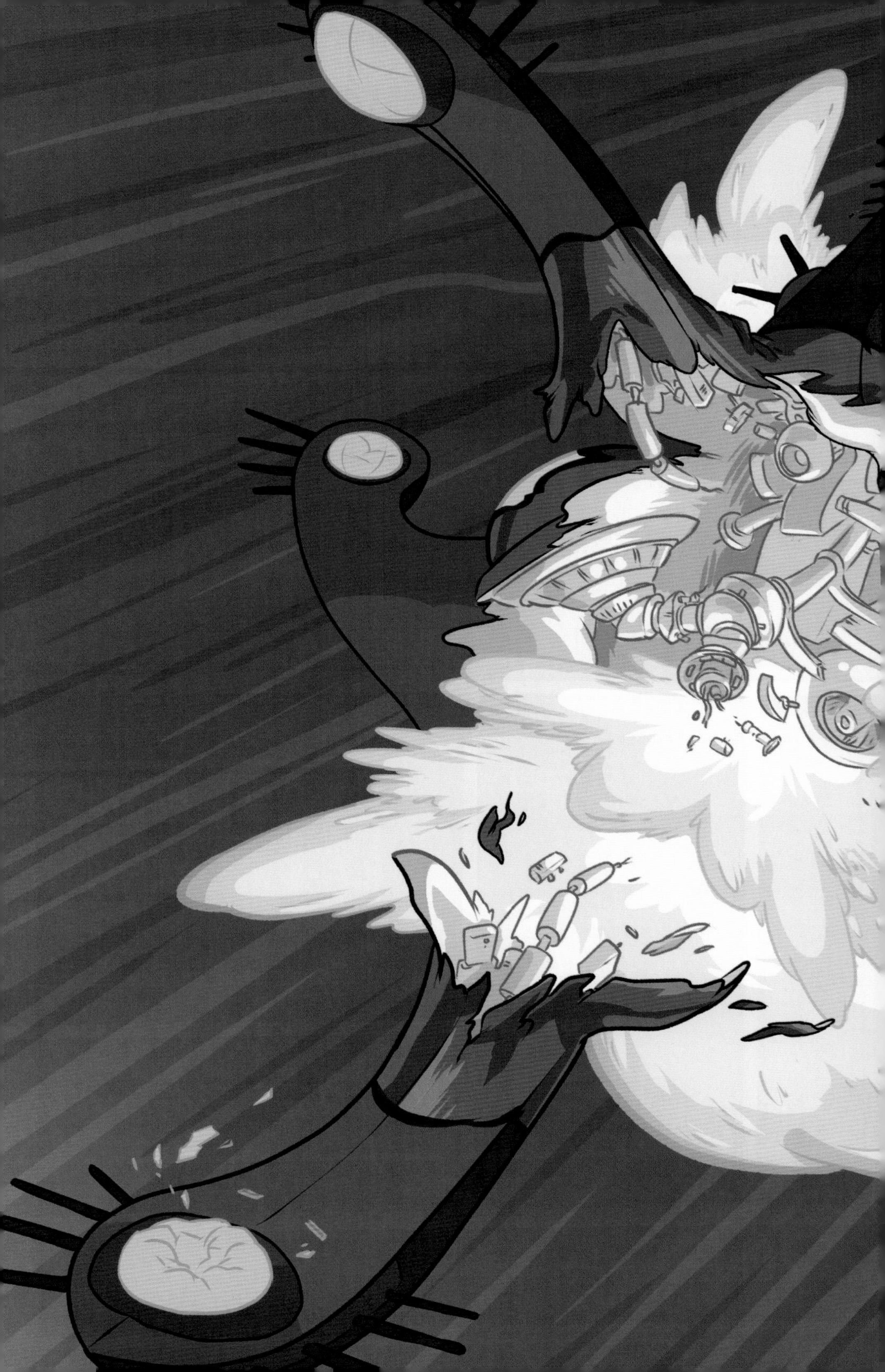

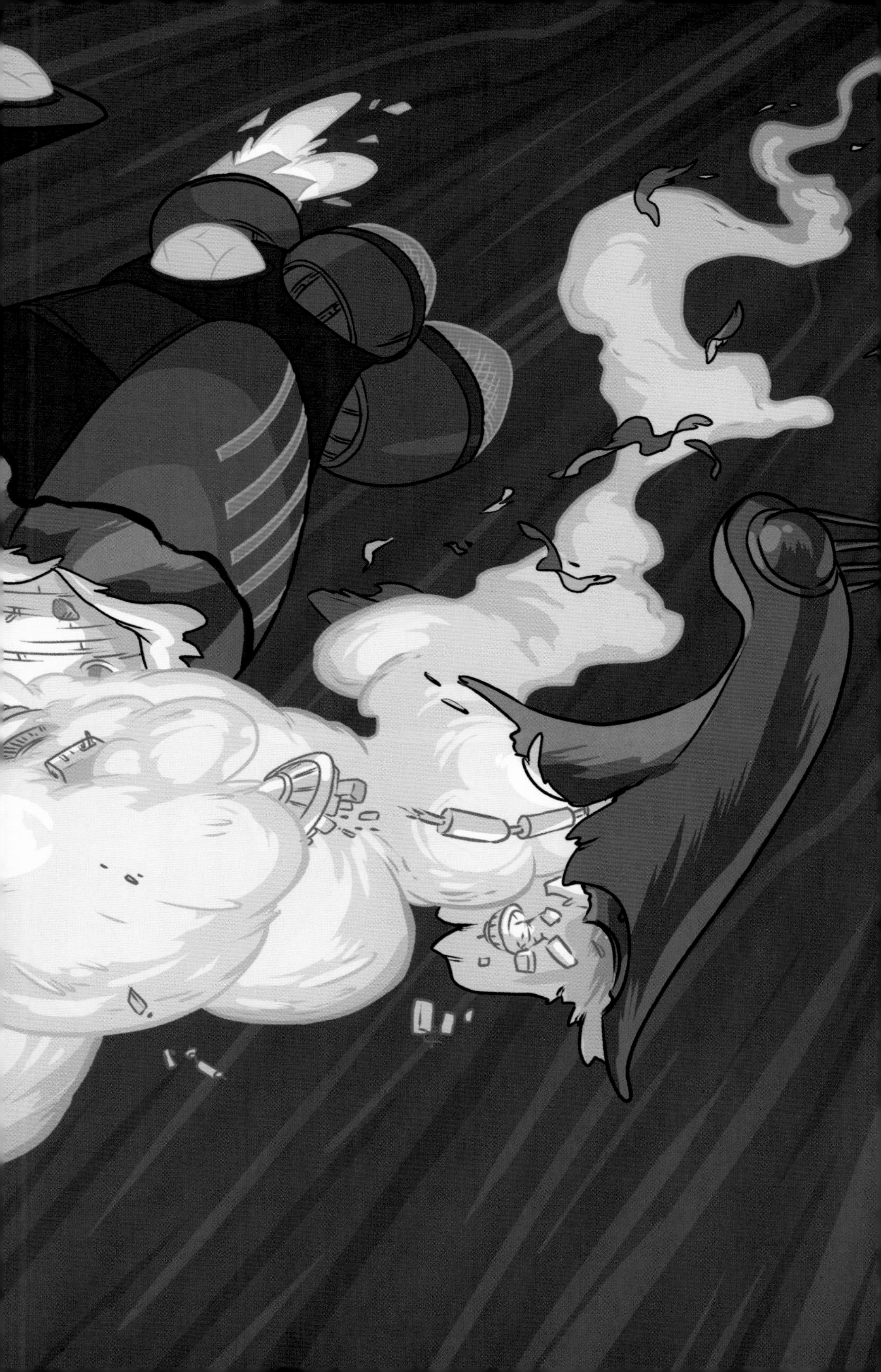

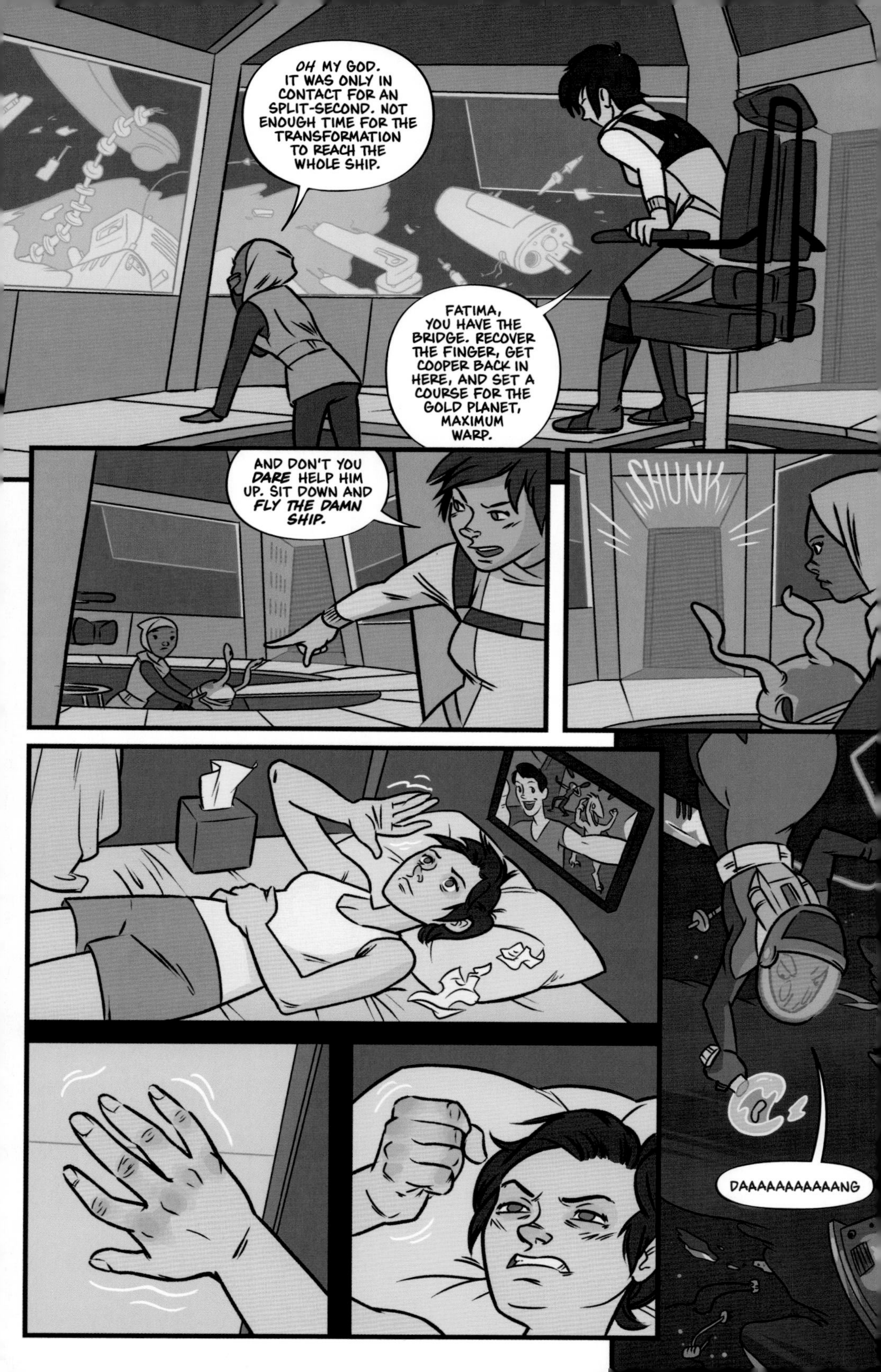
OH MY GOD. IT WAS ONLY IN CONTACT FOR AN SPLIT-SECOND. NOT ENOUGH TIME FOR THE TRANSFORMATION TO REACH THE WHOLE SHIP.
FATIMA, YOU HAVE THE BRIDGE. RECOVER THE FINGER, GET COOPER BACK IN HERE, AND SET A COURSE FOR THE GOLD PLANET, MAXIMUM WARP.
AND DON'T YOU *DARE* HELP HIM UP. SIT DOWN AND *FLY THE DAMN SHIP.*
SHUNK
DAAAAAAAAAAANG

"SCREW IT AND SCREW THEM. **LET'S DO IT.** LET'S SAVE EVERYONE."

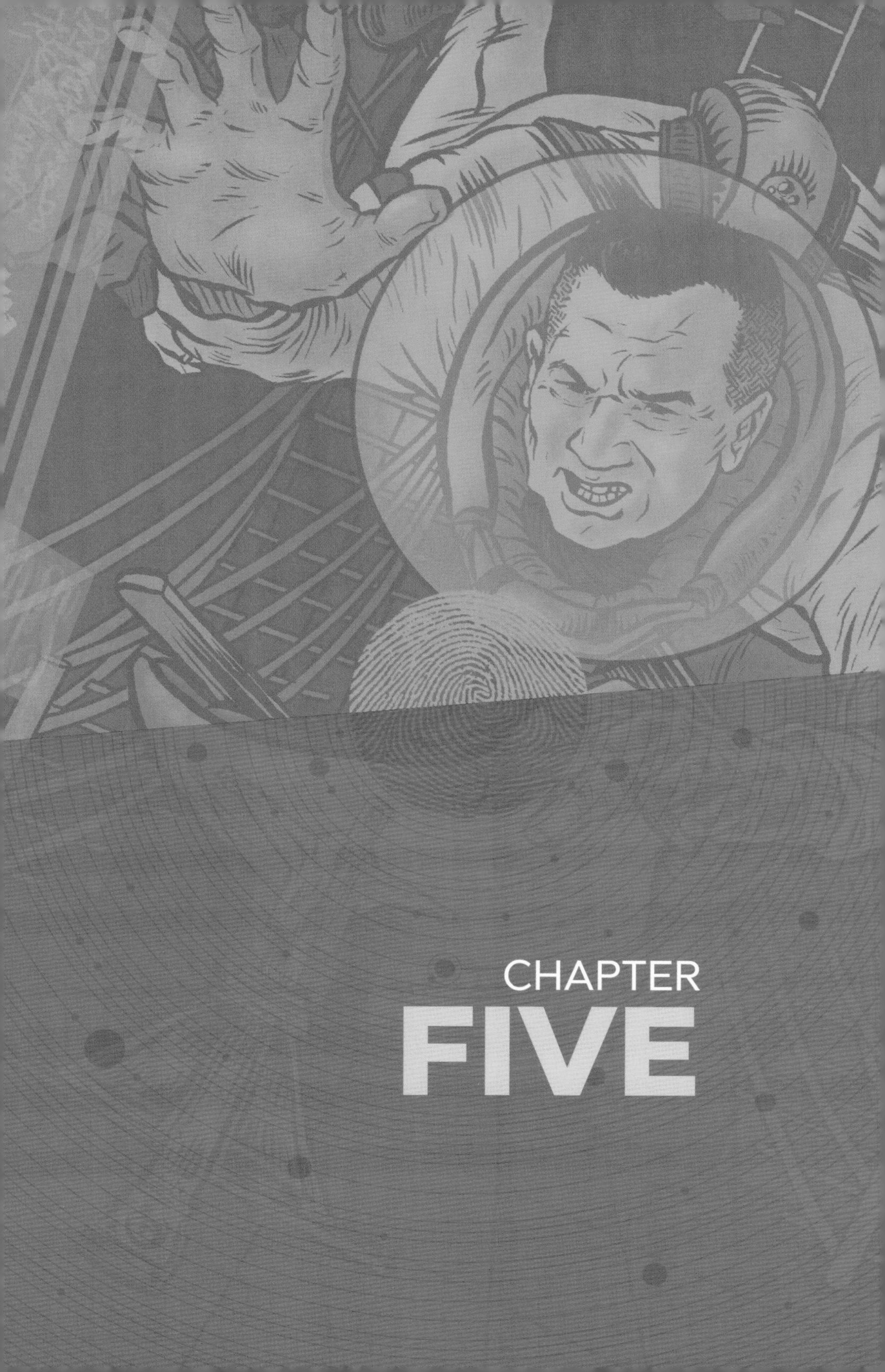

CHAPTER FIVE

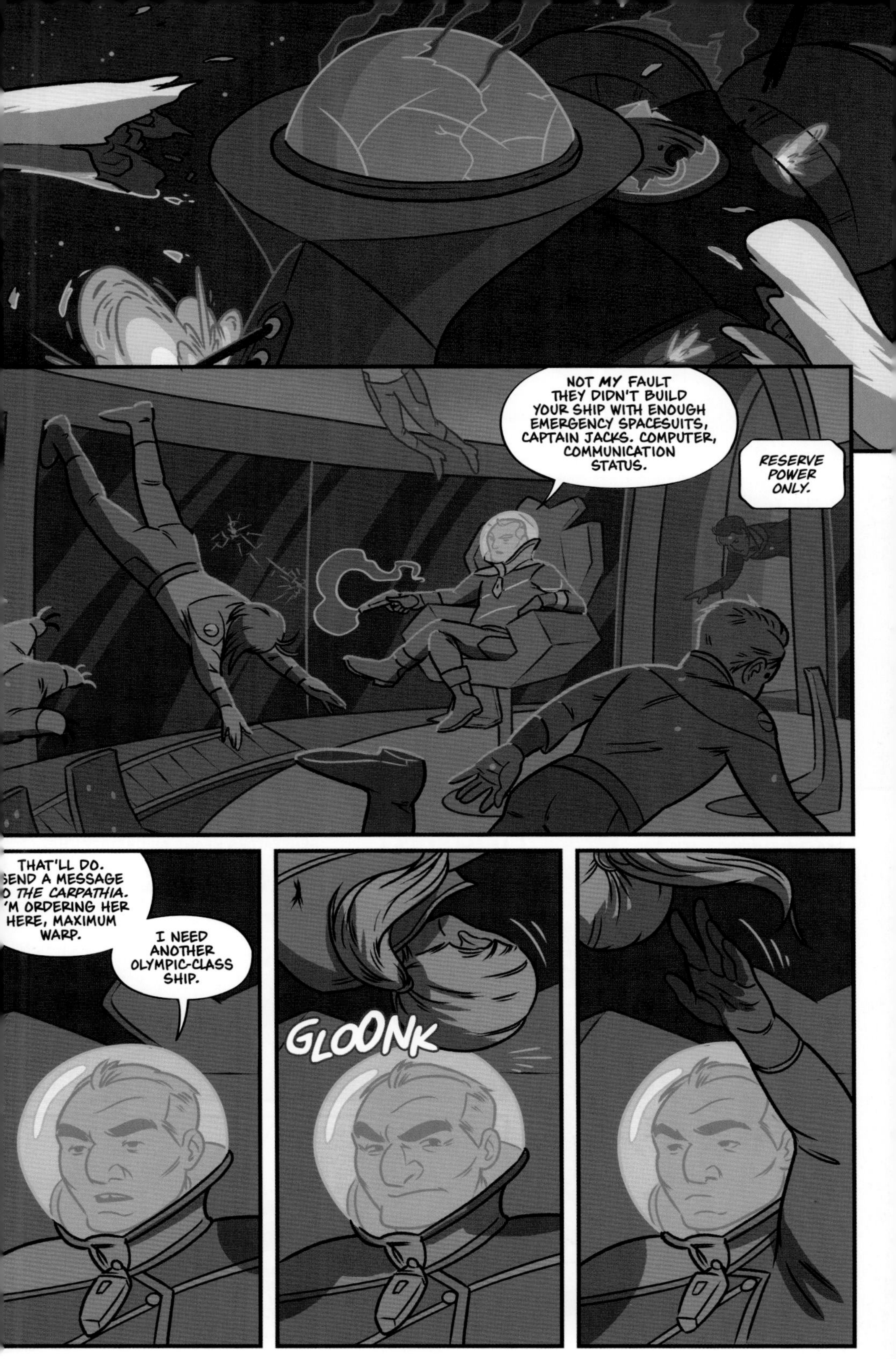
NOT MY FAULT THEY DIDN'T BUILD YOUR SHIP WITH ENOUGH EMERGENCY SPACESUITS, CAPTAIN JACKS. COMPUTER, COMMUNICATION STATUS.
RESERVE POWER ONLY.
THAT'LL DO. SEND A MESSAGE TO THE CARPATHIA. I'M ORDERING HER HERE, MAXIMUM WARP.
I NEED ANOTHER OLYMPIC-CLASS SHIP.
GLOONK

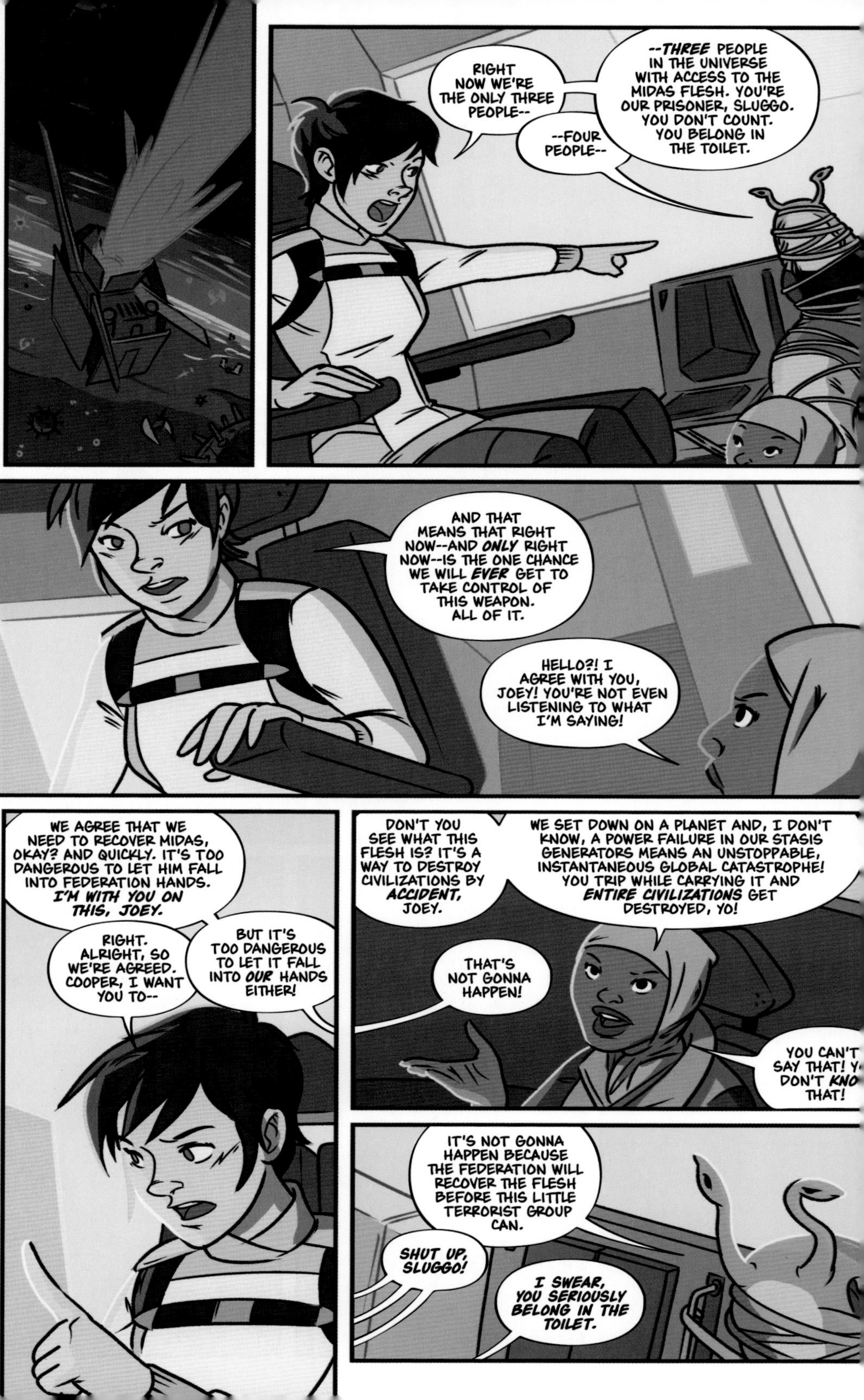
RIGHT NOW WE'RE THE ONLY THREE PEOPLE--
--FOUR PEOPLE--
--*THREE* PEOPLE IN THE UNIVERSE WITH ACCESS TO THE MIDAS FLESH. YOU'RE OUR PRISONER, SLUGGO. YOU DON'T COUNT. YOU BELONG IN THE TOILET.
AND THAT MEANS THAT RIGHT NOW--AND *ONLY* RIGHT NOW--IS THE ONE CHANCE WE WILL *EVER* GET TO TAKE CONTROL OF THIS WEAPON. ALL OF IT.
HELLO?! I AGREE WITH YOU, JOEY! YOU'RE NOT EVEN LISTENING TO WHAT I'M SAYING!
WE AGREE THAT WE NEED TO RECOVER MIDAS, OKAY? AND QUICKLY. IT'S TOO DANGEROUS TO LET HIM FALL INTO FEDERATION HANDS. *I'M WITH YOU ON THIS, JOEY.*
RIGHT. ALRIGHT, SO WE'RE AGREED. COOPER, I WANT YOU TO--
BUT IT'S TOO DANGEROUS TO LET IT FALL INTO *OUR* HANDS EITHER!
DON'T YOU SEE WHAT THIS FLESH IS? IT'S A WAY TO DESTROY CIVILIZATIONS BY *ACCIDENT*, JOEY.
WE SET DOWN ON A PLANET AND, I DON'T KNOW, A POWER FAILURE IN OUR STASIS GENERATORS MEANS AN UNSTOPPABLE, INSTANTANEOUS GLOBAL CATASTROPHE! YOU TRIP WHILE CARRYING IT AND *ENTIRE CIVILIZATIONS* GET DESTROYED, YO!
THAT'S NOT GONNA HAPPEN!
IT'S NOT GONNA HAPPEN BECAUSE THE FEDERATION WILL RECOVER THE FLESH BEFORE THIS LITTLE TERRORIST GROUP CAN.
SHUT UP, SLUGGO!
I SWEAR, YOU SERIOUSLY BELONG IN THE TOILET.

HEY, UM... YOU GUYS REALIZE I CAN HEAR WHAT YOU'RE SAYING, RIGHT? WE, UH--WE 'TILL ALL AGREED THAT I PICK UP MIDAS'S BODY? I'VE ALMOST GOT THE BLOOD TAKEN CARE OF.

YES. GO AHEAD, COOPER. BRIDGE OUT.

NO, LEAVE THE CHANNEL OPEN! I WANT COOPER'S INPUT ON THIS TOO. COOPER, TELL ME WHAT YOU THINK OF THESE TWO OPTIONS, OKAY?

ALRIGHT...

OPTION ONE: WE TAKE THE BODY AND USE IT TO DESTROY THE FEDERATION, LIKE WE PLANNED. I GUESS WE DROP IT ON THEIR HOMEWORLD?

SOUNDS REASONABLE, ASSUMING WE CAN MAKE IT THERE. IT'S A MILITARIZED PLANET, SUPER WELL-DEFENDED, BUT THAT IS WHAT WE PLANNED TO DO INITIALLY. AND I'LL REMIND YOU IT'S NOTHING THEY DIDN'T DO TO ME FIRST.

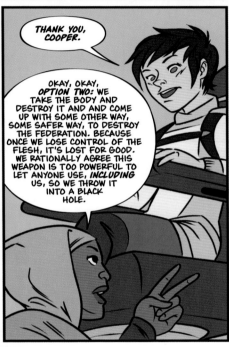

THANK YOU, COOPER.

OKAY, OKAY, *OPTION TWO*: WE TAKE THE BODY AND DESTROY IT AND AND COME UP WITH SOME OTHER WAY, SOME SAFER WAY, TO DESTROY THE FEDERATION. BECAUSE ONCE WE LOSE CONTROL OF THE FLESH, IT'S LOST FOR GOOD. WE RATIONALLY AGREE THIS WEAPON IS TOO POWERFUL TO LET ANYONE USE, *INCLUDING* US, SO WE THROW IT INTO A BLACK HOLE.

I MEAN, THAT DOES SOLVE THE PROBLEM. NOTHING COMES OUT OF A BLACK HOLE. BUT HOW DO 'E GO ABOUT DESTROYING THE FEDERATION SOME OTHER WAY?

I DON'T KNOW COOPER, *WE THINK OF A WAY*. BECAUSE IF WE DON'T AND THIS FLESH GETS OUT OF OUR CONTROL, IT'S OVER. FOR *EVERYONE*. WE CAN'T RISK THAT!

...YEAH ACTUALLY ON THAT SUBJECT I'D LOVE TO HAVE A CONVERSATION ABOUT RISK SOMETIME SOON?

YOU KNOW, BEFORE ONE WRONG MOVE TURNS ME INTO THE MOST AWESOME-LOOKING GOLD STATUE EVER?

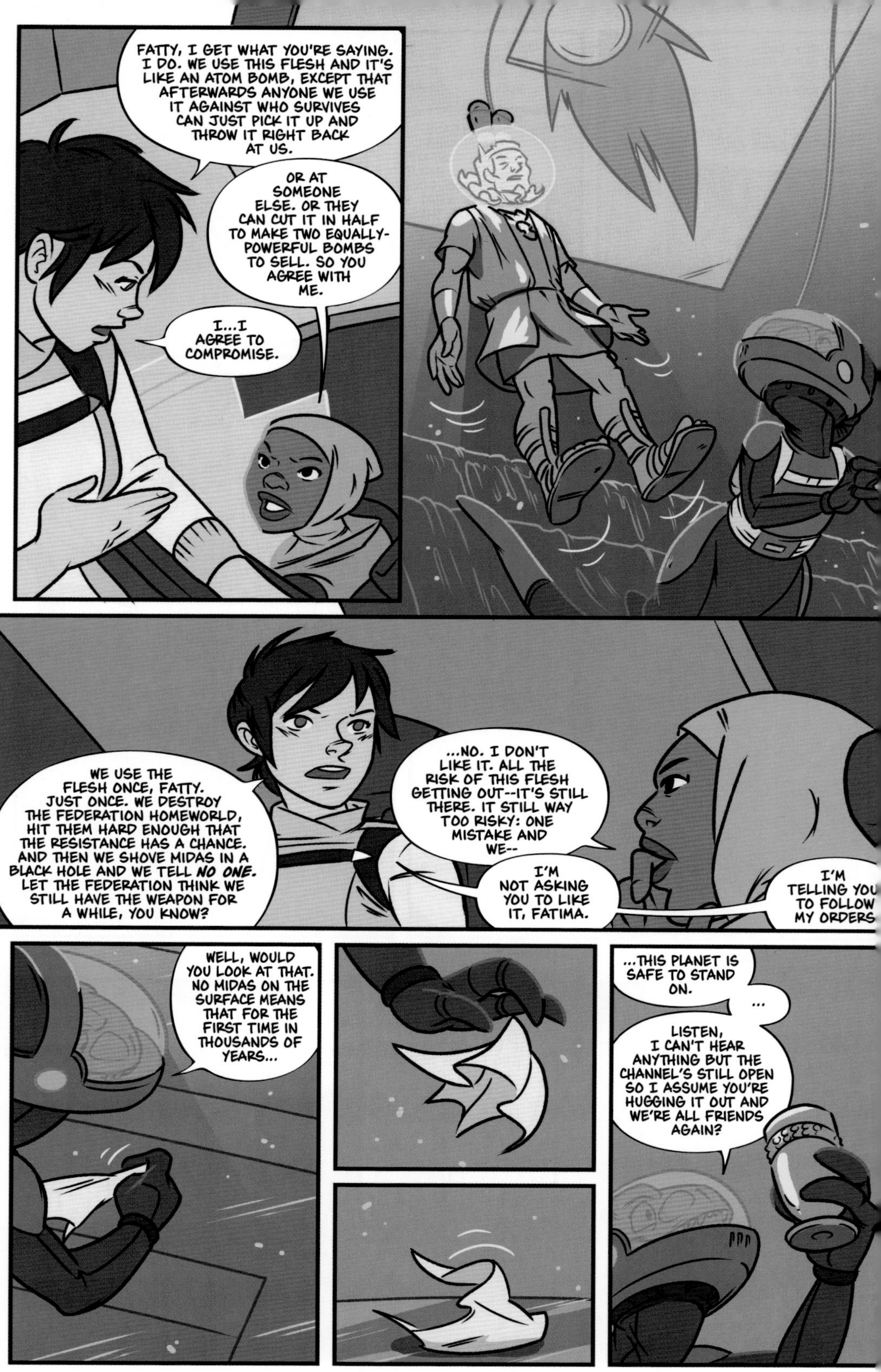
FATTY, I GET WHAT YOU'RE SAYING. I DO. WE USE THIS FLESH AND IT'S LIKE AN ATOM BOMB, EXCEPT THAT AFTERWARDS ANYONE WE USE IT AGAINST WHO SURVIVES CAN JUST PICK IT UP AND THROW IT RIGHT BACK AT US.
OR AT SOMEONE ELSE. OR THEY CAN CUT IT IN HALF TO MAKE TWO EQUALLY-POWERFUL BOMBS TO SELL. SO YOU AGREE WITH ME.
I...I AGREE TO COMPROMISE.
WE USE THE FLESH ONCE, FATTY. JUST ONCE. WE DESTROY THE FEDERATION HOMEWORLD, HIT THEM HARD ENOUGH THAT THE RESISTANCE HAS A CHANCE. AND THEN WE SHOVE MIDAS IN A BLACK HOLE AND WE TELL *NO ONE.* LET THE FEDERATION THINK WE STILL HAVE THE WEAPON FOR A WHILE, YOU KNOW?
...NO. I DON'T LIKE IT. ALL THE RISK OF THIS FLESH GETTING OUT--IT'S STILL THERE. IT STILL WAY TOO RISKY: ONE MISTAKE AND WE--
I'M NOT ASKING YOU TO LIKE IT, FATIMA.
I'M TELLING YOU TO FOLLOW MY ORDERS
WELL, WOULD YOU LOOK AT THAT. NO MIDAS ON THE SURFACE MEANS THAT FOR THE FIRST TIME IN THOUSANDS OF YEARS...
...THIS PLANET IS SAFE TO STAND ON.
...
LISTEN, I CAN'T HEAR ANYTHING BUT THE CHANNEL'S STILL OPEN SO I ASSUME YOU'RE HUGGING IT OUT AND WE'RE ALL FRIENDS AGAIN?

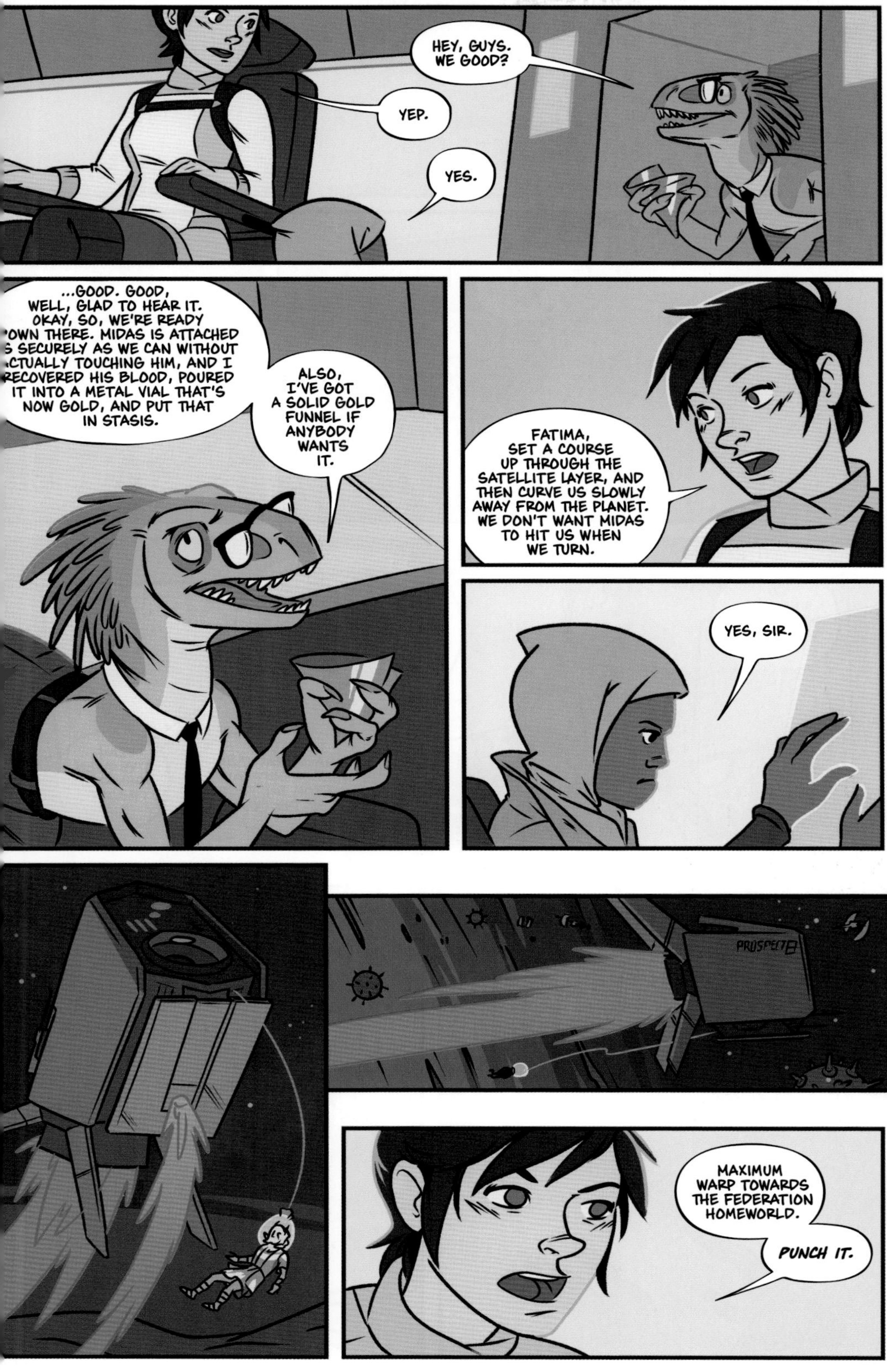
HEY, GUYS. WE GOOD?
YEP.
YES.
...GOOD. GOOD, WELL, GLAD TO HEAR IT. OKAY, SO, WE'RE READY 'OWN THERE. MIDAS IS ATTACHED S SECURELY AS WE CAN WITHOUT CTUALLY TOUCHING HIM, AND I RECOVERED HIS BLOOD, POURED IT INTO A METAL VIAL THAT'S NOW GOLD, AND PUT THAT IN STASIS.
ALSO, I'VE GOT A SOLID GOLD FUNNEL IF ANYBODY WANTS IT.
FATIMA, SET A COURSE UP THROUGH THE SATELLITE LAYER, AND THEN CURVE US SLOWLY AWAY FROM THE PLANET. WE DON'T WANT MIDAS TO HIT US WHEN WE TURN.
YES, SIR.
MAXIMUM WARP TOWARDS THE FEDERATION HOMEWORLD.
PUNCH IT.

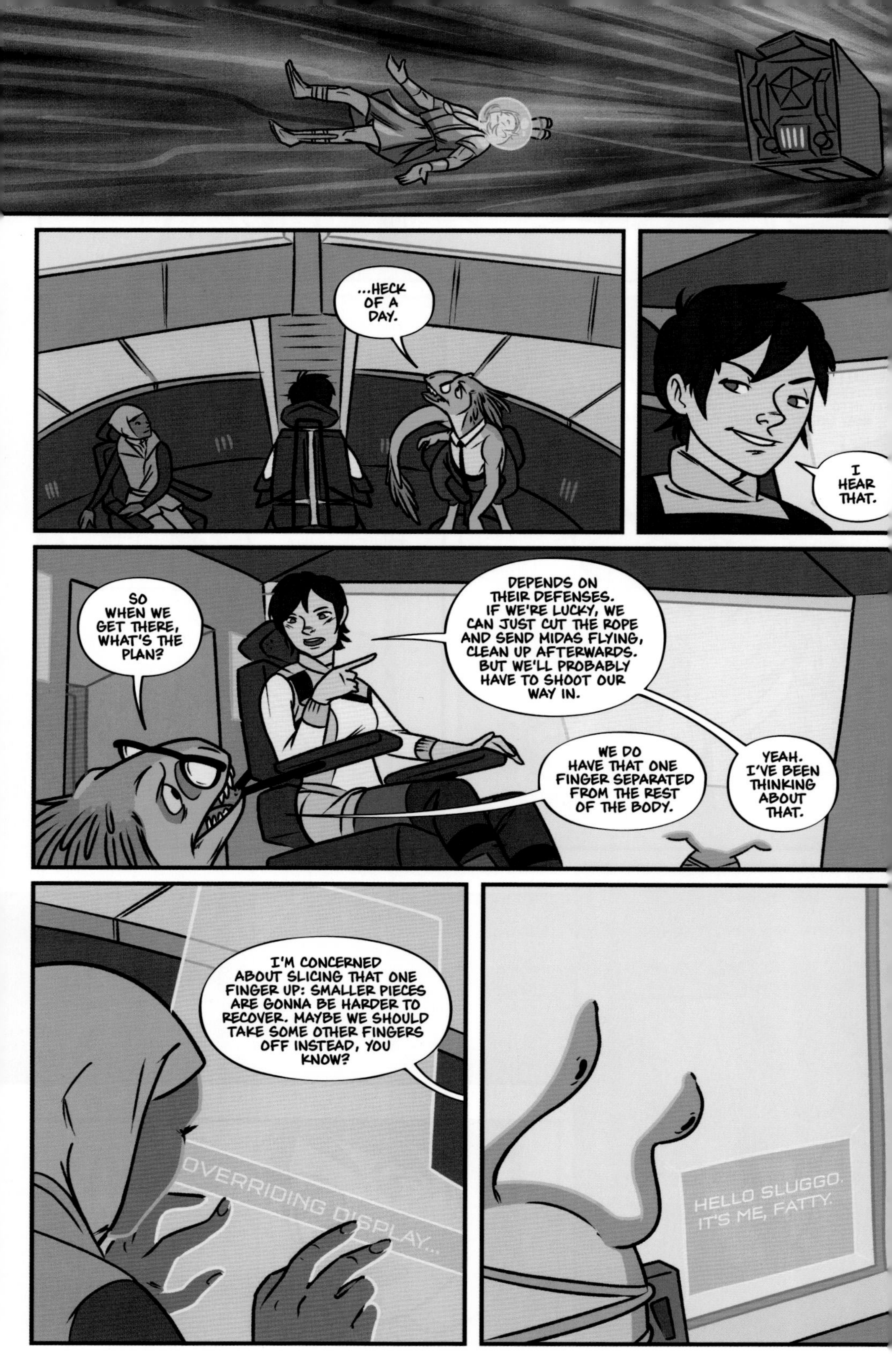
...HECK OF A DAY.
I HEAR THAT.
SO WHEN WE GET THERE, WHAT'S THE PLAN?
DEPENDS ON THEIR DEFENSES. IF WE'RE LUCKY, WE CAN JUST CUT THE ROPE AND SEND MIDAS FLYING, CLEAN UP AFTERWARDS. BUT WE'LL PROBABLY HAVE TO SHOOT OUR WAY IN.
WE DO HAVE THAT ONE FINGER SEPARATED FROM THE REST OF THE BODY.
YEAH. I'VE BEEN THINKING ABOUT THAT.
I'M CONCERNED ABOUT SLICING THAT ONE FINGER UP: SMALLER PIECES ARE GONNA BE HARDER TO RECOVER. MAYBE WE SHOULD TAKE SOME OTHER FINGERS OFF INSTEAD, YOU KNOW?
OVERRIDING DISPLAY...
HELLO SLUGGO. IT'S ME, FATTY.

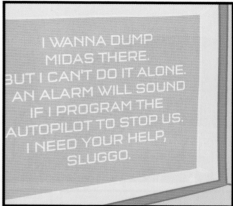

OKAY, SO YOU BELIEVE THE FEDERATION IS A FORCE OF GOOD, AND I DON'T. BUT WE BOTH THINK THE FLESH SHOULDN'T BE USED BY THE PROSPECT. I'VE SET A COURSE THAT BRINGS US PAST A BLACK HOLE ON OUR WAY TO FEDERATION SPACE.

I WANNA DUMP MIDAS THERE. BUT I CAN'T DO IT ALONE. AN ALARM WILL SOUND IF I PROGRAM THE AUTOPILOT TO STOP US. I NEED YOUR HELP, SLUGGO.

IF I GIVE YOU A WAY TO BREAK FREE OF YOUR BONDS, WILL YOU STOP THIS SHIP WHEN THE DISPLAY TELLS YOU TO? YOU'LL STILL BE OUR PRISONER, BUT THE WEAPON WILL BE DESTROYED. WILL YOU HELP? COUGH ONCE IF YES. :)

ＥAHEMＥ

ANYWAY, THAT WOULD GIVE US A COUPLE OF GOOD SHOTS, AND IF WE USE THEM WELL--

THEY WON'T KNOW WHAT HIT THEM.

THANKS SLUGGO. I KNEW THAT GOOD KID I REMEMBER FROM SCHOOL SURVIVED IN THERE SOMEWHERE. :P

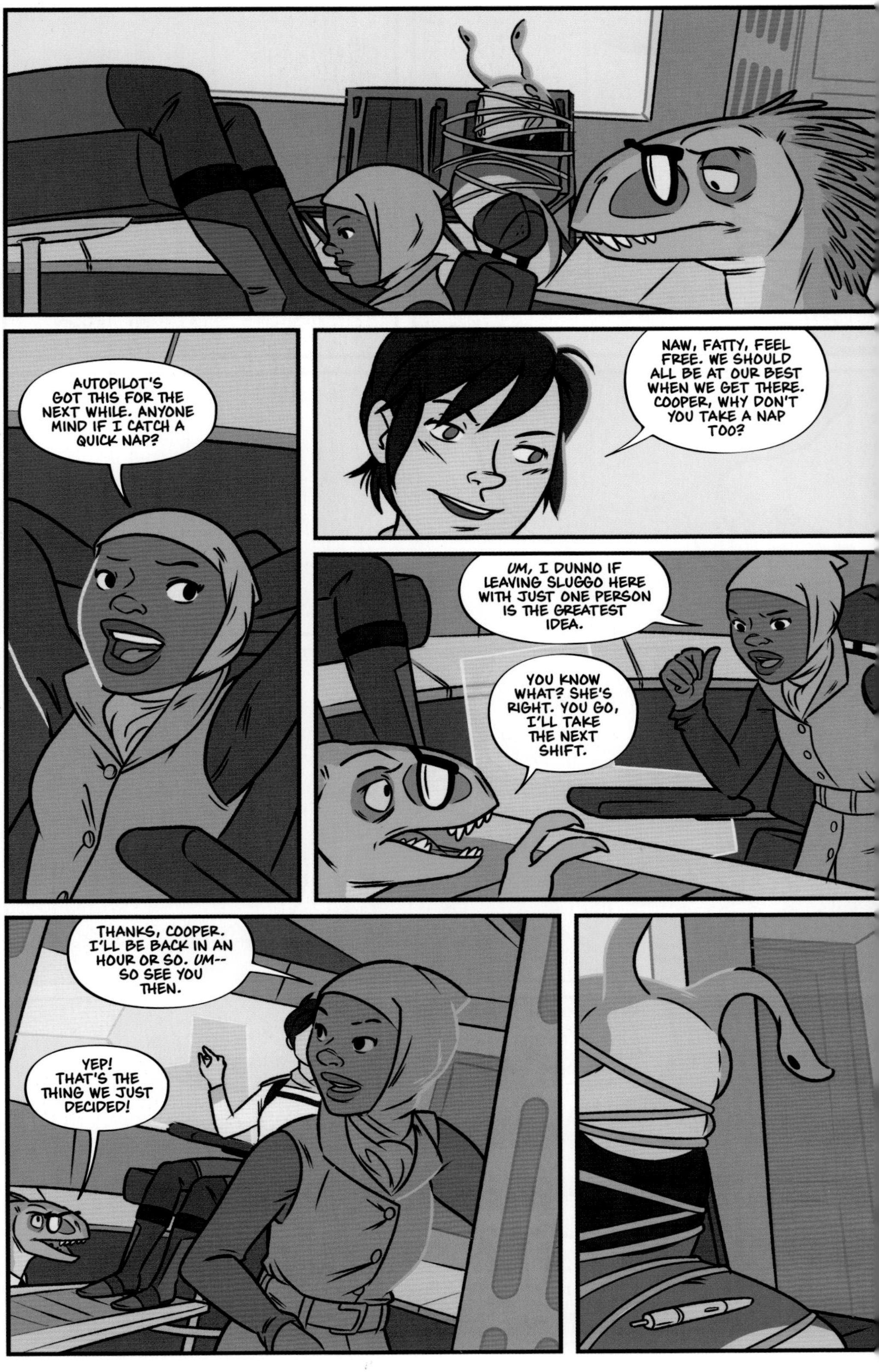
AUTOPILOT'S GOT THIS FOR THE NEXT WHILE. ANYONE MIND IF I CATCH A QUICK NAP?
NAW, FATTY, FEEL FREE. WE SHOULD ALL BE AT OUR BEST WHEN WE GET THERE. COOPER, WHY DON'T YOU TAKE A NAP TOO?
UM, I DUNNO IF LEAVING SLUGGO HERE WITH JUST ONE PERSON IS THE GREATEST IDEA.
YOU KNOW WHAT? SHE'S RIGHT. YOU GO, I'LL TAKE THE NEXT SHIFT.
THANKS, COOPER. I'LL BE BACK IN AN HOUR OR SO. UM-- SO SEE YOU THEN.
YEP! THAT'S THE THING WE JUST DECIDED!

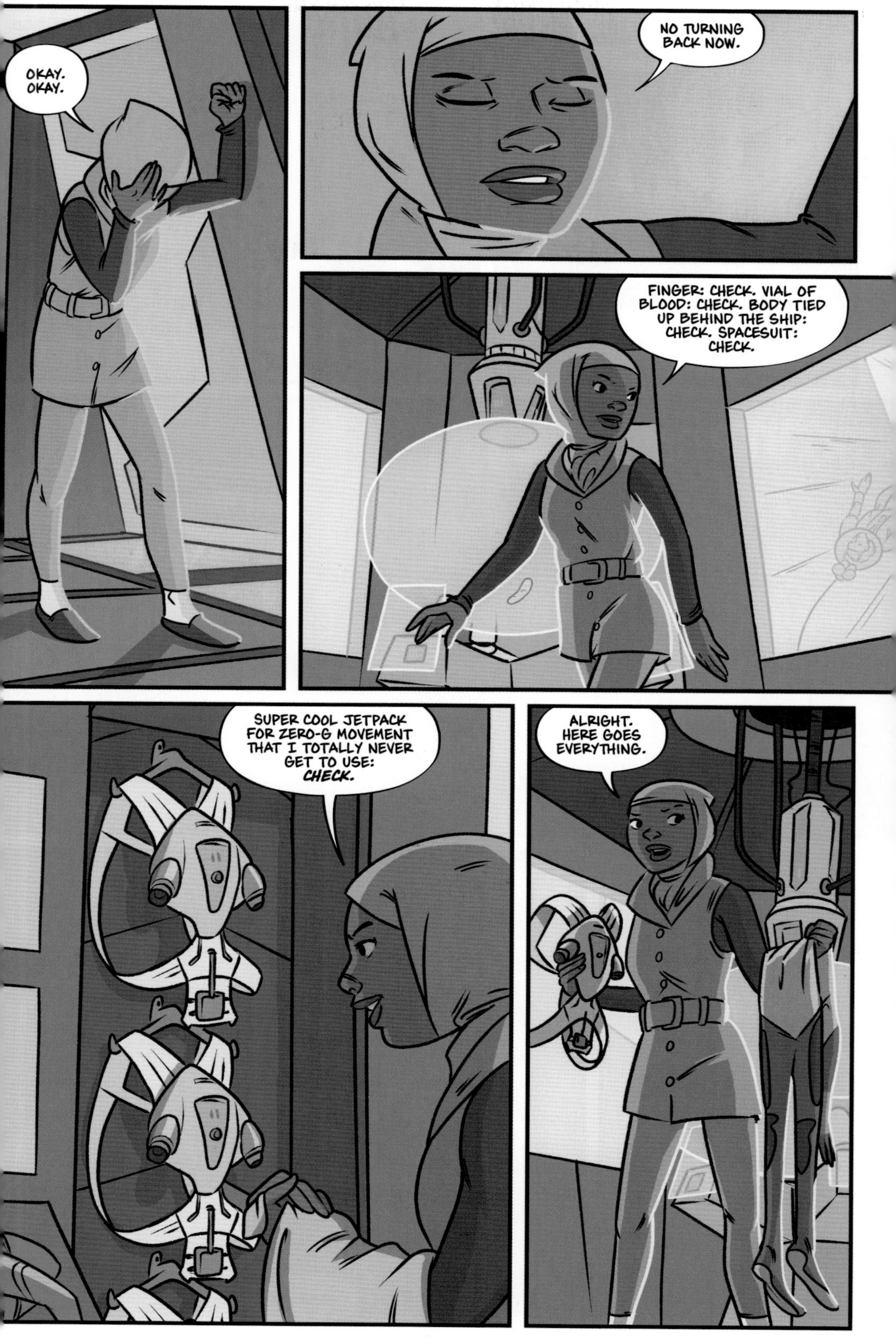
OKAY.
OKAY.
NO TURNING BACK NOW.
FINGER: CHECK. VIAL OF BLOOD: CHECK. BODY TIED UP BEHIND THE SHIP: CHECK. SPACESUIT: CHECK.
SUPER COOL JETPACK FOR ZERO-G MOVEMENT THAT I TOTALLY NEVER GET TO USE: *CHECK.*
ALRIGHT. HERE GOES EVERYTHING.

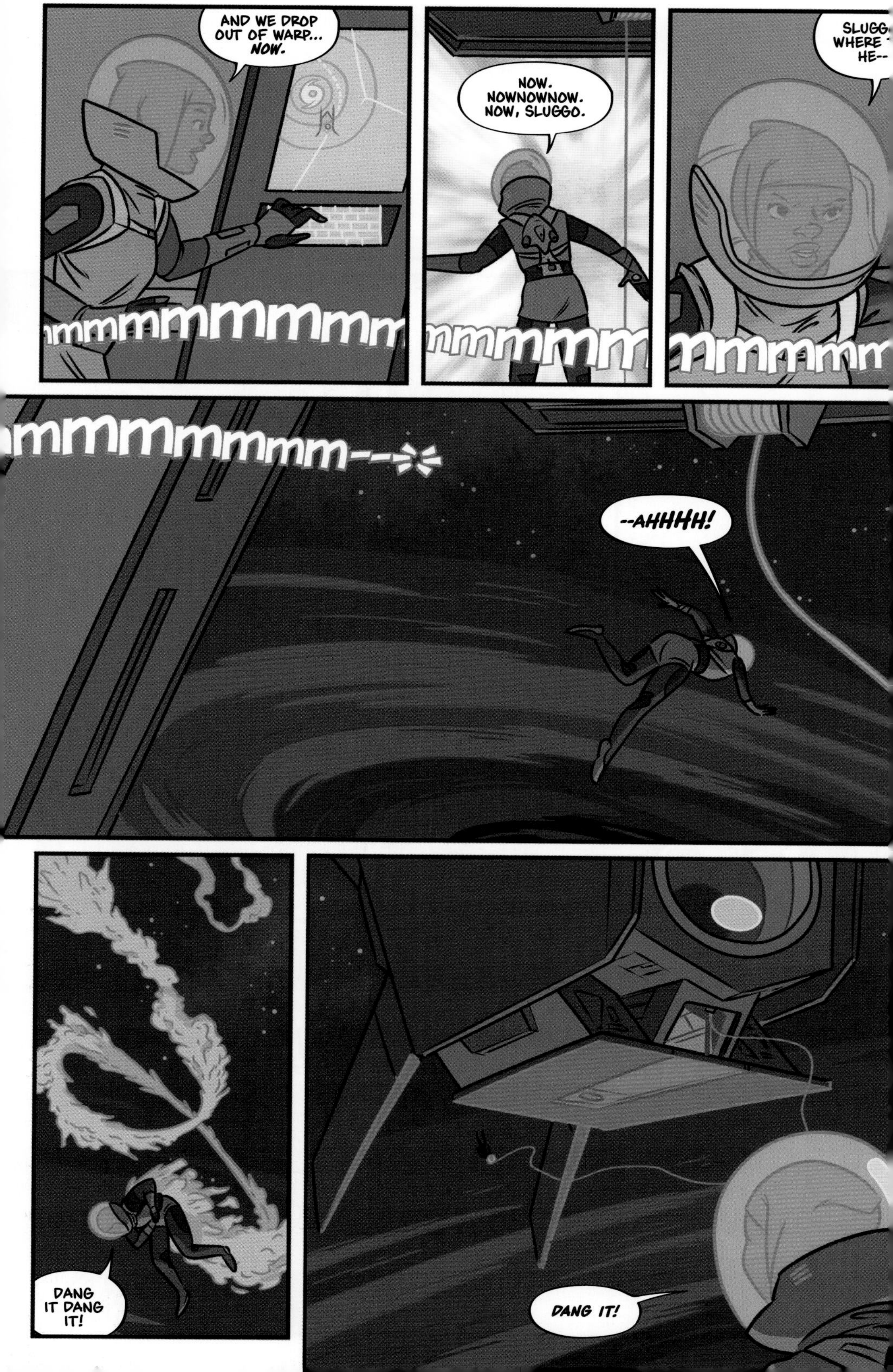
AND WE DROP OUT OF WARP... NOW.
mmmmmmmmmm
NOW. NOWNOWNOW. NOW, SLUGGO.
mmmmmmmm
mmmmmm
mmmmmmmmm--
--AHHHH!
DANG IT DANG IT!
DANG IT!

I GAVE HIM A SMOOTH DROP OUT OF WARP, NOT THIS RIDICULOUS--

OOF!

COME ON, COME ON--

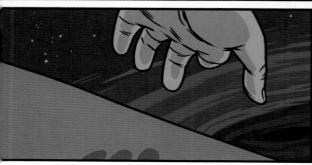

WHOOP!

OFF YOU GO, KING MIDAS!

AW YES! YOU'LL GET YOUR FINGER AND BODY JUICE TOO IN JUST ONE SECOND, DUDE!

REST IN PIECES!

...HUH?

COMPUTER, WHY'S GRAVITY OFF?

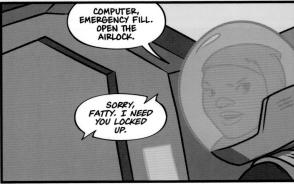

COMPUTER, EMERGENCY FILL. OPEN THE AIRLOCK.

SORRY, FATTY. I NEED YOU LOCKED UP.

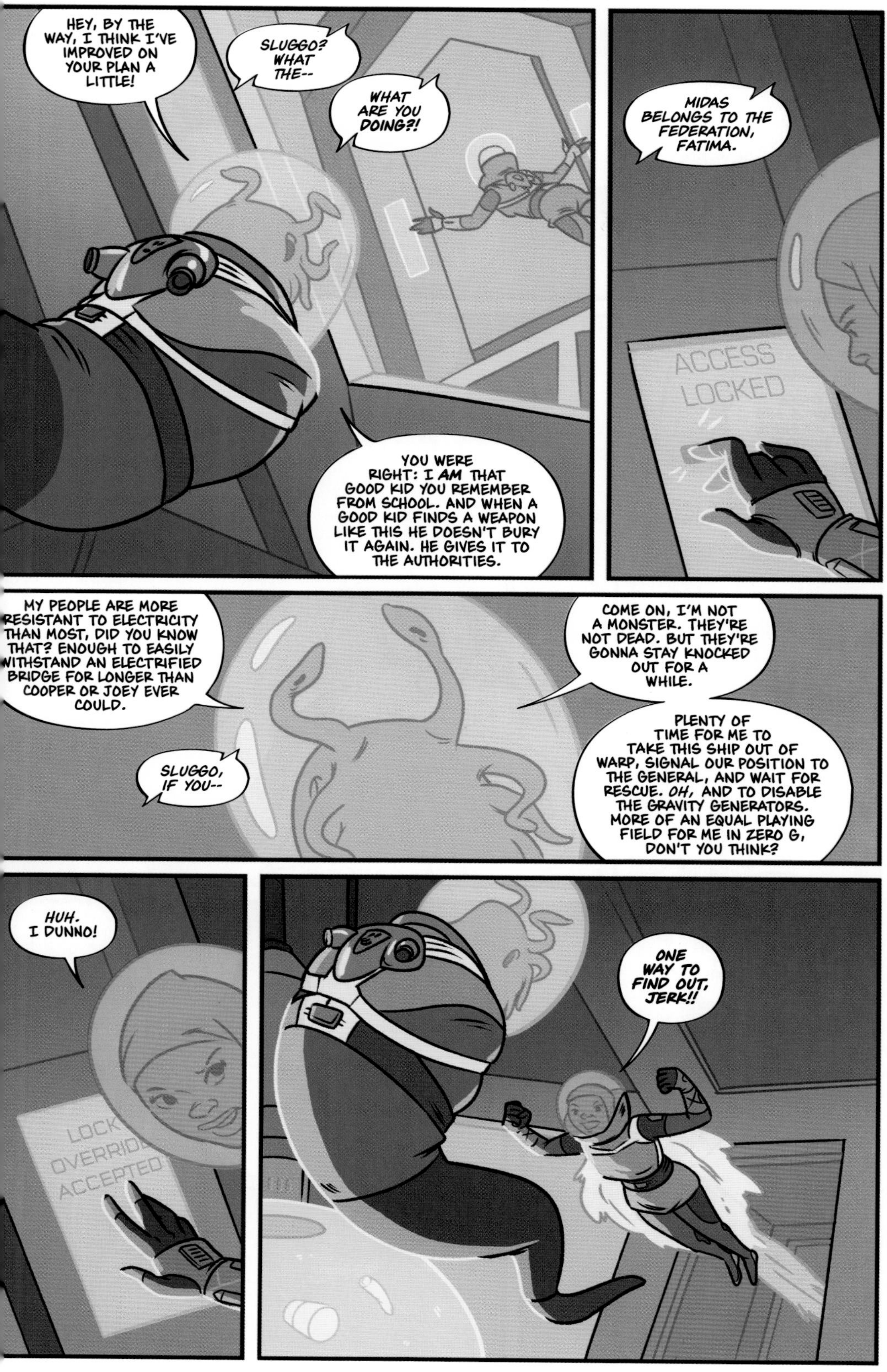
HEY, BY THE WAY, I THINK I'VE IMPROVED ON YOUR PLAN A LITTLE!
SLUGGO? WHAT THE--
WHAT ARE YOU DOING?!
YOU WERE RIGHT: I *AM* THAT GOOD KID YOU REMEMBER FROM SCHOOL. AND WHEN A GOOD KID FINDS A WEAPON LIKE THIS HE DOESN'T BURY IT AGAIN. HE GIVES IT TO THE AUTHORITIES.
MIDAS BELONGS TO THE FEDERATION, FATIMA.
ACCESS LOCKED
MY PEOPLE ARE MORE RESISTANT TO ELECTRICITY THAN MOST, DID YOU KNOW THAT? ENOUGH TO EASILY WITHSTAND AN ELECTRIFIED BRIDGE FOR LONGER THAN COOPER OR JOEY EVER COULD.
SLUGGO, IF YOU--
COME ON, I'M NOT A MONSTER. THEY'RE NOT DEAD. BUT THEY'RE GONNA STAY KNOCKED OUT FOR A WHILE.
PLENTY OF TIME FOR ME TO TAKE THIS SHIP OUT OF WARP, SIGNAL OUR POSITION TO THE GENERAL, AND WAIT FOR RESCUE. *OH,* AND TO DISABLE THE GRAVITY GENERATORS. MORE OF AN EQUAL PLAYING FIELD FOR ME IN ZERO G, DON'T YOU THINK?
HUH. I DUNNO!
LOCK OVERRIDE ACCEPTED
ONE WAY TO FIND OUT, JERK!!

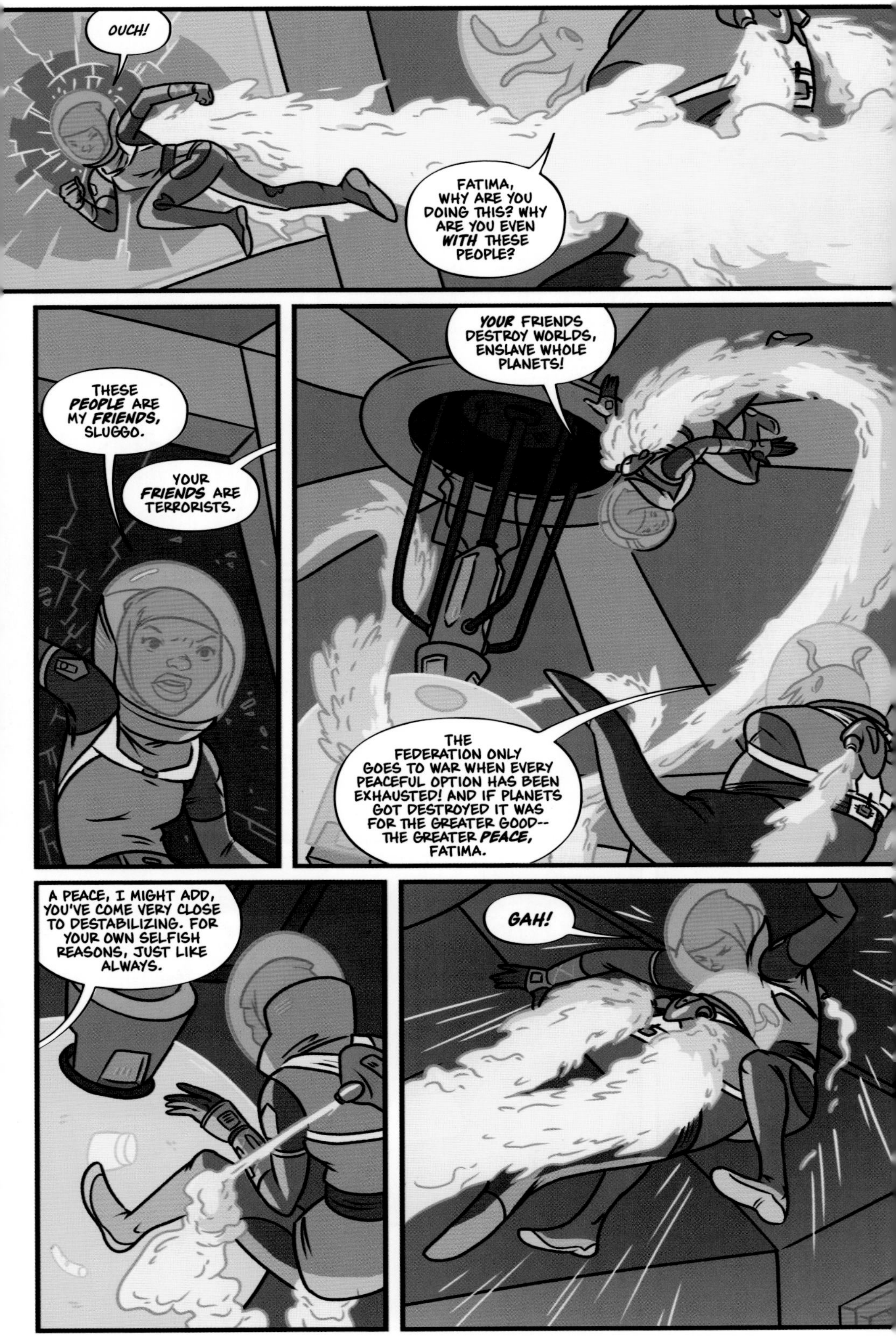
OUCH!
FATIMA, WHY ARE YOU DOING THIS? WHY ARE YOU EVEN *WITH* THESE PEOPLE?
THESE *PEOPLE* ARE MY *FRIENDS*, SLUGGO.
YOUR *FRIENDS* ARE TERRORISTS.
YOUR FRIENDS DESTROY WORLDS, ENSLAVE WHOLE PLANETS!
THE FEDERATION ONLY GOES TO WAR WHEN EVERY PEACEFUL OPTION HAS BEEN EXHAUSTED! AND IF PLANETS GOT DESTROYED IT WAS FOR THE GREATER GOOD-- THE GREATER *PEACE*, FATIMA.
A PEACE, I MIGHT ADD, YOU'VE COME VERY CLOSE TO DESTABILIZING. FOR YOUR OWN SELFISH REASONS, JUST LIKE ALWAYS.
GAH!

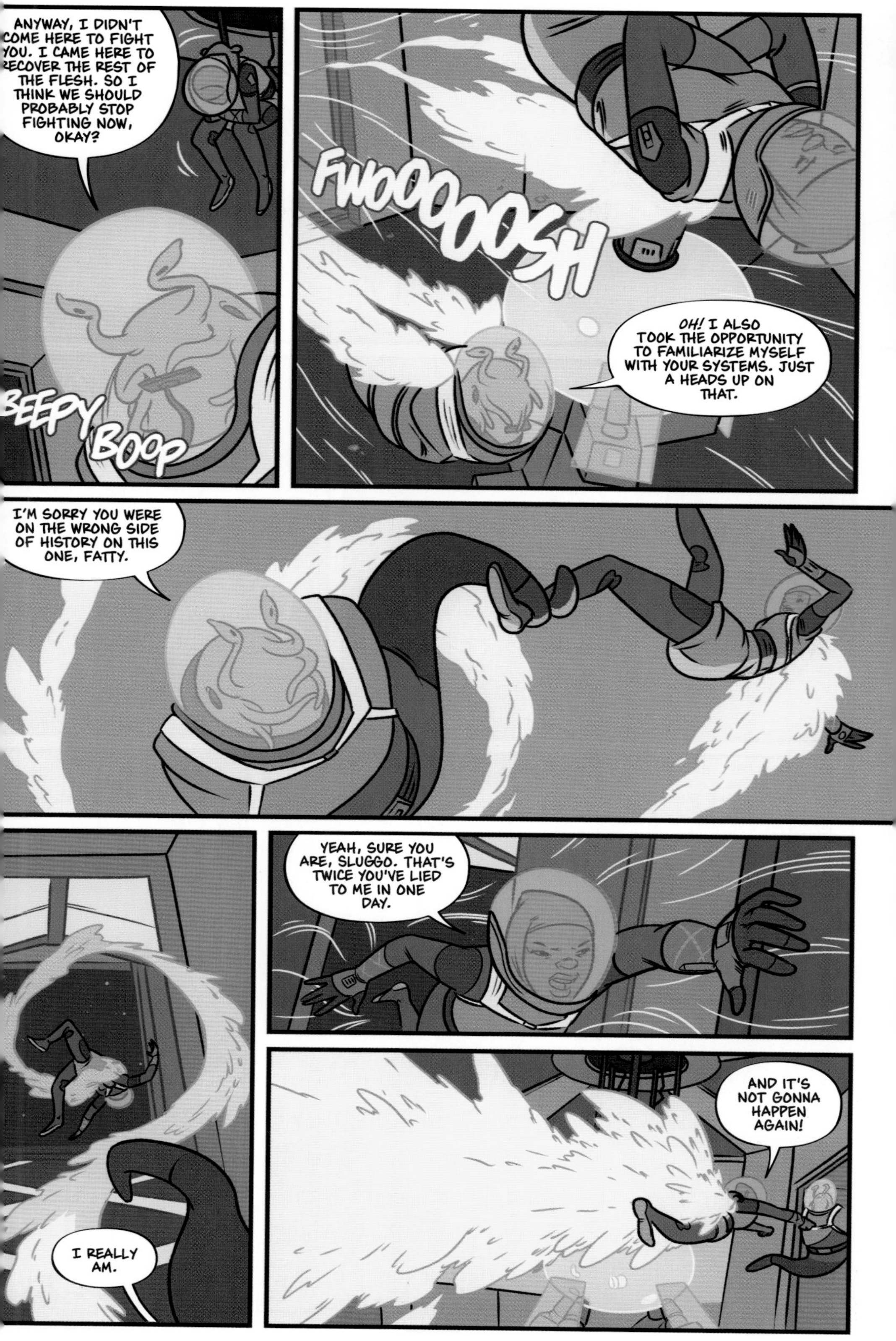
ANYWAY, I DIDN'T COME HERE TO FIGHT YOU. I CAME HERE TO RECOVER THE REST OF THE FLESH. SO I THINK WE SHOULD PROBABLY STOP FIGHTING NOW, OKAY?
BEEPY BOOP
FWOOOOOOSH
OH! I ALSO TOOK THE OPPORTUNITY TO FAMILIARIZE MYSELF WITH YOUR SYSTEMS. JUST A HEADS UP ON THAT.
I'M SORRY YOU WERE ON THE WRONG SIDE OF HISTORY ON THIS ONE, FATTY.
I REALLY AM.
YEAH, SURE YOU ARE, SLUGGO. THAT'S TWICE YOU'VE LIED TO ME IN ONE DAY.
AND IT'S NOT GONNA HAPPEN AGAIN!

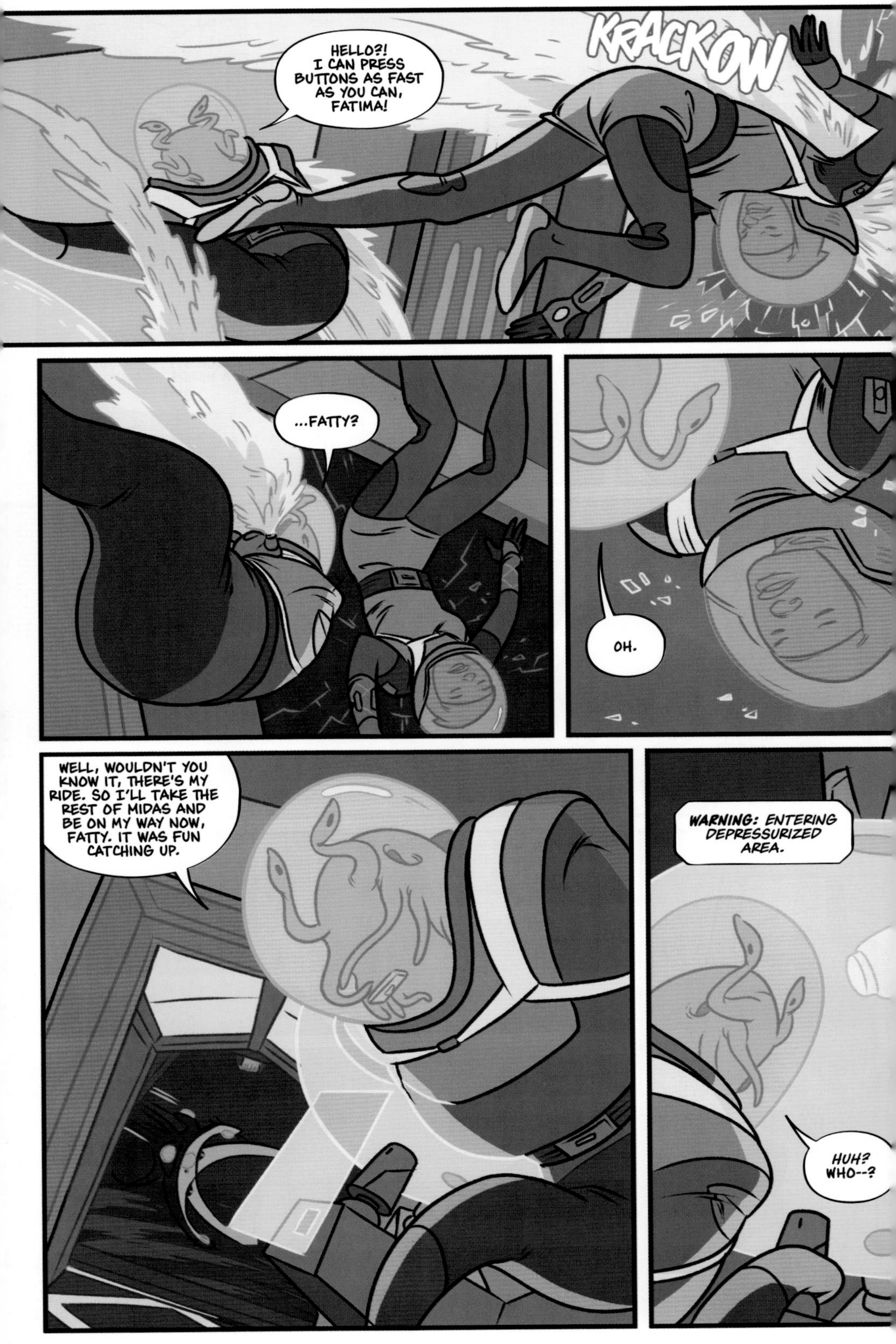
HELLO?! I CAN PRESS BUTTONS AS FAST AS YOU CAN, FATIMA!
KRACKOW
...FATTY?
OH.
WELL, WOULDN'T YOU KNOW IT, THERE'S MY RIDE. SO I'LL TAKE THE REST OF MIDAS AND BE ON MY WAY NOW, FATTY. IT WAS FUN CATCHING UP.
WARNING: ENTERING DEPRESSURIZED AREA.
HUH? WHO--?

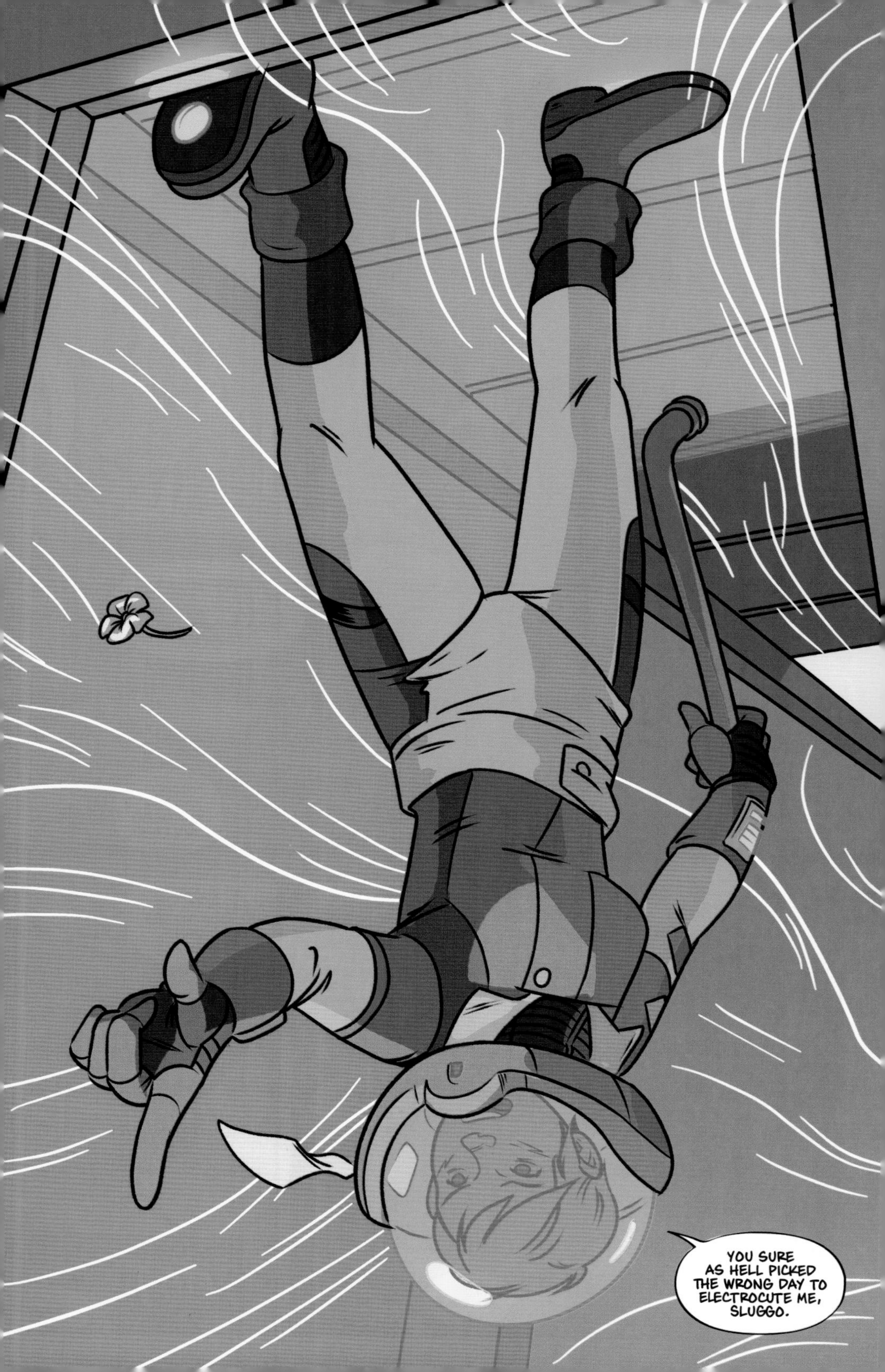
YOU SURE AS HELL PICKED THE WRONG DAY TO ELECTROCUTE ME, SLUGGO.

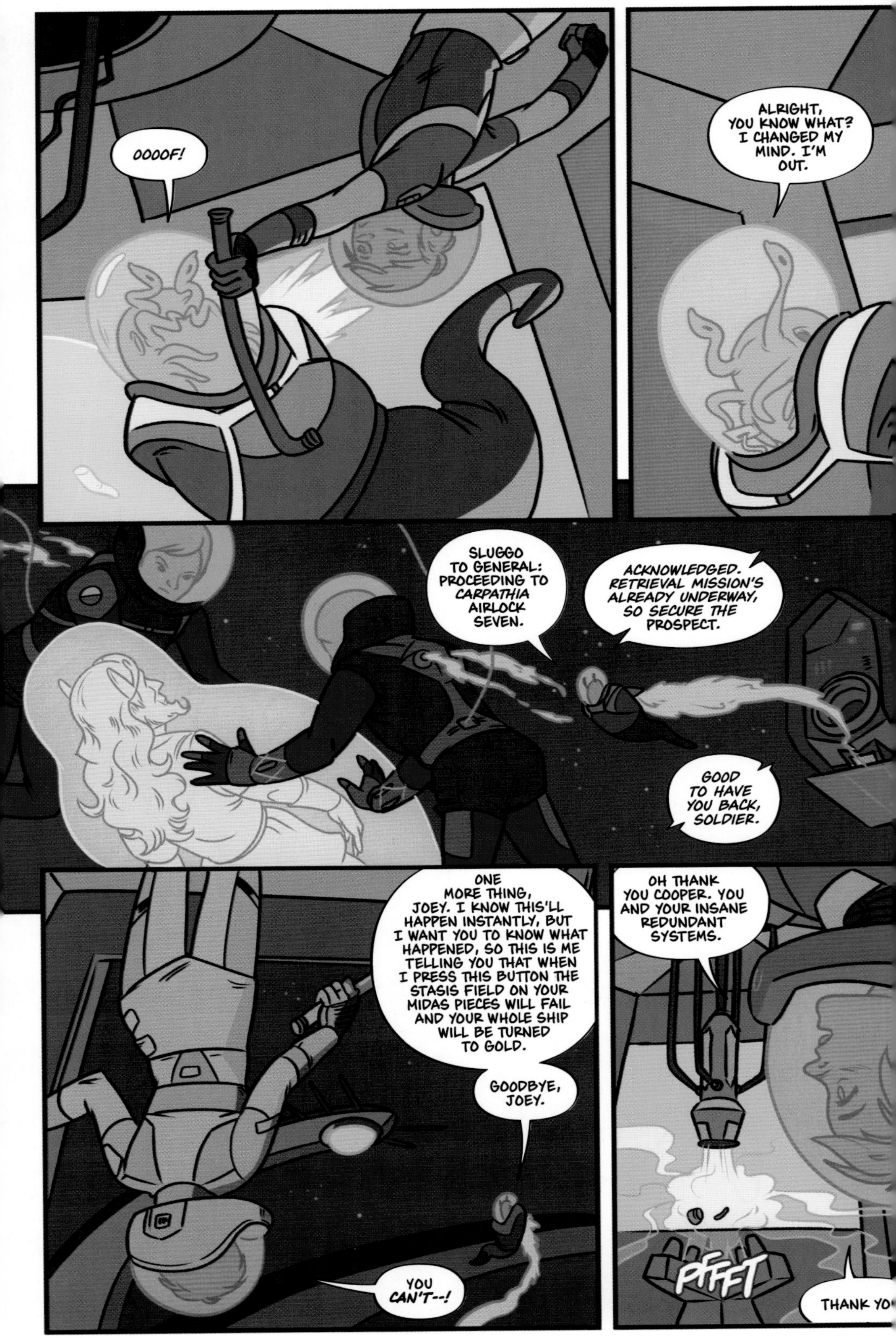
OOOOF!
ALRIGHT, YOU KNOW WHAT? I CHANGED MY MIND. I'M OUT.
SLUGGO TO GENERAL: PROCEEDING TO CARPATHIA AIRLOCK SEVEN.
ACKNOWLEDGED. RETRIEVAL MISSION'S ALREADY UNDERWAY, SO SECURE THE PROSPECT.
GOOD TO HAVE YOU BACK, SOLDIER.
ONE MORE THING, JOEY. I KNOW THIS'LL HAPPEN INSTANTLY, BUT I WANT YOU TO KNOW WHAT HAPPENED, SO THIS IS ME TELLING YOU THAT WHEN I PRESS THIS BUTTON THE STASIS FIELD ON YOUR MIDAS PIECES WILL FAIL AND YOUR WHOLE SHIP WILL BE TURNED TO GOLD.
GOODBYE, JOEY.
YOU CAN'T--!
OH THANK YOU COOPER. YOU AND YOUR INSANE REDUNDANT SYSTEMS.
PFFFT

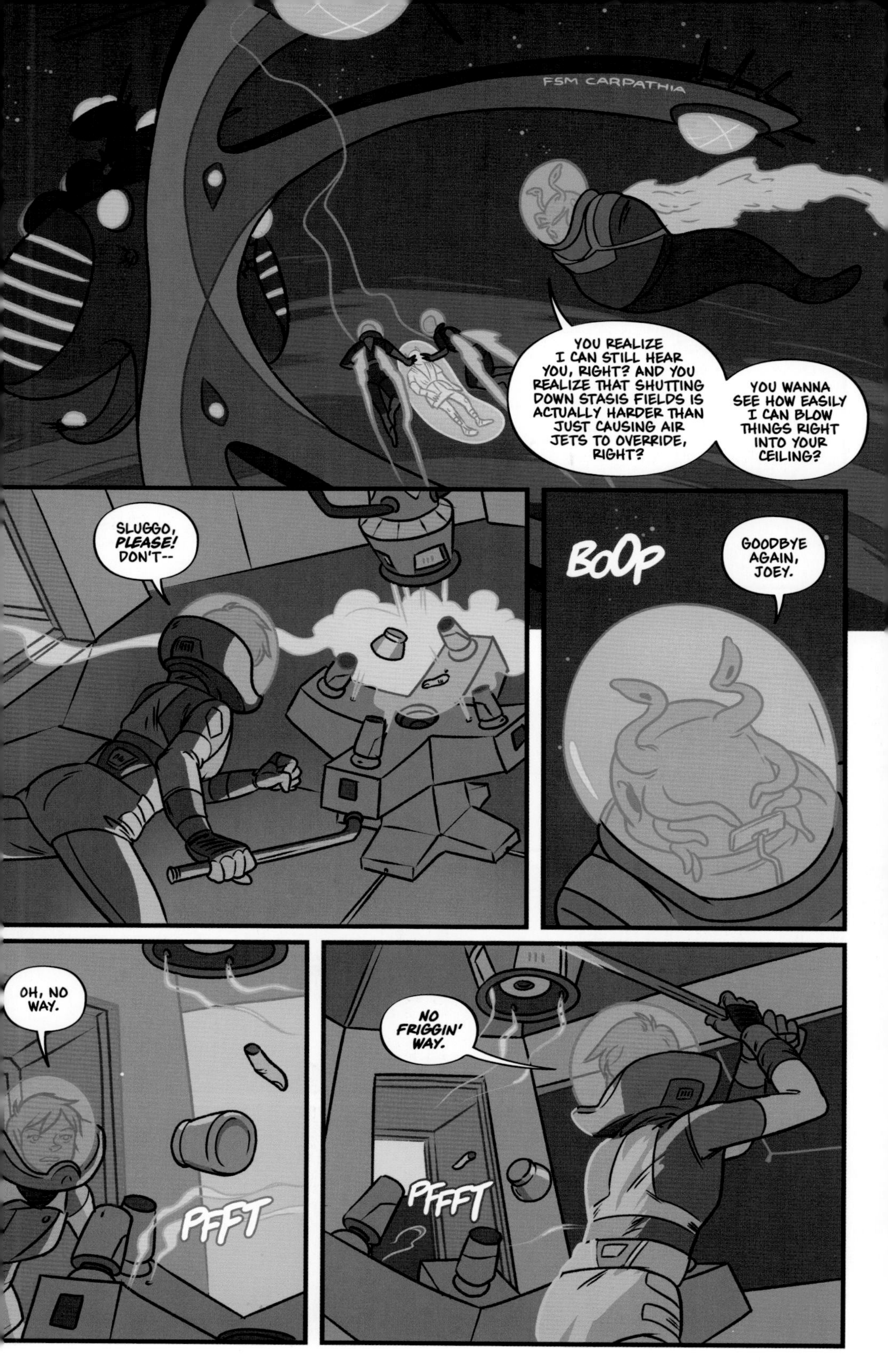
FSM CARPATHIA
YOU REALIZE I CAN STILL HEAR YOU, RIGHT? AND YOU REALIZE THAT SHUTTING DOWN STASIS FIELDS IS ACTUALLY HARDER THAN JUST CAUSING AIR JETS TO OVERRIDE, RIGHT?
YOU WANNA SEE HOW EASILY I CAN BLOW THINGS RIGHT INTO YOUR CEILING?
SLUGGO, *PLEASE!* DON'T--
BOOP
GOODBYE AGAIN, JOEY.
OH, NO WAY.
PFFT
NO FRIGGIN' WAY.
PFFFT

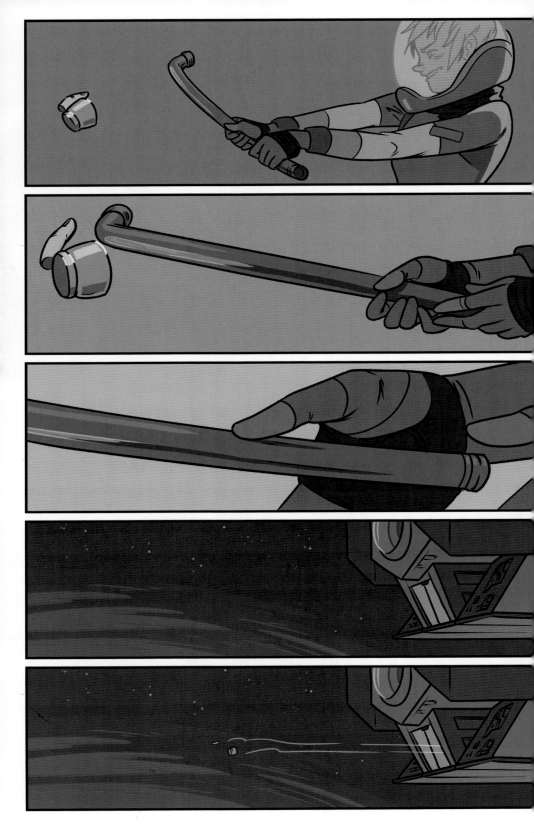

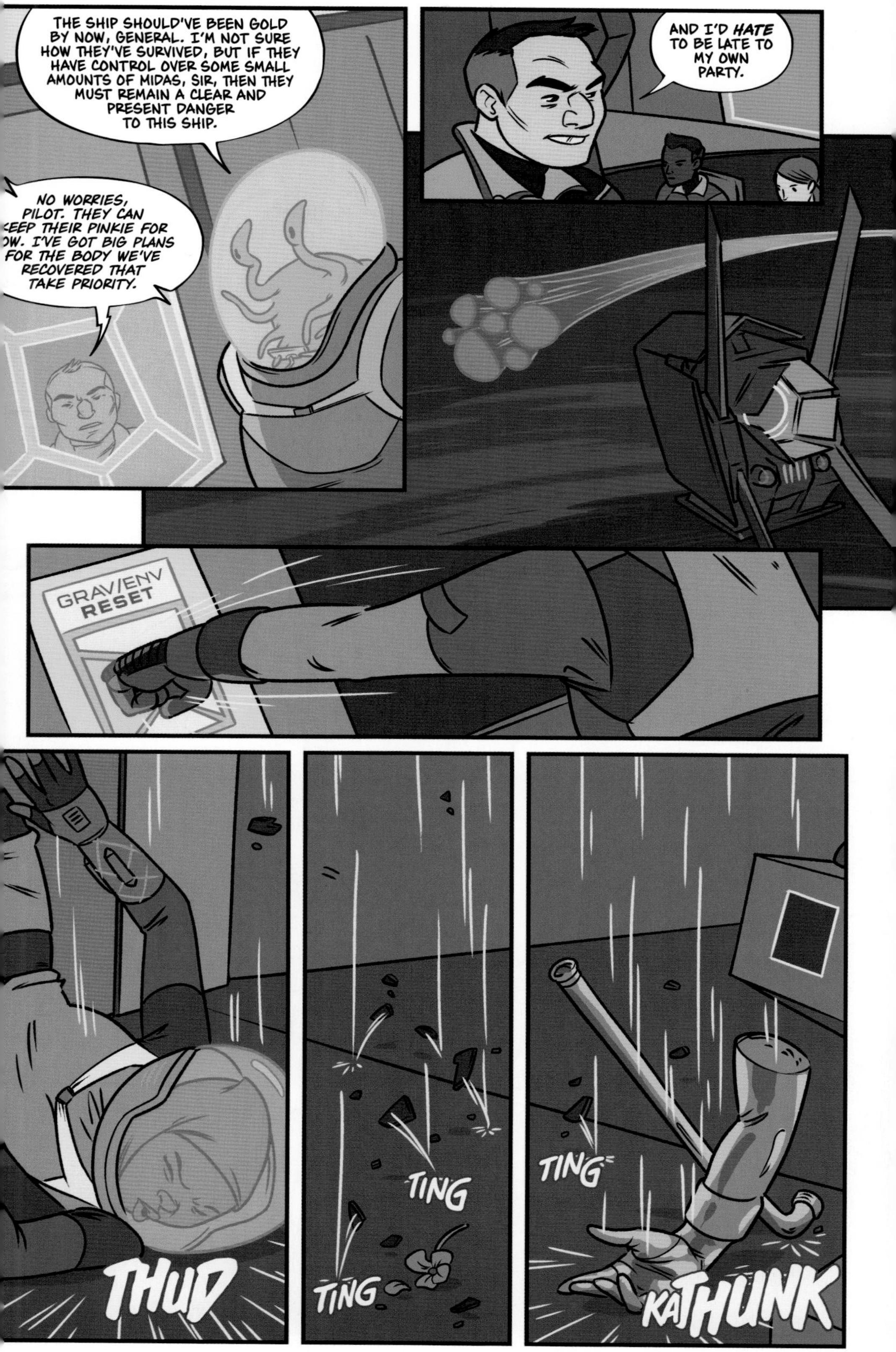
THE SHIP SHOULD'VE BEEN GOLD BY NOW, GENERAL. I'M NOT SURE HOW THEY'VE SURVIVED, BUT IF THEY HAVE CONTROL OVER SOME SMALL AMOUNTS OF MIDAS, SIR, THEN THEY MUST REMAIN A CLEAR AND PRESENT DANGER TO THIS SHIP.
NO WORRIES, PILOT. THEY CAN KEEP THEIR PINKIE FOR NOW. I'VE GOT BIG PLANS FOR THE BODY WE'VE RECOVERED THAT TAKE PRIORITY.
AND I'D HATE TO BE LATE TO MY OWN PARTY.
GRAV/ENV RESET
THUD
TING
TING
TING
KATHUNK

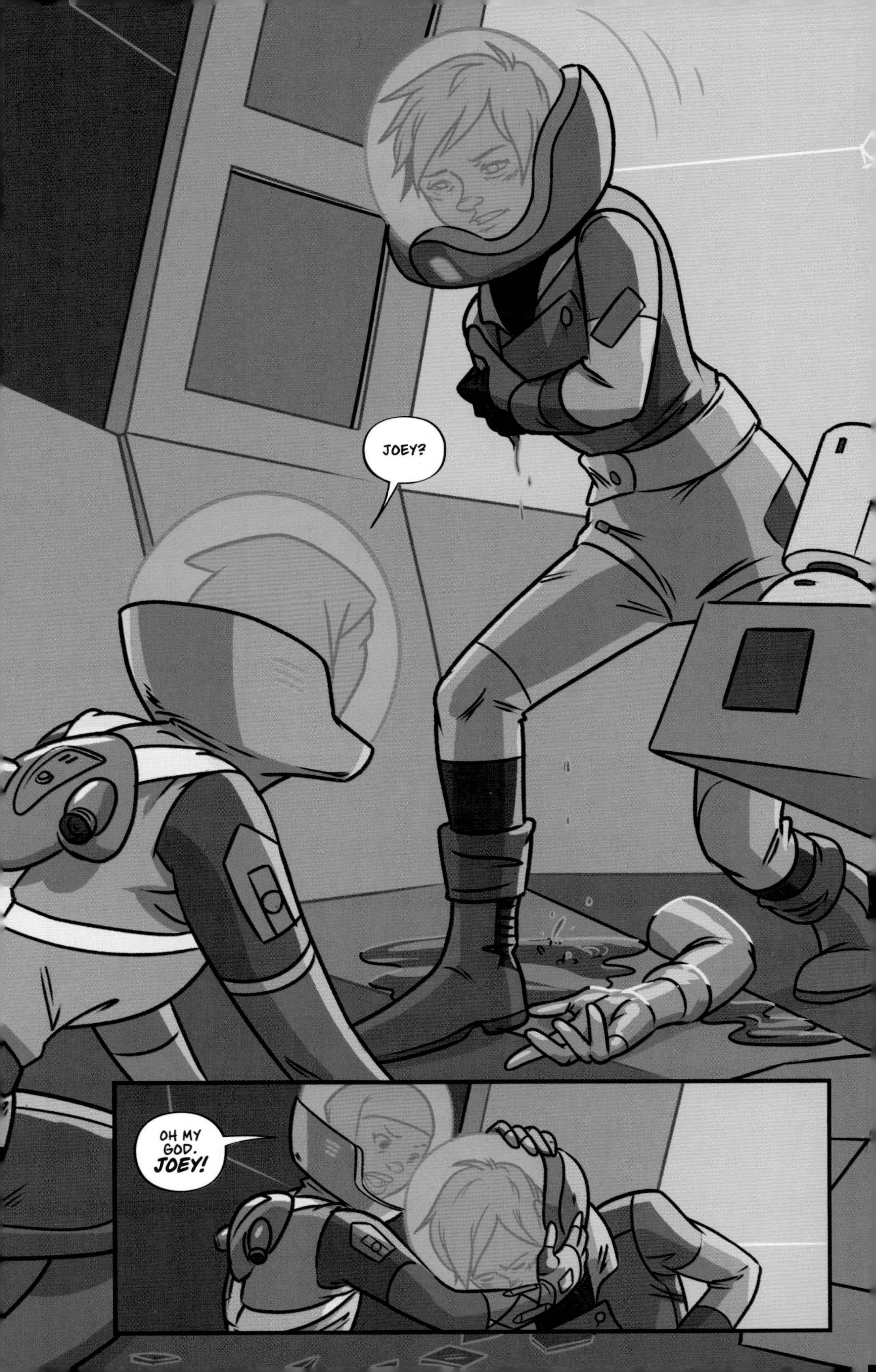
JOEY?
OH MY GOD. JOEY!

"REST IN PIECES!"

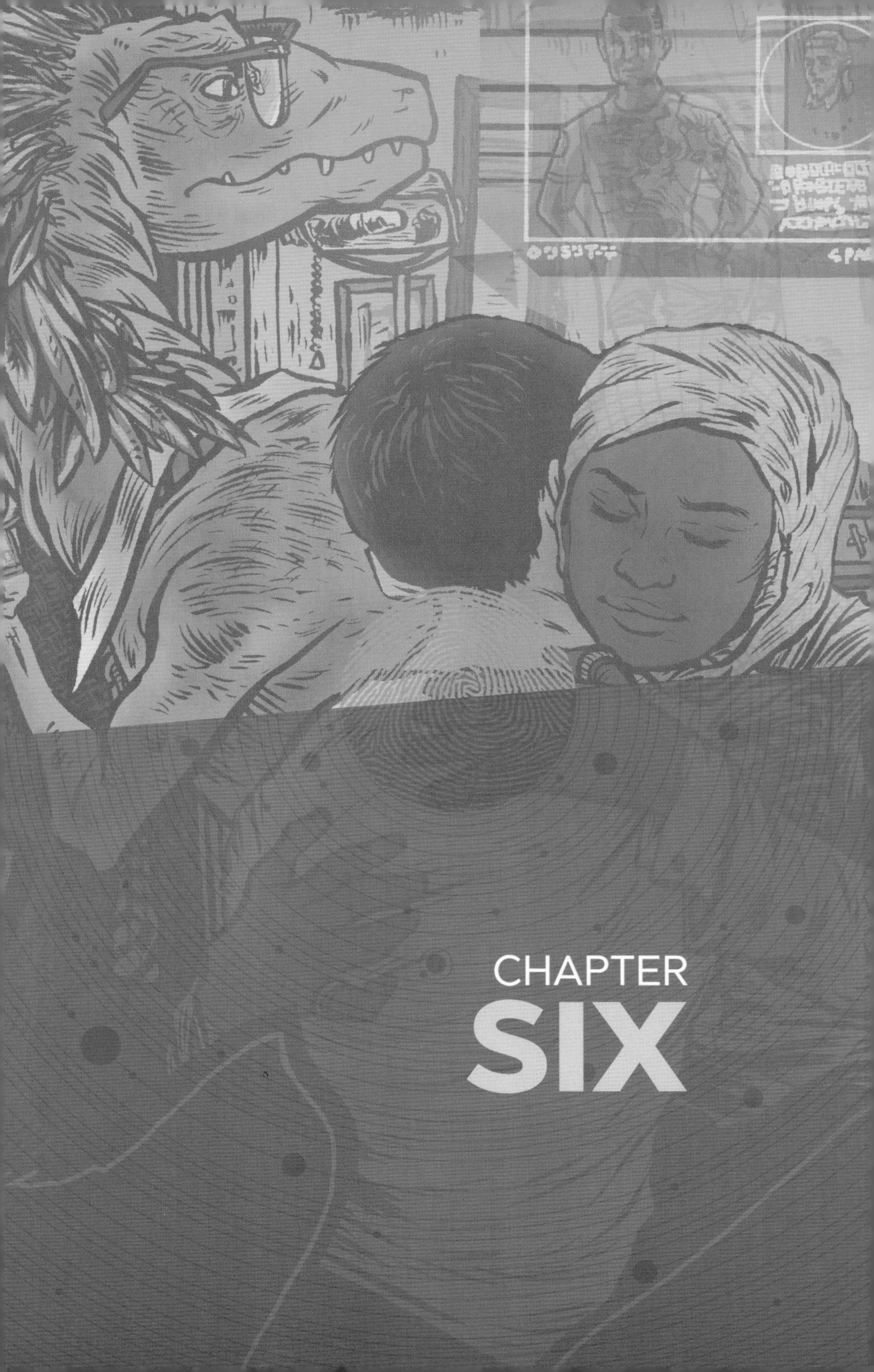

CHAPTER SIX

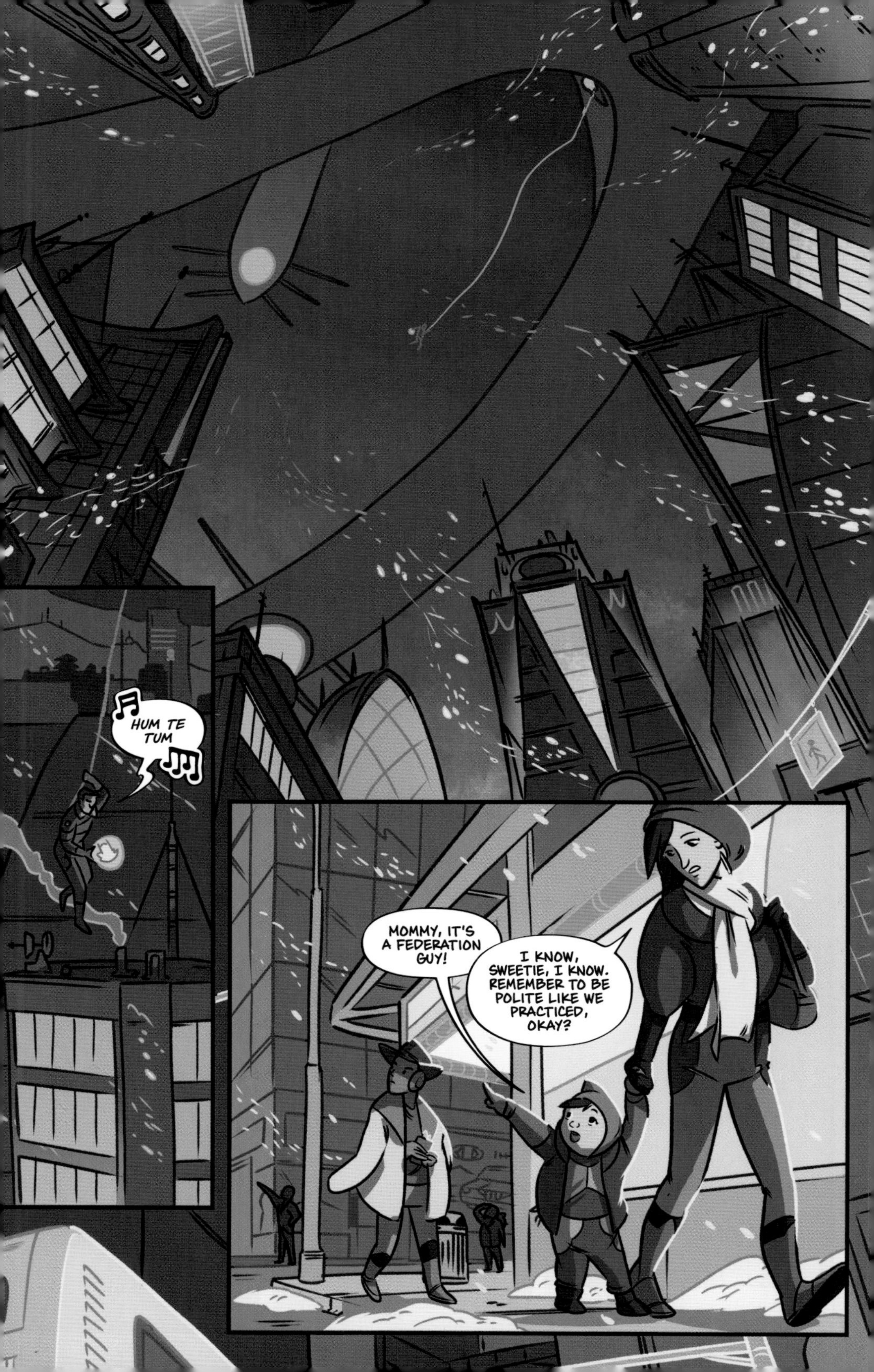
HUM TE TUM
MOMMY, IT'S A FEDERATION GUY!
I KNOW, SWEETIE, I KNOW. REMEMBER TO BE POLITE LIKE WE PRACTICED, OKAY?

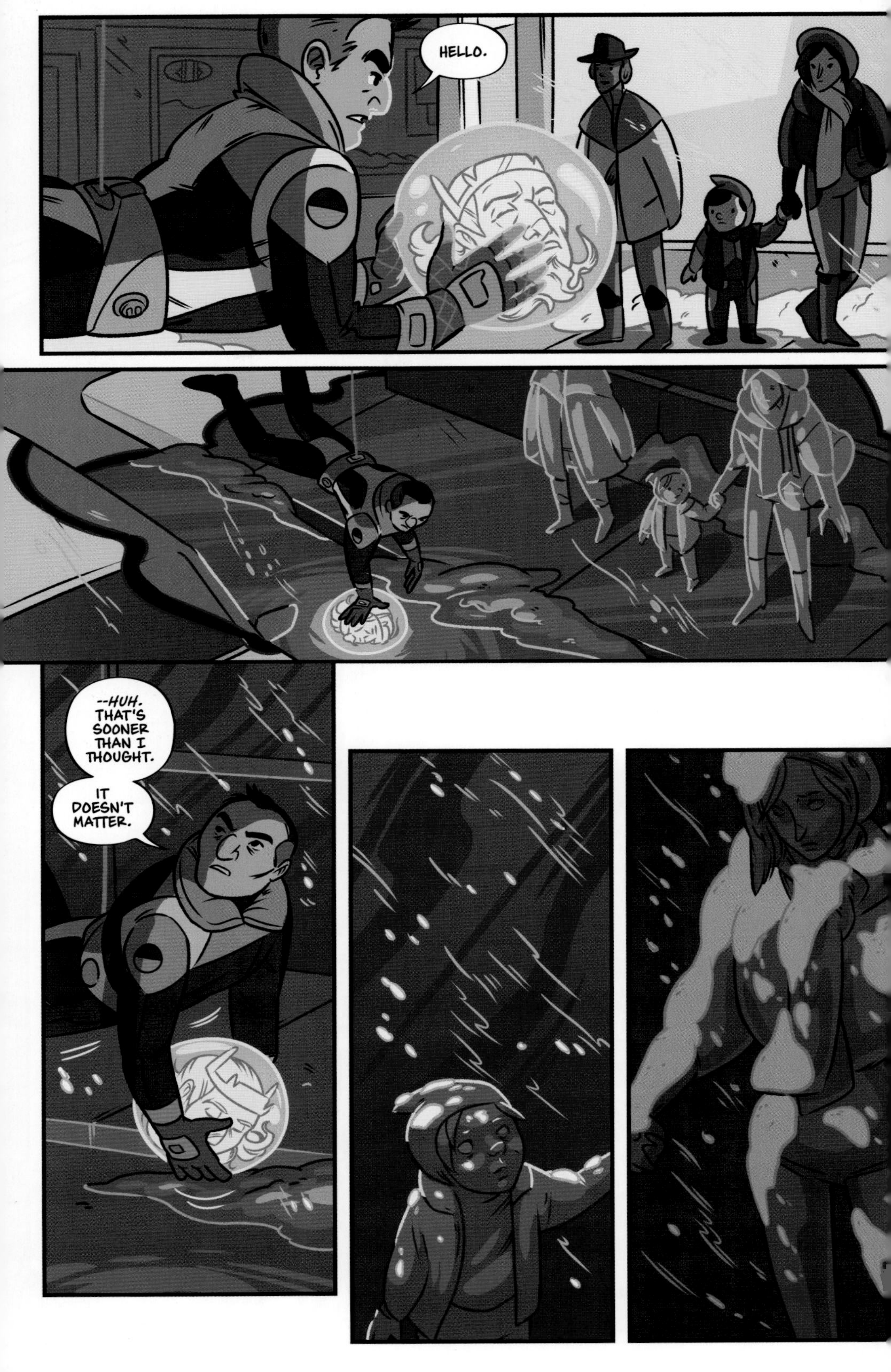
HELLO.
--HUH. THAT'S SOONER THAN I THOUGHT.
IT DOESN'T MATTER.

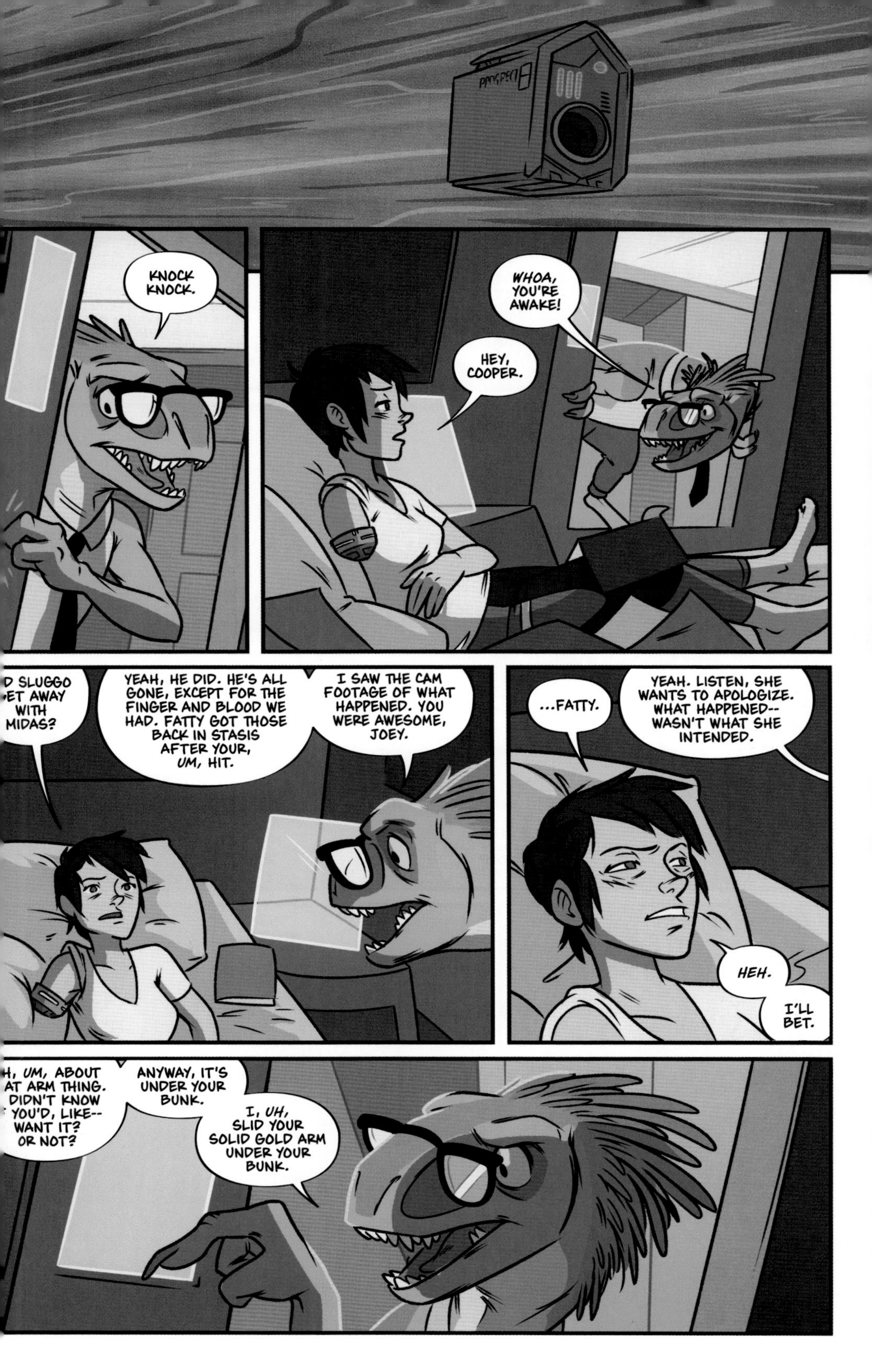
KNOCK KNOCK.
WHOA, YOU'RE AWAKE!
HEY, COOPER.
D SLUGGO ET AWAY WITH MIDAS?
YEAH, HE DID. HE'S ALL GONE, EXCEPT FOR THE FINGER AND BLOOD WE HAD. FATTY GOT THOSE BACK IN STASIS AFTER YOUR, UM, HIT.
I SAW THE CAM FOOTAGE OF WHAT HAPPENED. YOU WERE AWESOME, JOEY.
...FATTY.
YEAH. LISTEN, SHE WANTS TO APOLOGIZE. WHAT HAPPENED-- WASN'T WHAT SHE INTENDED.
HEH.
I'LL BET.
H, UM, ABOUT AT ARM THING. DIDN'T KNOW YOU'D, LIKE-- WANT IT? OR NOT?
ANYWAY, IT'S UNDER YOUR BUNK.
I, UH, SLID YOUR SOLID GOLD ARM UNDER YOUR BUNK.

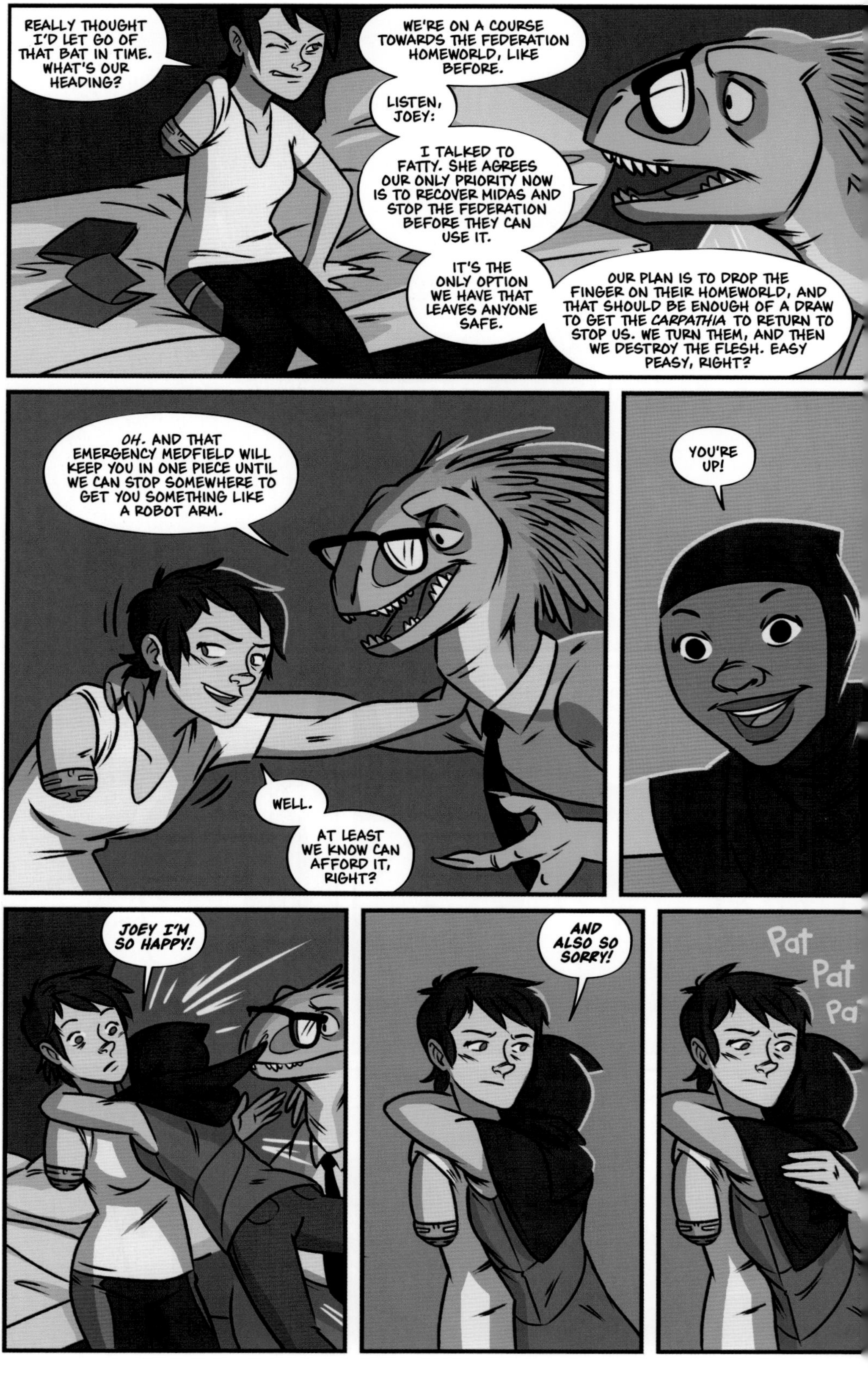
REALLY THOUGHT I'D LET GO OF THAT BAT IN TIME. WHAT'S OUR HEADING?
WE'RE ON A COURSE TOWARDS THE FEDERATION HOMEWORLD, LIKE BEFORE.
LISTEN, JOEY:
I TALKED TO FATTY. SHE AGREES OUR ONLY PRIORITY NOW IS TO RECOVER MIDAS AND STOP THE FEDERATION BEFORE THEY CAN USE IT.
IT'S THE ONLY OPTION WE HAVE THAT LEAVES ANYONE SAFE.
OUR PLAN IS TO DROP THE FINGER ON THEIR HOMEWORLD, AND THAT SHOULD BE ENOUGH OF A DRAW TO GET THE *CARPATHIA* TO RETURN TO STOP US. WE TURN THEM, AND THEN WE DESTROY THE FLESH. EASY PEASY, RIGHT?
OH. AND THAT EMERGENCY MEDFIELD WILL KEEP YOU IN ONE PIECE UNTIL WE CAN STOP SOMEWHERE TO GET YOU SOMETHING LIKE A ROBOT ARM.
WELL.
AT LEAST WE KNOW CAN AFFORD IT, RIGHT?
YOU'RE UP!
JOEY I'M SO HAPPY!
AND ALSO SO SORRY!
Pat
Pat

FATTY, WHAT YOU DID--

--WAS A *BETRAYAL*. I KNOW, AND I'M SORRY, JOEY. THINGS GOT OUT OF CONTROL. THE STAKES ARE JUST SO RIDICULOUSLY HIGH, YOU KNOW? FATE-OF-EVERY-LIVING-BEING HIGH. I WAS, YOU KNOW...

...I WAS TRYING TO SAVE THEM.

BUT THAT HASN'T CHANGED.

BUT THE CIRCUMSTANCES HAVE. THE FEDERATION HAS MIDAS, AND THAT MEANS THE ONLY WAY TO SAVE EVERYONE IS TO STOP THEM AND DESTROY THE FLESH. WE'RE ON THE SAME SIDE, JOEY. IT WON'T HAPPEN AGAIN.

I PROMISE.

THANK YOU. I ACCEPT YOUR APOLOGY.

AND I'M SORRY TOO, FATIMA. I SHOULD'VE LISTENED MORE TO WHAT YOU WERE--

GUYS, PICKING UP A TRANSMISSION FROM THE CARPATHIA.

IT LOOKS LIKE IT'S DIRECTED SPECIFICALLY TOWARDS US, BUT IT'S WEIRD. IT'S BEING PIGGYBACKED ON A NAV FREQUENCY.

SOMEONE TRYING TO HIDE THE TRANSMISSION?

PUT IT THROUGH.

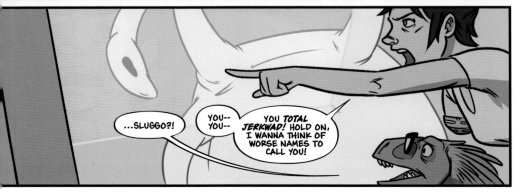

...SLUGGO?!

YOU-- YOU--

YOU *TOTAL JERKWAD!* HOLD ON, I WANNA THINK OF WORSE NAMES TO CALL YOU!

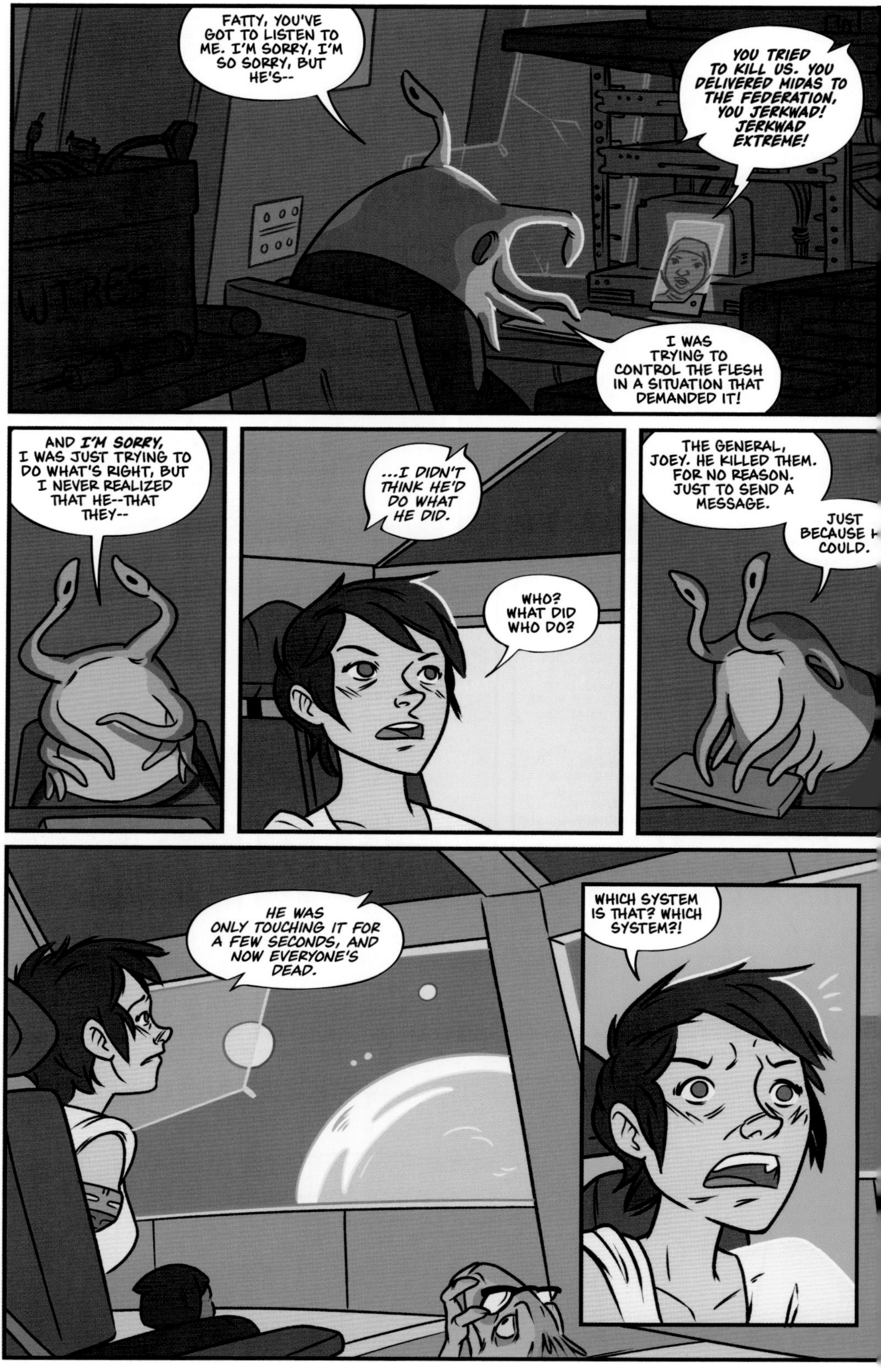
FATTY, YOU'VE GOT TO LISTEN TO ME. I'M SORRY, I'M SO SORRY, BUT HE'S--
YOU TRIED TO KILL US. YOU DELIVERED MIDAS TO THE FEDERATION, YOU JERKWAD! JERKWAD EXTREME!
I WAS TRYING TO CONTROL THE FLESH IN A SITUATION THAT DEMANDED IT!
WIRES
AND I'M SORRY, I WAS JUST TRYING TO DO WHAT'S RIGHT, BUT I NEVER REALIZED THAT HE--THAT THEY--
...I DIDN'T THINK HE'D DO WHAT HE DID.
WHO? WHAT DID WHO DO?
THE GENERAL, JOEY. HE KILLED THEM. FOR NO REASON. JUST TO SEND A MESSAGE.
HE WAS ONLY TOUCHING IT FOR A FEW SECONDS, AND NOW EVERYONE'S DEAD.
WHICH SYSTEM IS THAT? WHICH SYSTEM?!

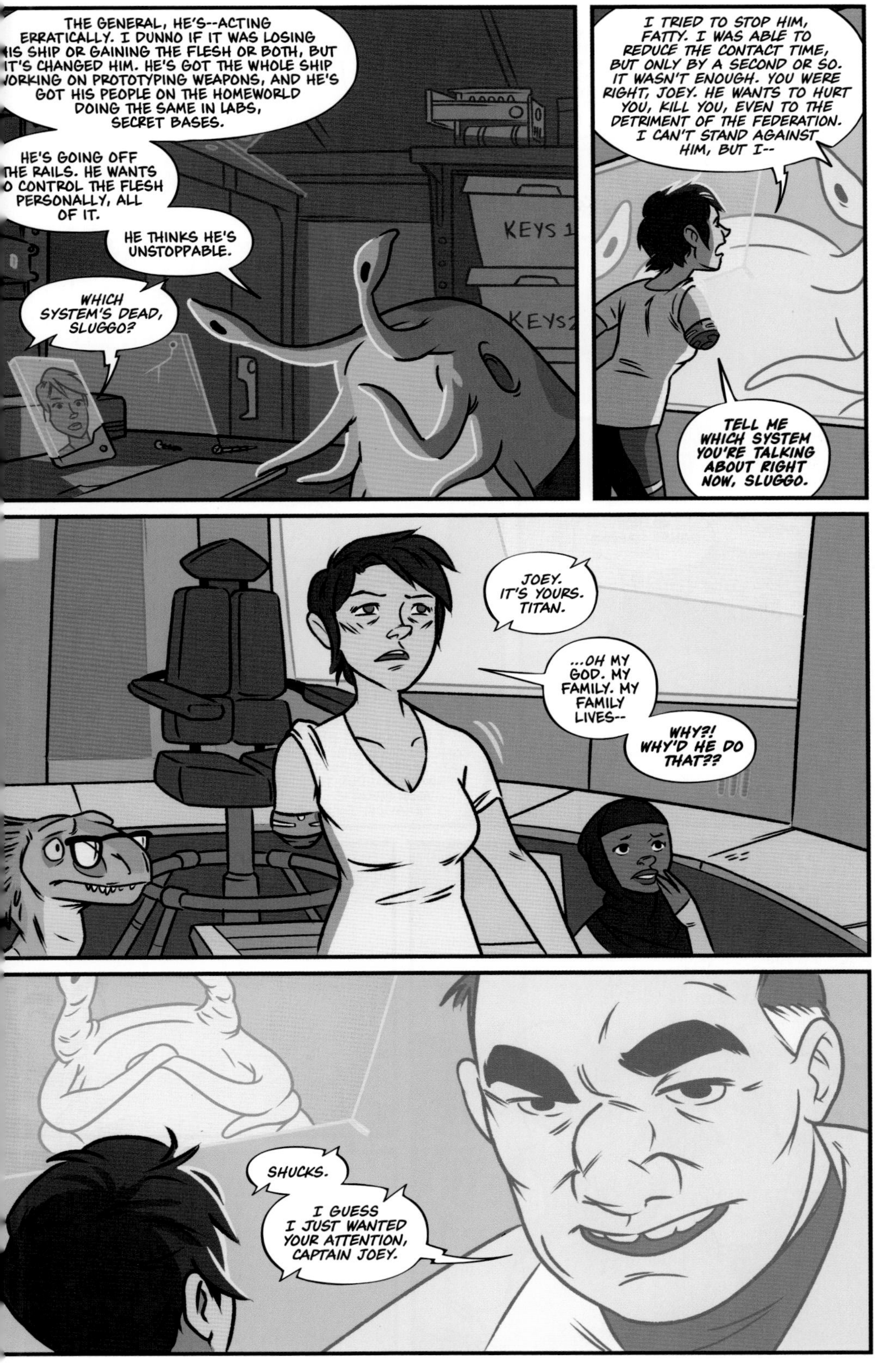
THE GENERAL, HE'S--ACTING ERRATICALLY. I DUNNO IF IT WAS LOSING HIS SHIP OR GAINING THE FLESH OR BOTH, BUT IT'S CHANGED HIM. HE'S GOT THE WHOLE SHIP WORKING ON PROTOTYPING WEAPONS, AND HE'S GOT HIS PEOPLE ON THE HOMEWORLD DOING THE SAME IN LABS, SECRET BASES.
HE'S GOING OFF THE RAILS. HE WANTS TO CONTROL THE FLESH PERSONALLY, ALL OF IT.
HE THINKS HE'S UNSTOPPABLE.
WHICH SYSTEM'S DEAD, SLUGGO?
KEYS 1
KEYS 2
I TRIED TO STOP HIM, FATTY. I WAS ABLE TO REDUCE THE CONTACT TIME, BUT ONLY BY A SECOND OR SO. IT WASN'T ENOUGH. YOU WERE RIGHT, JOEY. HE WANTS TO HURT YOU, KILL YOU, EVEN TO THE DETRIMENT OF THE FEDERATION. I CAN'T STAND AGAINST HIM, BUT I--
TELL ME WHICH SYSTEM YOU'RE TALKING ABOUT RIGHT NOW, SLUGGO.
JOEY. IT'S YOURS. TITAN.
...OH MY GOD. MY FAMILY. MY FAMILY LIVES--
WHY?! WHY'D HE DO THAT??
SHUCKS.
I GUESS I JUST WANTED YOUR ATTENTION, CAPTAIN JOEY.

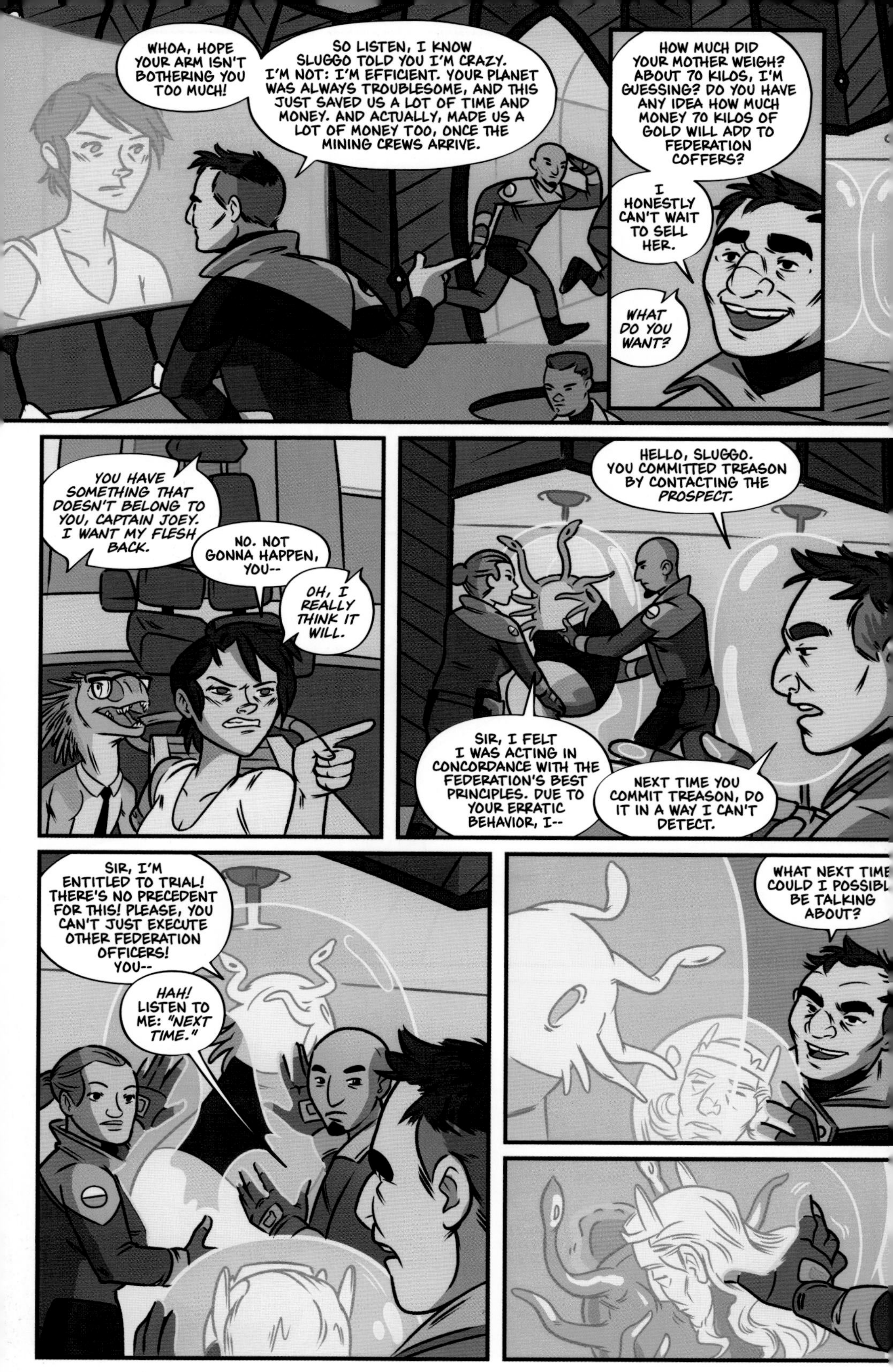
WHOA, HOPE YOUR ARM ISN'T BOTHERING YOU TOO MUCH!
SO LISTEN, I KNOW SLUGGO TOLD YOU I'M CRAZY. I'M NOT: I'M EFFICIENT. YOUR PLANET WAS ALWAYS TROUBLESOME, AND THIS JUST SAVED US A LOT OF TIME AND MONEY. AND ACTUALLY, MADE US A LOT OF MONEY TOO, ONCE THE MINING CREWS ARRIVE.
HOW MUCH DID YOUR MOTHER WEIGH? ABOUT 70 KILOS, I'M GUESSING? DO YOU HAVE ANY IDEA HOW MUCH MONEY 70 KILOS OF GOLD WILL ADD TO FEDERATION COFFERS?
I HONESTLY CAN'T WAIT TO SELL HER.
WHAT DO YOU WANT?
YOU HAVE SOMETHING THAT DOESN'T BELONG TO YOU, CAPTAIN JOEY. I WANT MY FLESH BACK.
NO. NOT GONNA HAPPEN, YOU--
OH, I REALLY THINK IT WILL.
HELLO, SLUGGO. YOU COMMITTED TREASON BY CONTACTING THE PROSPECT.
SIR, I FELT I WAS ACTING IN CONCORDANCE WITH THE FEDERATION'S BEST PRINCIPLES. DUE TO YOUR ERRATIC BEHAVIOR, I--
NEXT TIME YOU COMMIT TREASON, DO IT IN A WAY I CAN'T DETECT.
SIR, I'M ENTITLED TO TRIAL! THERE'S NO PRECEDENT FOR THIS! PLEASE, YOU CAN'T JUST EXECUTE OTHER FEDERATION OFFICERS! YOU--
HAH! LISTEN TO ME: "NEXT TIME."
WHAT NEXT TIME COULD I POSSIBL BE TALKING ABOUT?

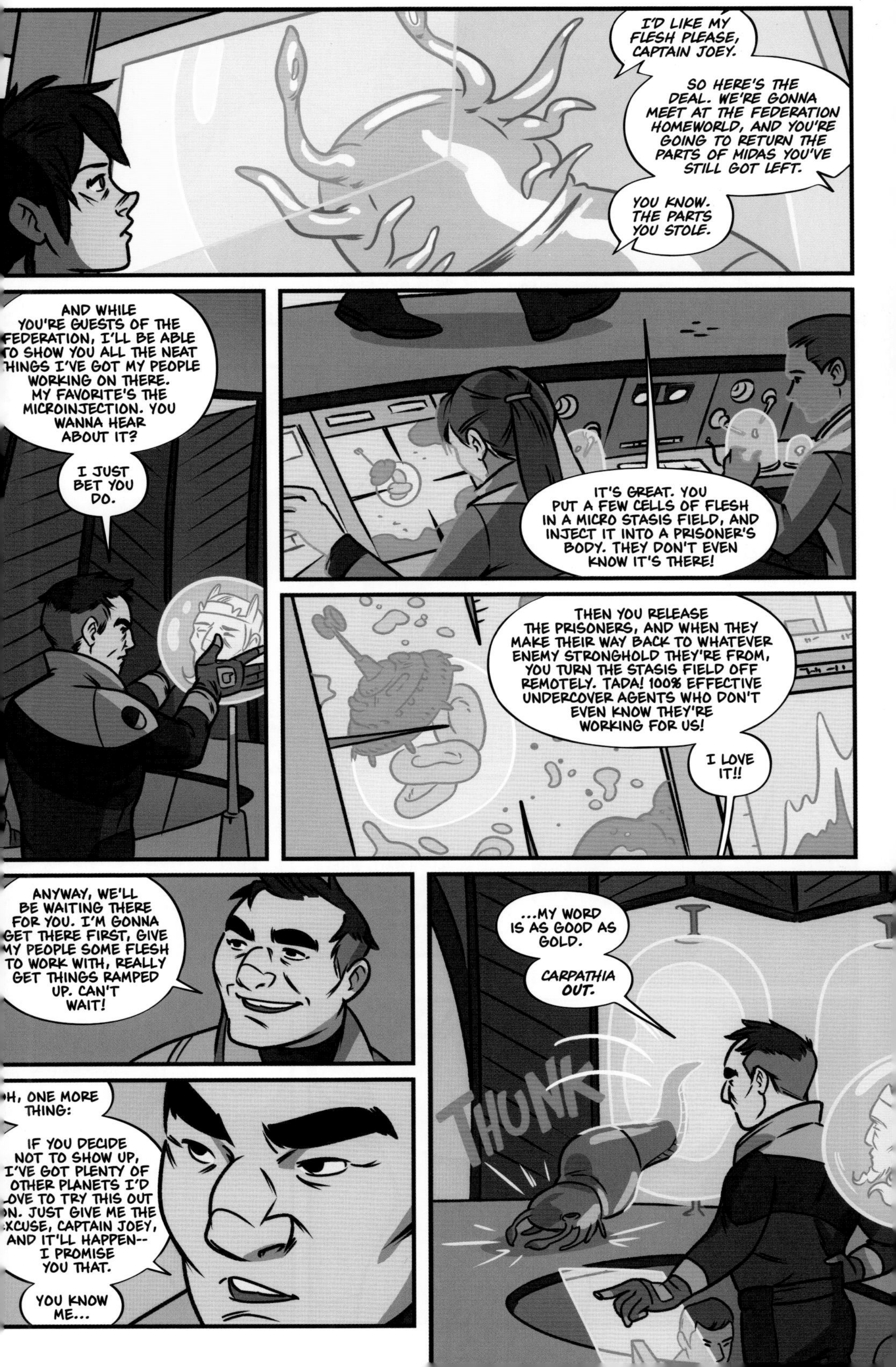
I'D LIKE MY FLESH PLEASE, CAPTAIN JOEY.
SO HERE'S THE DEAL. WE'RE GONNA MEET AT THE FEDERATION HOMEWORLD, AND YOU'RE GOING TO RETURN THE PARTS OF MIDAS YOU'VE STILL GOT LEFT.
YOU KNOW. THE PARTS YOU STOLE.
AND WHILE YOU'RE GUESTS OF THE FEDERATION, I'LL BE ABLE TO SHOW YOU ALL THE NEAT THINGS I'VE GOT MY PEOPLE WORKING ON THERE. MY FAVORITE'S THE MICROINJECTION. YOU WANNA HEAR ABOUT IT?
I JUST BET YOU DO.
IT'S GREAT. YOU PUT A FEW CELLS OF FLESH IN A MICRO STASIS FIELD, AND INJECT IT INTO A PRISONER'S BODY. THEY DON'T EVEN KNOW IT'S THERE!
THEN YOU RELEASE THE PRISONERS, AND WHEN THEY MAKE THEIR WAY BACK TO WHATEVER ENEMY STRONGHOLD THEY'RE FROM, YOU TURN THE STASIS FIELD OFF REMOTELY. TADA! 100% EFFECTIVE UNDERCOVER AGENTS WHO DON'T EVEN KNOW THEY'RE WORKING FOR US!
I LOVE IT!!
ANYWAY, WE'LL BE WAITING THERE FOR YOU. I'M GONNA GET THERE FIRST, GIVE MY PEOPLE SOME FLESH TO WORK WITH, REALLY GET THINGS RAMPED UP. CAN'T WAIT!
H, ONE MORE THING:
IF YOU DECIDE NOT TO SHOW UP, I'VE GOT PLENTY OF OTHER PLANETS I'D LOVE TO TRY THIS OUT N. JUST GIVE ME THE XCUSE, CAPTAIN JOEY, AND IT'LL HAPPEN-- I PROMISE YOU THAT.
YOU KNOW ME...
...MY WORD IS AS GOOD AS GOLD.
CARPATHIA OUT.
THUNK

I'M SO SORRY, JOEY.

I DON'T KNOW HOW HE COULD'VE--

NOT NOW. I APPRECIATE IT, FRIENDS, I DO--BUT WE SIMPLY DON'T HAVE THE TIME. WE CAUSED THIS PROBLEM, AND WE NEED TO FIX IT, AND RIGHT NOW IS OUR LAST CHANCE *EVER* TO DO THAT.

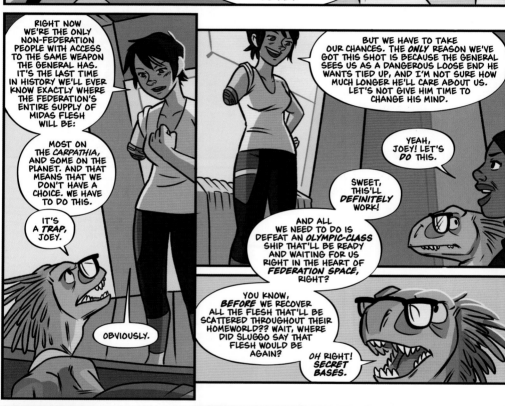

RIGHT NOW WE'RE THE ONLY NON-FEDERATION PEOPLE WITH ACCESS TO THE SAME WEAPON THE GENERAL HAS. IT'S THE LAST TIME IN HISTORY WE'LL EVER KNOW EXACTLY WHERE THE FEDERATION'S ENTIRE SUPPLY OF MIDAS FLESH WILL BE:

MOST ON THE *CARPATHIA*, AND SOME ON THE PLANET. AND THAT MEANS THAT WE DON'T HAVE A CHOICE. WE HAVE TO DO THIS.

IT'S A *TRAP*, JOEY.

OBVIOUSLY.

BUT WE HAVE TO TAKE OUR CHANCES. THE *ONLY* REASON WE'VE GOT THIS SHOT IS BECAUSE THE GENERAL SEES US AS A DANGEROUS LOOSE END HE WANTS TIED UP, AND I'M NOT SURE HOW MUCH LONGER HE'LL CARE ABOUT US. LET'S NOT GIVE HIM TIME TO CHANGE HIS MIND.

YEAH, JOEY! LET'S *DO* THIS.

SWEET, THIS'LL *DEFINITELY* WORK!

AND ALL WE NEED TO DO IS DEFEAT AN *OLYMPIC-CLASS* SHIP THAT'LL BE READY AND WAITING FOR US RIGHT IN THE HEART OF *FEDERATION SPACE*, RIGHT?

YOU KNOW, *BEFORE* WE RECOVER ALL THE FLESH THAT'LL BE SCATTERED THROUGHOUT THEIR HOMEWORLD?? WAIT, WHERE DID SLUGGO SAY THAT FLESH WOULD BE AGAIN?

OH RIGHT! *SECRET BASES.*

...RIGHT. COOPER, YOU'RE EXACTLY RIGHT. THAT'S WHAT HE'S EXPECTING, ISN'T IT? ATTACK THE SHIP, RECOVER THE BODY, SEARCH THE HOMEWORLD. HE THINKS WE WANT TO CONTROL THE FLESH AS BADLY AS HE DOES!

UM. DON'T WE?

I DUNNO, FATTY.

WHAT IF WE DON'T?

WHAT IF WE *IGNORED* MIDAS AND WENT FOR THE PLANET FIRST? WE TURN IT TO GOLD AND WHATEVER FLESH THE GENERAL'S DISTRIBUTED THERE IS LOST. AND UNTRACEABLE, SINCE THERE'LL BE NO SHOCKWAVES TO LEAD ANYONE TO IT.

HECK, WITH ANY LUCK, IT'LL BE BURIED IN SOME "SECRET BASE" BENEATH TONS OF SOLID-GOLD GROUND NOBODY CAN EVER TOUCH AGAIN.

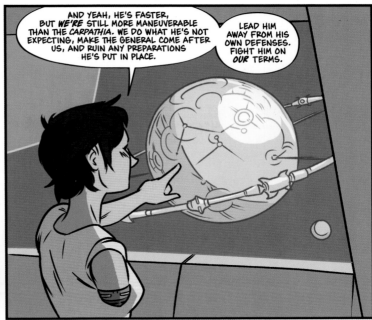

AND YEAH, HE'S FASTER, BUT *WE'RE* STILL MORE MANEUVERABLE THAN THE *CARPATHIA*. WE DO WHAT HE'S NOT EXPECTING, MAKE THE GENERAL COME AFTER US, AND RUIN ANY PREPARATIONS HE'S PUT IN PLACE.

LEAD HIM AWAY FROM HIS OWN DEFENSES. FIGHT HIM ON *OUR* TERMS.

THAT PLANET-- *FEDERATION HOMEWORLD*-- IS GONNA BE SURROUNDED BY SHIPS. INSANELY *OVER-POWERED* SHIPS.

SURE.

THEN I GUESS IT'S REAL LUCKY FOR US THAT WE'VE GOT A DOOMSDAY DEVICE ON BOARD, HUH?

WE CAN *DO* THIS. WE CAN PUT THIS GENIE BACK IN THE BOTTLE.

LET'S USE THE FEW HOURS WE'VE GOT. LET'S SLICE THAT FINGER UP, LET'S MAKE OURSELVES SOME WEAPONS, AND LET'S GO SAVE THE WHOLE FREAKIN' GALAXY.

...I GUESS IT REALLY IS OUR ONLY MOVE. WHAT DO YOU SAY, FATTY?

LET'S.

LATER.

REPORT.

A BUNCH OF WARSHIPS IN ORBIT AROUND THE HOMEWORLD, BUT NO SIGN OF THE *CARPATHI*--

--WAIT, WAIT, I'M PICKING UP A SPATIAL DISTORTION THAT I HAVEN'T SEEN BEFORE!

IT'S THEM: THEY WERE HIDING IN WARP, JOEY! I--I DON'T KNOW HOW THAT'S POSSIBLE!

EVASIVE!

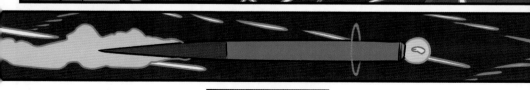

THEY'VE WEAPONIZED HIM TOO--WE'VE GOT MIDAS INBOUND, GUYS!

DOWN HARD TO PORT! GET US OUT OF RANGE, FATTY!

ON IT!

IT'S TRACKING US! AND IT'S TOO CLOSE--IF WE FIRE AT IT WE RISK BLOWING UP THE FLESH AND GETTING HIT BY THE BLOOD!

LAUNCH FLAK! COOPER, ARE YOU READY DOWN THERE?

READY.

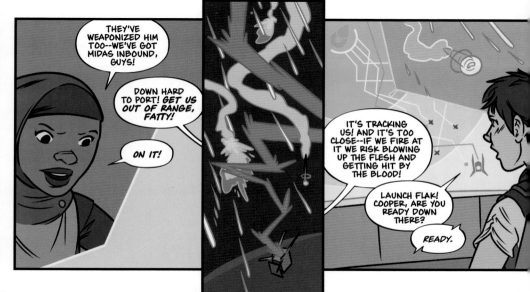

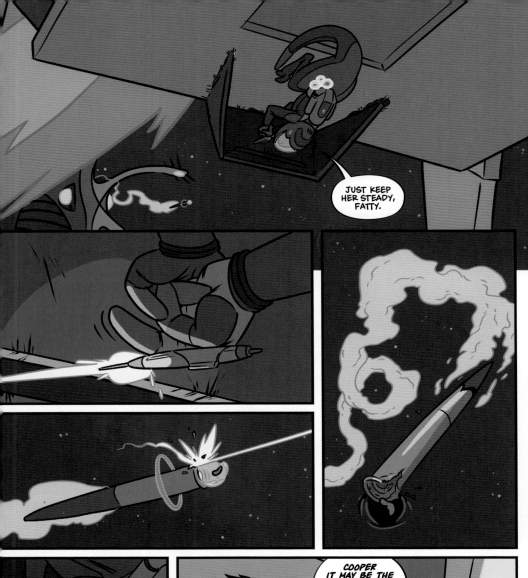

JUST KEEP HER STEADY, FATTY.

COOPER IT MAY BE THE FACT YOU JUST SAVED ALL OUR LIVES TALKING BUT REAL TALK:

I SERIOUSLY LOVE YOU!

AS A FRIEND, BUT COME ON, THAT'S STILL REALLY GREAT

GOT IT! DIRECT HIT TO ITS STASIS FIELD, GUYS. THAT GOLD MISSILE ISN'T TRACKING ANYONE NOW.

BUT, UH, I'VE ONLY GOT TWO MORE SHOTS.

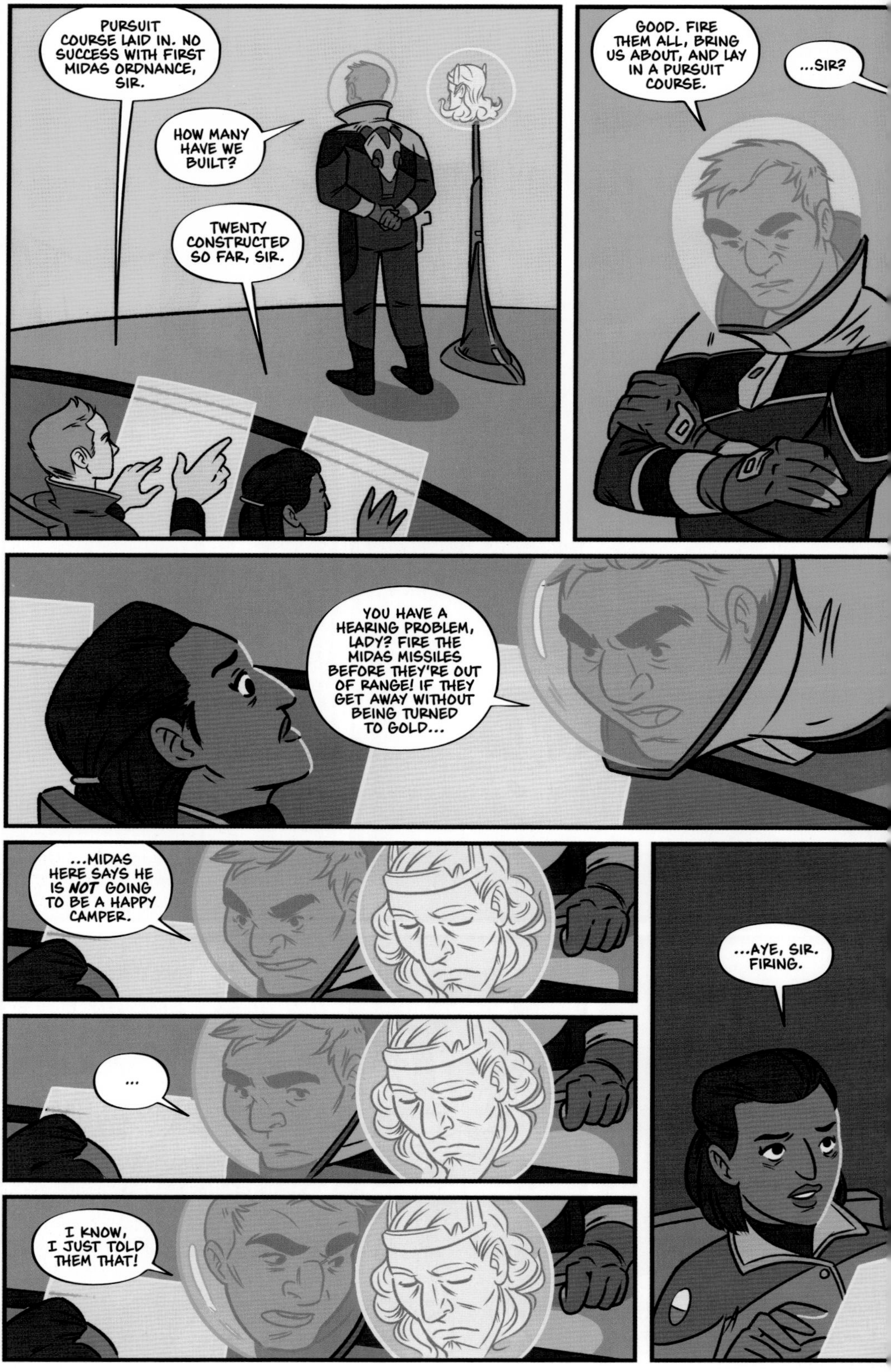
PURSUIT COURSE LAID IN. NO SUCCESS WITH FIRST MIDAS ORDNANCE, SIR.
HOW MANY HAVE WE BUILT?
TWENTY CONSTRUCTED SO FAR, SIR.
GOOD. FIRE THEM ALL, BRING US ABOUT, AND LAY IN A PURSUIT COURSE.
...SIR?
YOU HAVE A HEARING PROBLEM, LADY? FIRE THE MIDAS MISSILES BEFORE THEY'RE OUT OF RANGE! IF THEY GET AWAY WITHOUT BEING TURNED TO GOLD...
...MIDAS HERE SAYS HE IS *NOT* GOING TO BE A HAPPY CAMPER.
...
I KNOW, I JUST TOLD THEM THAT!
...AYE, SIR. FIRING.

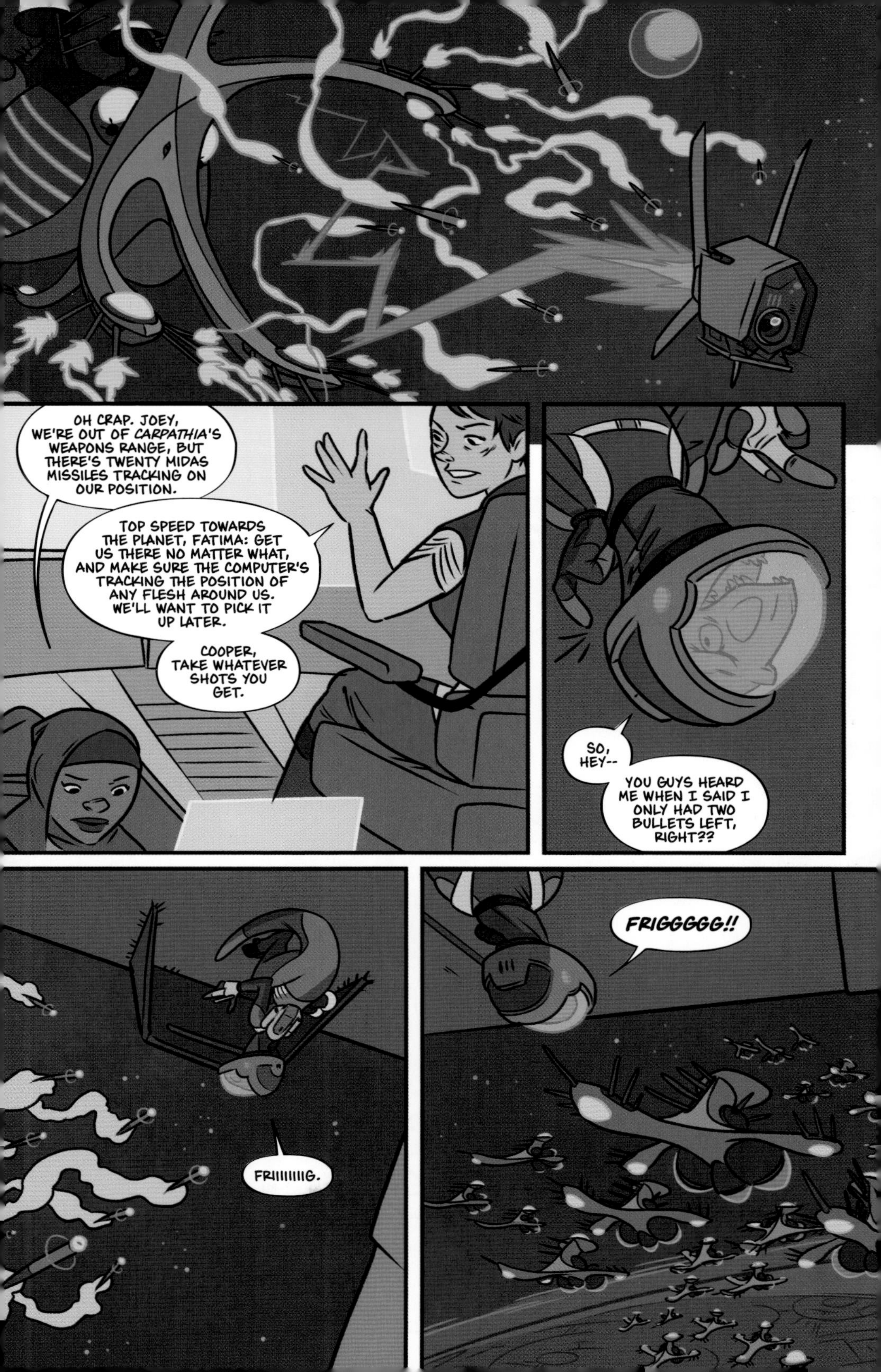

OH CRAP. JOEY, WE'RE OUT OF *CARPATHIA*'S WEAPONS RANGE, BUT THERE'S TWENTY MIDAS MISSILES TRACKING ON OUR POSITION.
TOP SPEED TOWARDS THE PLANET, FATIMA: GET US THERE NO MATTER WHAT, AND MAKE SURE THE COMPUTER'S TRACKING THE POSITION OF ANY FLESH AROUND US. WE'LL WANT TO PICK IT UP LATER.
COOPER, TAKE WHATEVER SHOTS YOU GET.
SO, HEY--
YOU GUYS HEARD ME WHEN I SAID I ONLY HAD TWO BULLETS LEFT, RIGHT??
FRIIIIIIIG.
FRIGGGGG!!

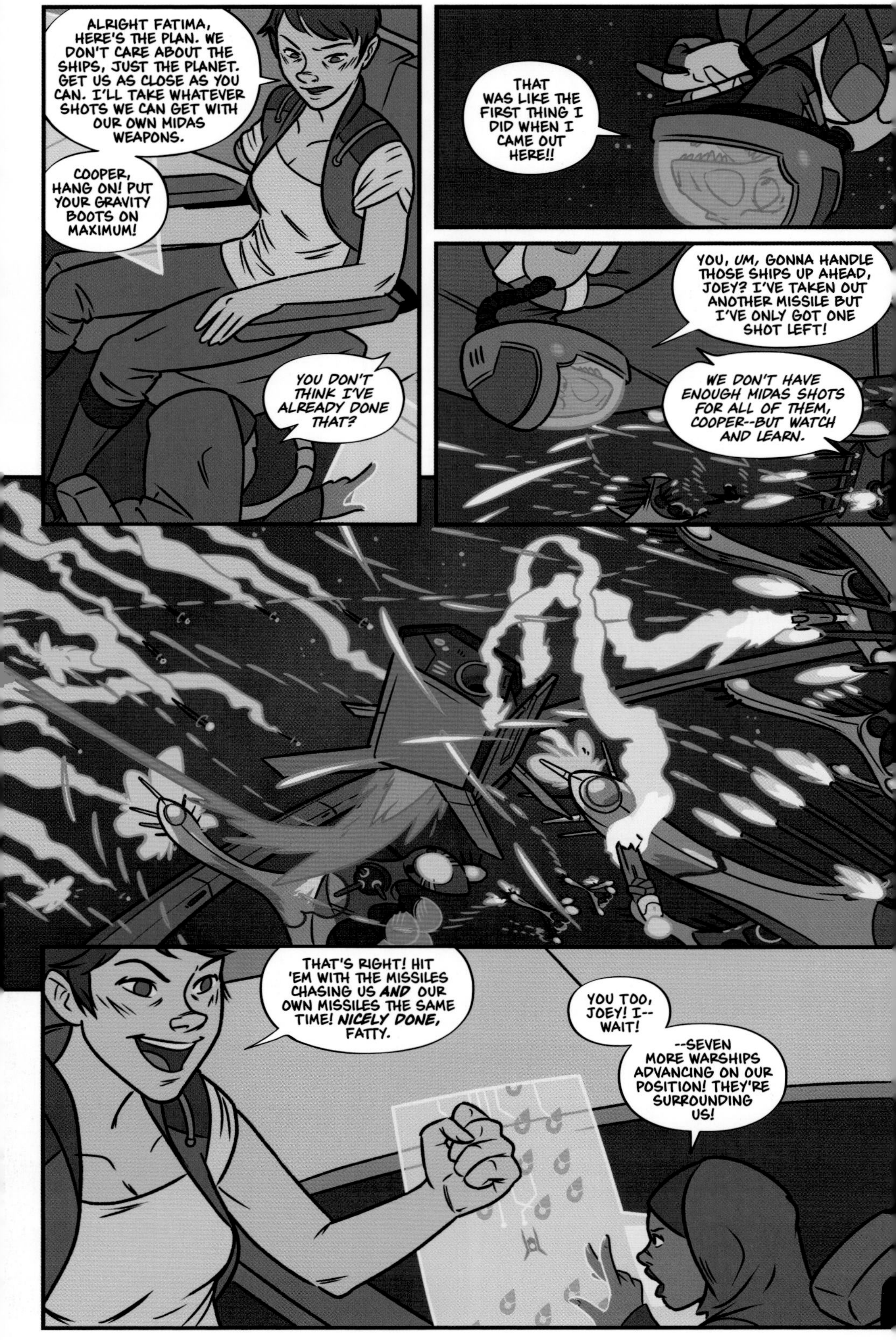
ALRIGHT FATIMA, HERE'S THE PLAN. WE DON'T CARE ABOUT THE SHIPS, JUST THE PLANET. GET US AS CLOSE AS YOU CAN. I'LL TAKE WHATEVER SHOTS WE CAN GET WITH OUR OWN MIDAS WEAPONS.
COOPER, HANG ON! PUT YOUR GRAVITY BOOTS ON MAXIMUM!
YOU DON'T THINK I'VE ALREADY DONE THAT?
THAT WAS LIKE THE FIRST THING I DID WHEN I CAME OUT HERE!!
YOU, UM, GONNA HANDLE THOSE SHIPS UP AHEAD, JOEY? I'VE TAKEN OUT ANOTHER MISSILE BUT I'VE ONLY GOT ONE SHOT LEFT!
WE DON'T HAVE ENOUGH MIDAS SHOTS FOR ALL OF THEM, COOPER--BUT WATCH AND LEARN.
THAT'S RIGHT! HIT 'EM WITH THE MISSILES CHASING US AND OUR OWN MISSILES THE SAME TIME! NICELY DONE, FATTY.
YOU TOO, JOEY! I--WAIT!
--SEVEN MORE WARSHIPS ADVANCING ON OUR POSITION! THEY'RE SURROUNDING US!

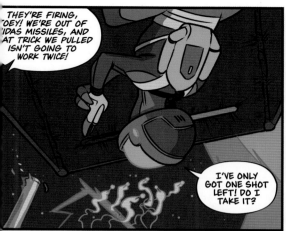

THEY'RE FIRING, JOEY! WE'RE OUT OF 'IDAS MISSILES, AND AT TRICK WE PULLED ISN'T GOING TO WORK TWICE!

I'VE ONLY GOT ONE SHOT LEFT! DO I TAKE IT?

HANG TIGHT, COOPER!

FATTY, I'M TARGETING EVERY MISSILE BEHIND US AT ONCE. GIVE US ALL THE SPEED WE'VE GOT!

WHAT? JOEY!!

NOW, FATTY!

PROSPECT8

HOLY GEEZ!!

FATTY, MAXIMUM SPEED! KEEP US CLEAR OF ANY BLOOD!!

AHHHHH!

I'M DOING IT, AHHHH!

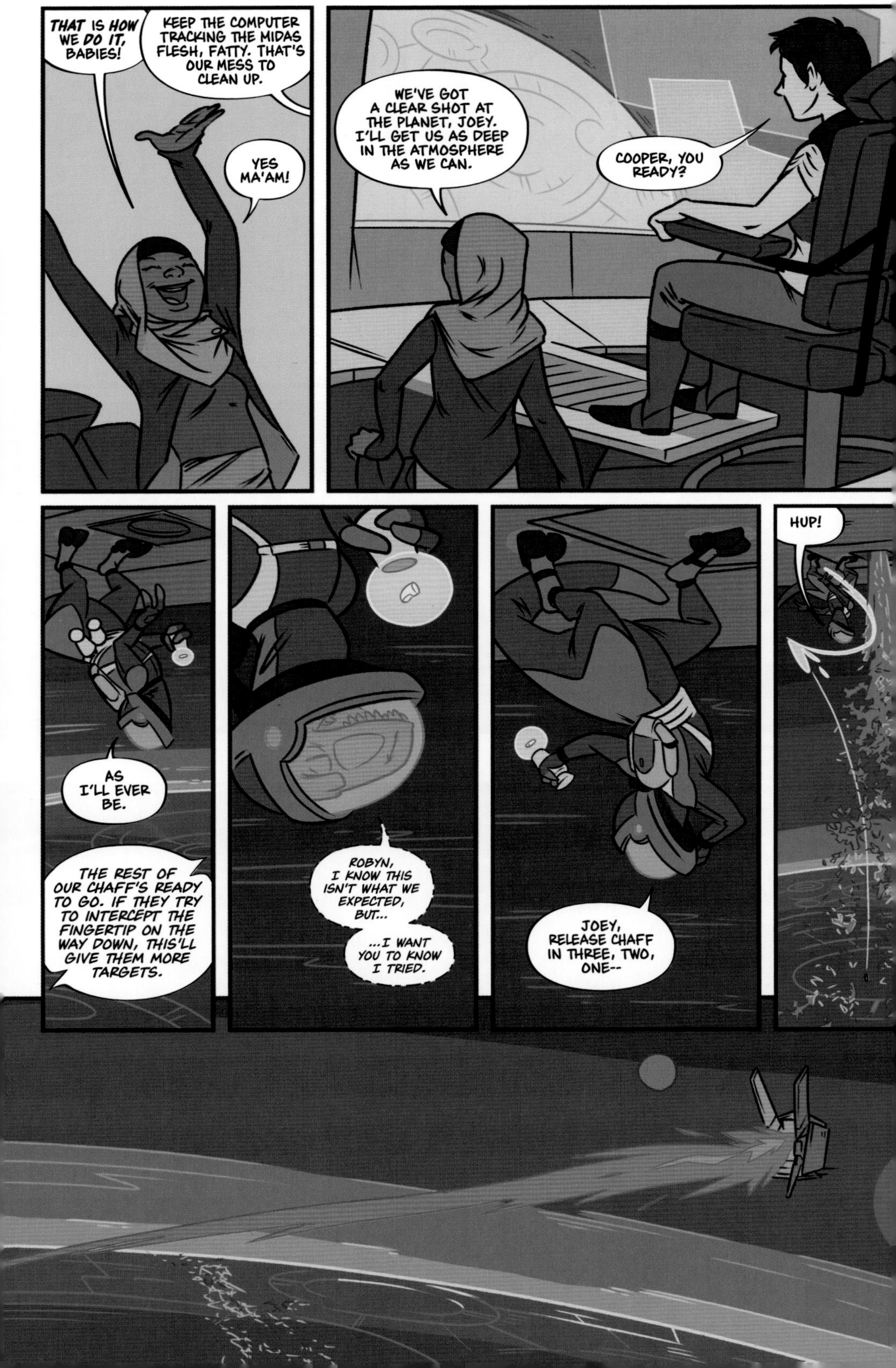
THAT IS HOW WE DO IT, BABIES!
KEEP THE COMPUTER TRACKING THE MIDAS FLESH, FATTY. THAT'S OUR MESS TO CLEAN UP.
YES MA'AM!
WE'VE GOT A CLEAR SHOT AT THE PLANET, JOEY. I'LL GET US AS DEEP IN THE ATMOSPHERE AS WE CAN.
COOPER, YOU READY?
AS I'LL EVER BE.
THE REST OF OUR CHAFF'S READY TO GO. IF THEY TRY TO INTERCEPT THE FINGERTIP ON THE WAY DOWN, THIS'LL GIVE THEM MORE TARGETS.
ROBYN, I KNOW THIS ISN'T WHAT WE EXPECTED, BUT...
...I WANT YOU TO KNOW I TRIED.
JOEY, RELEASE CHAFF IN THREE, TWO, ONE--
HUP!

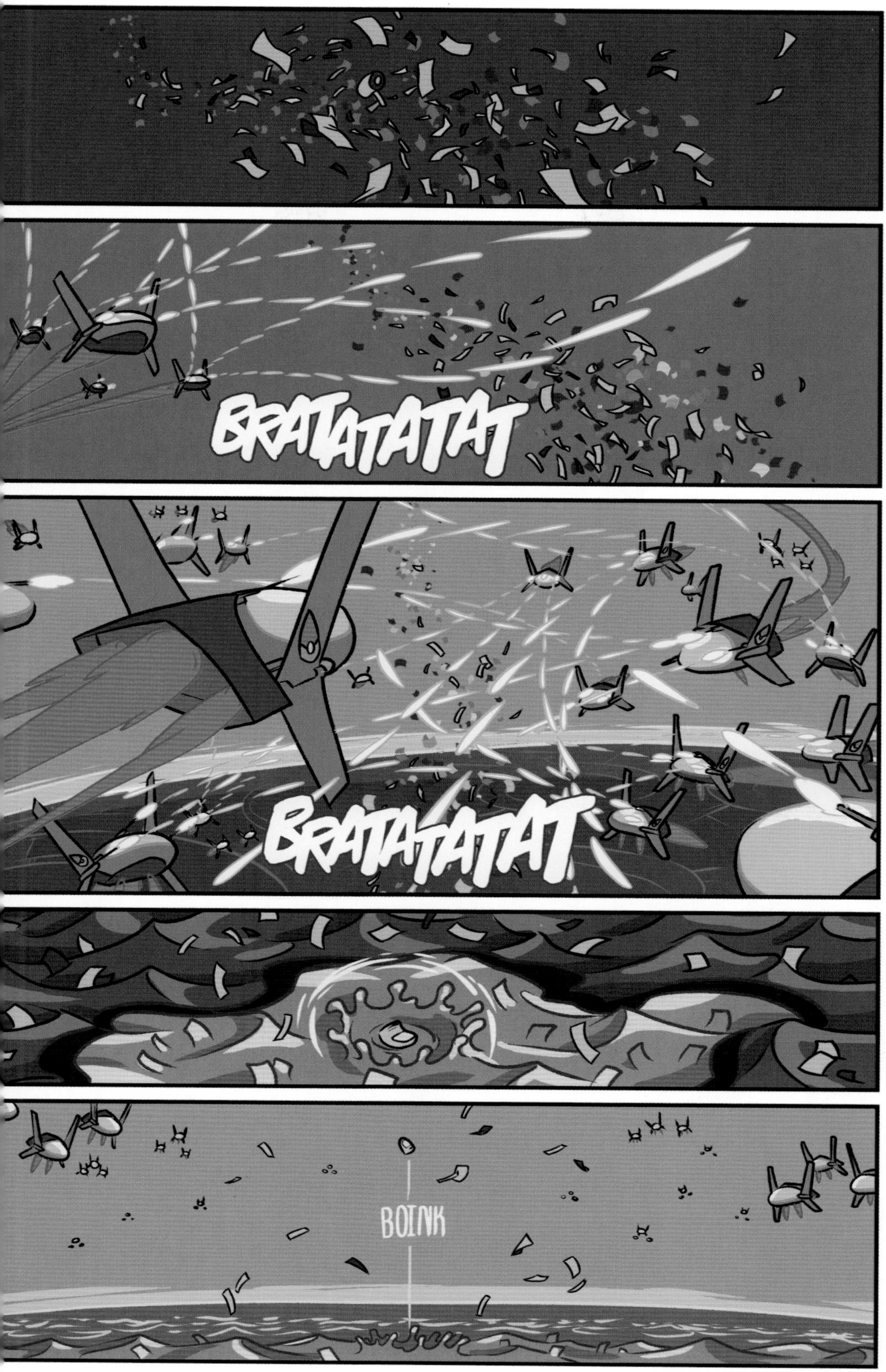
BRATATATAT
BRATATATAT
BOINK

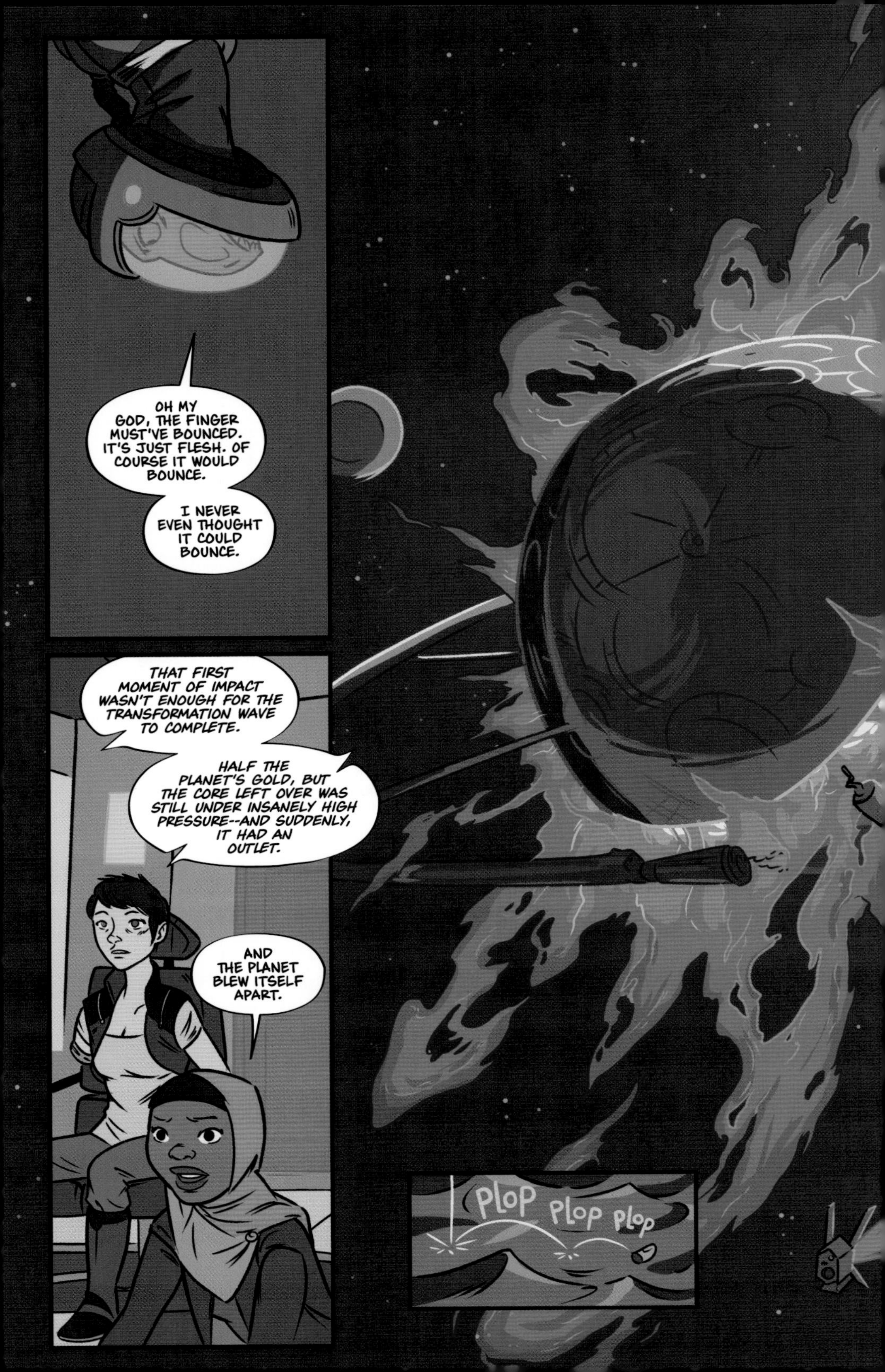
OH MY GOD, THE FINGER MUST'VE BOUNCED. IT'S JUST FLESH. OF COURSE IT WOULD BOUNCE.
I NEVER EVEN THOUGHT IT COULD BOUNCE.
THAT FIRST MOMENT OF IMPACT WASN'T ENOUGH FOR THE TRANSFORMATION WAVE TO COMPLETE.
HALF THE PLANET'S GOLD, BUT THE CORE LEFT OVER WAS STILL UNDER INSANELY HIGH PRESSURE--AND SUDDENLY, IT HAD AN OUTLET.
AND THE PLANET BLEW ITSELF APART.
PLOP PLOP PLOP

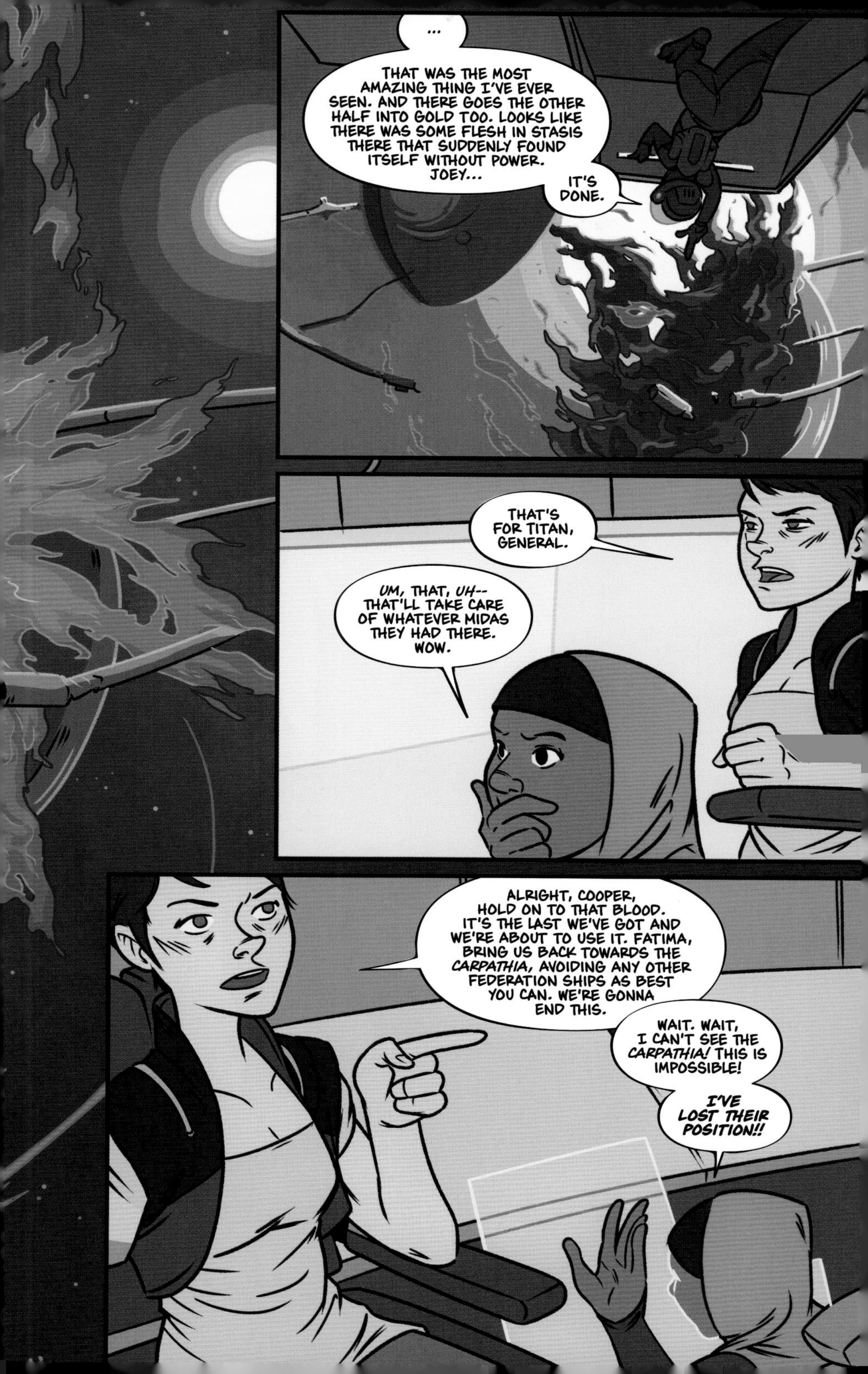
...
THAT WAS THE MOST AMAZING THING I'VE EVER SEEN. AND THERE GOES THE OTHER HALF INTO GOLD TOO. LOOKS LIKE THERE WAS SOME FLESH IN STASIS THERE THAT SUDDENLY FOUND ITSELF WITHOUT POWER. JOEY...
IT'S DONE.
THAT'S FOR TITAN, GENERAL.
UM, THAT, *UH*-- THAT'LL TAKE CARE OF WHATEVER MIDAS THEY HAD THERE. WOW.
ALRIGHT, COOPER, HOLD ON TO THAT BLOOD. IT'S THE LAST WE'VE GOT AND WE'RE ABOUT TO USE IT. FATIMA, BRING US BACK TOWARDS THE *CARPATHIA*, AVOIDING ANY OTHER FEDERATION SHIPS AS BEST YOU CAN. WE'RE GONNA END THIS.
WAIT. WAIT, I CAN'T SEE THE *CARPATHIA!* THIS IS IMPOSSIBLE!
I'VE LOST THEIR POSITION!!

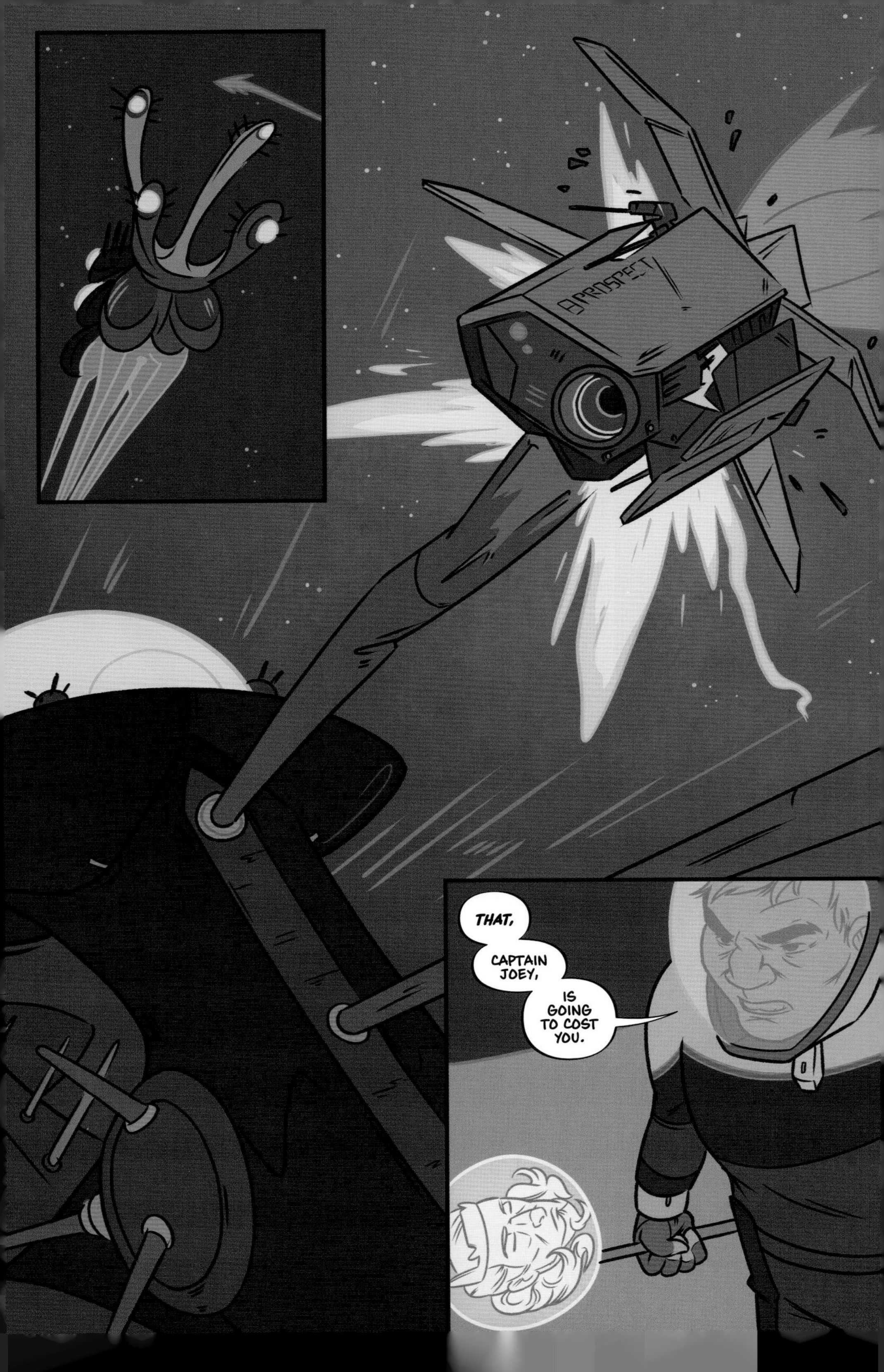
PROSPECT
THAT,
CAPTAIN JOEY,
IS GOING TO COST YOU.

"HOLY GEEZ!!"

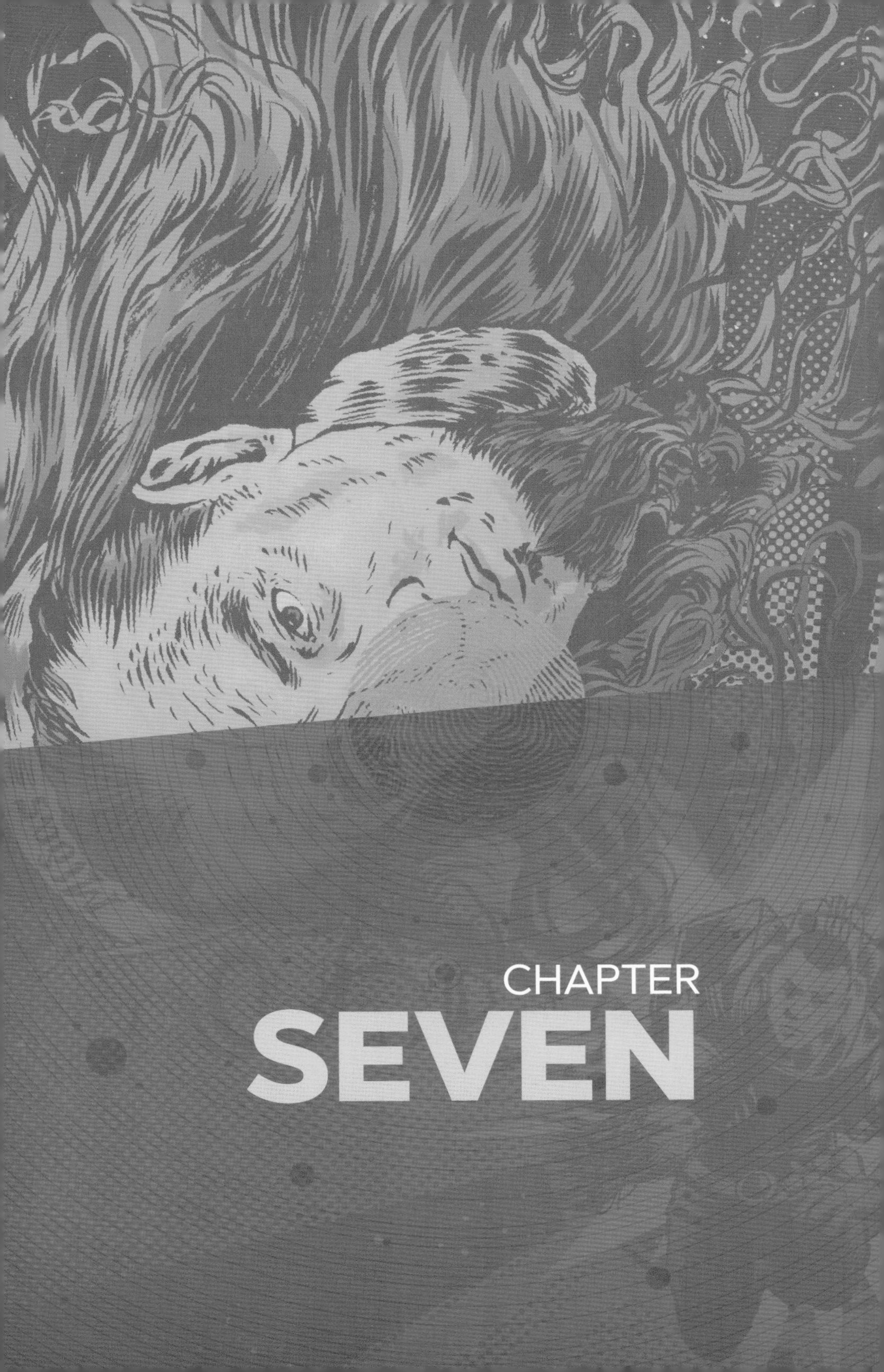

CHAPTER SEVEN

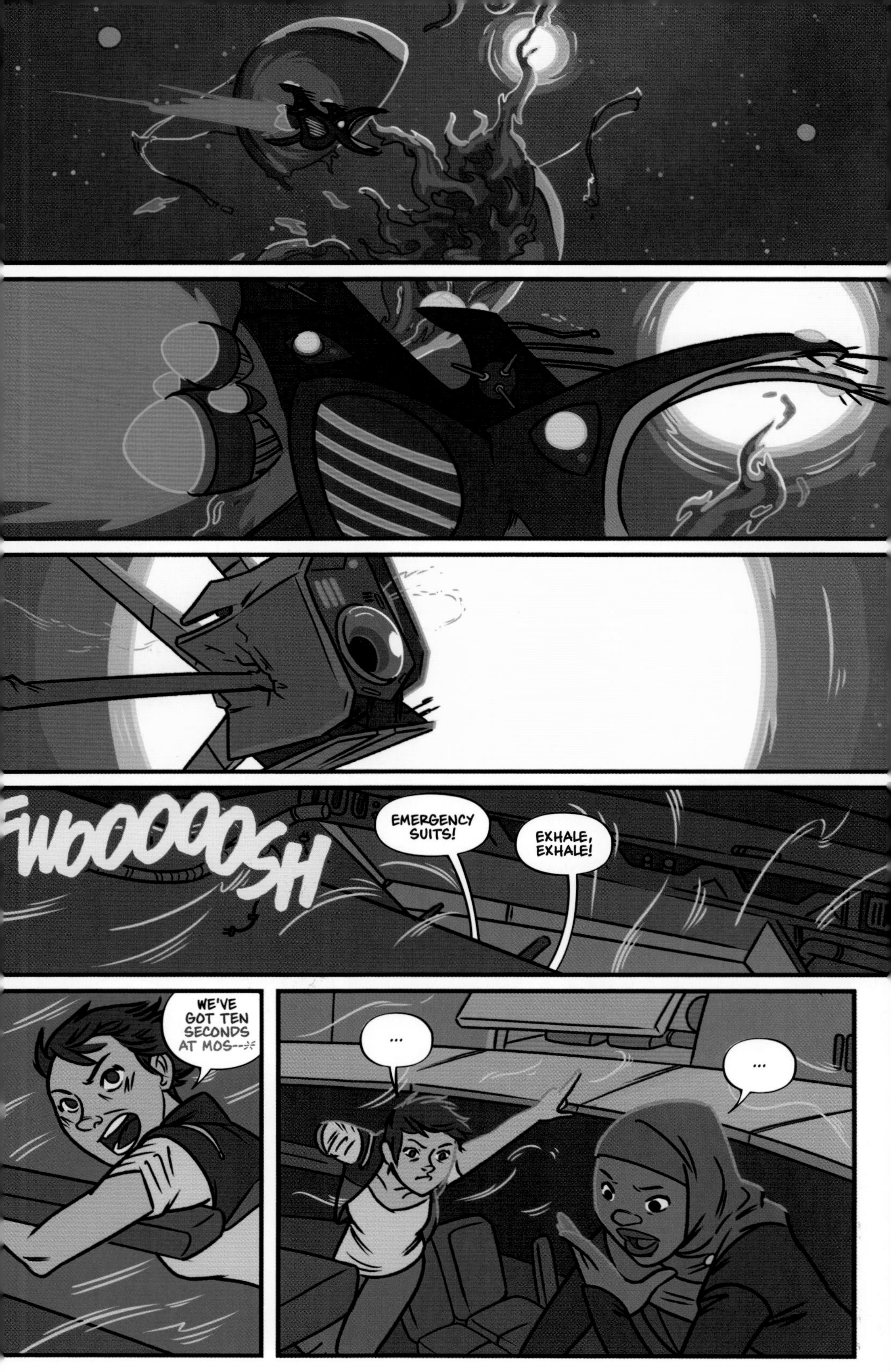
FWOOOOOSH
EMERGENCY SUITS!
EXHALE, EXHALE!
WE'VE GOT TEN SECONDS AT MOS--
...
...

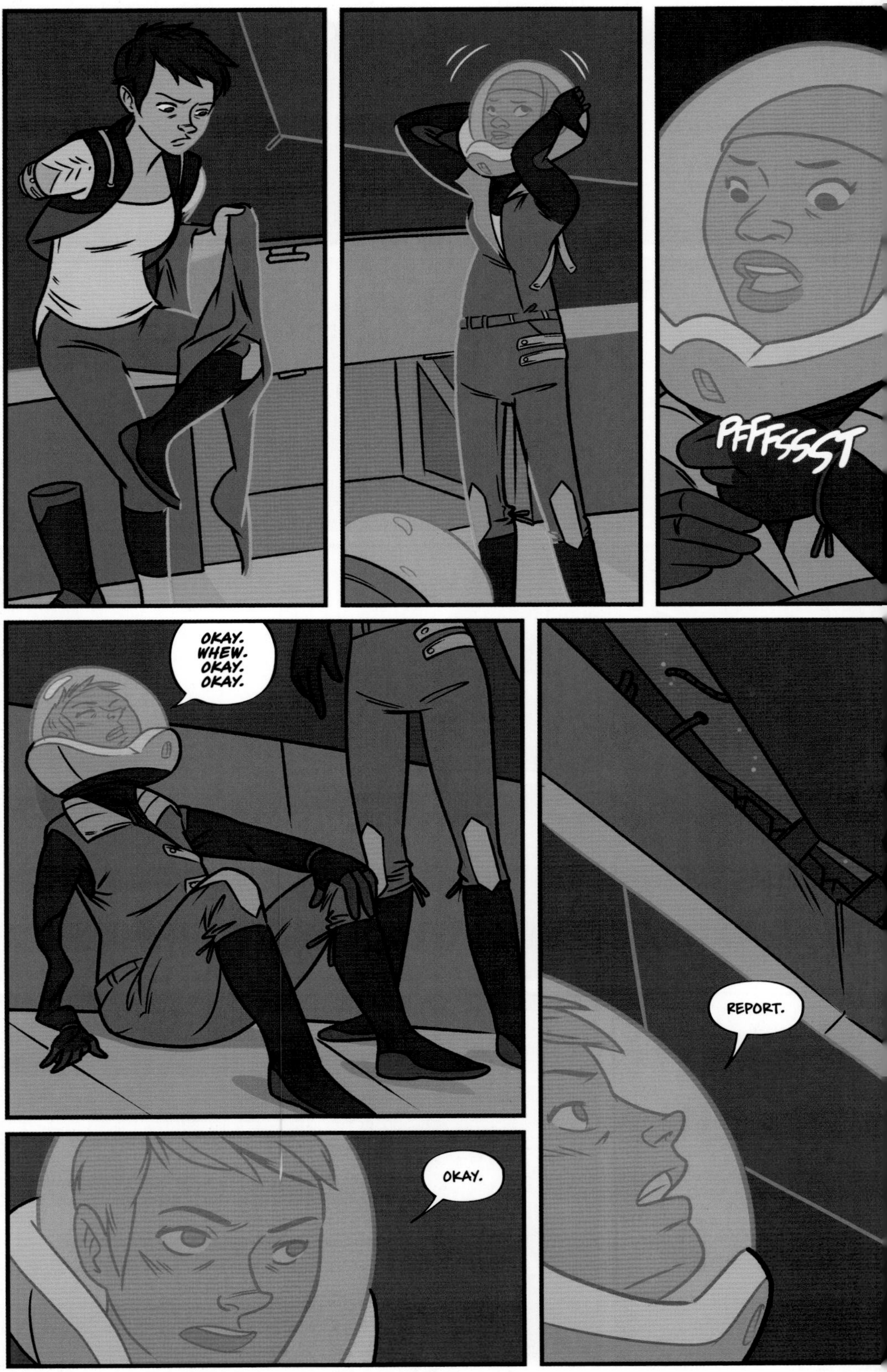
PFFFSSST
OKAY. WHEW. OKAY. OKAY.
REPORT.
OKAY.

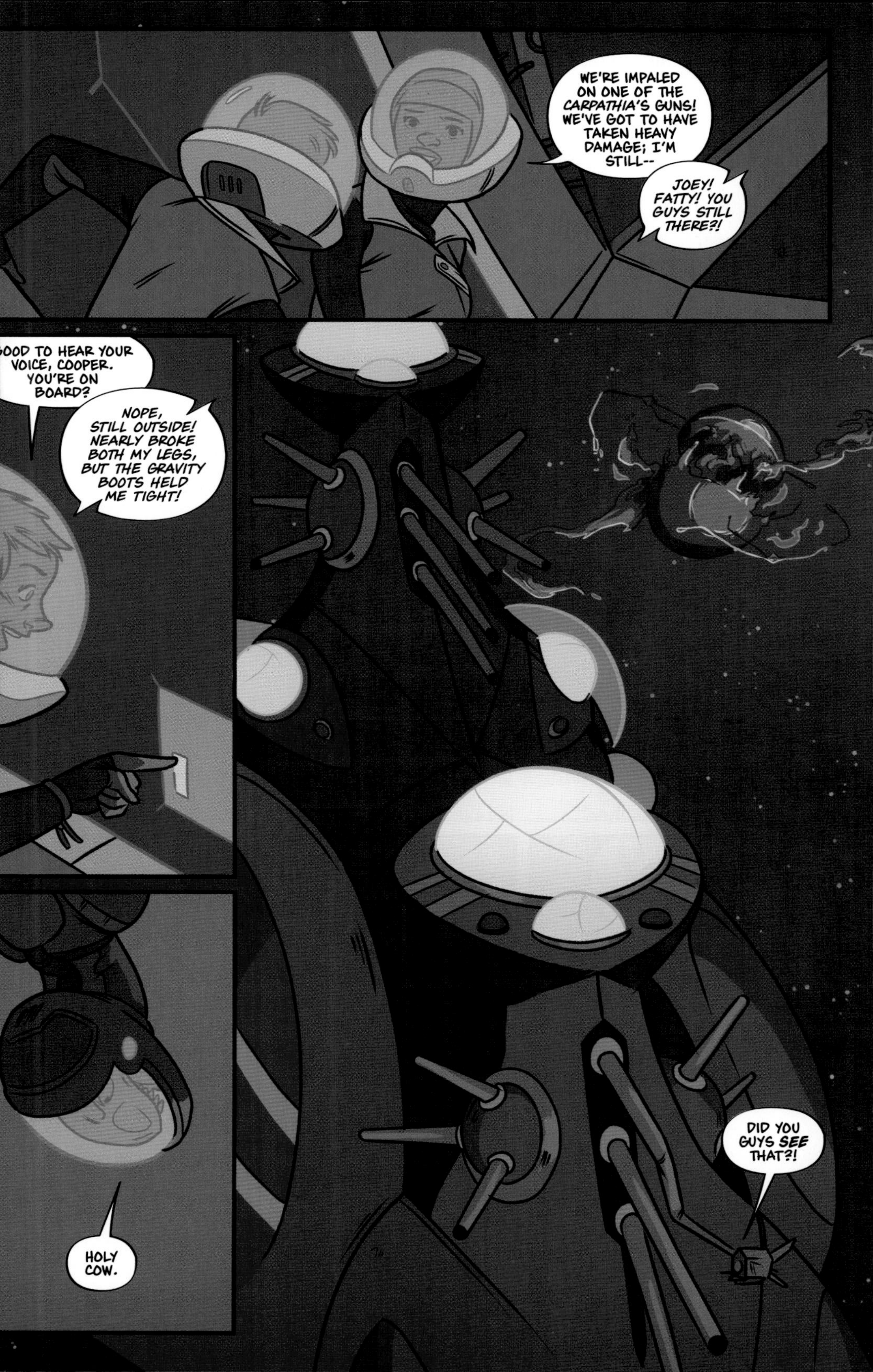
WE'RE IMPALED ON ONE OF THE CARPATHIA'S GUNS! WE'VE GOT TO HAVE TAKEN HEAVY DAMAGE; I'M STILL--
JOEY! FATTY! YOU GUYS STILL THERE?!
GOOD TO HEAR YOUR VOICE, COOPER. YOU'RE ON BOARD?
NOPE, STILL OUTSIDE! NEARLY BROKE BOTH MY LEGS, BUT THE GRAVITY BOOTS HELD ME TIGHT!
HOLY COW.
DID YOU GUYS SEE THAT?!

OKAY SO, THE GOOD NEWS IS, *THAT'S* THE ONLY HULL BREACH. THE BAD AND WORSE NEWS IS THE *CARPATHIA'S* PUSHING US DIRECTLY INTO THE SUN, AND OUR ENGINES ARE DOWN, WHICH MEANS WE'RE NOT GONNA HAVE ENOUGH THRUST TO BREAK FREE.

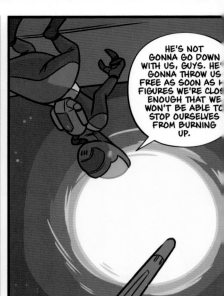

HE'S NOT GONNA GO DOWN WITH US, GUYS. HE'S GONNA THROW US FREE AS SOON AS HE FIGURES WE'RE CLOSE ENOUGH THAT WE WON'T BE ABLE TO STOP OURSELVES FROM BURNING UP.

AGREED. ALRIGHT COOPER, I WANT YOU TO WALK OVER AND HIT THE *CARPATHIA* WITH THAT LAST BIT OF MIDAS BLOOD.

...YOU'RE SURE?

THAT'LL TURN US TOO.

YEAH MAN. WE CAN'T RISK MISSING OUR CHANCE TO END THIS. THIS THING IS OUR FAULT. OUR RESPONSIBILITY.

I'M NOT SUICIDAL AND I'VE GOT AN IDEA TO BREAK THE *PROSPECT* FREE, BUT IF YOU SEE YOUR CHANCE, COOPER...

...I'M TELLING YOU TO TAKE IT.

HAH HAH, OKAY! I'LL JUST GET THINGS READY SO I CAN TURN MYSELF AND ALL MY FRIENDS INTO GOLD STATUES WITH SOME SPACE BLOOD!

THIS IS DEFINITELY A REAL THING THAT IS HAPPENING IN MY LIFE DUE TO THE REALLY EXCELLENT DECISIONS WE'VE MADE!

FATIMA, CAN WE OPEN ALL INTERIOR BULKHEADS *EXCEPT* THE ONE LEADING TO THE BRIDGE?

YEAH, I THINK SO.

DO IT.

I'M VENTING OUR WASTE CO_2 FROM STORAGE BACK INTO THE SHIP.

THAT'LL MAKE THE AIR IN THE REST OF THE SHIP TOXIC.

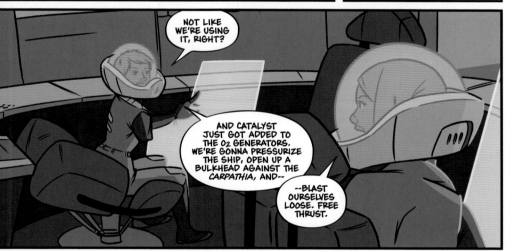

NOT LIKE WE'RE USING IT, RIGHT?

AND CATALYST JUST GOT ADDED TO THE O_2 GENERATORS. WE'RE GONNA PRESSURIZE THE SHIP, OPEN UP A BULKHEAD AGAINST THE *CARPATHIA*, AND--

--BLAST OURSELVES LOOSE. FREE THRUST.

I LOVE IT. ALTHOUGH I DID HAVE SOME HOUSEPLANTS IN MY QUARTERS THAT I'D HOPED WOULD SURVIVE THIS TRIP.

YES. WELL. THEY'RE GOING TO BE BURIED IN SPACE NOW. THEY WILL BE SPACE PLANTS.

IT IS HONESTLY THE MOST EXCITING DEATH A PLANT COULD HOPE FOR.

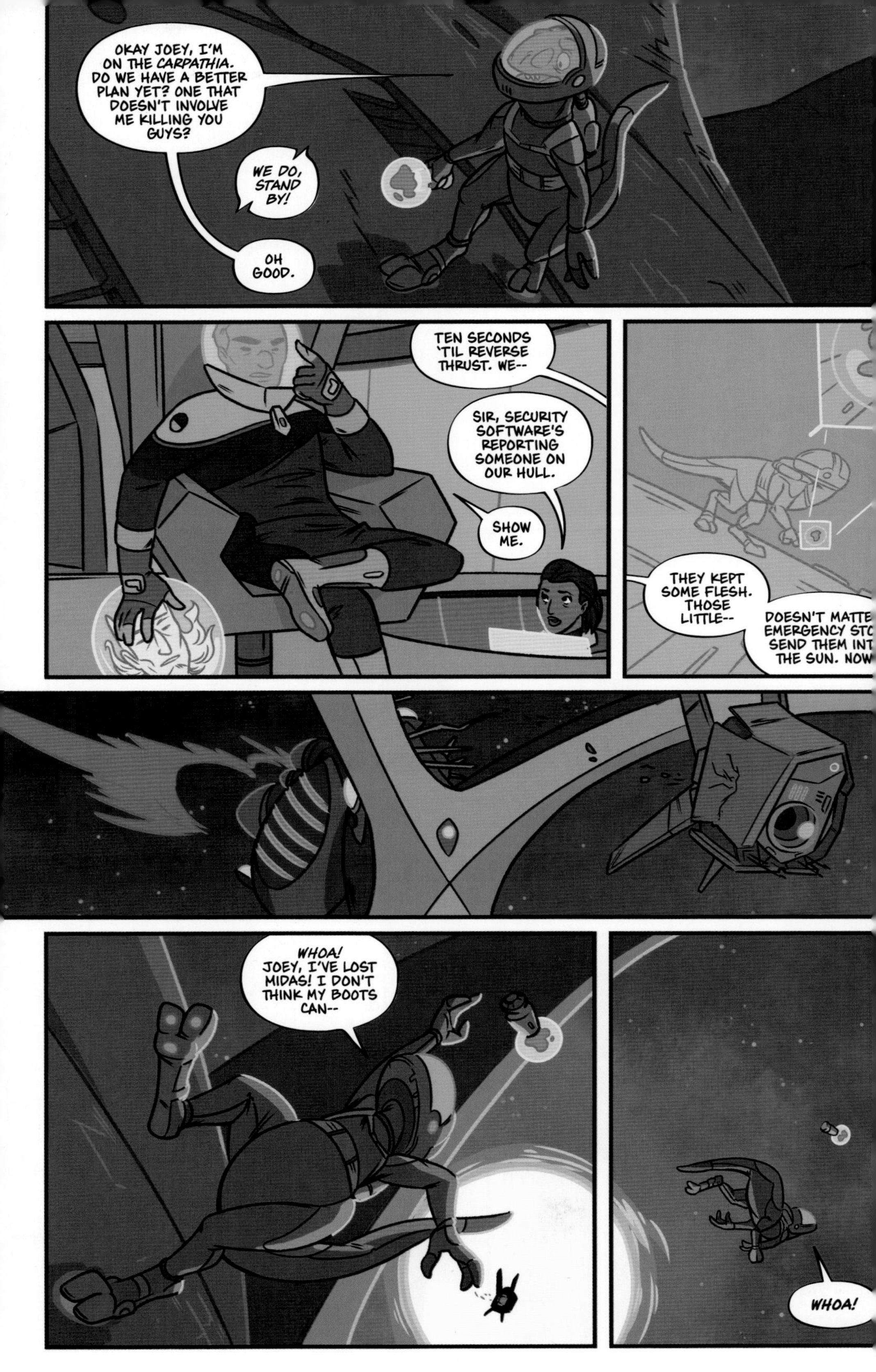
OKAY JOEY, I'M ON THE *CARPATHIA*. DO WE HAVE A BETTER PLAN YET? ONE THAT DOESN'T INVOLVE ME KILLING YOU GUYS?
WE DO, STAND BY!
OH GOOD.
TEN SECONDS 'TIL REVERSE THRUST. WE--
SIR, SECURITY SOFTWARE'S REPORTING SOMEONE ON OUR HULL.
SHOW ME.
THEY KEPT SOME FLESH. THOSE LITTLE--
DOESN'T MATTE EMERGENCY STO SEND THEM INT THE SUN. NOW
WHOA! JOEY, I'VE LOST MIDAS! I DON'T THINK MY BOOTS CAN--
WHOA!

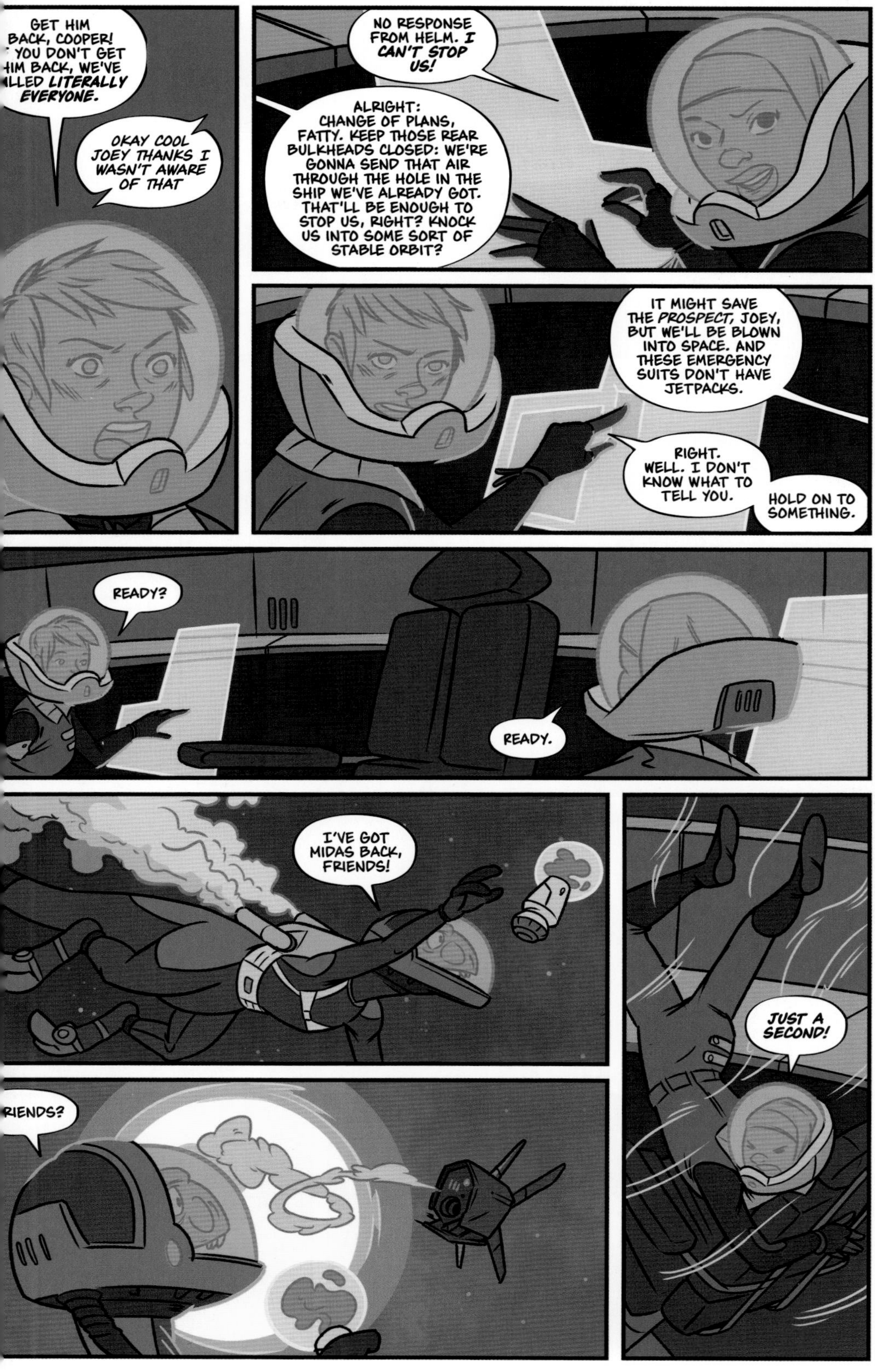
GET HIM BACK, COOPER! 'F YOU DON'T GET HIM BACK, WE'VE ..LLED *LITERALLY EVERYONE.*
OKAY COOL JOEY THANKS I WASN'T AWARE OF THAT
NO RESPONSE FROM HELM. *I CAN'T STOP US!*
ALRIGHT: CHANGE OF PLANS, FATTY. KEEP THOSE REAR BULKHEADS CLOSED: WE'RE GONNA SEND THAT AIR THROUGH THE HOLE IN THE SHIP WE'VE ALREADY GOT. THAT'LL BE ENOUGH TO STOP US, RIGHT? KNOCK US INTO SOME SORT OF STABLE ORBIT?
IT MIGHT SAVE THE *PROSPECT,* JOEY, BUT WE'LL BE BLOWN INTO SPACE. AND THESE EMERGENCY SUITS DON'T HAVE JETPACKS.
RIGHT. WELL. I DON'T KNOW WHAT TO TELL YOU.
HOLD ON TO SOMETHING.
READY?
READY.
I'VE GOT MIDAS BACK, FRIENDS!
..RIENDS?
JUST A SECOND!

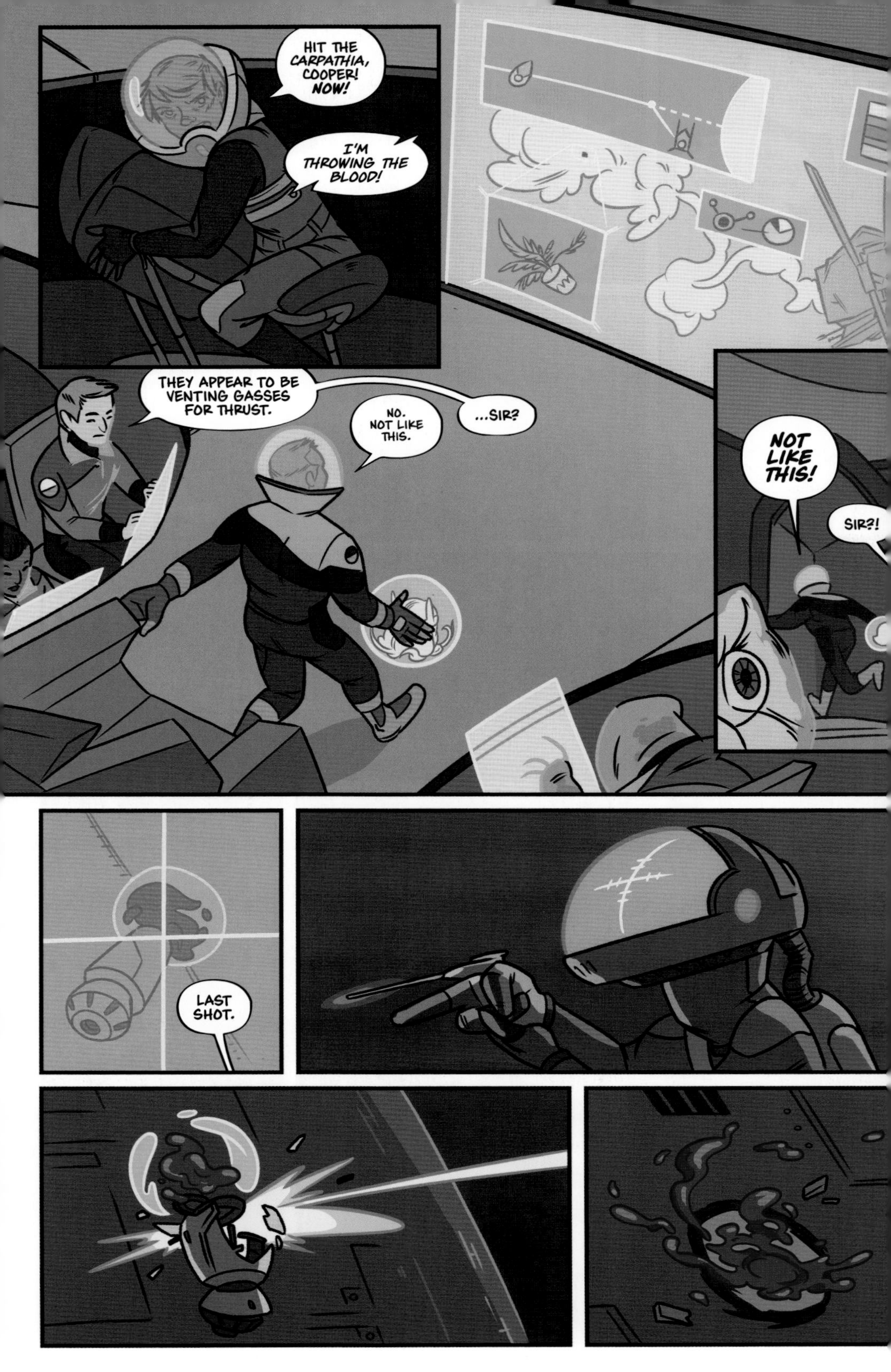
HIT THE CARPATHIA, COOPER! NOW!
I'M THROWING THE BLOOD!
THEY APPEAR TO BE VENTING GASSES FOR THRUST.
NO. NOT LIKE THIS.
...SIR?
NOT LIKE THIS!
SIR?!
LAST SHOT.

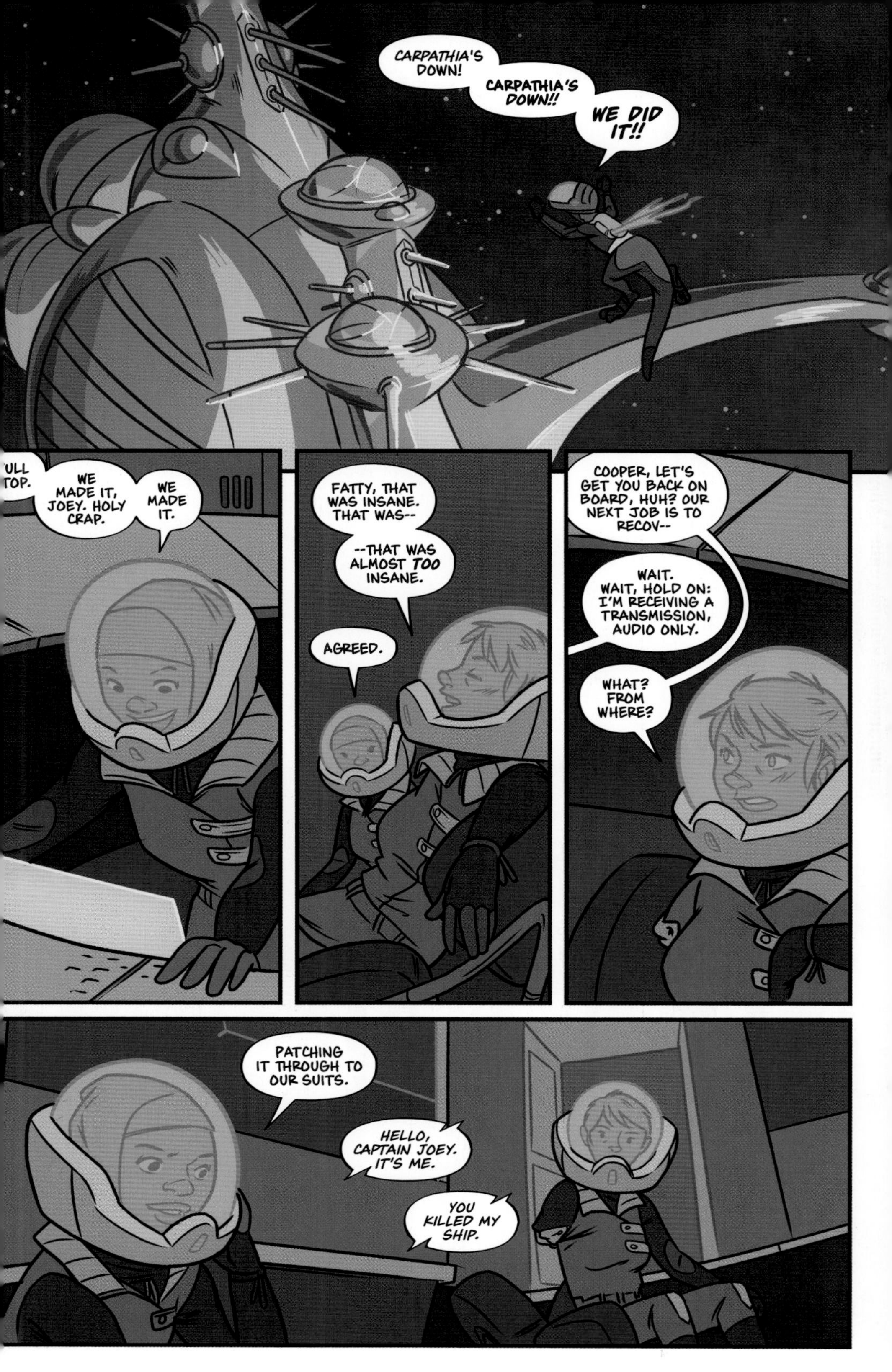
CARPATHIA'S DOWN!
CARPATHIA'S DOWN!!
WE DID IT!!
ULL TOP.
WE MADE IT, JOEY. HOLY CRAP.
WE MADE IT.
FATTY, THAT WAS INSANE. THAT WAS--
--THAT WAS ALMOST TOO INSANE.
AGREED.
COOPER, LET'S GET YOU BACK ON BOARD, HUH? OUR NEXT JOB IS TO RECOV--
WAIT. WAIT, HOLD ON: I'M RECEIVING A TRANSMISSION, AUDIO ONLY.
WHAT? FROM WHERE?
PATCHING IT THROUGH TO OUR SUITS.
HELLO, CAPTAIN JOEY. IT'S ME.
YOU KILLED MY SHIP.

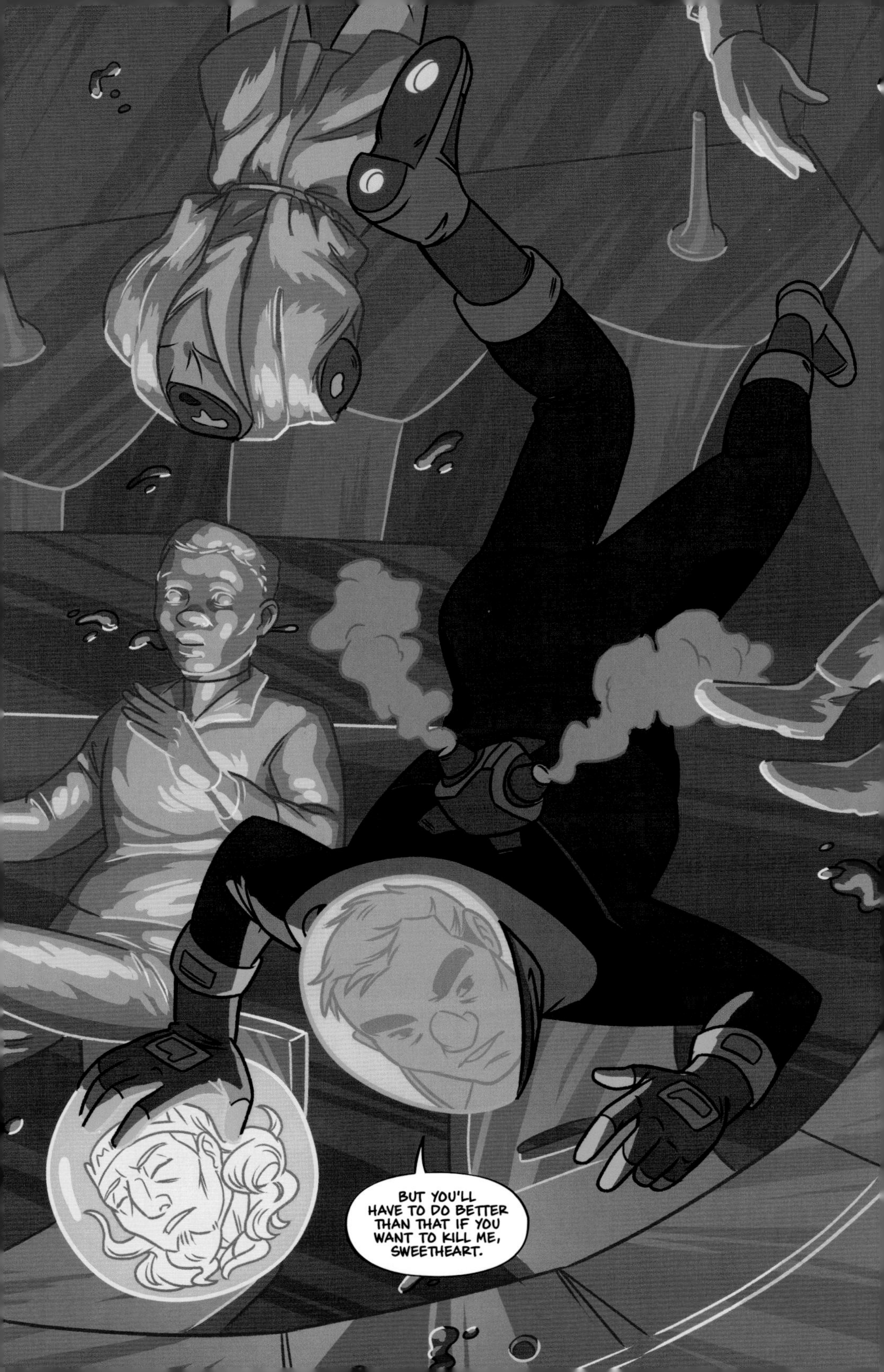
BUT YOU'LL HAVE TO DO BETTER THAN THAT IF YOU WANT TO KILL ME, SWEETHEART.

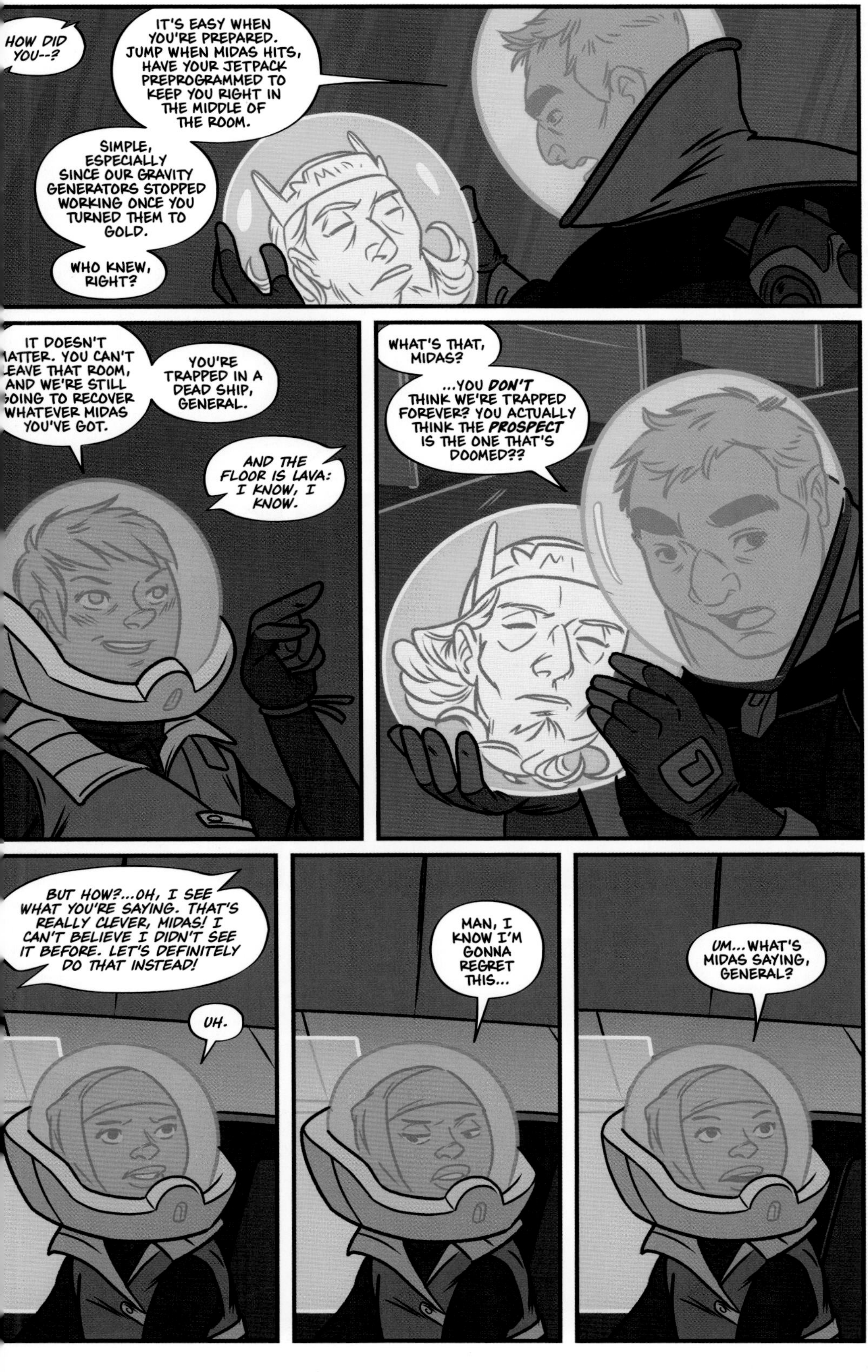
HOW DID YOU--?
IT'S EASY WHEN YOU'RE PREPARED. JUMP WHEN MIDAS HITS, HAVE YOUR JETPACK PREPROGRAMMED TO KEEP YOU RIGHT IN THE MIDDLE OF THE ROOM.
SIMPLE, ESPECIALLY SINCE OUR GRAVITY GENERATORS STOPPED WORKING ONCE YOU TURNED THEM TO GOLD.
WHO KNEW, RIGHT?
IT DOESN'T MATTER. YOU CAN'T LEAVE THAT ROOM, AND WE'RE STILL GOING TO RECOVER WHATEVER MIDAS YOU'VE GOT.
YOU'RE TRAPPED IN A DEAD SHIP, GENERAL.
AND THE FLOOR IS LAVA: I KNOW, I KNOW.
WHAT'S THAT, MIDAS?
...YOU DON'T THINK WE'RE TRAPPED FOREVER? YOU ACTUALLY THINK THE PROSPECT IS THE ONE THAT'S DOOMED??
BUT HOW?...OH, I SEE WHAT YOU'RE SAYING. THAT'S REALLY CLEVER, MIDAS! I CAN'T BELIEVE I DIDN'T SEE IT BEFORE. LET'S DEFINITELY DO THAT INSTEAD!
UH.
MAN, I KNOW I'M GONNA REGRET THIS...
UM...WHAT'S MIDAS SAYING, GENERAL?

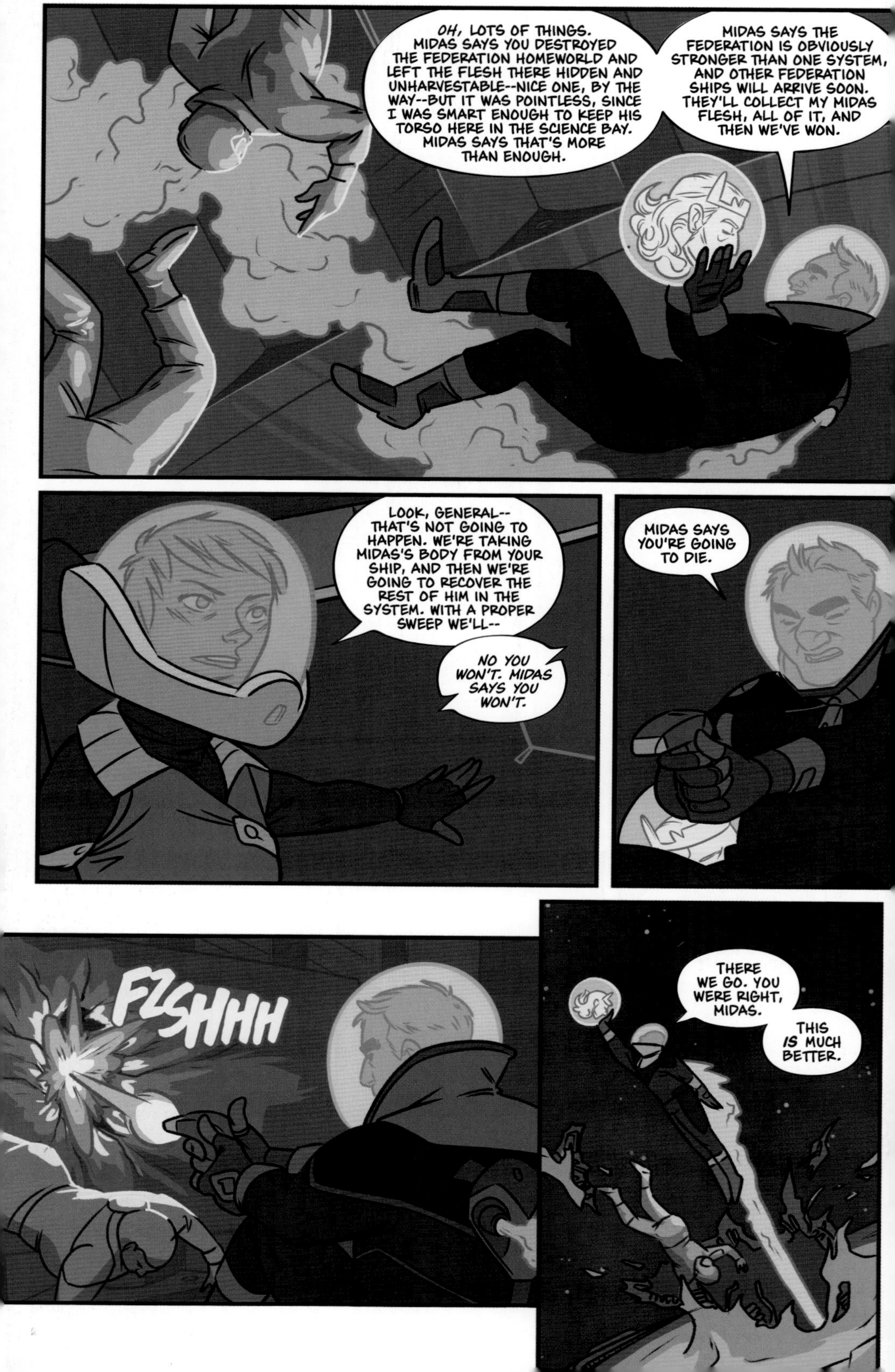

OH, LOTS OF THINGS. MIDAS SAYS YOU DESTROYED THE FEDERATION HOMEWORLD AND LEFT THE FLESH THERE HIDDEN AND UNHARVESTABLE--NICE ONE, BY THE WAY--BUT IT WAS POINTLESS, SINCE I WAS SMART ENOUGH TO KEEP HIS TORSO HERE IN THE SCIENCE BAY. MIDAS SAYS THAT'S MORE THAN ENOUGH.
MIDAS SAYS THE FEDERATION IS OBVIOUSLY STRONGER THAN ONE SYSTEM, AND OTHER FEDERATION SHIPS WILL ARRIVE SOON. THEY'LL COLLECT MY MIDAS FLESH, ALL OF IT, AND THEN WE'VE WON.
LOOK, GENERAL--THAT'S NOT GOING TO HAPPEN. WE'RE TAKING MIDAS'S BODY FROM YOUR SHIP, AND THEN WE'RE GOING TO RECOVER THE REST OF HIM IN THE SYSTEM. WITH A PROPER SWEEP WE'LL--
NO YOU WON'T. MIDAS SAYS YOU WON'T.
MIDAS SAYS YOU'RE GOING TO DIE.
FZSHHH
THERE WE GO. YOU WERE RIGHT, MIDAS.
THIS IS MUCH BETTER.

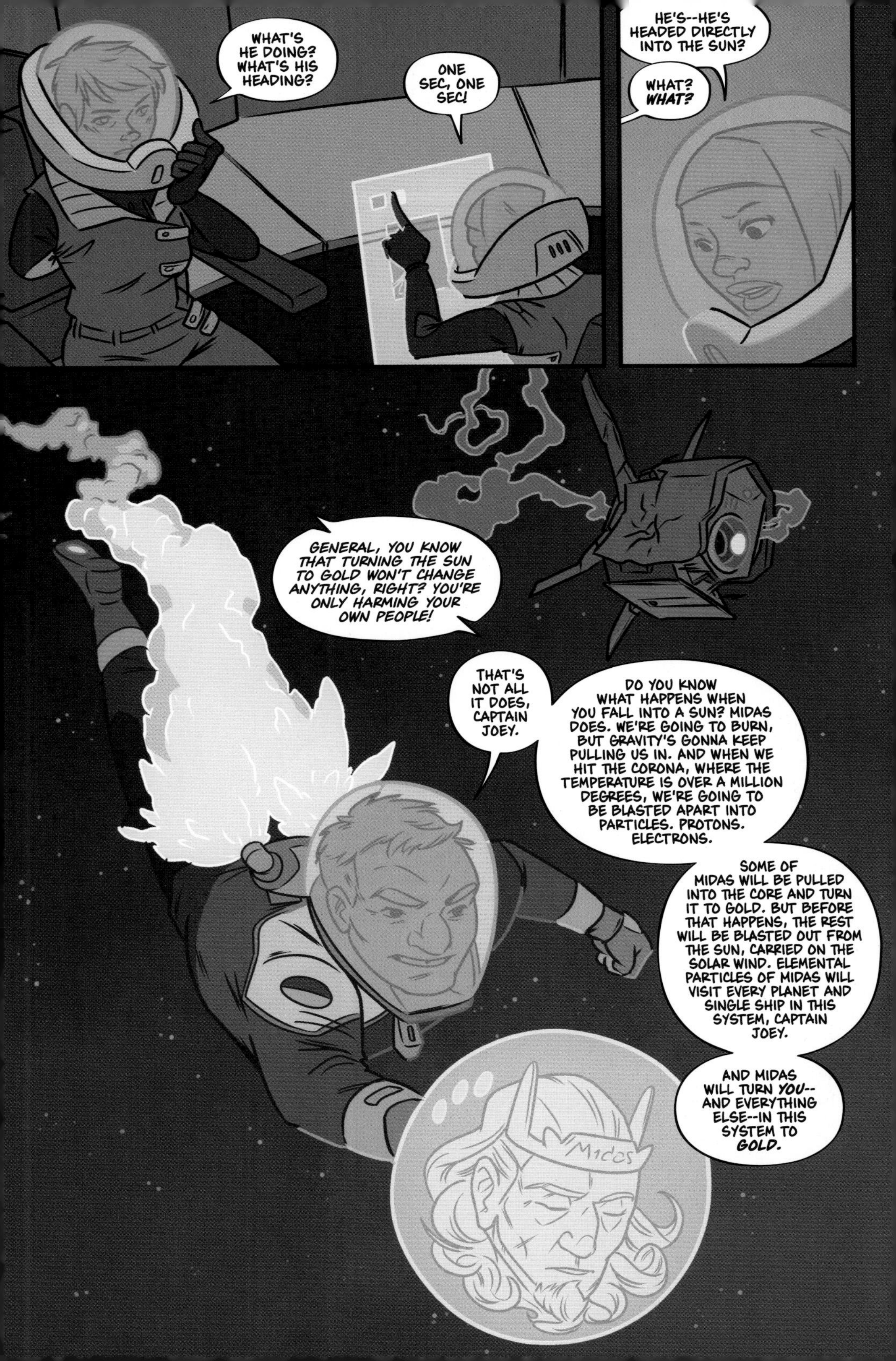

WHAT'S HE DOING? WHAT'S HIS HEADING?
ONE SEC, ONE SEC!
HE'S--HE'S HEADED DIRECTLY INTO THE SUN?
WHAT? *WHAT?*
GENERAL, YOU KNOW THAT TURNING THE SUN TO GOLD WON'T CHANGE ANYTHING, RIGHT? YOU'RE ONLY HARMING YOUR OWN PEOPLE!
THAT'S NOT ALL IT DOES, CAPTAIN JOEY.
DO YOU KNOW WHAT HAPPENS WHEN YOU FALL INTO A SUN? MIDAS DOES. WE'RE GOING TO BURN, BUT GRAVITY'S GONNA KEEP PULLING US IN. AND WHEN WE HIT THE CORONA, WHERE THE TEMPERATURE IS OVER A MILLION DEGREES, WE'RE GOING TO BE BLASTED APART INTO PARTICLES. PROTONS. ELECTRONS.
SOME OF MIDAS WILL BE PULLED INTO THE CORE AND TURN IT TO GOLD. BUT BEFORE THAT HAPPENS, THE REST WILL BE BLASTED OUT FROM THE SUN, CARRIED ON THE SOLAR WIND. ELEMENTAL PARTICLES OF MIDAS WILL VISIT EVERY PLANET AND SINGLE SHIP IN THIS SYSTEM, CAPTAIN JOEY.
AND MIDAS WILL TURN *YOU*--AND EVERYTHING ELSE--IN THIS SYSTEM TO *GOLD.*
Midas

GENERAL, THERE ARE OTHER SHIPS IN THE SYSTEM! YOU CAN'T--

THEY'RE DEAD ALREADY. AND THE FEDERATION WILL SURVIVE. WE'LL HARVEST MIDAS'S PARTICLES, HIS TORSO, AND KEEP THEM FROM OTHERS. AND YOU--THE ONLY PEOPLE IN THE UNIVERSE WHO CAN STOP US, THE ONLY PEOPLE I'VE HAD TROUBLE GETTING OUT OF THE PICTURE...

...WELL, YOU'LL BE GOLD.

NO!

GOODBYE, CAPTAIN JOEY.

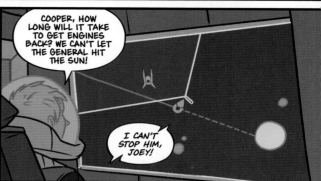

COOPER, HOW LONG WILL IT TAKE TO GET ENGINES BACK? WE CAN'T LET THE GENERAL HIT THE SUN!

I CAN'T STOP HIM, JOEY!

HE'S ALREADY CLOSER TO THE SUN THAN WE CAN ESCAPE FROM! WE GO AFTER HIM AND IT'S A ONE-WAY TRIP FOR US TOO. NOTHING CHANGES!!

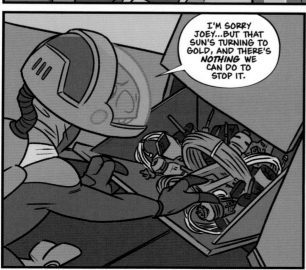

I'M SORRY JOEY...BUT THAT SUN'S TURNING TO GOLD, AND THERE'S *NOTHING* WE CAN DO TO STOP IT.

COOPER. COOPER, LISTEN TO ME.

I NEED AN IDEA IN THE NEXT TWO MINUTES OR WE'RE ALL DEAD.

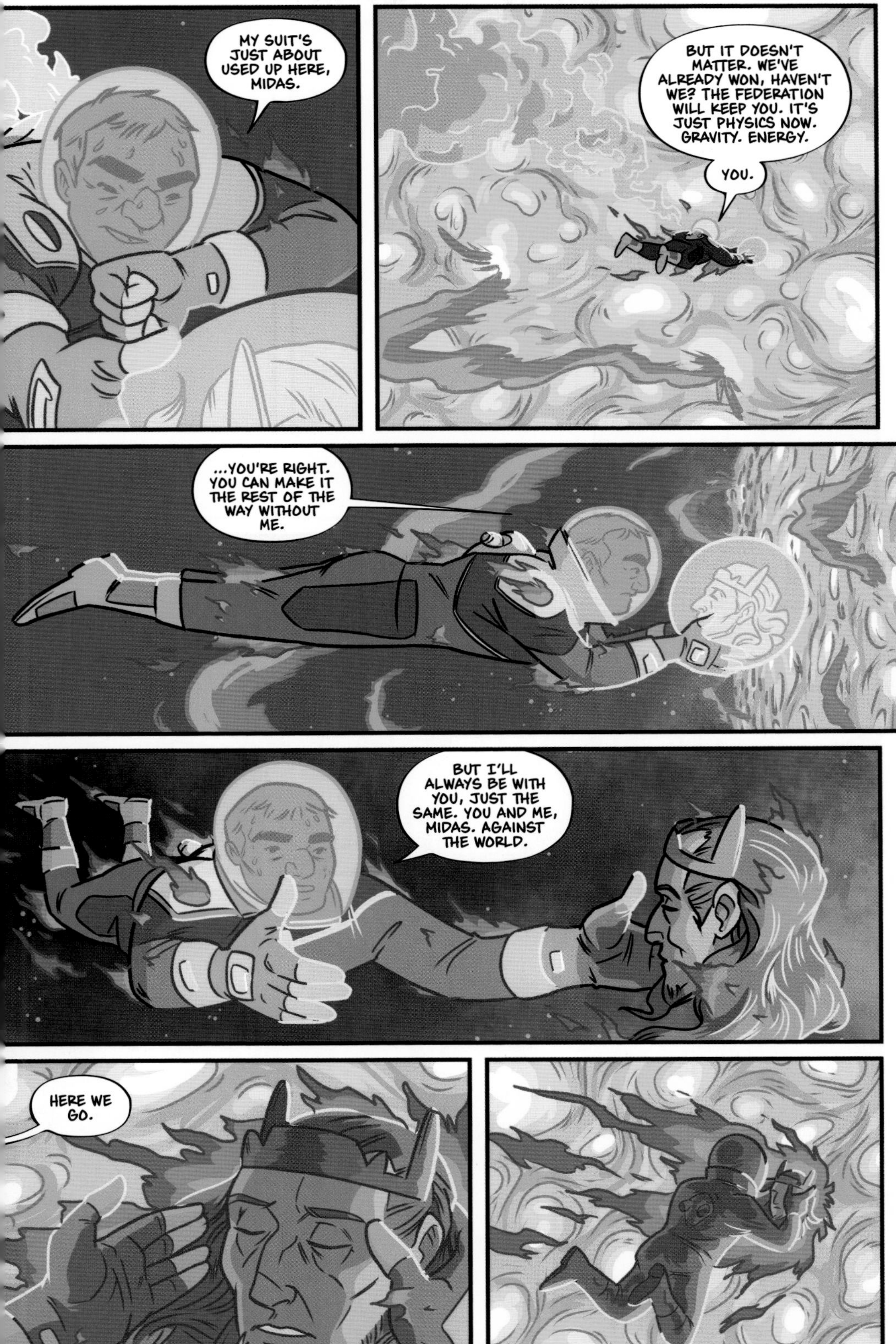
MY SUIT'S JUST ABOUT USED UP HERE, MIDAS.
BUT IT DOESN'T MATTER. WE'VE ALREADY WON, HAVEN'T WE? THE FEDERATION WILL KEEP YOU. IT'S JUST PHYSICS NOW. GRAVITY. ENERGY.
YOU.
...YOU'RE RIGHT. YOU CAN MAKE IT THE REST OF THE WAY WITHOUT ME.
BUT I'LL ALWAYS BE WITH YOU, JUST THE SAME. YOU AND ME, MIDAS. AGAINST THE WORLD.
HERE WE GO.

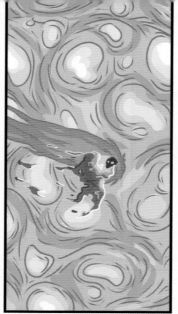
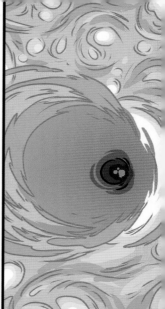

COMPUTER'S PROJECTING SOLAR WIND WILL HIT IN UNDER A MINUTE!

I KNOW, I KNOW! FATIMA, HELP ME FIND WHERE THE BATTERIES ENDED UP! JOEY, DISABLE GRAVITY!

SOLAR WIND IMPACT IN THREE SECONDS.

ALRIGHT, ALL THE POWER WE'VE GOT ON THE SHIP IS GONNA BE RUNNING THROUGH HERE AND INTO THE WALLS. SO, UM...

...NOBODY TOUCH ANYTHING?

ZZZZTTTTTTT

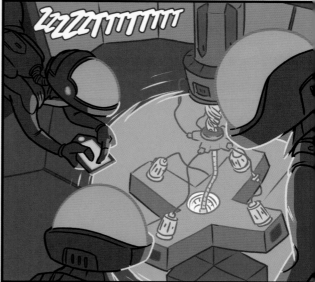

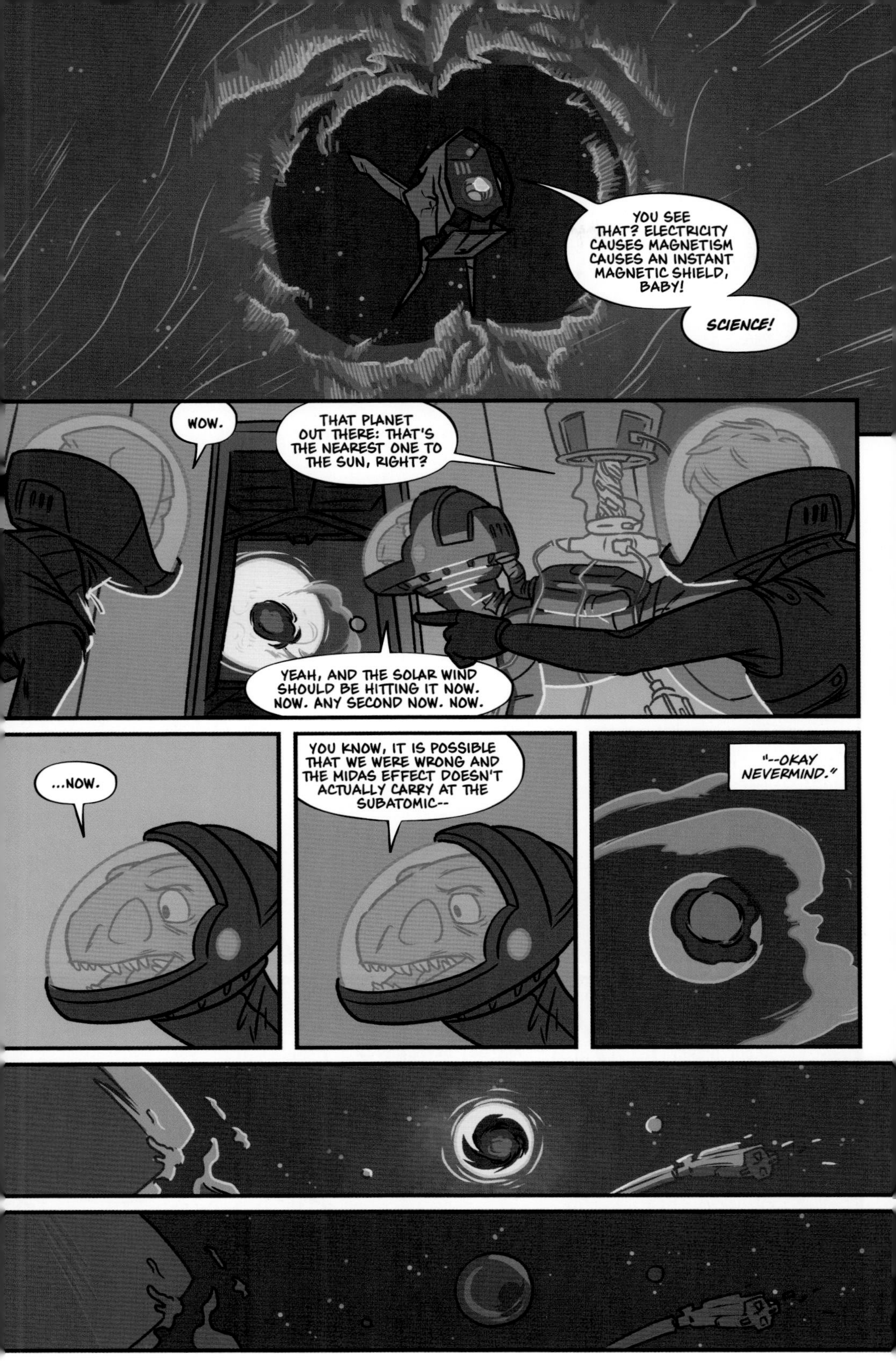
YOU SEE THAT? ELECTRICITY CAUSES MAGNETISM CAUSES AN INSTANT MAGNETIC SHIELD, BABY!
SCIENCE!
WOW.
THAT PLANET OUT THERE: THAT'S THE NEAREST ONE TO THE SUN, RIGHT?
YEAH, AND THE SOLAR WIND SHOULD BE HITTING IT NOW. NOW. ANY SECOND NOW. NOW.
...NOW.
YOU KNOW, IT IS POSSIBLE THAT WE WERE WRONG AND THE MIDAS EFFECT DOESN'T ACTUALLY CARRY AT THE SUBATOMIC--
"--OKAY NEVERMIND."

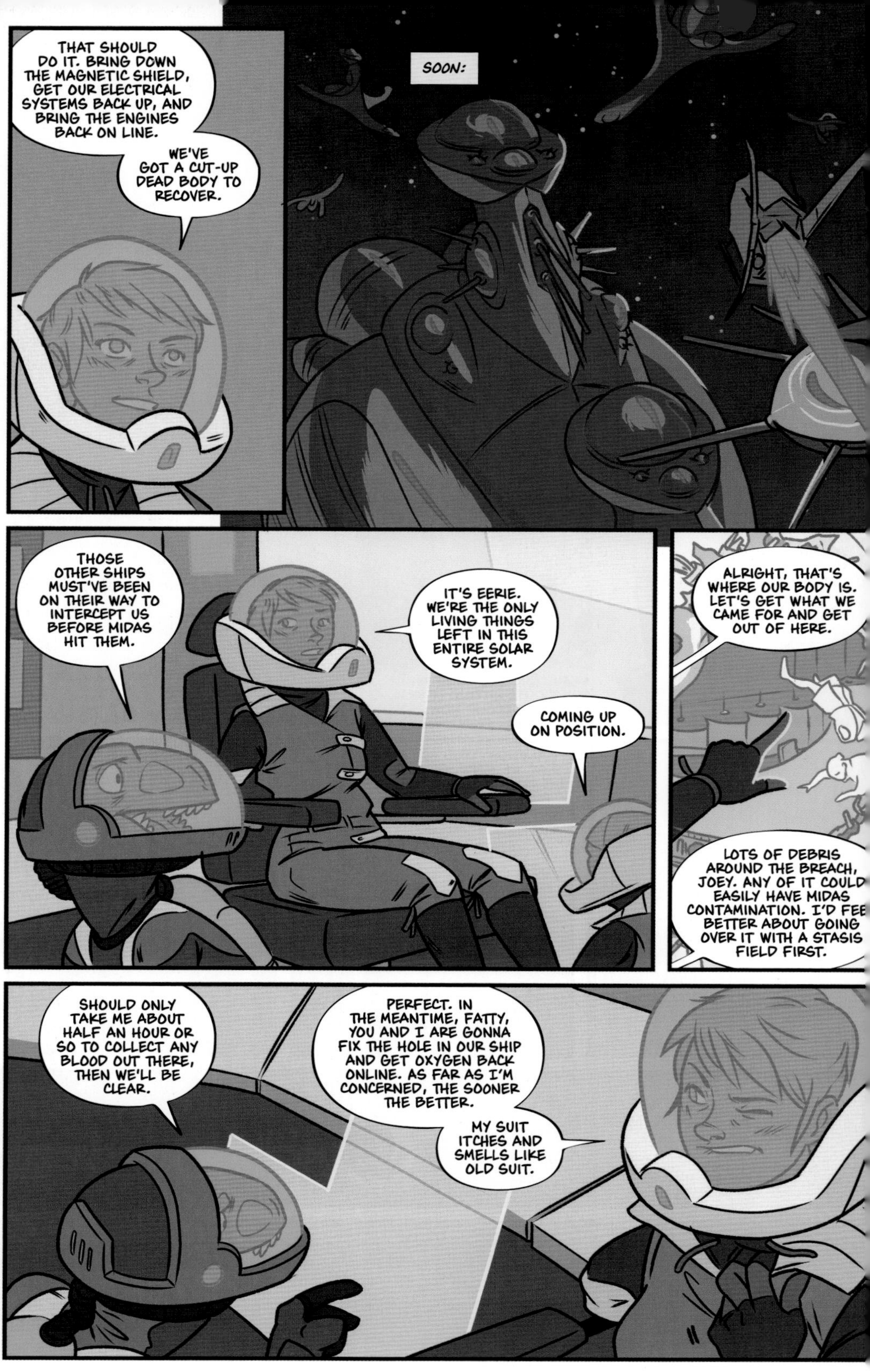
THAT SHOULD DO IT. BRING DOWN THE MAGNETIC SHIELD, GET OUR ELECTRICAL SYSTEMS BACK UP, AND BRING THE ENGINES BACK ON LINE.
WE'VE GOT A CUT-UP DEAD BODY TO RECOVER.
SOON:
THOSE OTHER SHIPS MUST'VE BEEN ON THEIR WAY TO INTERCEPT US BEFORE MIDAS HIT THEM.
IT'S EERIE. WE'RE THE ONLY LIVING THINGS LEFT IN THIS ENTIRE SOLAR SYSTEM.
COMING UP ON POSITION.
ALRIGHT, THAT'S WHERE OUR BODY IS. LET'S GET WHAT WE CAME FOR AND GET OUT OF HERE.
LOTS OF DEBRIS AROUND THE BREACH, JOEY. ANY OF IT COULD EASILY HAVE MIDAS CONTAMINATION. I'D FEE BETTER ABOUT GOING OVER IT WITH A STASIS FIELD FIRST.
SHOULD ONLY TAKE ME ABOUT HALF AN HOUR OR SO TO COLLECT ANY BLOOD OUT THERE, THEN WE'LL BE CLEAR.
PERFECT. IN THE MEANTIME, FATTY, YOU AND I ARE GONNA FIX THE HOLE IN OUR SHIP AND GET OXYGEN BACK ONLINE. AS FAR AS I'M CONCERNED, THE SOONER THE BETTER.
MY SUIT ITCHES AND SMELLS LIKE OLD SUIT.

YOU REALLY THINK WE CAN COLLECT ALL OF MIDAS'S BLOOD IN THIS SYSTEM, JOEY? ALL OF IT?

I DO.

HEY! ALMOST DONE OVER HERE!

ALMOST DONE HERE TOO, THANKS COOPER!

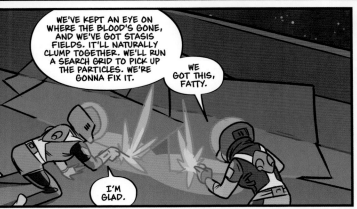

WE'VE KEPT AN EYE ON WHERE THE BLOOD'S GONE, AND WE'VE GOT STASIS FIELDS. IT'LL NATURALLY CLUMP TOGETHER. WE'LL RUN A SEARCH GRID TO PICK UP THE PARTICLES. WE'RE GONNA FIX IT.

WE GOT THIS, FATTY.

I'M GLAD.

...I'M STILL REALLY SORRY ABOUT YOUR ARM, JOEY.

DID I EVER TELL YOU HOW I'D DRAW UP THESE PLANS FOR A ROBOT ARM WHEN I WAS A KID? IT HAD A LASER POINTER, A CAN OPENER, KNIVES THAT POP OUT OF MY KNUCKLES... I'LL BE FINE, FATTY.

HECK. I'LL BE BETTER THAN FINE, ONCE I GET THOSE KNIVES THAT POP OUT OF MY KNUCKLES.

THAT SHOULD DO IT. WE CAN BEGIN REPRESSURIZING THE BRID--

I'VE GOT THE LAST OF THE BLOOD CLEAN OUT HERE!

--SCRATCH THAT. WE'RE ON OUR WAY OVER, COOPER. C'MON, FATTY.

LET'S GO GET MIDAS.

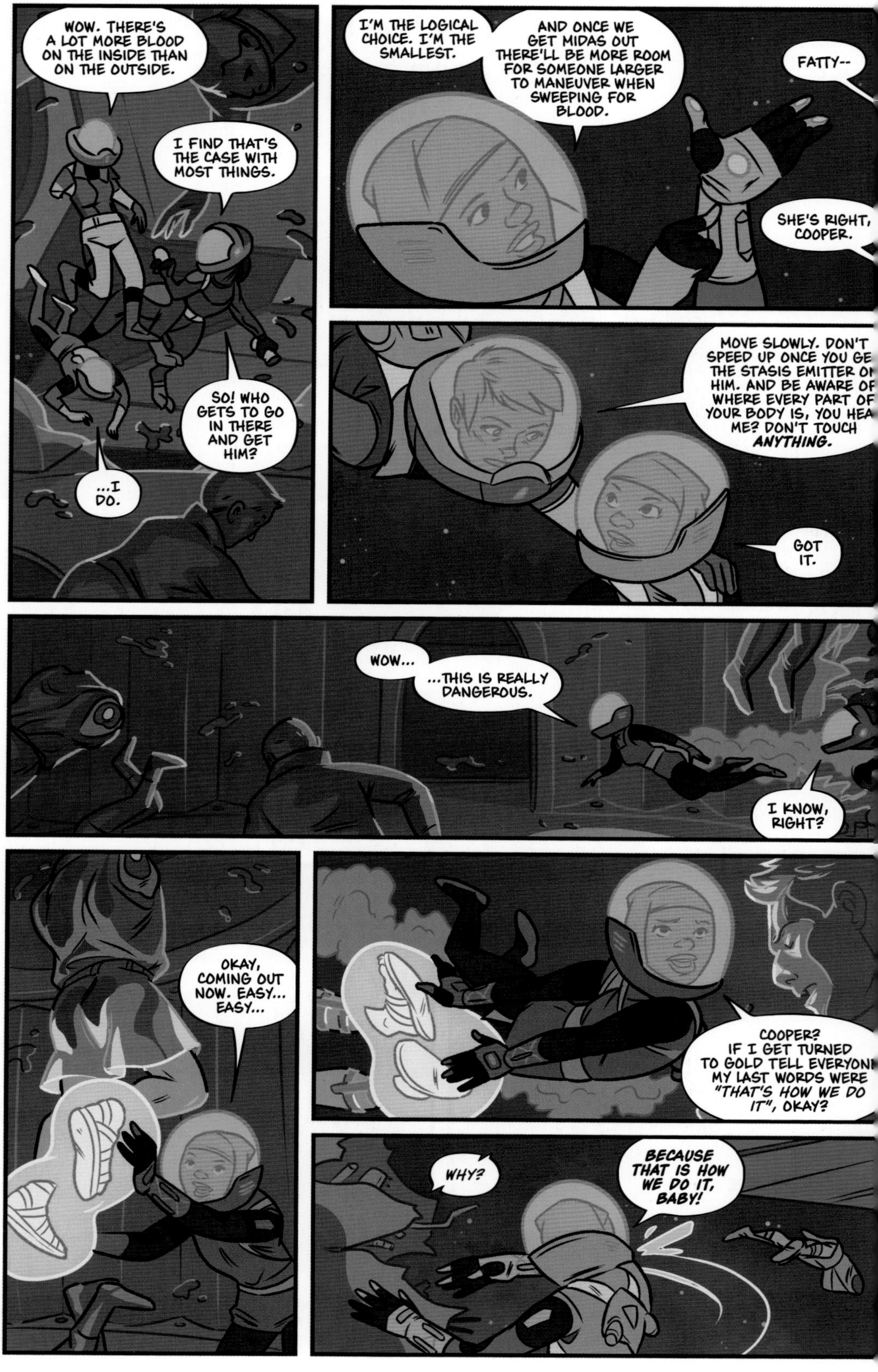
WOW. THERE'S A LOT MORE BLOOD ON THE INSIDE THAN ON THE OUTSIDE.
I FIND THAT'S THE CASE WITH MOST THINGS.
SO! WHO GETS TO GO IN THERE AND GET HIM?
...I DO.
I'M THE LOGICAL CHOICE. I'M THE SMALLEST.
AND ONCE WE GET MIDAS OUT THERE'LL BE MORE ROOM FOR SOMEONE LARGER TO MANEUVER WHEN SWEEPING FOR BLOOD.
FATTY--
SHE'S RIGHT, COOPER.
MOVE SLOWLY. DON'T SPEED UP ONCE YOU GE THE STASIS EMITTER ON HIM. AND BE AWARE OF WHERE EVERY PART OF YOUR BODY IS, YOU HEA ME? DON'T TOUCH *ANYTHING.*
GOT IT.
WOW...
...THIS IS REALLY DANGEROUS.
I KNOW, RIGHT?
OKAY, COMING OUT NOW. EASY... EASY...
COOPER? IF I GET TURNED TO GOLD TELL EVERYON MY LAST WORDS WERE *"THAT'S HOW WE DO IT"*, OKAY?
WHY?
BECAUSE THAT IS HOW WE DO IT, BABY!

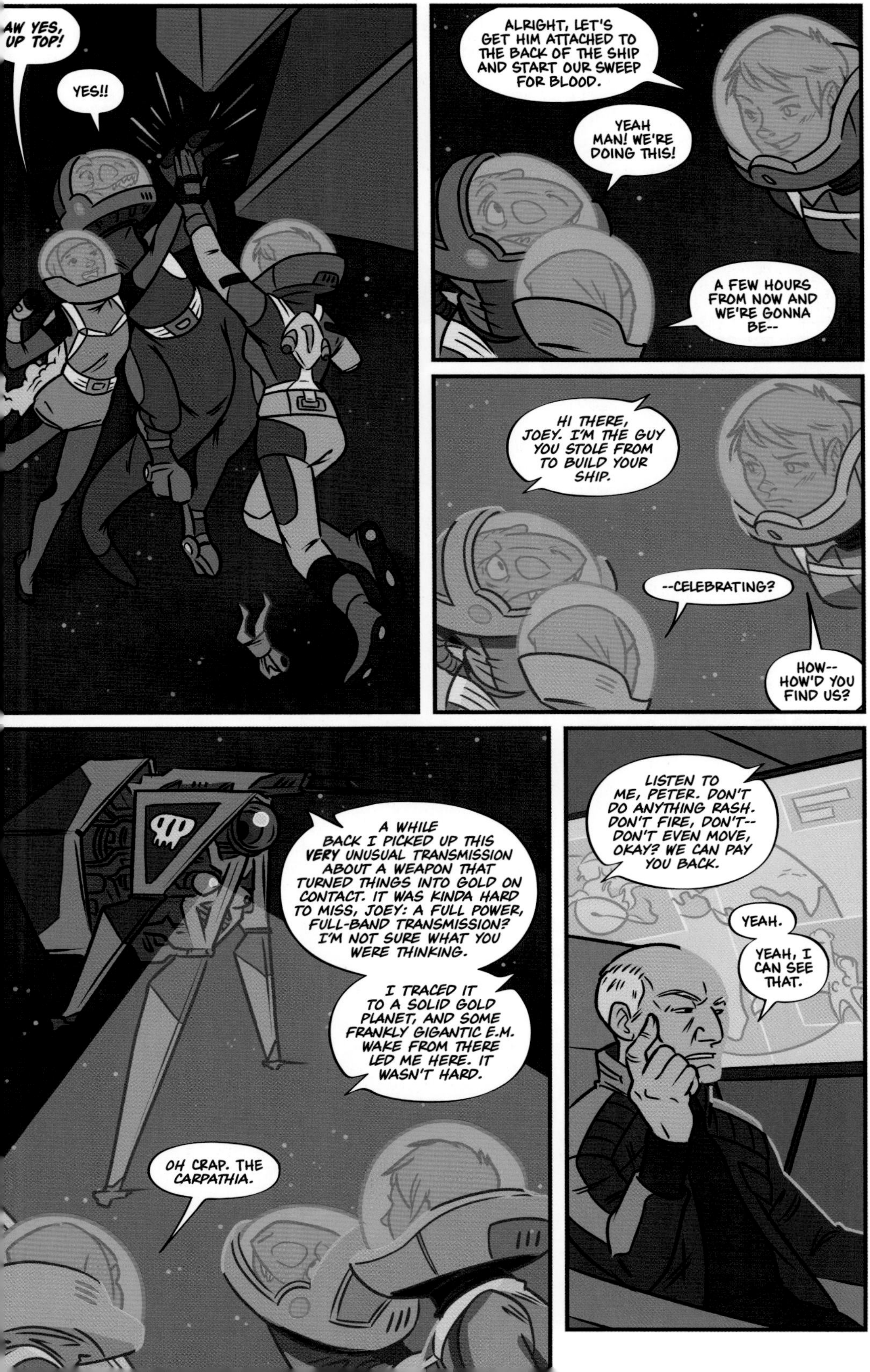
AW YES, UP TOP!
YES!!
ALRIGHT, LET'S GET HIM ATTACHED TO THE BACK OF THE SHIP AND START OUR SWEEP FOR BLOOD.
YEAH MAN! WE'RE DOING THIS!
A FEW HOURS FROM NOW AND WE'RE GONNA BE--
HI THERE, JOEY. I'M THE GUY YOU STOLE FROM TO BUILD YOUR SHIP.
--CELEBRATING?
HOW-- HOW'D YOU FIND US?
A WHILE BACK I PICKED UP THIS VERY UNUSUAL TRANSMISSION ABOUT A WEAPON THAT TURNED THINGS INTO GOLD ON CONTACT. IT WAS KINDA HARD TO MISS, JOEY: A FULL POWER, FULL-BAND TRANSMISSION? I'M NOT SURE WHAT YOU WERE THINKING.
I TRACED IT TO A SOLID GOLD PLANET, AND SOME FRANKLY GIGANTIC E.M. WAKE FROM THERE LED ME HERE. IT WASN'T HARD.
OH CRAP. THE CARPATHIA.
LISTEN TO ME, PETER. DON'T DO ANYTHING RASH. DON'T FIRE, DON'T-- DON'T EVEN MOVE, OKAY? WE CAN PAY YOU BACK.
YEAH.
YEAH, I CAN SEE THAT.

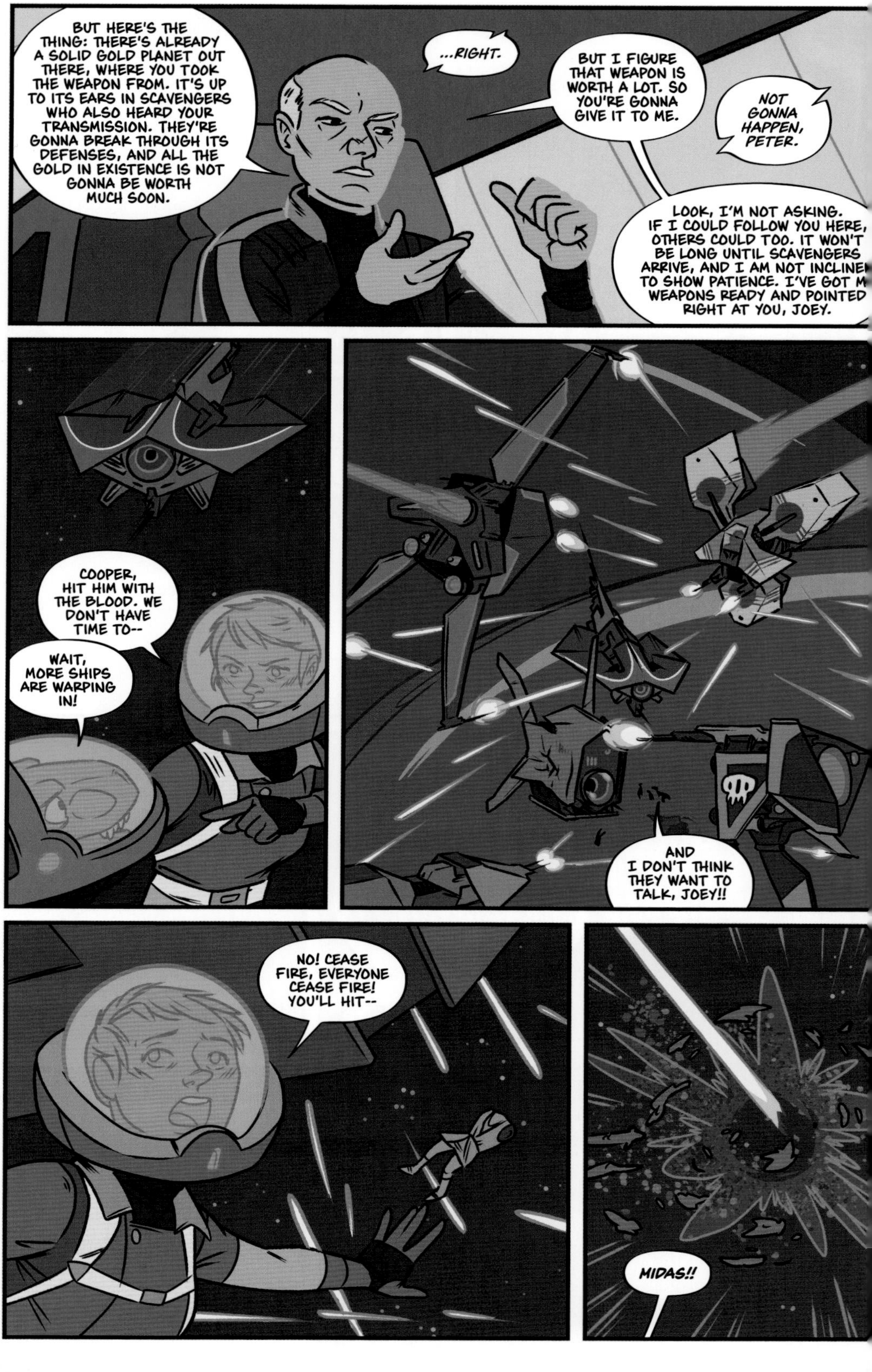
BUT HERE'S THE THING: THERE'S ALREADY A SOLID GOLD PLANET OUT THERE, WHERE YOU TOOK THE WEAPON FROM. IT'S UP TO ITS EARS IN SCAVENGERS WHO ALSO HEARD YOUR TRANSMISSION. THEY'RE GONNA BREAK THROUGH ITS DEFENSES, AND ALL THE GOLD IN EXISTENCE IS NOT GONNA BE WORTH MUCH SOON.
...RIGHT.
BUT I FIGURE THAT WEAPON IS WORTH A LOT. SO YOU'RE GONNA GIVE IT TO ME.
NOT GONNA HAPPEN, PETER.
LOOK, I'M NOT ASKING. IF I COULD FOLLOW YOU HERE, OTHERS COULD TOO. IT WON'T BE LONG UNTIL SCAVENGERS ARRIVE, AND I AM NOT INCLINE TO SHOW PATIENCE. I'VE GOT M WEAPONS READY AND POINTED RIGHT AT YOU, JOEY.
COOPER, HIT HIM WITH THE BLOOD. WE DON'T HAVE TIME TO--
WAIT, MORE SHIPS ARE WARPING IN!
AND I DON'T THINK THEY WANT TO TALK, JOEY!!
NO! CEASE FIRE, EVERYONE CEASE FIRE! YOU'LL HIT--
MIDAS!!

"I'LL JUST GET THINGS READY SO I CAN TURN MYSELF AND ALL MY FRIENDS INTO GOLD STATUES WITH SOME SPACE BLOOD."

CHAPTER
EIGHT

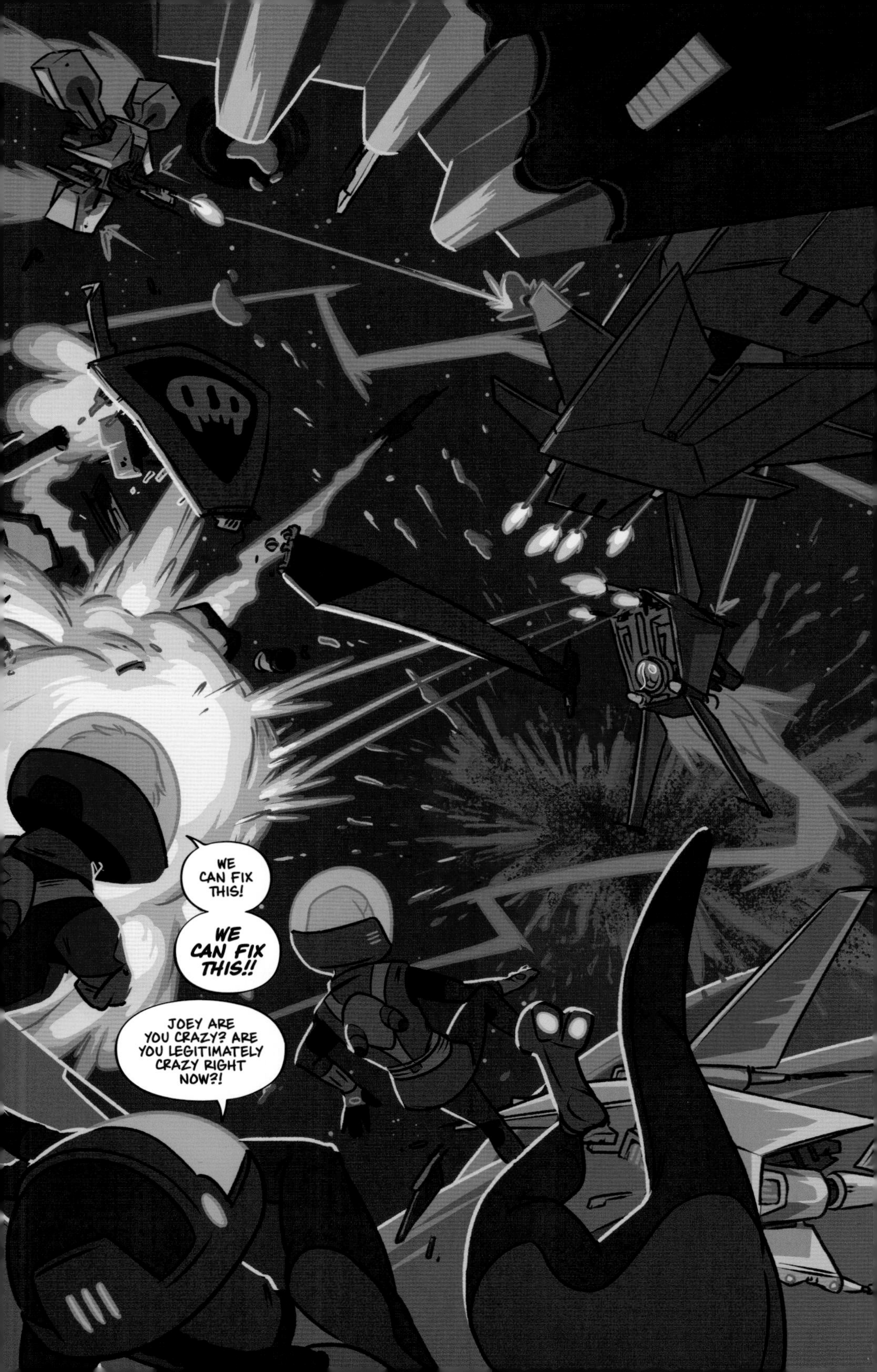
WE CAN FIX THIS!
WE CAN FIX THIS!!
JOEY ARE YOU CRAZY? ARE YOU LEGITIMATELY CRAZY RIGHT NOW?!

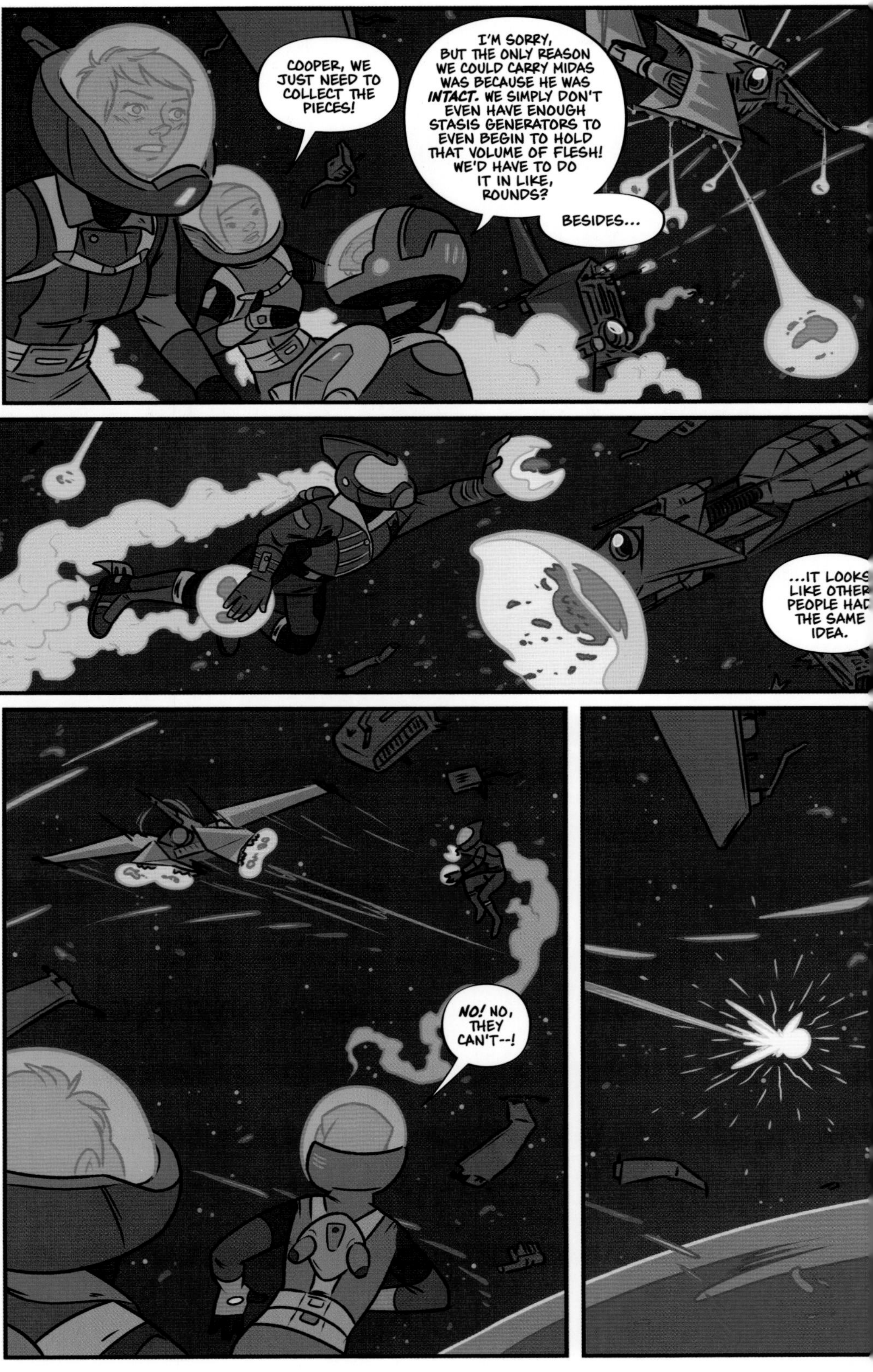
COOPER, WE JUST NEED TO COLLECT THE PIECES!
I'M SORRY, BUT THE ONLY REASON WE COULD CARRY MIDAS WAS BECAUSE HE WAS *INTACT.* WE SIMPLY DON'T EVEN HAVE ENOUGH STASIS GENERATORS TO EVEN BEGIN TO HOLD THAT VOLUME OF FLESH! WE'D HAVE TO DO IT IN LIKE, ROUNDS?
BESIDES...
...IT LOOKS LIKE OTHER PEOPLE HAD THE SAME IDEA.
NO! NO, THEY CAN'T--!

OH MY GOD. HE'S GONE.

HE'S REALLY GONE.

NO. *NO,* WE CAN GET HIM BACK. THERE'S GOTTA BE A WAY. IF WE CAN TRACK THEM, *FIND* THEM--

JOEY, *LISTEN TO ME.* BY THE TIME WE GET BACK IN THE *PROSPECT,* FINDING THOSE SHIPS IS GONNA BE A NIGHTMARE.

AND UNLESS WE FIND THEM AND DESTROY THEM WHILE *ALSO* DESTROYING EVERY ONE OF THESE SHIPS HERE *AND* ALL THOSE THAT COME AFTERWARD, MORE FLESH IS GOING TO GET OUT THERE.

HE'S RIGHT. MIDAS IS OUT OF OUR CONTROL. OUT OF ANYONE'S.

NO, WE FIX IT. WE'LL FIX IT FATTY, OKAY?

I WILL *NOT* BE RESPONSIBLE FOR THIS. I'M NOT GONNA BE THE ONE WHO DESTROYED EVERYTHING.

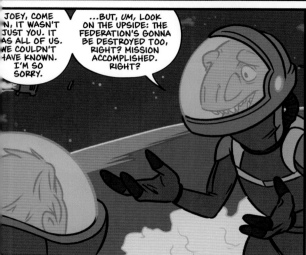

JOEY, COME ON, IT WASN'T JUST YOU. IT WAS ALL OF US. WE COULDN'T HAVE KNOWN. I'M SO SORRY.

...BUT, UM, LOOK ON THE UPSIDE: THE FEDERATION'S GONNA BE DESTROYED TOO, RIGHT? MISSION ACCOMPLISHED. RIGHT?

COOPER, THAT IS NOT HELPING.

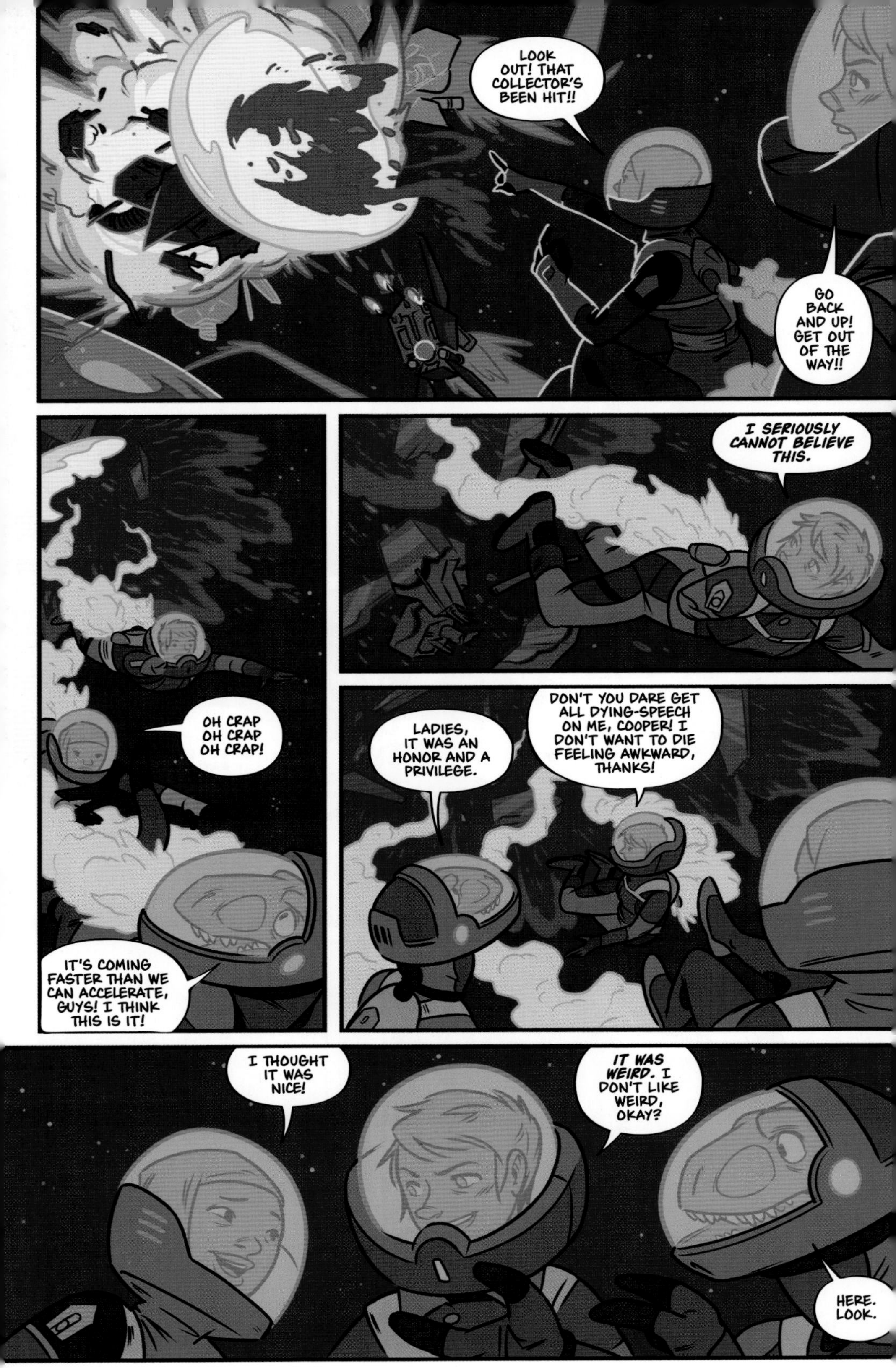
LOOK OUT! THAT COLLECTOR'S BEEN HIT!!
GO BACK AND UP! GET OUT OF THE WAY!!
OH CRAP OH CRAP OH CRAP!
IT'S COMING FASTER THAN WE CAN ACCELERATE, GUYS! I THINK THIS IS IT!
I SERIOUSLY CANNOT BELIEVE THIS.
LADIES, IT WAS AN HONOR AND A PRIVILEGE.
DON'T YOU DARE GET ALL DYING-SPEECH ON ME, COOPER! I DON'T WANT TO DIE FEELING AWKWARD, THANKS!
I THOUGHT IT WAS NICE!
IT WAS WEIRD. I DON'T LIKE WEIRD, OKAY?
HERE. LOOK.

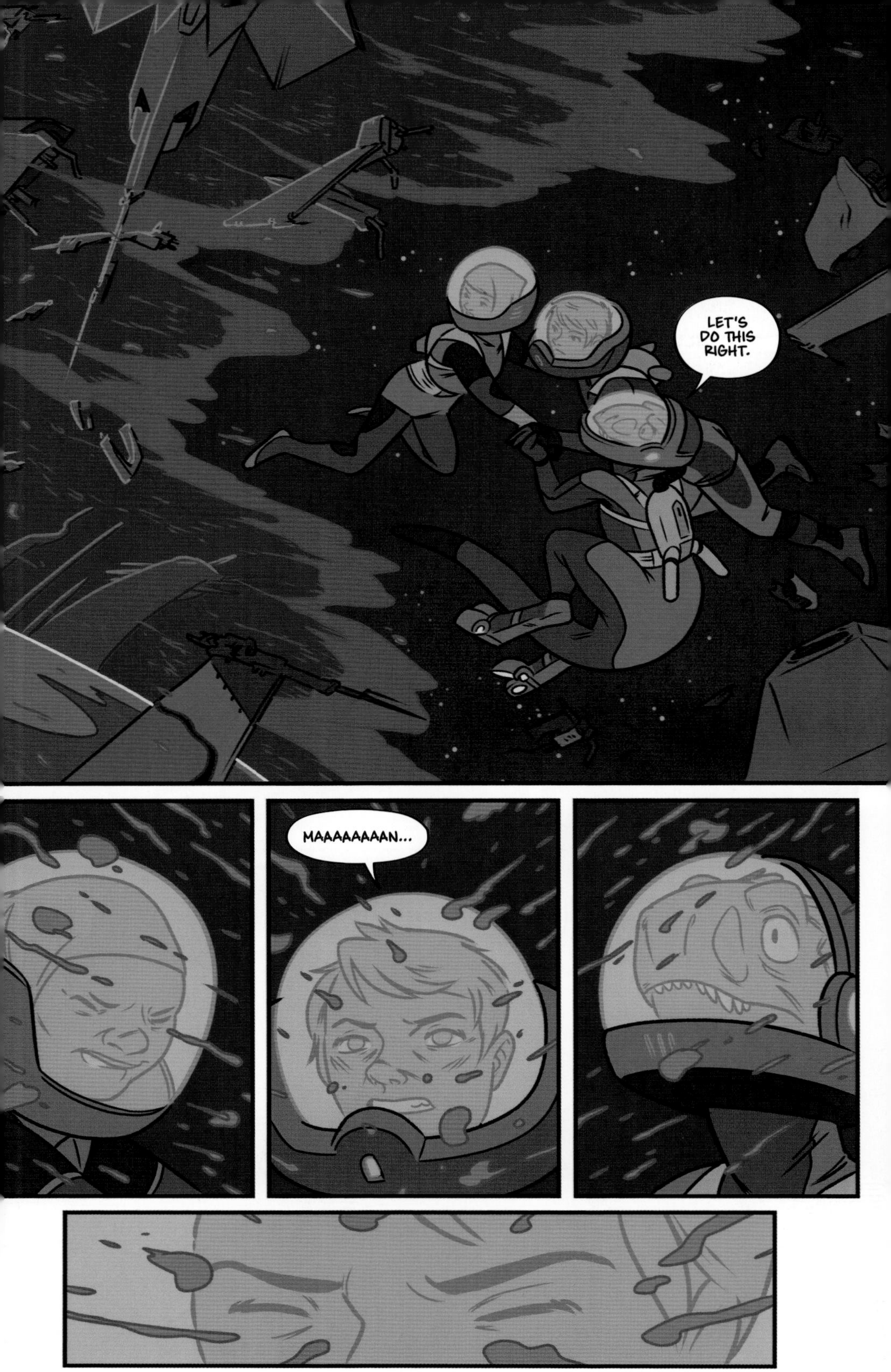
LET'S DO THIS RIGHT.
MAAAAAAAAN...

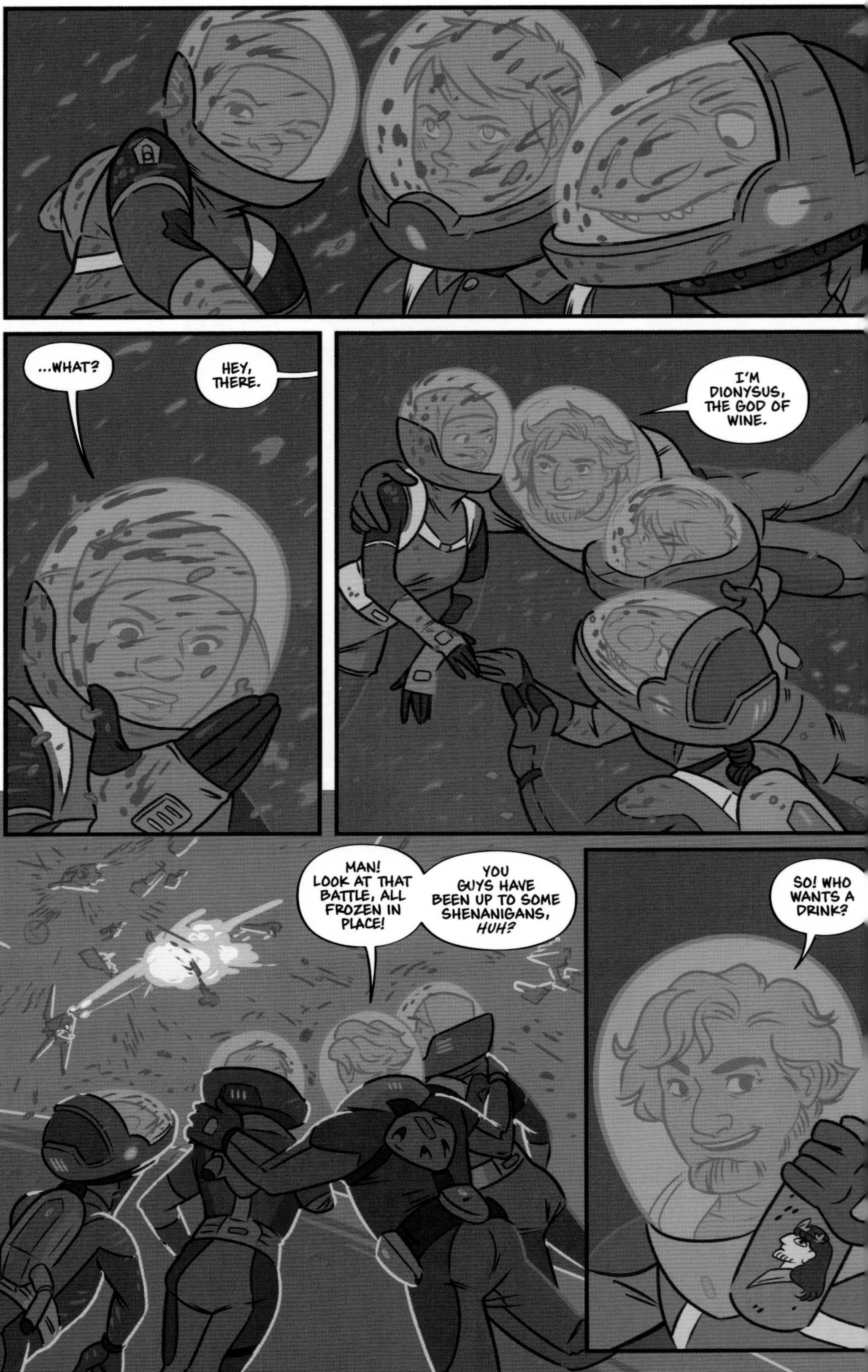

...WHAT?
HEY, THERE.
I'M DIONYSUS, THE GOD OF WINE.
MAN! LOOK AT THAT BATTLE, ALL FROZEN IN PLACE!
YOU GUYS HAVE BEEN UP TO SOME SHENANIGANS, *HUH?*
SO! WHO WANTS A DRINK?

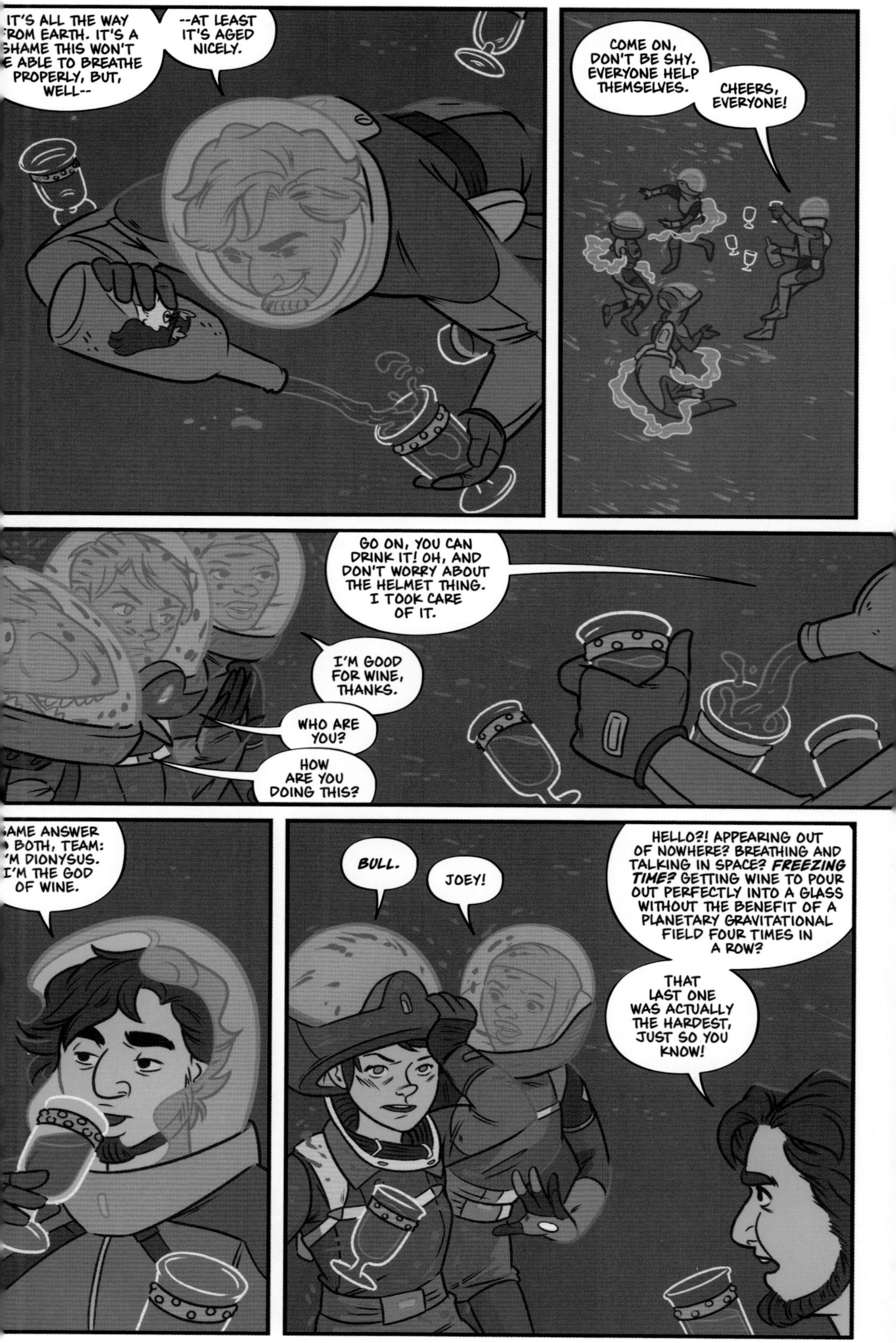

IT'S ALL THE WAY FROM EARTH. IT'S A SHAME THIS WON'T E ABLE TO BREATHE PROPERLY, BUT, WELL--
--AT LEAST IT'S AGED NICELY.
COME ON, DON'T BE SHY. EVERYONE HELP THEMSELVES.
CHEERS, EVERYONE!
GO ON, YOU CAN DRINK IT! OH, AND DON'T WORRY ABOUT THE HELMET THING. I TOOK CARE OF IT.
I'M GOOD FOR WINE, THANKS.
WHO ARE YOU?
HOW ARE YOU DOING THIS?
AME ANSWER BOTH, TEAM: 'M DIONYSUS. I'M THE GOD OF WINE.
BULL.
JOEY!
HELLO?! APPEARING OUT OF NOWHERE? BREATHING AND TALKING IN SPACE? FREEZING TIME? GETTING WINE TO POUR OUT PERFECTLY INTO A GLASS WITHOUT THE BENEFIT OF A PLANETARY GRAVITATIONAL FIELD FOUR TIMES IN A ROW?
THAT LAST ONE WAS ACTUALLY THE HARDEST, JUST SO YOU KNOW!

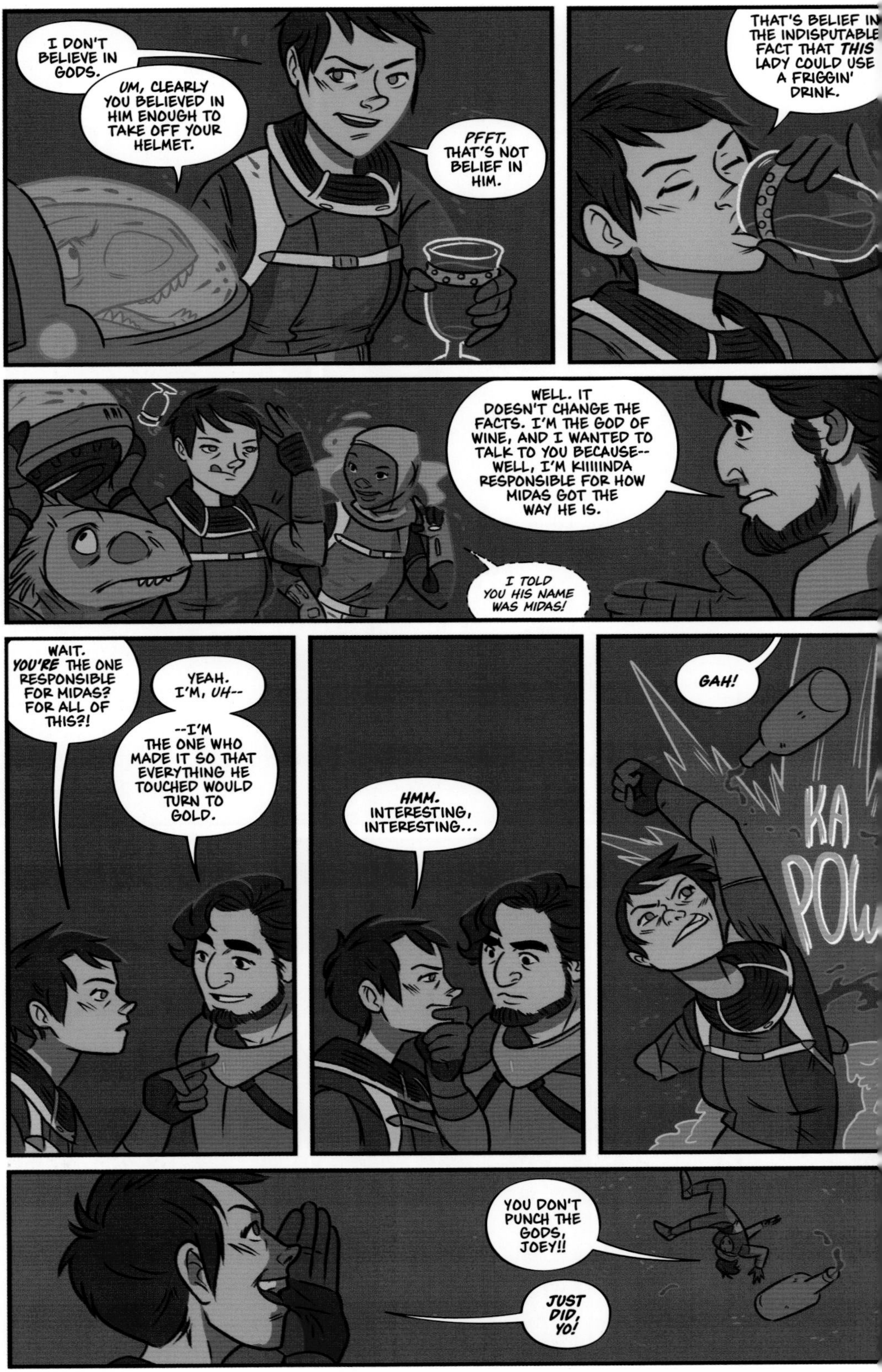
I DON'T BELIEVE IN GODS.
UM, CLEARLY YOU BELIEVED IN HIM ENOUGH TO TAKE OFF YOUR HELMET.
PFFT, THAT'S NOT BELIEF IN HIM.
THAT'S BELIEF IN THE INDISPUTABLE FACT THAT THIS LADY COULD USE A FRIGGIN' DRINK.
WELL. IT DOESN'T CHANGE THE FACTS. I'M THE GOD OF WINE, AND I WANTED TO TALK TO YOU BECAUSE-- WELL, I'M KIIIIINDA RESPONSIBLE FOR HOW MIDAS GOT THE WAY HE IS.
I TOLD YOU HIS NAME WAS MIDAS!
WAIT. YOU'RE THE ONE RESPONSIBLE FOR MIDAS? FOR ALL OF THIS?!
YEAH. I'M, UH--
--I'M THE ONE WHO MADE IT SO THAT EVERYTHING HE TOUCHED WOULD TURN TO GOLD.
HMM. INTERESTING, INTERESTING...
GAH!
KA POW
YOU DON'T PUNCH THE GODS, JOEY!!
JUST DID, YO!

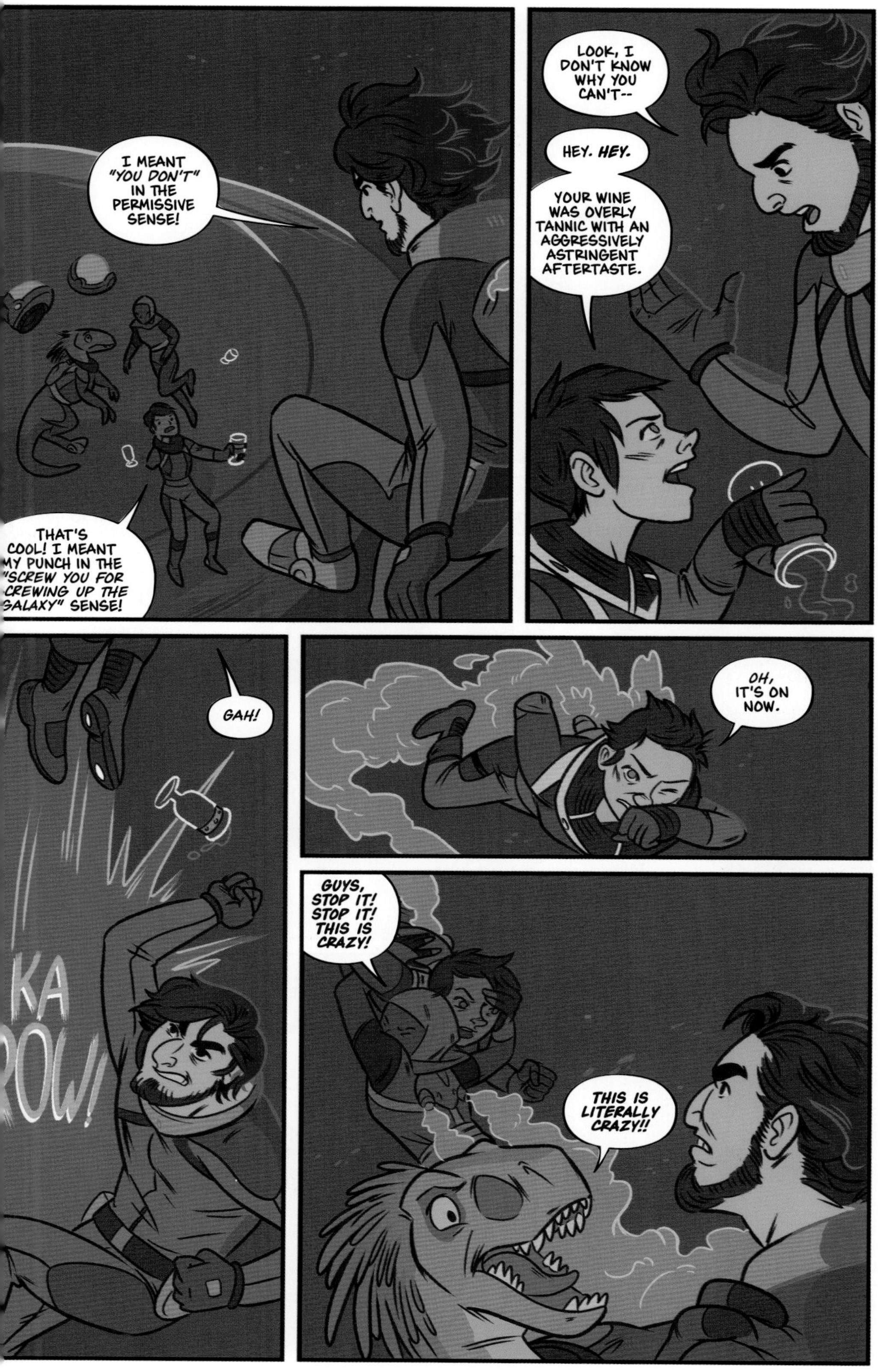
I MEANT "YOU DON'T" IN THE PERMISSIVE SENSE!
THAT'S COOL! I MEANT MY PUNCH IN THE "SCREW YOU FOR SCREWING UP THE GALAXY" SENSE!
LOOK, I DON'T KNOW WHY YOU CAN'T--
HEY. HEY.
YOUR WINE WAS OVERLY TANNIC WITH AN AGGRESSIVELY ASTRINGENT AFTERTASTE.
GAH!
KA ROW!
OH, IT'S ON NOW.
GUYS, STOP IT! STOP IT! THIS IS CRAZY!
THIS IS LITERALLY CRAZY!!

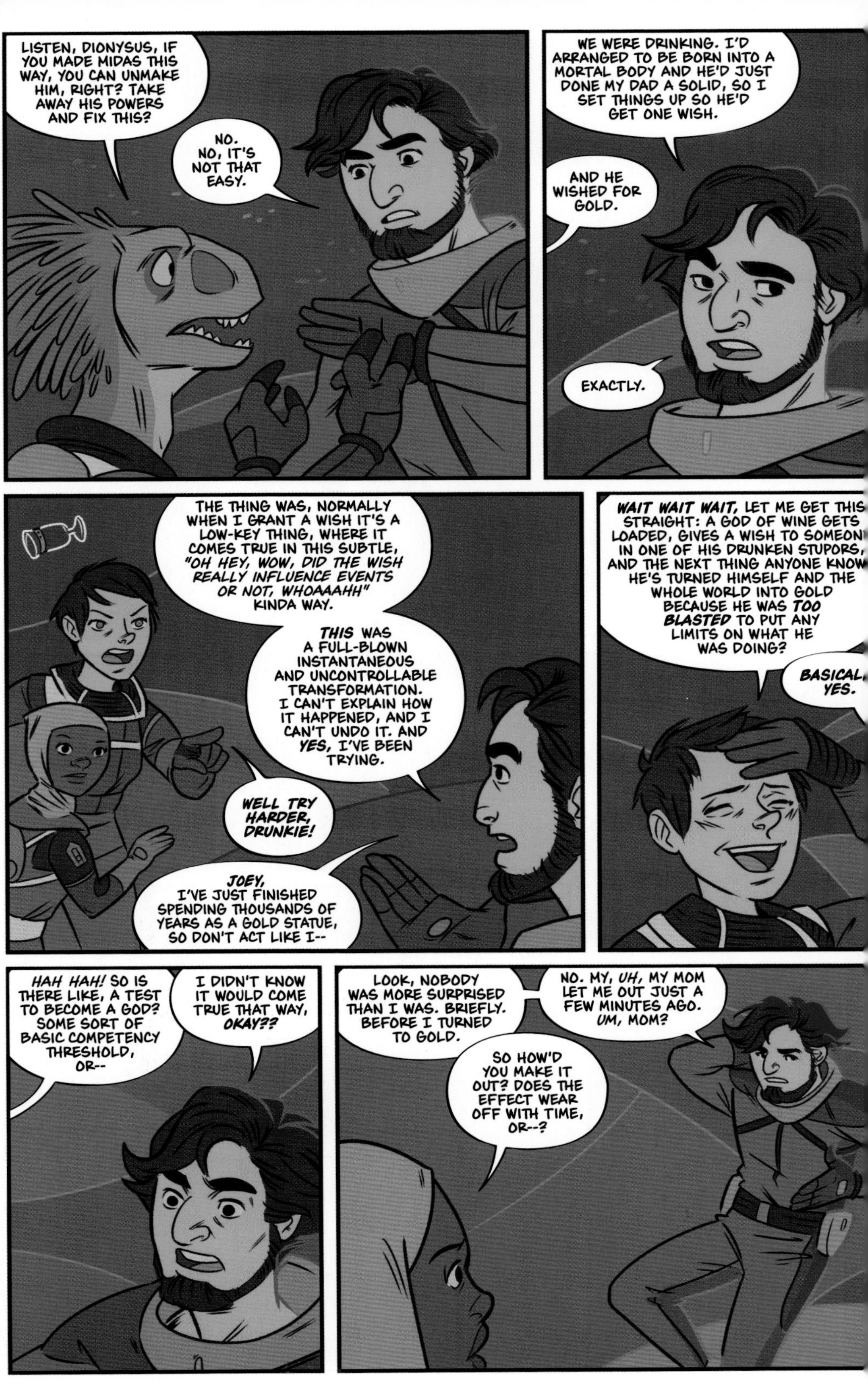
LISTEN, DIONYSUS, IF YOU MADE MIDAS THIS WAY, YOU CAN UNMAKE HIM, RIGHT? TAKE AWAY HIS POWERS AND FIX THIS?
NO. NO, IT'S NOT THAT EASY.
WE WERE DRINKING. I'D ARRANGED TO BE BORN INTO A MORTAL BODY AND HE'D JUST DONE MY DAD A SOLID, SO I SET THINGS UP SO HE'D GET ONE WISH.
AND HE WISHED FOR GOLD.
EXACTLY.
THE THING WAS, NORMALLY WHEN I GRANT A WISH IT'S A LOW-KEY THING, WHERE IT COMES TRUE IN THIS SUBTLE, *"OH HEY, WOW, DID THE WISH REALLY INFLUENCE EVENTS OR NOT, WHOAAAHH"* KINDA WAY.
THIS WAS A FULL-BLOWN INSTANTANEOUS AND UNCONTROLLABLE TRANSFORMATION. I CAN'T EXPLAIN HOW IT HAPPENED, AND I CAN'T UNDO IT. AND *YES*, I'VE BEEN TRYING.
WELL TRY HARDER, DRUNKIE!
JOEY, I'VE JUST FINISHED SPENDING THOUSANDS OF YEARS AS A GOLD STATUE, SO DON'T ACT LIKE I--
WAIT WAIT WAIT, LET ME GET THIS STRAIGHT: A GOD OF WINE GETS LOADED, GIVES A WISH TO SOMEON IN ONE OF HIS DRUNKEN STUPORS, AND THE NEXT THING ANYONE KNOW HE'S TURNED HIMSELF AND THE WHOLE WORLD INTO GOLD BECAUSE HE WAS *TOO BLASTED* TO PUT ANY LIMITS ON WHAT HE WAS DOING?
BASICAL YES.
HAH HAH! SO IS THERE LIKE, A TEST TO BECOME A GOD? SOME SORT OF BASIC COMPETENCY THRESHOLD, OR--
I DIDN'T KNOW IT WOULD COME TRUE THAT WAY, *OKAY??*
LOOK, NOBODY WAS MORE SURPRISED THAN I WAS. BRIEFLY. BEFORE I TURNED TO GOLD.
SO HOW'D YOU MAKE IT OUT? DOES THE EFFECT WEAR OFF WITH TIME, OR--?
NO. MY, *UH*, MY MOM LET ME OUT JUST A FEW MINUTES AGO. *UM, MOM?*

HELLO, DIONYSUS. HELLO, OTHER LIFE.

COOPER, FATIMA, JOEY, MAY I INTRODUCE MY MOM, *ANANKE*: CO-CREATOR OF THE UNIVERSE AND GOD OF NATURAL LAW.

OH MY GOD, I'M GONNA PUNCH HER TOO.

JOEY!

SO RARELY DOES MORTAL LIFE UNDERSTAND THE LARGER PICTURE OF THEIR ACTIONS: HOW THEY GOT HERE, HOW THEY'VE ALTERED THE COURSE OF THE LIVES THAT COME AFTER THEM. YOU THREE WERE CRITICAL TO THE STORY OF THIS UNIVERSE, AND I WANTED YOU TO KNOW.

I WANTED YOU TO SEE.

BUT-- SEE WHAT? THAT MIDAS WAS A STUPID ACCIDENT AND WE LET HIM OUT?

NO.

I WANTED YOU TO SEE HOW THE UNIVERSE ENDS.

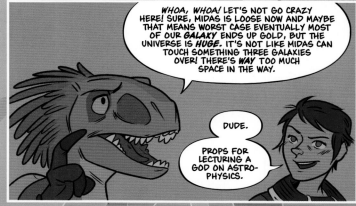

WHOA, WHOA! LET'S NOT GO CRAZY HERE! SURE, MIDAS IS LOOSE NOW AND MAYBE THAT MEANS WORST CASE EVENTUALLY MOST OF OUR *GALAXY* ENDS UP GOLD, BUT THE UNIVERSE IS *HUGE*. IT'S NOT LIKE MIDAS CAN TOUCH SOMETHING THREE GALAXIES OVER! THERE'S *WAY* TOO MUCH SPACE IN THE WAY.

DUDE.

PROPS FOR LECTURING A GOD ON ASTRO-PHYSICS.

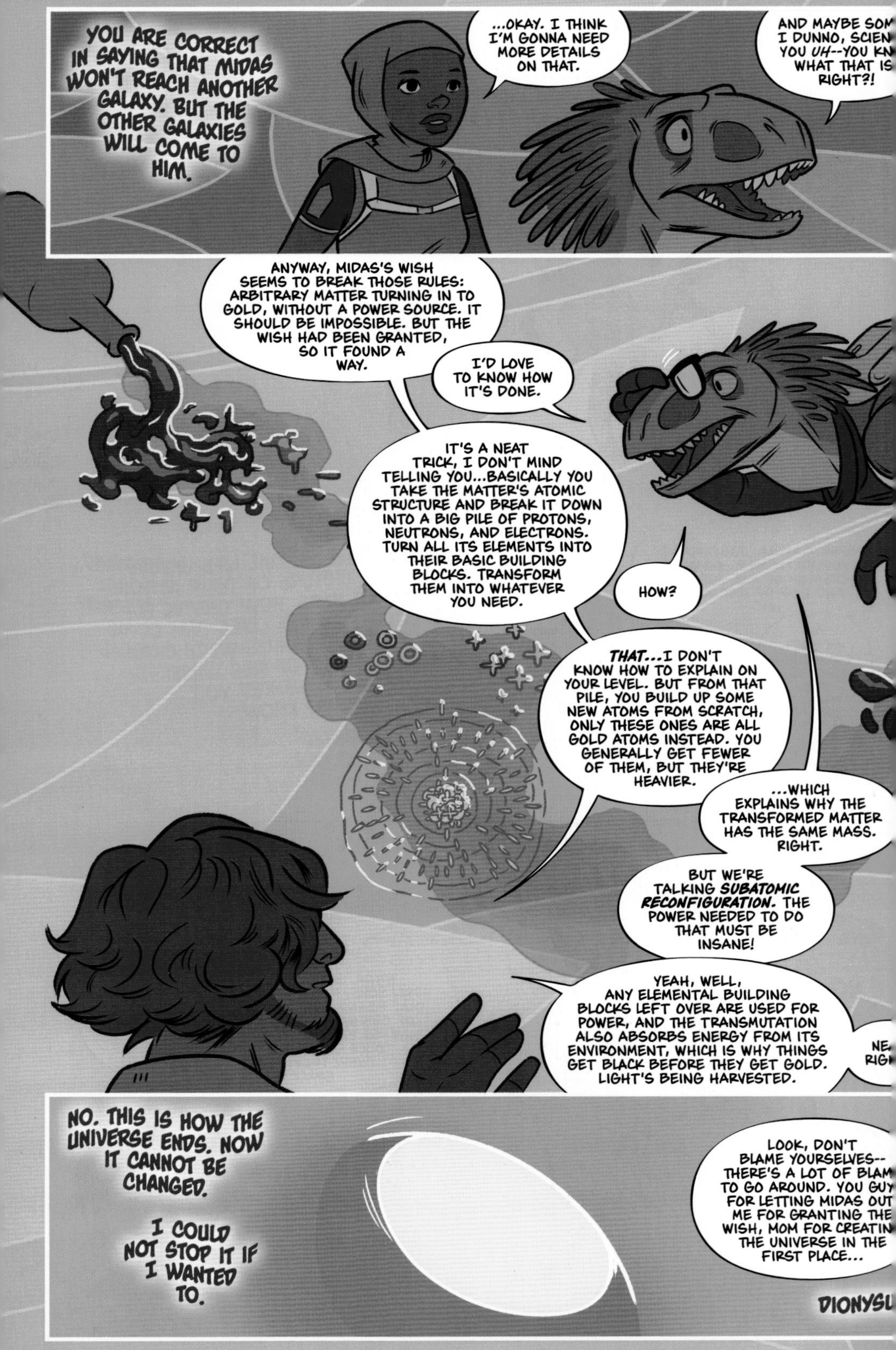
YOU ARE CORRECT IN SAYING THAT MIDAS WON'T REACH ANOTHER GALAXY. BUT THE OTHER GALAXIES WILL COME TO HIM.
...OKAY. I THINK I'M GONNA NEED MORE DETAILS ON THAT.
AND MAYBE SOM I DUNNO, SCIEN YOU UH--YOU KN WHAT THAT IS RIGHT?!
ANYWAY, MIDAS'S WISH SEEMS TO BREAK THOSE RULES: ARBITRARY MATTER TURNING IN TO GOLD, WITHOUT A POWER SOURCE. IT SHOULD BE IMPOSSIBLE. BUT THE WISH HAD BEEN GRANTED, SO IT FOUND A WAY.
I'D LOVE TO KNOW HOW IT'S DONE.
IT'S A NEAT TRICK, I DON'T MIND TELLING YOU...BASICALLY YOU TAKE THE MATTER'S ATOMIC STRUCTURE AND BREAK IT DOWN INTO A BIG PILE OF PROTONS, NEUTRONS, AND ELECTRONS. TURN ALL ITS ELEMENTS INTO THEIR BASIC BUILDING BLOCKS. TRANSFORM THEM INTO WHATEVER YOU NEED.
HOW?
THAT...I DON'T KNOW HOW TO EXPLAIN ON YOUR LEVEL. BUT FROM THAT PILE, YOU BUILD UP SOME NEW ATOMS FROM SCRATCH, ONLY THESE ONES ARE ALL GOLD ATOMS INSTEAD. YOU GENERALLY GET FEWER OF THEM, BUT THEY'RE HEAVIER.
...WHICH EXPLAINS WHY THE TRANSFORMED MATTER HAS THE SAME MASS. RIGHT.
BUT WE'RE TALKING SUBATOMIC RECONFIGURATION. THE POWER NEEDED TO DO THAT MUST BE INSANE!
YEAH, WELL, ANY ELEMENTAL BUILDING BLOCKS LEFT OVER ARE USED FOR POWER, AND THE TRANSMUTATION ALSO ABSORBS ENERGY FROM ITS ENVIRONMENT, WHICH IS WHY THINGS GET BLACK BEFORE THEY GET GOLD. LIGHT'S BEING HARVESTED.
NE RIG
NO. THIS IS HOW THE UNIVERSE ENDS. NOW IT CANNOT BE CHANGED.
I COULD NOT STOP IT IF I WANTED TO.
LOOK, DON'T BLAME YOURSELVES-- THERE'S A LOT OF BLAM TO GO AROUND. YOU GUY FOR LETTING MIDAS OUT ME FOR GRANTING THE WISH, MOM FOR CREATIN THE UNIVERSE IN THE FIRST PLACE...
DIONYSU

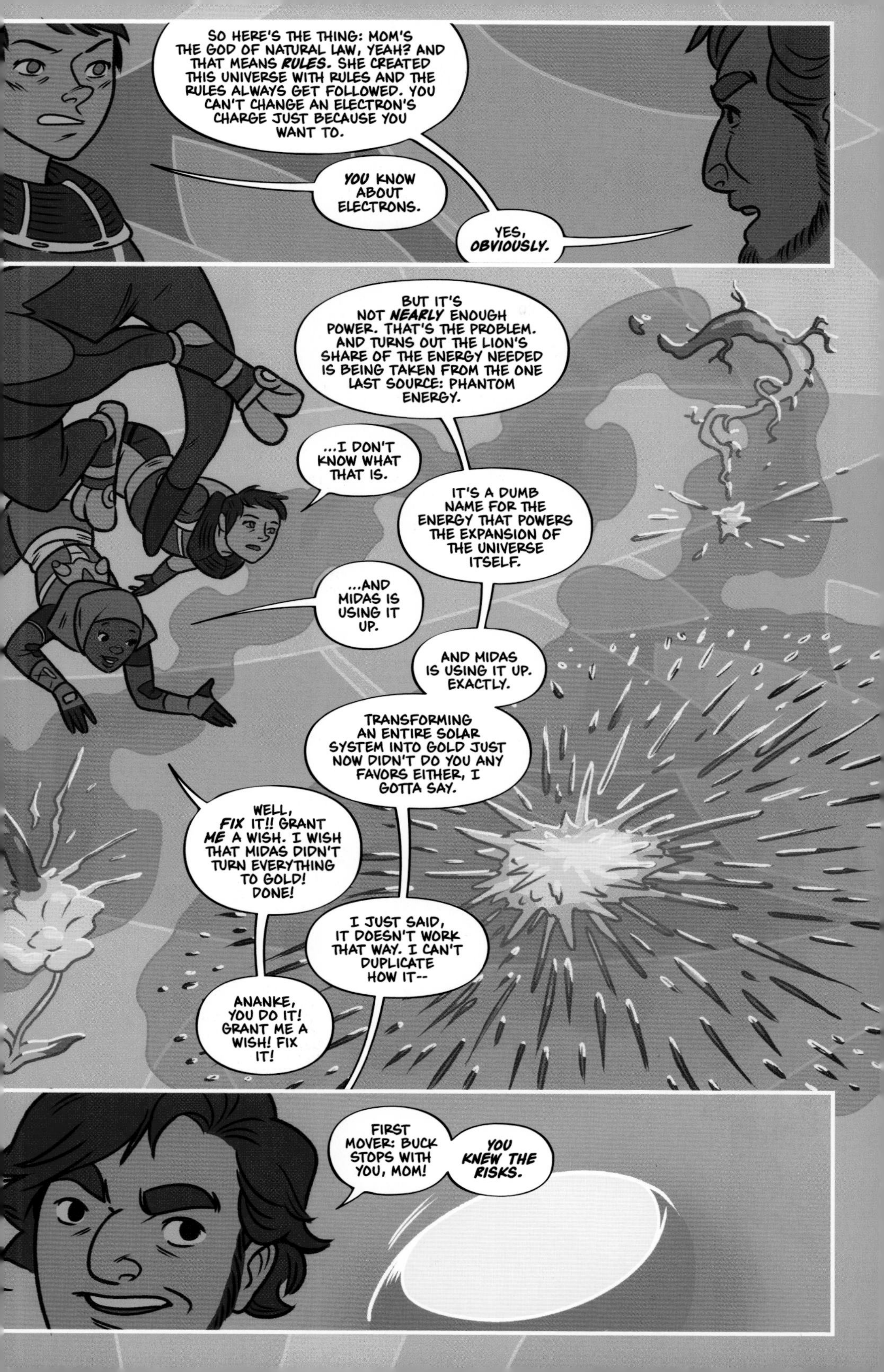
SO HERE'S THE THING: MOM'S THE GOD OF NATURAL LAW, YEAH? AND THAT MEANS *RULES.* SHE CREATED THIS UNIVERSE WITH RULES AND THE RULES ALWAYS GET FOLLOWED. YOU CAN'T CHANGE AN ELECTRON'S CHARGE JUST BECAUSE YOU WANT TO.
YOU KNOW ABOUT ELECTRONS.
YES, *OBVIOUSLY.*
BUT IT'S NOT *NEARLY* ENOUGH POWER. THAT'S THE PROBLEM. AND TURNS OUT THE LION'S SHARE OF THE ENERGY NEEDED IS BEING TAKEN FROM THE ONE LAST SOURCE: PHANTOM ENERGY.
...I DON'T KNOW WHAT THAT IS.
IT'S A DUMB NAME FOR THE ENERGY THAT POWERS THE EXPANSION OF THE UNIVERSE ITSELF.
...AND MIDAS IS USING IT UP.
AND MIDAS IS USING IT UP. EXACTLY.
TRANSFORMING AN ENTIRE SOLAR SYSTEM INTO GOLD JUST NOW DIDN'T DO YOU ANY FAVORS EITHER, I GOTTA SAY.
WELL, *FIX* IT!! GRANT *ME* A WISH. I WISH THAT MIDAS DIDN'T TURN EVERYTHING TO GOLD! DONE!
I JUST SAID, IT DOESN'T WORK THAT WAY. I CAN'T DUPLICATE HOW IT--
ANANKE, YOU DO IT! GRANT ME A WISH! FIX IT!
FIRST MOVER: BUCK STOPS WITH YOU, MOM!
YOU KNEW THE RISKS.

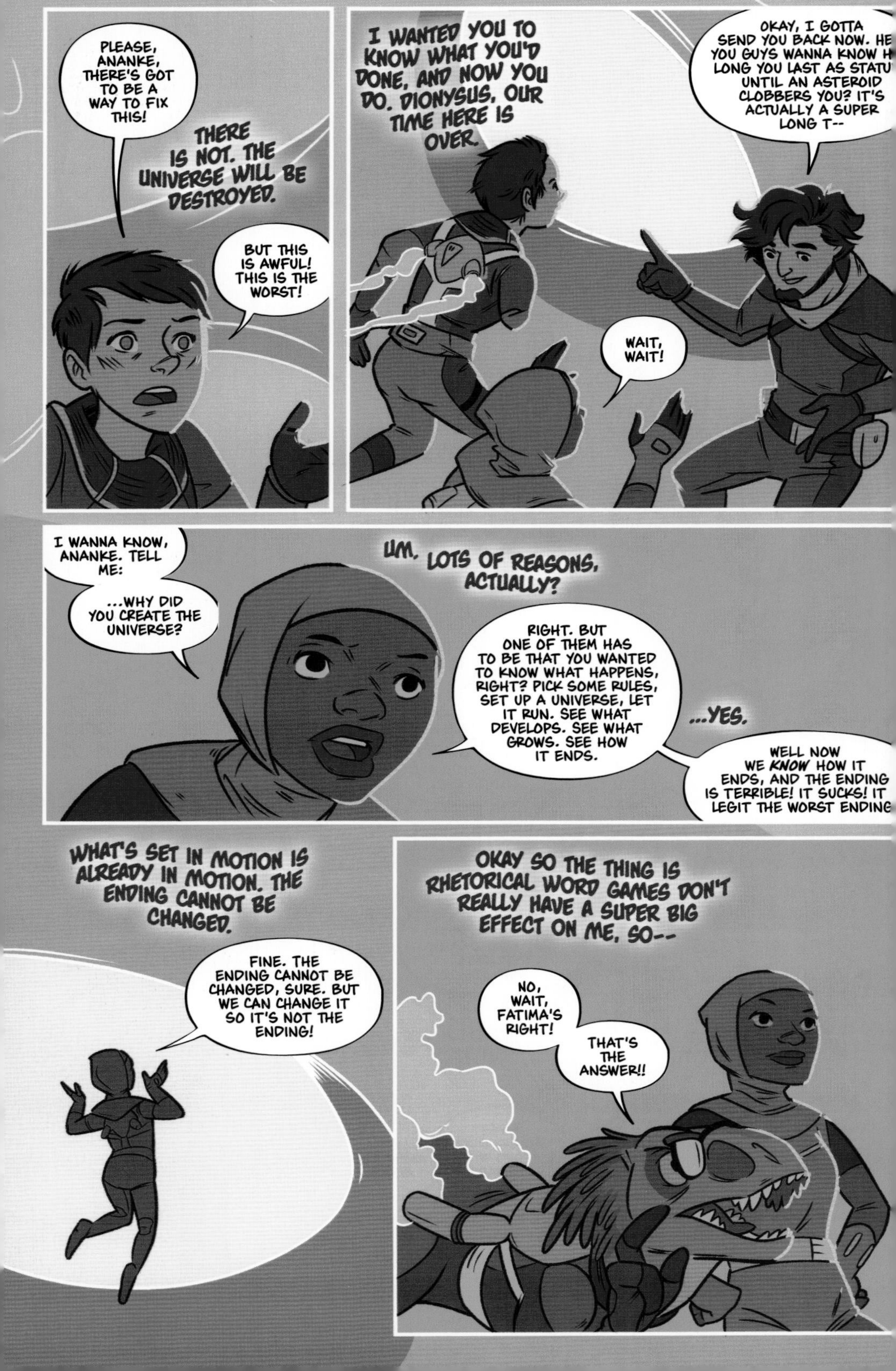
PLEASE, ANANKE, THERE'S GOT TO BE A WAY TO FIX THIS!
THERE IS NOT. THE UNIVERSE WILL BE DESTROYED.
BUT THIS IS AWFUL! THIS IS THE WORST!
I WANTED YOU TO KNOW WHAT YOU'D DONE, AND NOW YOU DO. DIONYSUS, OUR TIME HERE IS OVER.
OKAY, I GOTTA SEND YOU BACK NOW. HE YOU GUYS WANNA KNOW H LONG YOU LAST AS STATU UNTIL AN ASTEROID CLOBBERS YOU? IT'S ACTUALLY A SUPER LONG T--
WAIT, WAIT!
I WANNA KNOW, ANANKE. TELL ME:
...WHY DID YOU CREATE THE UNIVERSE?
UM. LOTS OF REASONS, ACTUALLY?
RIGHT. BUT ONE OF THEM HAS TO BE THAT YOU WANTED TO KNOW WHAT HAPPENS, RIGHT? PICK SOME RULES, SET UP A UNIVERSE, LET IT RUN. SEE WHAT DEVELOPS. SEE WHAT GROWS. SEE HOW IT ENDS.
...YES.
WELL NOW WE KNOW HOW IT ENDS, AND THE ENDING IS TERRIBLE! IT SUCKS! IT LEGIT THE WORST ENDING
WHAT'S SET IN MOTION IS ALREADY IN MOTION. THE ENDING CANNOT BE CHANGED.
FINE. THE ENDING CANNOT BE CHANGED, SURE. BUT WE CAN CHANGE IT SO IT'S NOT THE ENDING!
OKAY SO THE THING IS RHETORICAL WORD GAMES DON'T REALLY HAVE A SUPER BIG EFFECT ON ME, SO--
NO, WAIT, FATIMA'S RIGHT!
THAT'S THE ANSWER!!

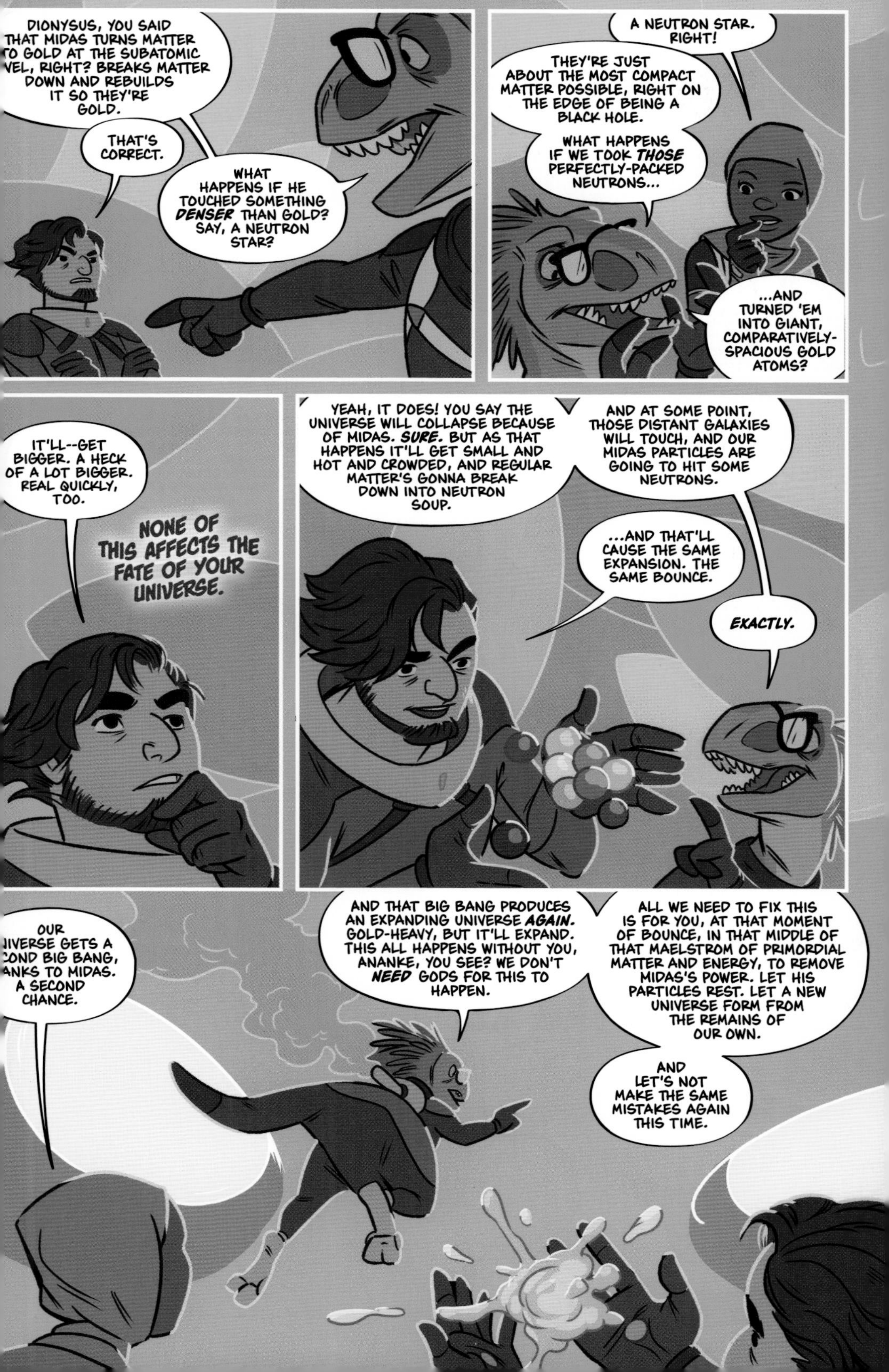

DIONYSUS, YOU SAID THAT MIDAS TURNS MATTER TO GOLD AT THE SUBATOMIC LEVEL, RIGHT? BREAKS MATTER DOWN AND REBUILDS IT SO THEY'RE GOLD.
THAT'S CORRECT.
WHAT HAPPENS IF HE TOUCHED SOMETHING *DENSER* THAN GOLD? SAY, A NEUTRON STAR?
A NEUTRON STAR. RIGHT!
THEY'RE JUST ABOUT THE MOST COMPACT MATTER POSSIBLE, RIGHT ON THE EDGE OF BEING A BLACK HOLE.
WHAT HAPPENS IF WE TOOK *THOSE* PERFECTLY-PACKED NEUTRONS...
...AND TURNED 'EM INTO GIANT, COMPARATIVELY-SPACIOUS GOLD ATOMS?
IT'LL--GET BIGGER. A HECK OF A LOT BIGGER. REAL QUICKLY, TOO.
NONE OF THIS AFFECTS THE FATE OF YOUR UNIVERSE.
YEAH, IT DOES! YOU SAY THE UNIVERSE WILL COLLAPSE BECAUSE OF MIDAS. *SURE.* BUT AS THAT HAPPENS IT'LL GET SMALL AND HOT AND CROWDED, AND REGULAR MATTER'S GONNA BREAK DOWN INTO NEUTRON SOUP.
AND AT SOME POINT, THOSE DISTANT GALAXIES WILL TOUCH, AND OUR MIDAS PARTICLES ARE GOING TO HIT SOME NEUTRONS.
...AND THAT'LL CAUSE THE SAME EXPANSION. THE SAME BOUNCE.
EXACTLY.
OUR UNIVERSE GETS A SECOND BIG BANG, THANKS TO MIDAS. A SECOND CHANCE.
AND THAT BIG BANG PRODUCES AN EXPANDING UNIVERSE *AGAIN.* GOLD-HEAVY, BUT IT'LL EXPAND. THIS ALL HAPPENS WITHOUT YOU, ANANKE, YOU SEE? WE DON'T *NEED* GODS FOR THIS TO HAPPEN.
ALL WE NEED TO FIX THIS IS FOR YOU, AT THAT MOMENT OF BOUNCE, IN THAT MIDDLE OF THAT MAELSTROM OF PRIMORDIAL MATTER AND ENERGY, TO REMOVE MIDAS'S POWER. LET HIS PARTICLES REST. LET A NEW UNIVERSE FORM FROM THE REMAINS OF OUR OWN.
AND LET'S NOT MAKE THE SAME MISTAKES AGAIN THIS TIME.

I WILL...

DO IT DO IT DO IT!

...CONSIDER IT.

AW YEAH!

I WILL NOT BE PRESSURED INTO A DECISION. I HAVE MILLIONS OF YEARS TO DECIDE.

YOU KNOW, MOM, IT'S ACTUALLY NOT SUCH A BAD IDEA.

THAT SOUNDS LIKE A YES TO ME!

BUT NOW YOU STILL MUST RETURN.

RIGHT. TIME TO SEND US BACK.

BUT NOT AS GOLD STATUES. WE GET TO CLEAN THE BLOOD OFF US BEFORE WE GO BACK, COOL?

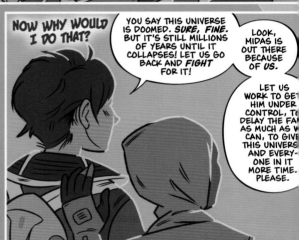

NOW WHY WOULD I DO THAT?

YOU SAY THIS UNIVERSE IS DOOMED. *SURE, FINE.* BUT IT'S STILL MILLIONS OF YEARS UNTIL IT COLLAPSES! LET US GO BACK AND *FIGHT* FOR IT!

LOOK, MIDAS IS OUT THERE BECAUSE OF *US.*

LET US WORK TO GET HIM UNDER CONTROL, TO DELAY THE FA[...] AS MUCH AS W[...] CAN, TO GIVE THIS UNIVERS[...] AND EVERY- ONE IN IT MORE TIME. PLEASE.

YOU WON'T BE ABLE TO STOP THIS. YOU KNOW THAT, RIGHT?

YEAH, MAYBE NOT. BUT I'M PRETTY DANG SURE WE SLOW IT DOWN. WE CAN STILL MAKE A DIFFERENCE. WE CAN STILL *SAVE* PEOPLE.

PLEASE. LET US TRY, ANANKE.

LET US DO WHAT WE CAN.

HMM.

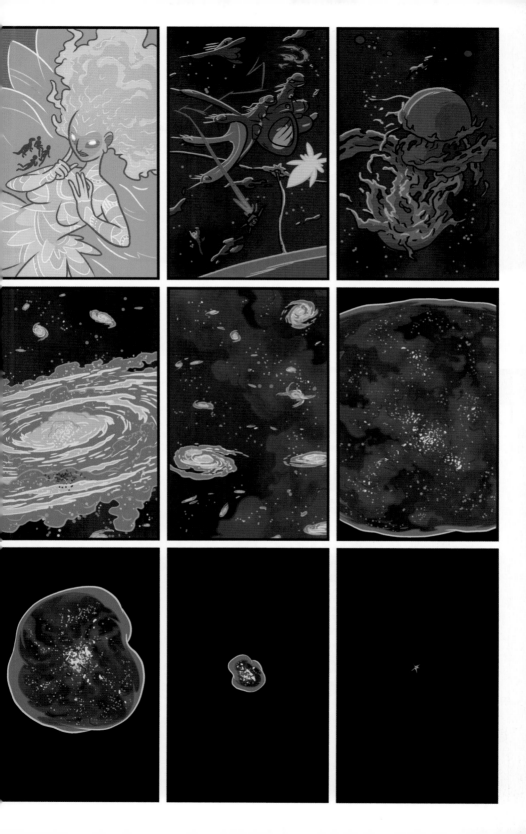

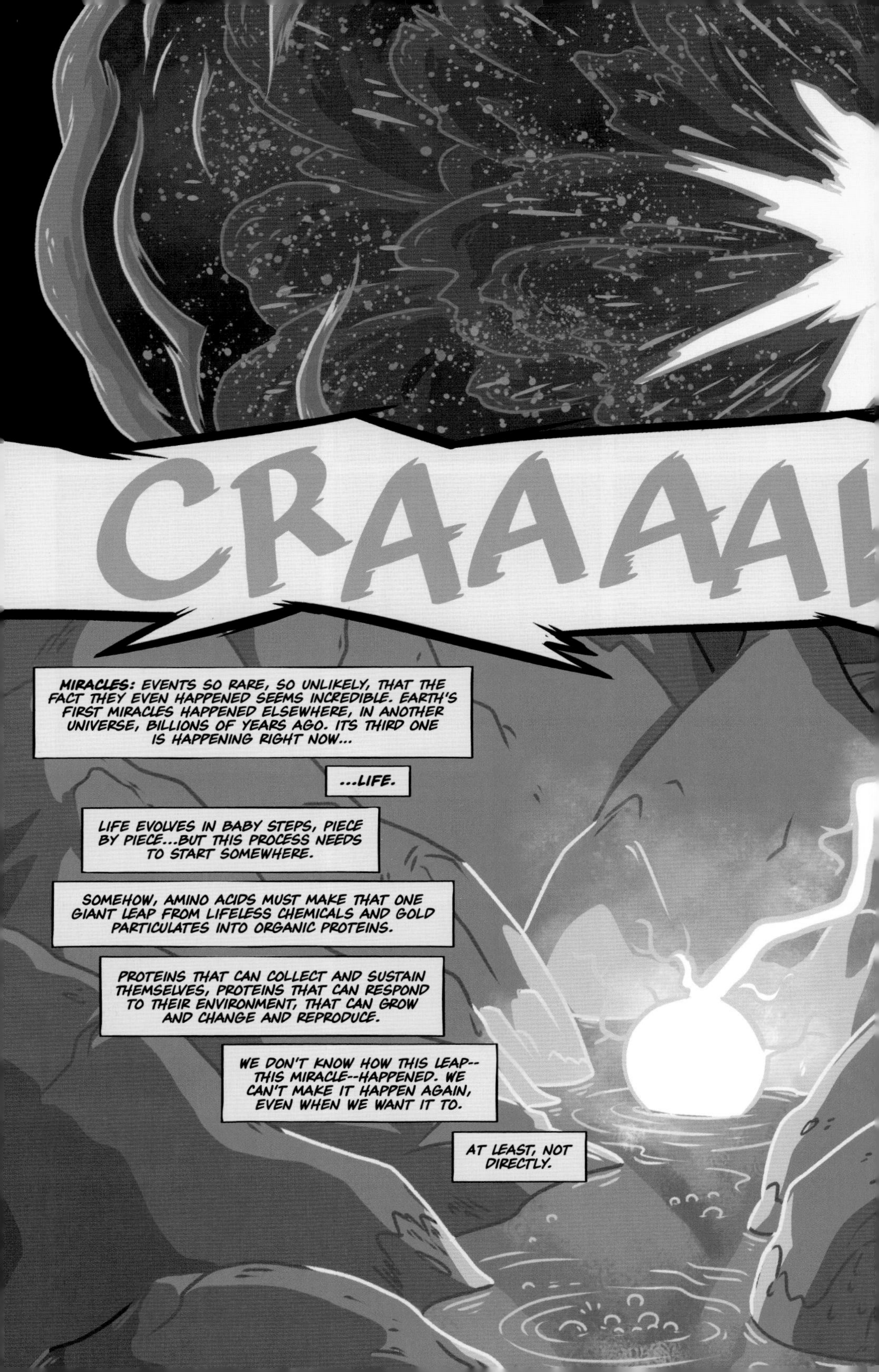
CRAAAA
MIRACLES: EVENTS SO RARE, SO UNLIKELY, THAT THE FACT THEY EVEN HAPPENED SEEMS INCREDIBLE. EARTH'S FIRST MIRACLES HAPPENED ELSEWHERE, IN ANOTHER UNIVERSE, BILLIONS OF YEARS AGO. ITS THIRD ONE IS HAPPENING RIGHT NOW...
...LIFE.
LIFE EVOLVES IN BABY STEPS, PIECE BY PIECE...BUT THIS PROCESS NEEDS TO START SOMEWHERE.
SOMEHOW, AMINO ACIDS MUST MAKE THAT ONE GIANT LEAP FROM LIFELESS CHEMICALS AND GOLD PARTICULATES INTO ORGANIC PROTEINS.
PROTEINS THAT CAN COLLECT AND SUSTAIN THEMSELVES, PROTEINS THAT CAN RESPOND TO THEIR ENVIRONMENT, THAT CAN GROW AND CHANGE AND REPRODUCE.
WE DON'T KNOW HOW THIS LEAP--THIS MIRACLE--HAPPENED. WE CAN'T MAKE IT HAPPEN AGAIN, EVEN WHEN WE WANT IT TO.
AT LEAST, NOT DIRECTLY.

KKKOW!
BUT WE CAN AT LEAST SET UP CIRCUMSTANCES WHERE THEY COULD HAPPEN.
AND SO WE SET UP THIS ONE. A NEW UNIVERSE, HEAVY WITH GOLD.
A NEW WORLD.

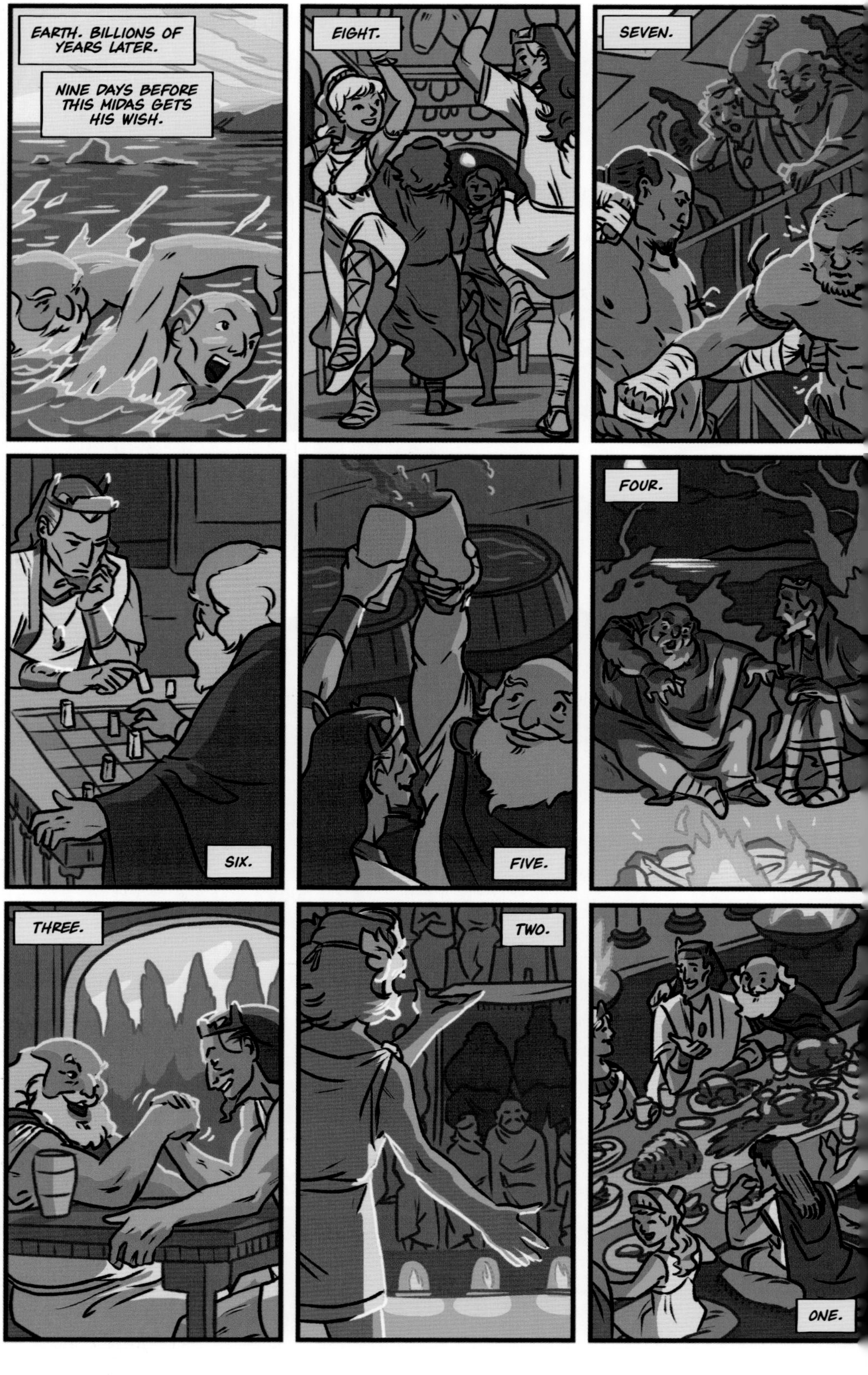
EARTH. BILLIONS OF YEARS LATER.
NINE DAYS BEFORE THIS MIDAS GETS HIS WISH.
EIGHT.
SEVEN.
SIX.
FIVE.
FOUR.
THREE.
TWO.
ONE.

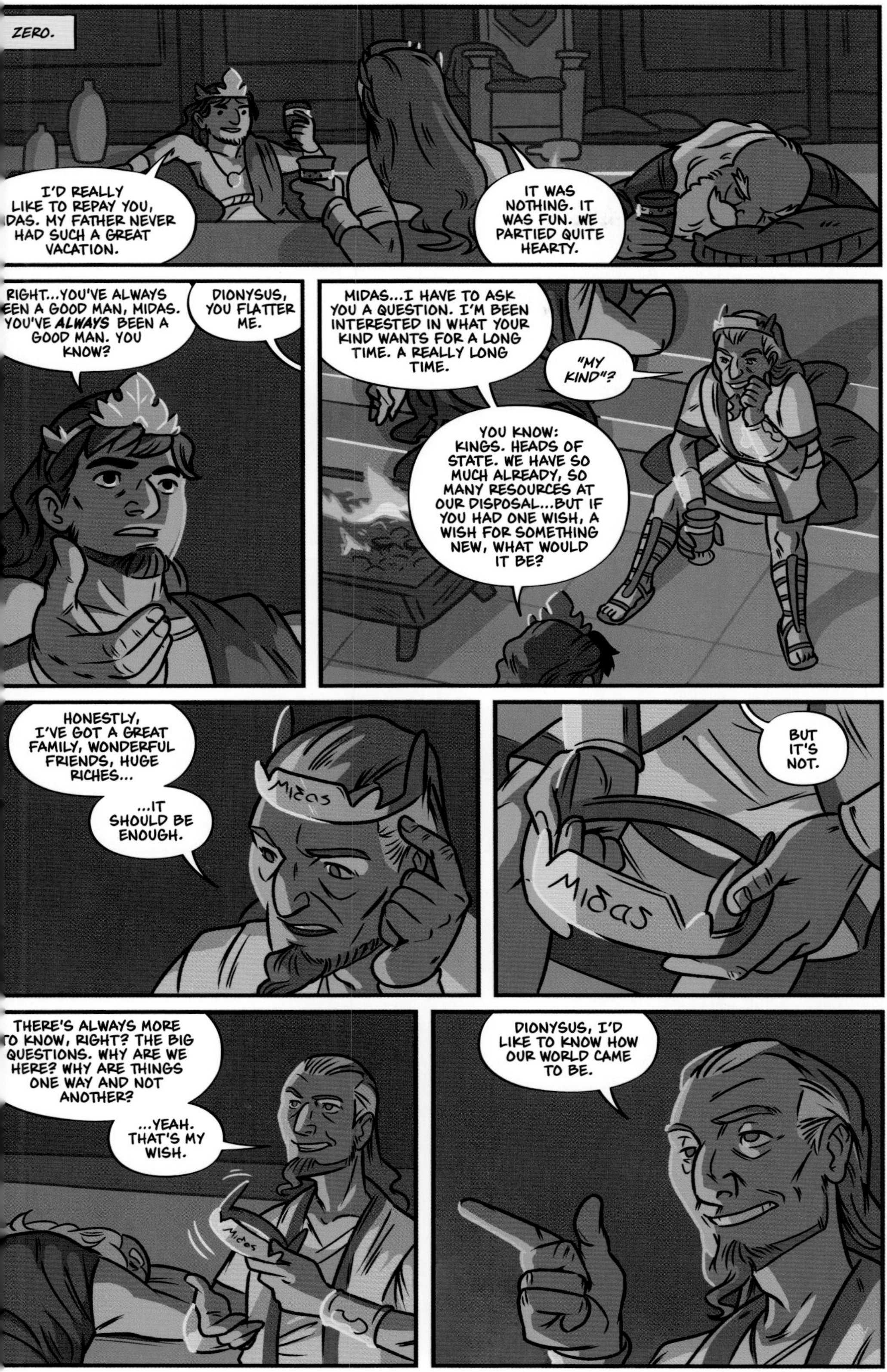
ZERO.
I'D REALLY LIKE TO REPAY YOU, MIDAS. MY FATHER NEVER HAD SUCH A GREAT VACATION.
IT WAS NOTHING. IT WAS FUN. WE PARTIED QUITE HEARTY.
RIGHT...YOU'VE ALWAYS BEEN A GOOD MAN, MIDAS. YOU'VE ALWAYS BEEN A GOOD MAN. YOU KNOW?
DIONYSUS, YOU FLATTER ME.
MIDAS...I HAVE TO ASK YOU A QUESTION. I'M BEEN INTERESTED IN WHAT YOUR KIND WANTS FOR A LONG TIME. A REALLY LONG TIME.
"MY KIND"?
YOU KNOW: KINGS. HEADS OF STATE. WE HAVE SO MUCH ALREADY, SO MANY RESOURCES AT OUR DISPOSAL...BUT IF YOU HAD ONE WISH, A WISH FOR SOMETHING NEW, WHAT WOULD IT BE?
HONESTLY, I'VE GOT A GREAT FAMILY, WONDERFUL FRIENDS, HUGE RICHES...
...IT SHOULD BE ENOUGH.
MIDAS
BUT IT'S NOT.
MIDAS
THERE'S ALWAYS MORE TO KNOW, RIGHT? THE BIG QUESTIONS. WHY ARE WE HERE? WHY ARE THINGS ONE WAY AND NOT ANOTHER?
...YEAH. THAT'S MY WISH.
MIDAS
DIONYSUS, I'D LIKE TO KNOW HOW OUR WORLD CAME TO BE.

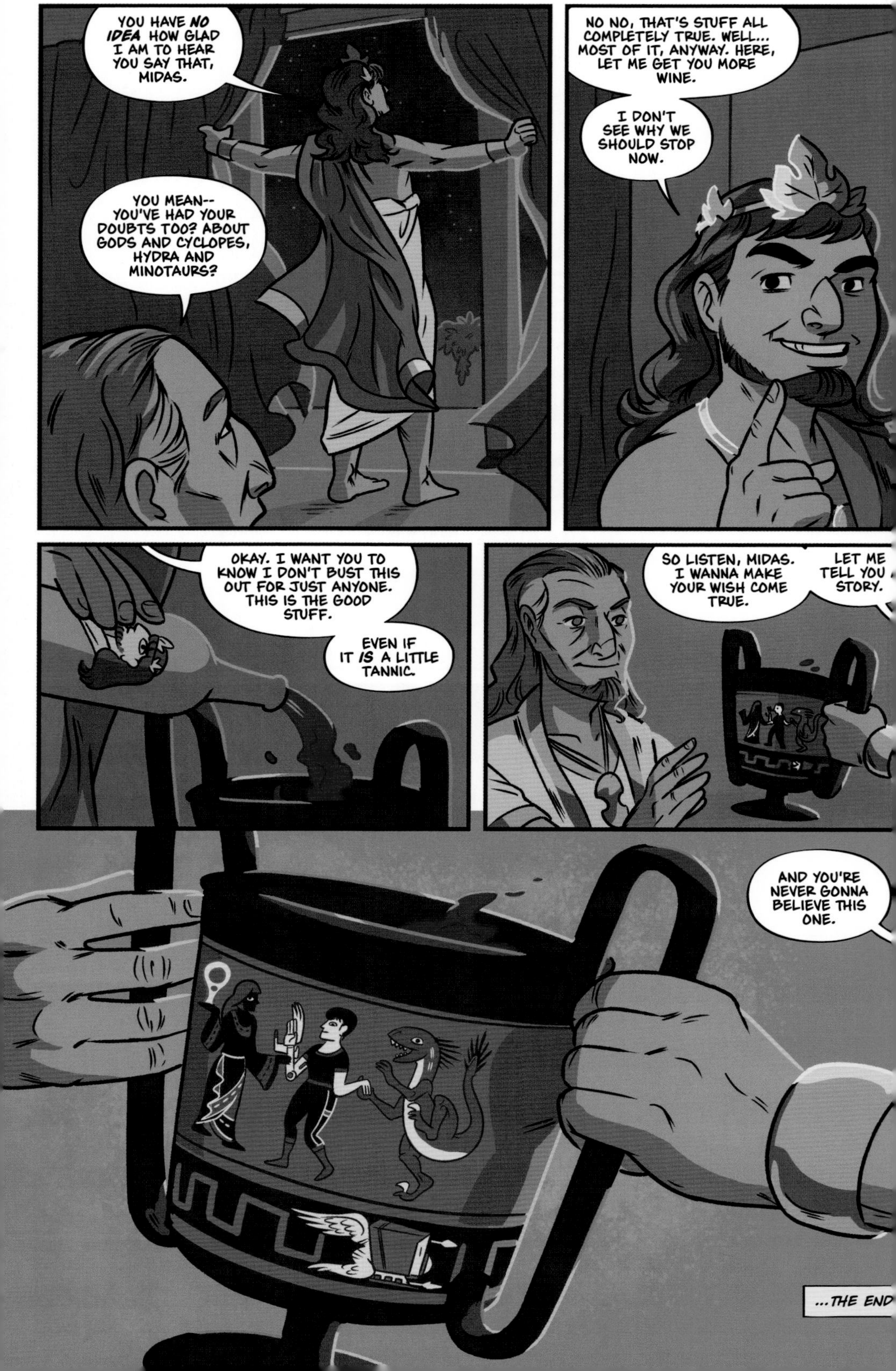
YOU HAVE NO IDEA HOW GLAD I AM TO HEAR YOU SAY THAT, MIDAS.
YOU MEAN-- YOU'VE HAD YOUR DOUBTS TOO? ABOUT GODS AND CYCLOPES, HYDRA AND MINOTAURS?
NO NO, THAT'S STUFF ALL COMPLETELY TRUE. WELL... MOST OF IT, ANYWAY. HERE, LET ME GET YOU MORE WINE.
I DON'T SEE WHY WE SHOULD STOP NOW.
OKAY. I WANT YOU TO KNOW I DON'T BUST THIS OUT FOR JUST ANYONE. THIS IS THE GOOD STUFF.
EVEN IF IT IS A LITTLE TANNIC.
SO LISTEN, MIDAS. I WANNA MAKE YOUR WISH COME TRUE.
LET ME TELL YOU STORY.
AND YOU'RE NEVER GONNA BELIEVE THIS ONE.
...THE END

"MAN!
YOU GUYS
HAVE BEEN
UP TO SOME
SHENANIGANS,
HUH?"

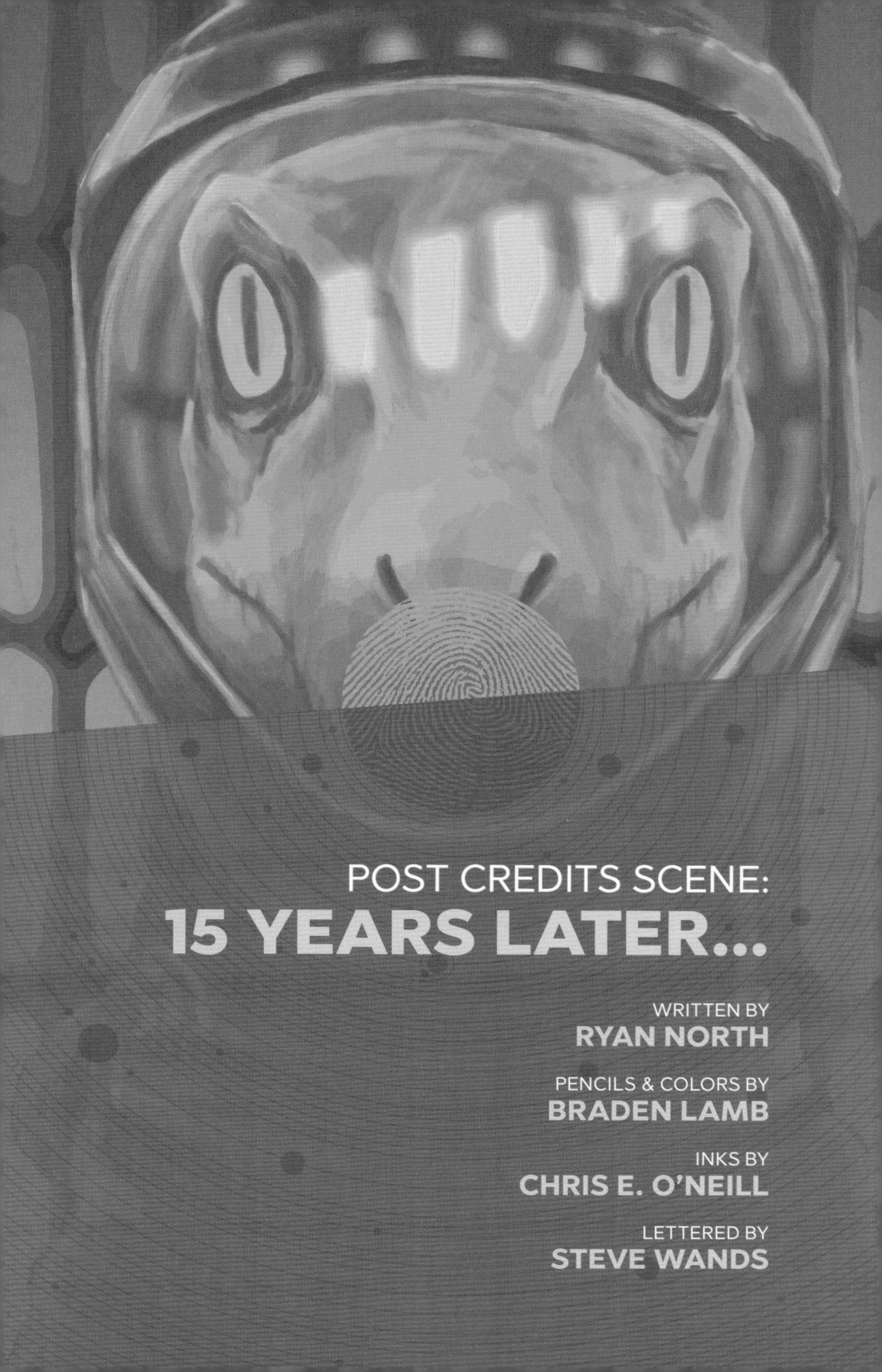

POST CREDITS SCENE:
15 YEARS LATER...

WRITTEN BY
RYAN NORTH

PENCILS & COLORS BY
BRADEN LAMB

INKS BY
CHRIS E. O'NEILL

LETTERED BY
STEVE WANDS

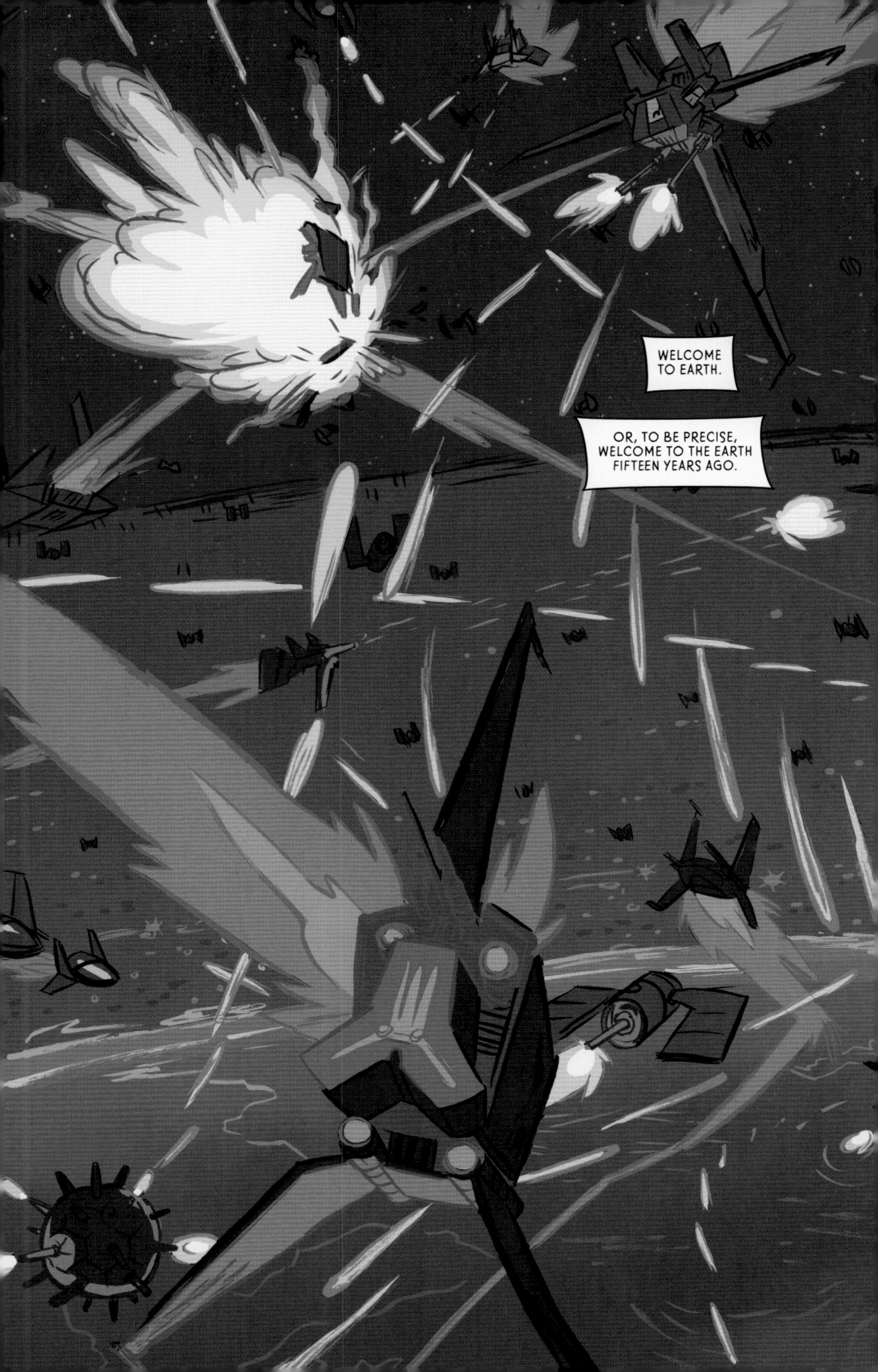
WELCOME TO EARTH.
OR, TO BE PRECISE, WELCOME TO THE EARTH FIFTEEN YEARS AGO.

OF COURSE, WE DIDN'T KNOW THIS PLANET WAS CALLED "EARTH" BACK THEN, BECAUSE WE HADN'T TRANSLATED THE GOLD TEXTS THE EARTH PEOPLE LEFT BEHIND. CAN ANYONE TELL ME **WHY** THERE WERE SO MANY GOLD BOOKS LEFT HERE?

BECAUSE WHEN THE MIDAS TRANSFORMATION HAPPENED, IT HAPPENED REALLY FAST?

THAT'S RIGHT. WE KNOW THAT W EVERYTHING WAS TURNED TO G IT WAS A SURPRISE, AND SOME THOSE SURPRISED PEOPLE WE READING. SO WHATEVER THEY V READING WAS PRESERVED THAT AND CENTURIES AND CENTUR LATER WE CAN STILL READ TH WORDS ON THE PAGE!

DIFFERENT THIN TURN INTO DIFFER DENSITIES OF GC WHICH LETS US T "INK" GOLD FRC "PAPER" GOLD

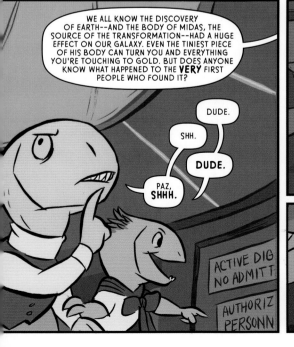

WE ALL KNOW THE DISCOVERY OF EARTH--AND THE BODY OF MIDAS, THE SOURCE OF THE TRANSFORMATION--HAD A HUGE EFFECT ON OUR GALAXY. EVEN THE TINIEST PIECE OF HIS BODY CAN TURN YOU AND EVERYTHING YOU'RE TOUCHING TO GOLD. BUT DOES ANYONE KNOW WHAT HAPPENED TO THE **VERY** FIRST PEOPLE WHO FOUND IT?

DUDE.

SHH.

DUDE.

PAZ, **SHHH.**

ACTIVE DIG NO ADMITT

AUTHORIZ PERSONN

NOBODY? IT SOUNDS SILLY NOW, BUT BACK THEN, HAVING A LOT OF GOLD COULD MAKE YOU **VERY** RICH. THERE WASN'T THAT MUCH OF IT! THE FIRST EXPLORERS HERE--

RICHARD, BY THE AUTHORITY VESTED IN ME, I HEREBY AUTHORIZE YOU...

HUH?

AUTHORIZE ME FOR WHAT?

LET'S F OUT

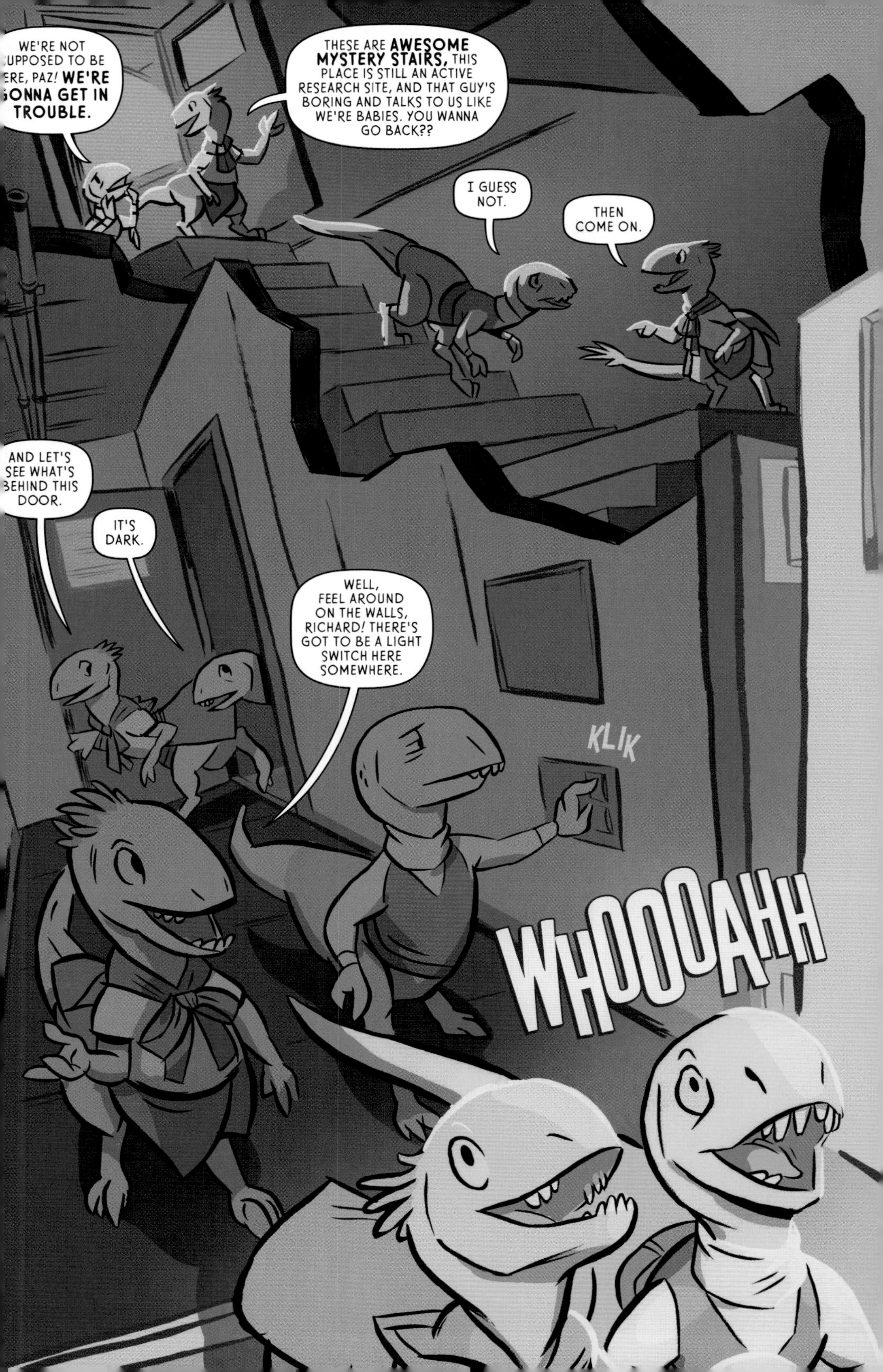

WE'RE NOT
UPPOSED TO BE
ERE, PAZ! WE'RE
GONNA GET IN
TROUBLE.
THESE ARE AWESOME MYSTERY STAIRS, THIS PLACE IS STILL AN ACTIVE RESEARCH SITE, AND THAT GUY'S BORING AND TALKS TO US LIKE WE'RE BABIES. YOU WANNA GO BACK??
I GUESS NOT.
THEN COME ON.
AND LET'S
SEE WHAT'S
BEHIND THIS
DOOR.
IT'S DARK.
WELL, FEEL AROUND ON THE WALLS, RICHARD! THERE'S GOT TO BE A LIGHT SWITCH HERE SOMEWHERE.
KLIK
WHOOOAHH

YOINK

HEY!

GAH!

MISS, YOU WON'T BELIEVE IT!!

MISS, YOU KNOW HOW EVERYONE'S BEEN TO ALL THESE PLANETS AND NEVER EVER FOUND PEOPLE LIKE US? WELL **GUESS WHAT, MISS??**

I WILL NOT GUESS WHAT, RICHARD. NOW YOU'RE BOTH GOING TO TALK TO THE TOUR GUIDE, AND YOU'RE GOING TO APOLOGIZE TO HIM FOR EMBARRASSING BOTH YOURSELF AND THE SCHOOL.

QUIET, PAZ. YOU'RE BOTH IN VERY, **VERY** BIG TROUBLE.

AND WHEN YOU'VE DONE THAT, YOU'RE BOTH GOING TO GR**AAAAHH!**

CHOMP

PAZ!!

YOUNG LADY, YOU ARE IN A **LOT** OF --

...

...OH GOOD!

TOLD YOU WE WEREN'T GONNA GET IN TROUBLE.

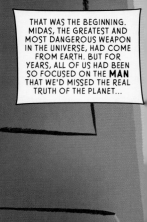

THAT WAS THE BEGINNING. MIDAS, THE GREATEST AND MOST DANGEROUS WEAPON IN THE UNIVERSE, HAD COME FROM EARTH. BUT FOR YEARS, ALL OF US HAD BEEN SO FOCUSED ON THE **MAN** THAT WE'D MISSED THE REAL TRUTH OF THE PLANET...

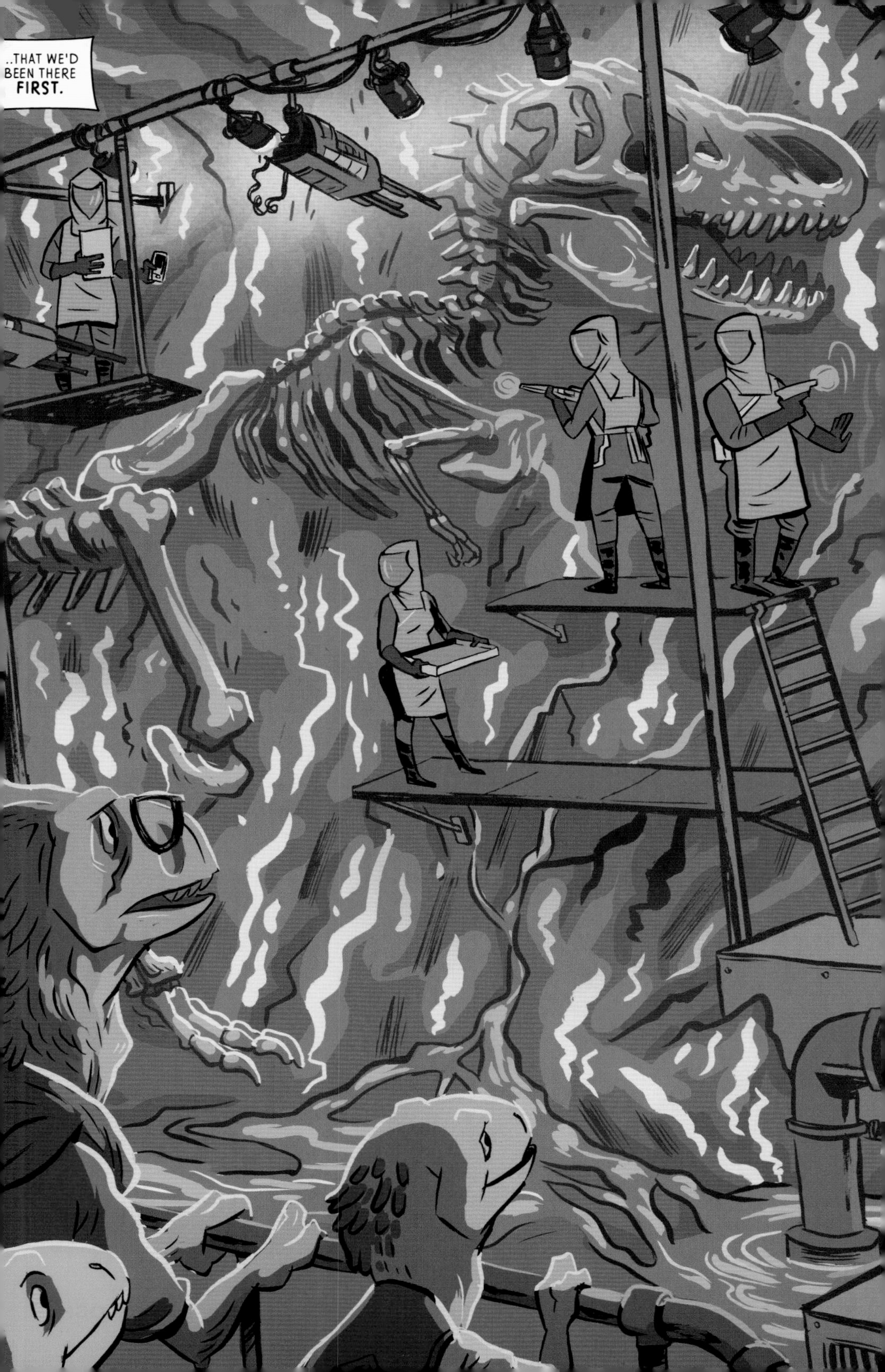
..THAT WE'D BEEN THERE FIRST.

MIDAS
ORIGINS

WITH AN ESSAY FROM **RYAN NORTH**
AND CONCEPT ART FROM **SHELLI PAROLINE,**
BRADEN LAMB, & JOHN KEOGH

ORIGINAL COOPER, JOEY, AND FATTY CHARACTER DESIGNS BY JOHN KEOGH

There's an old text file on my computer called "midas.txt." It looks like this:

THE NEXT MORNING:

Joey, putting down tablet computer: Finally.
Cooper: I know. I made it go as fast as I could.
They can look inside. It's just three men, perfectly preserved, covered in gold dust. It doesn't make any sense. It's got to be hidden. Let's see if we can get rid of some of this dust. We'll blow air on it. Whatever air coalesces into gold dust should be less than what's there. They do, and they reveal frozen Silenus, frozen Dionysus, and Midas. A corpse, perfectly preserved. Hair as vibrant as it was the last issue. Any microbe that would decay him has turned to gold. He looks like he's still alive. In fact, that's what everyone assumes. He's the only non-gold thing on the planet, and he stands out like a sore thumb.
Everyone, watching the viewscreen in shock. Of all the things they were expecting to find, a perfectly-preserved body was not one of them.
Fatima: He's still alive?!

END OF ISSUE THREE

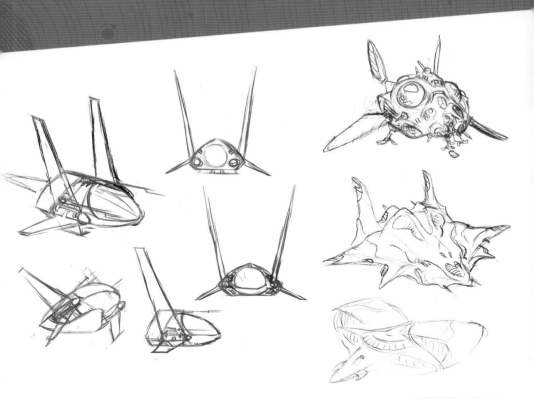

UNUSED SHIPS

LAMB I've been itching to draw sci fi stuff for ages, so I started out by exploring all the kinds of ships I might want to see in a comic. Not just the typical (but fun) clunky *Star Wars* stuff, but some bug-like design, and maybe living technology.

That's from the earliest draft of this story that I still have, then called *The Midas Planet*. It's a form of writing I do when I'm just trying to get ideas out. It's almost a comic script, only there's dialogue sometimes, description sometimes, and everything's mixed together in a big pile of text. It's a mess, but it's something I can read later to remember what I wanted when I sit down to tell an actual story.

The file is dated 2010, and I must've saved it over my very first draft, because I started this story in 2008 and at that point I didn't have any character names. They were just called "Navigator" and "Captain" and "Weapons." The Prospect was called "The Hero Ship." I came *this close* to actually calling it that in the comic before Braden suggested its actual name, which was approximately one billion times better.

And no, Midas wasn't actually alive. At this point, the cliffhanger on this issue was that they just *thought* he was alive, and then we'd all wait a month, and discover hah hah, okay, no, it was a huge fake-out and he's actually dead and our characters are just big ol' dummies.

I dropped this idea later.

vent
future candles/ lanterns
room
room
(Kitchen)
religious icon/ heirloom?
Joey
Fatima
Cooper
futon
coffee
BATH
tv
KITCH
to loft
work bench
toolchest
TOP VIEW OF ROOM
CONTROLS
Screen
Screen
door

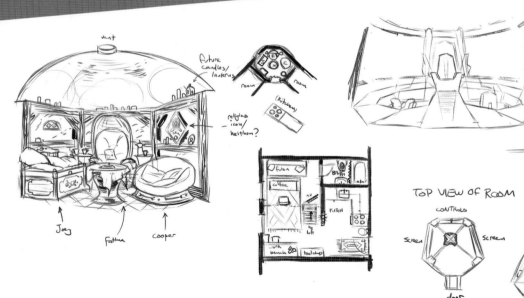

FATIMA'S APARTMENT

LAMB This flashback to Fatima's homeworld was an opportunity to explore another alien planet, and my initial inclination was to base it on Moroccan architecture. However, that gave the impression that we were just appropriating another culture and passing it off as exotic and alien, so instead the home became a New York/Paris loft.

But even that now-lost draft wasn't where this idea started. The comic you just read actually started here:

LATER: aliens discover midas's body and use him as a highly unstable source of gold, keeping him in vacuum suspension with magnetic fields. but their ship soon suffers a power failure, midas hits the floor, and the ship is transmuted. the ship drifts until drawn in by the gravitational field of a backwater planet, where it crashes and causes the planet to suffer the same fate as Earth. we join our story centuries later as our heroes, bounty hunters seeking the near-mythic Midas Flesh, successfully break quarantine and get past the defences erected around the planet. they are the first to land on the Second Golden Planet.

and here:

ryan what if aliens divided up the Midas Flesh with lasers into six pieces (torso, four limbs, and head) and distributed it across the galaxy for safe keeping. but one keeper of the Flesh is tempted! alarms go off and they find his body, a gold statue with an empty hand where the Midas Skull should be. the chase is on to track down the most dangerous weapon in the universe!!

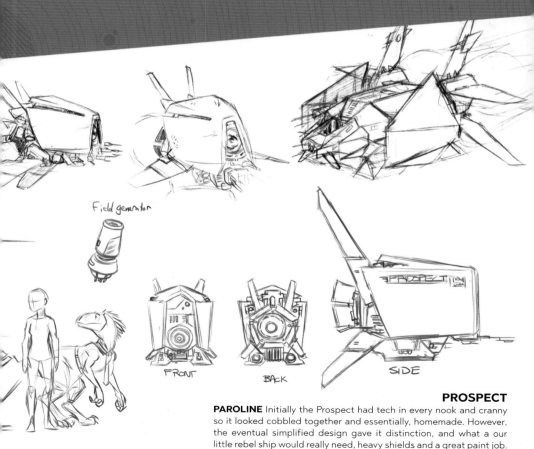

Field generator

FRONT

BACK

SIDE

PROSPECT

PAROLINE Initially the Prospect had tech in every nook and cranny so it looked cobbled together and essentially, homemade. However, the eventual simplified design gave it distinction, and what a our little rebel ship would really need, heavy shields and a great paint job.

Those are from an online comic I wrote *(Dinosaur Comics!)* where a talking T. rex named T-Rex walked through the idea of King Midas making his wish and it catastrophically coming true. T-Rex's version ended with Midas dying exactly as he did in here, but once that six-panel strip was done, I found I wanted to keep going and explore this idea. So if you hovered your mouse over the comic, you'd get the first text, and if you clicked the "contact" link, you'd get the second text as your email subject line. And if you looked up what I called this comic in my archives, you'd discover I'd written:

i am thinking of writing a comic about the Midas Flesh, can you tell

I started writing this comic the same day. But after I'd written the first issue and outlined the next few, I put it aside: the first issue worked, but after that I'd written myself into a corner and gotten stuck. Here's how a version from that time concludes, four issues in, with Fatima and Cooper floating in space near Earth:

Cooper: I don't know how we're going to pull this one out.
Fatty has an idea: they've got statis fields and they're solar powered - if we get near the sun, we can stasis our own heads.
That'll kill us.

But maybe in future someone will rescue us?
That's really our best hope?

ONE THOUSAND YEARS LATER

That's how it ends, exactly like that. You can tell the exact moment I walked away from the keyboard and said "Hah hah hah this is awful; I guess I'd better wait until I'm better at writing and can figure out a way to tell this story!"

I tinkered with the outline over the next couple of years, but never too seriously, because I couldn't see a way to make this comic happen. It was too big. Several years went by, and while I could never forget about my Midas comic idea, I never went back to it either. Then, one day, my editor Shannon asked me if there were any stories I wanted to tell. If there were any comics I'd like to run past BOOM! with the eye to them being produced as a new miniseries. If there was anything she could help me with.

As it so happened, there was one story that I'd wanted to tell for a very long time.

RYAN NORTH
Toronto
July 2014

CHARACTERS

LAMB The characters went through a few changes before we settled on something Shelli and I could easily sustain over our tenure on this project. We pushed toward a more animated look to enhance the fun, adventurous tone. Even then the characters evolved a little, becoming more detailed as the issues progressed. I'd love to say that it was a conscious choice, reflecting the increasing gravity of emotions, but really it's just what felt best.

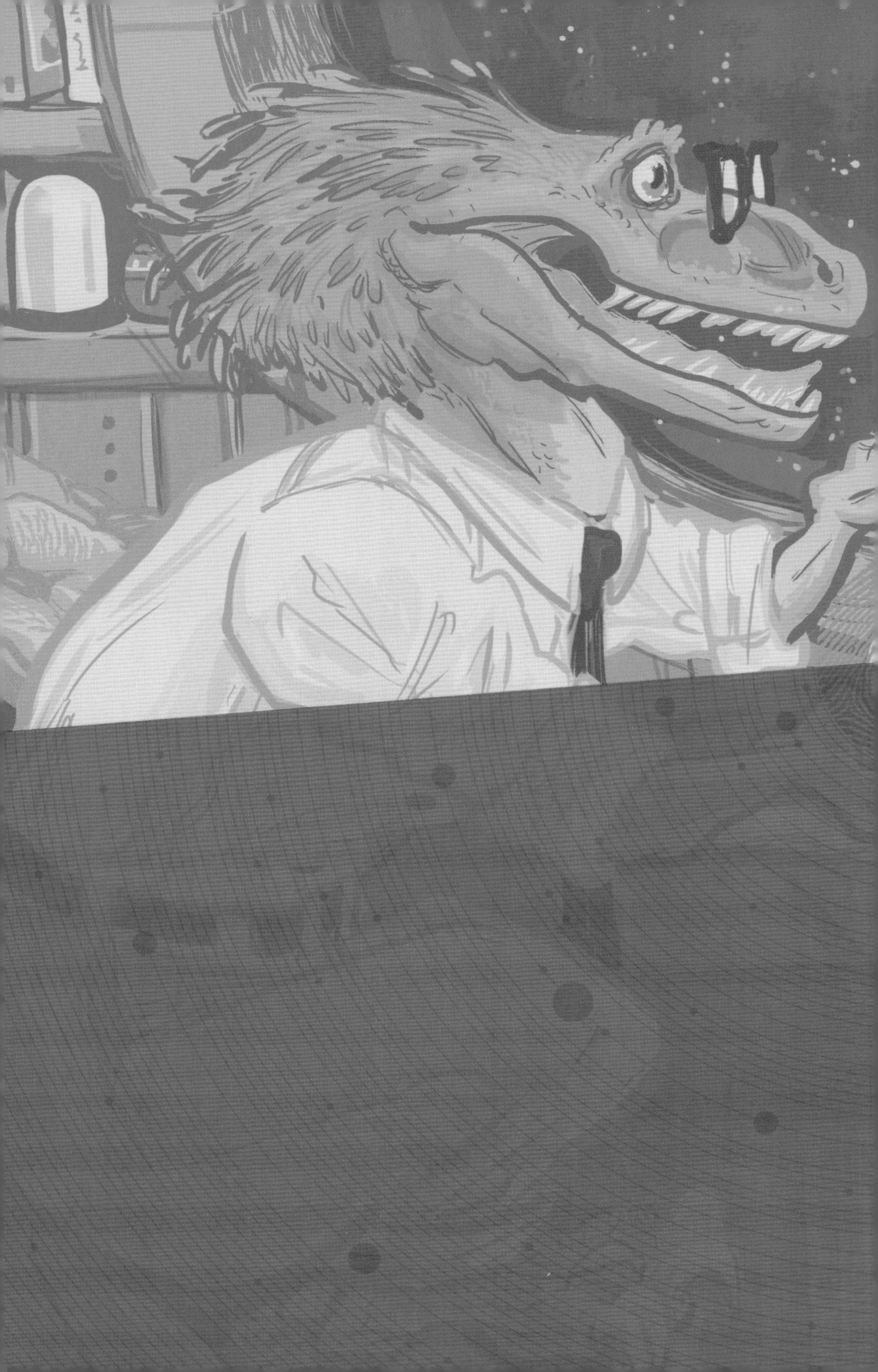

COVER
GALLERY

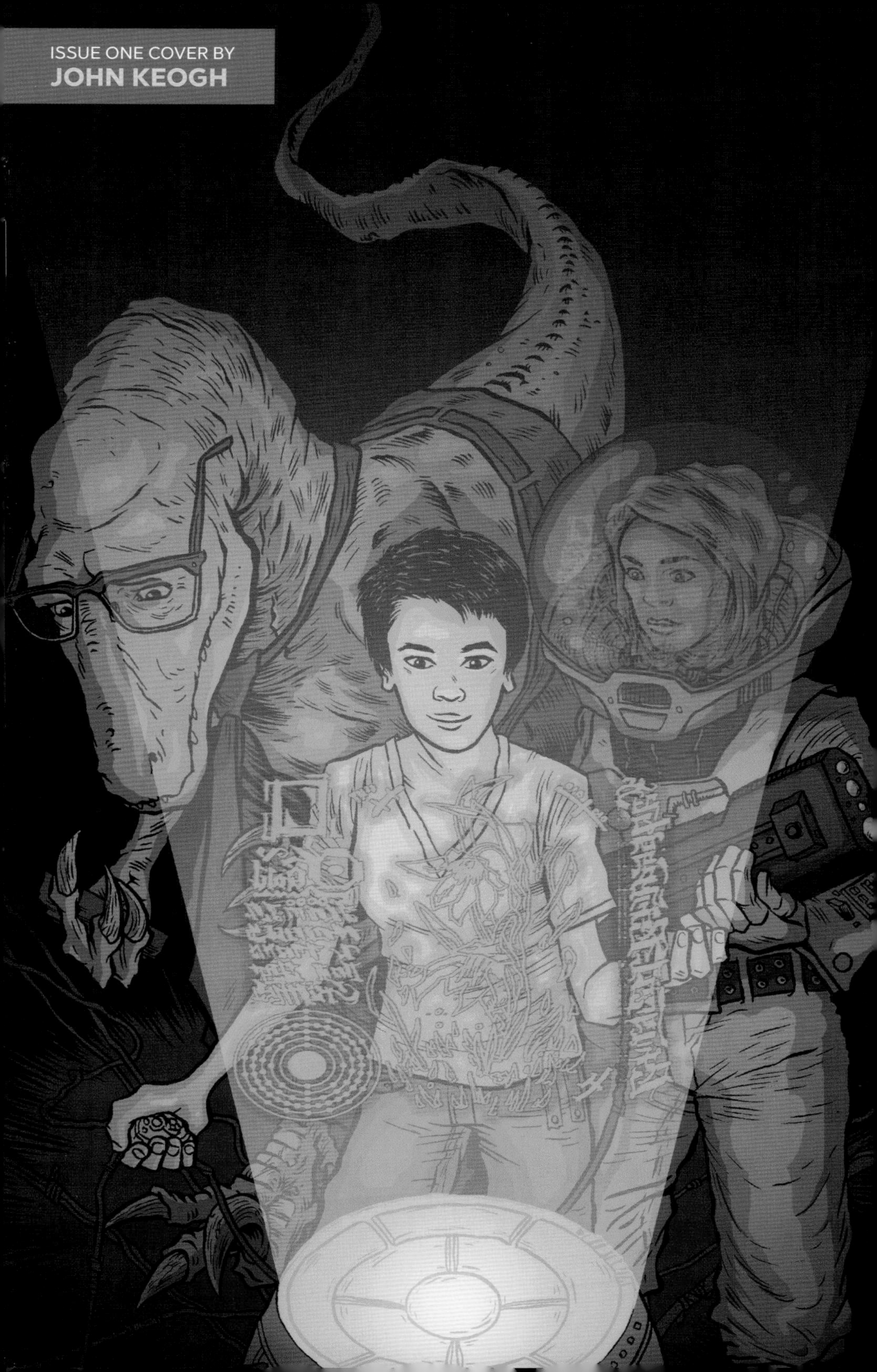

ISSUE ONE COVER BY
JOHN KEOGH

ISSUE ONE VARIANT COVER BY
LYLE PARTRIDGE

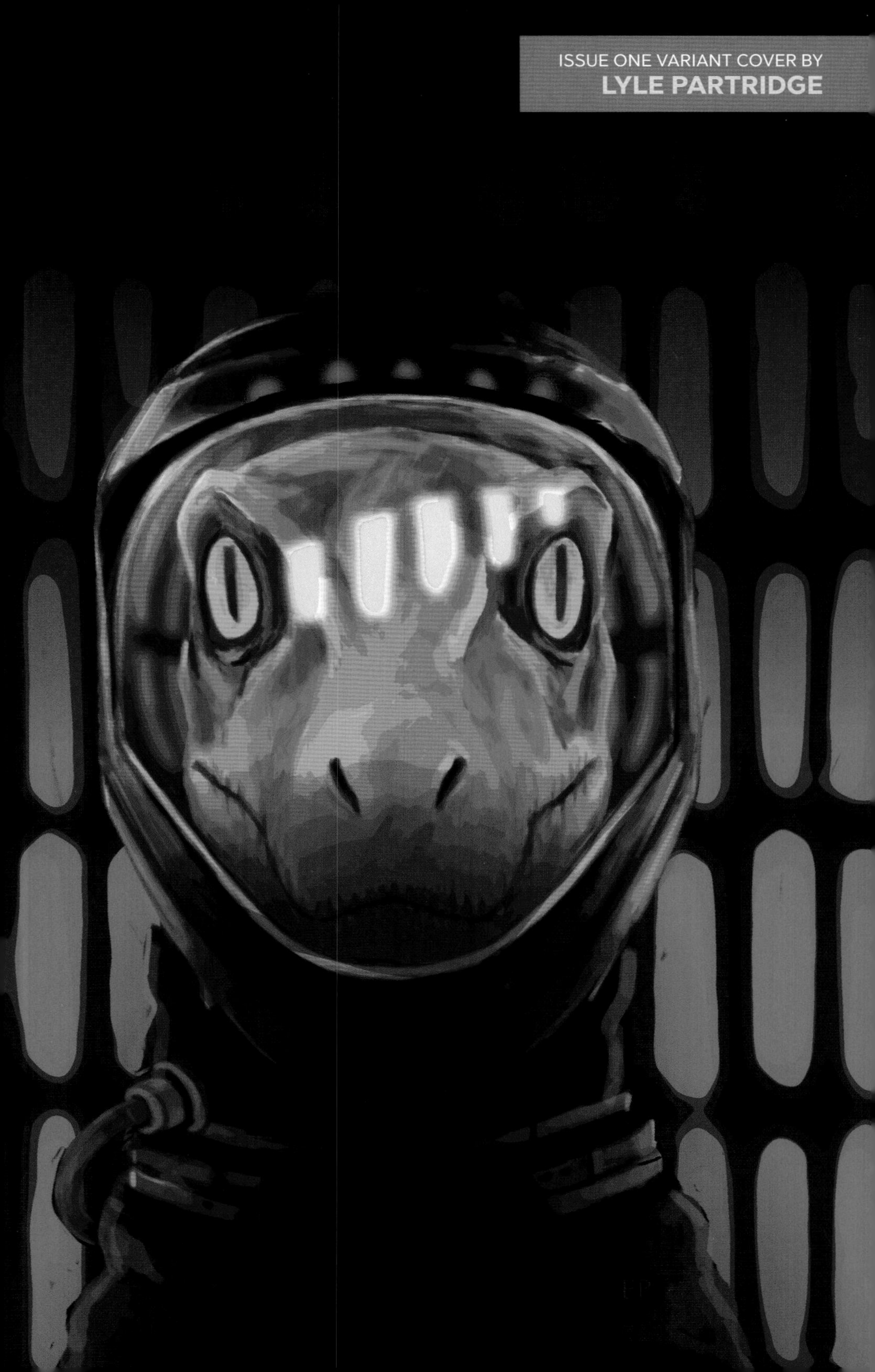

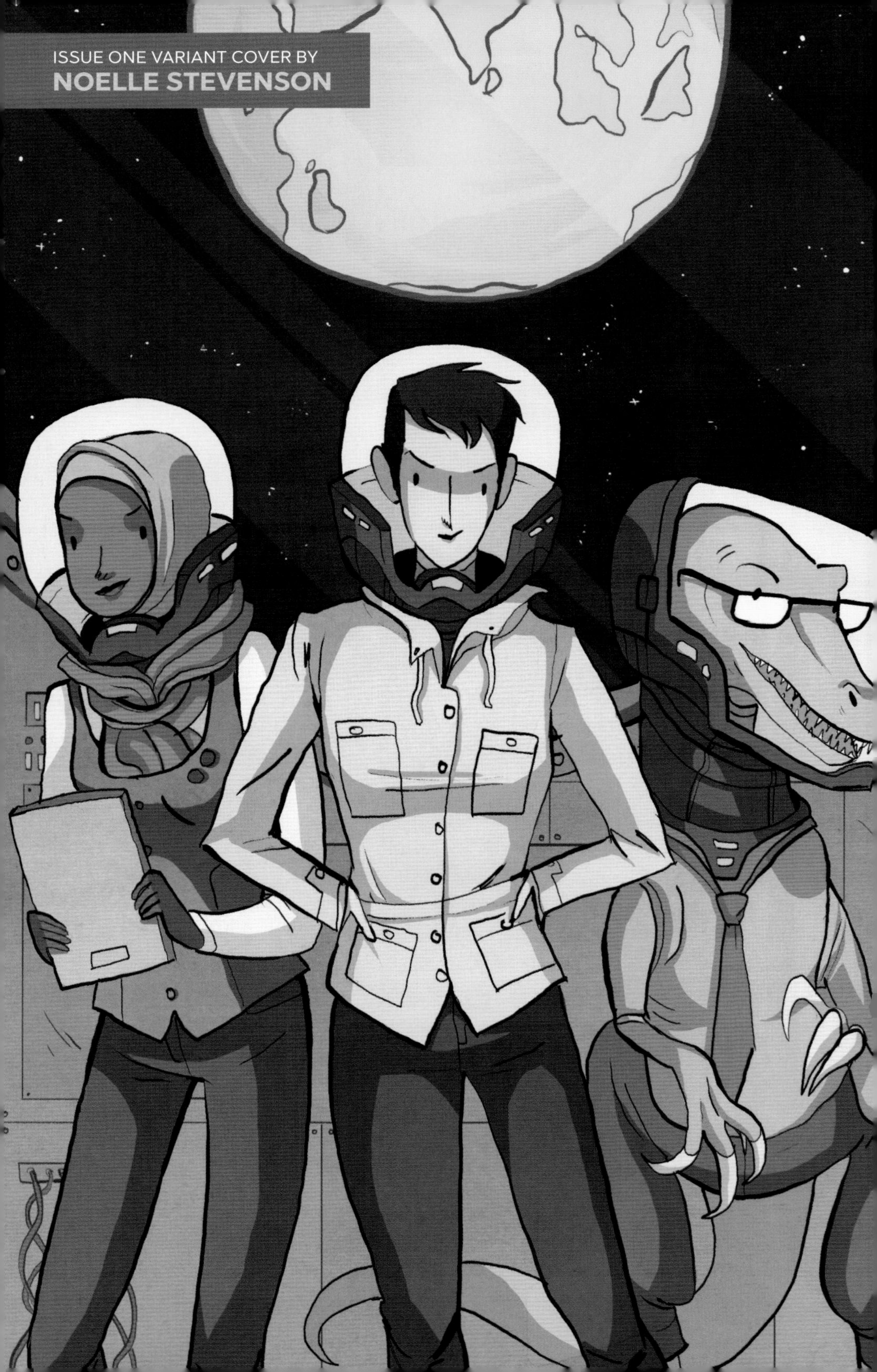

ISSUE ONE VARIANT COVER BY
NOELLE STEVENSON

ISSUE ONE WRITER'S VARIANT COVER BY
BROOKLYN ALLEN

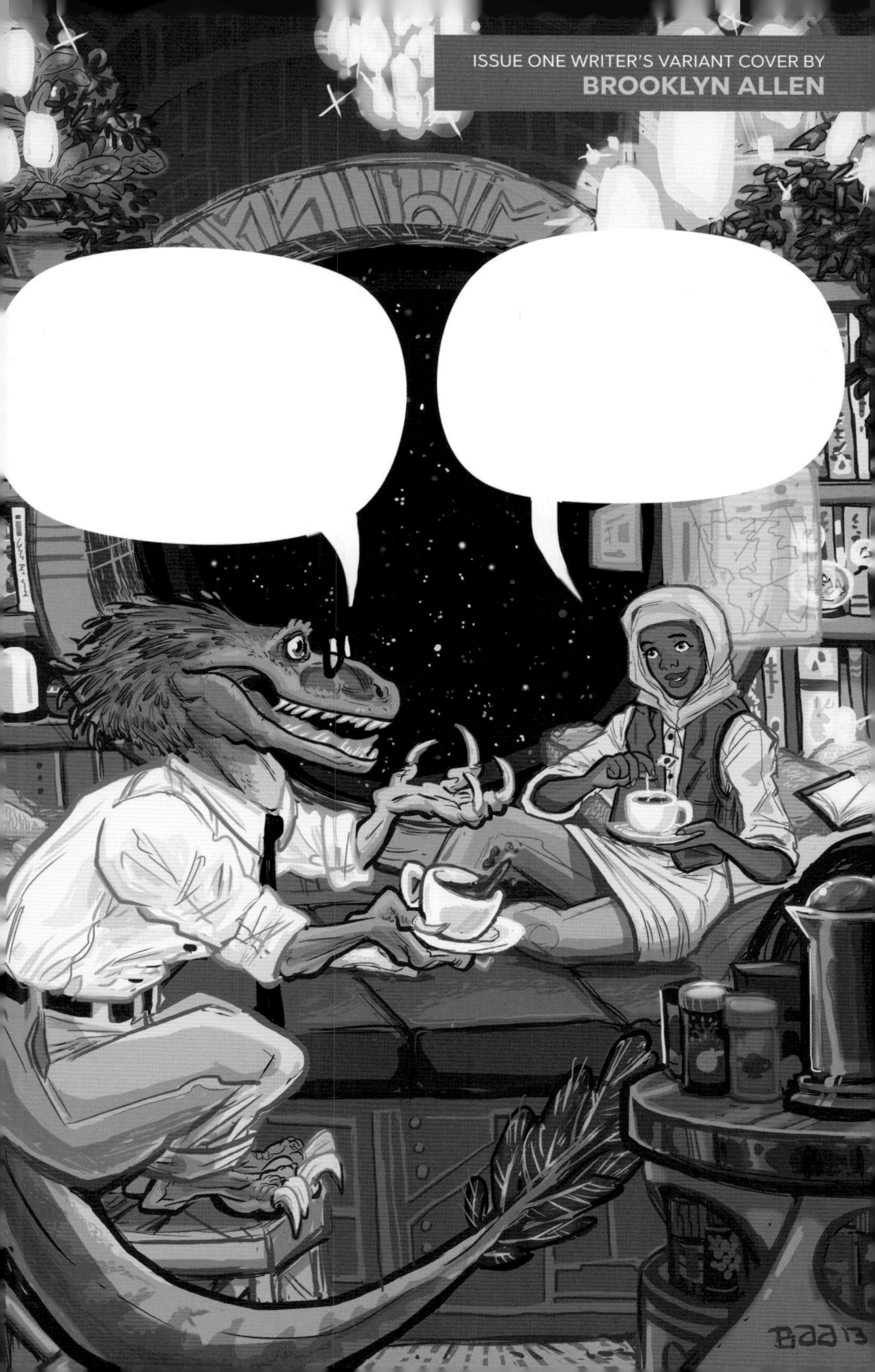
BAA '13

ISSUE ONE EMERALD CITY COMIC CON EXCLUSIVE COVER BY
CHIP ZDARSKY

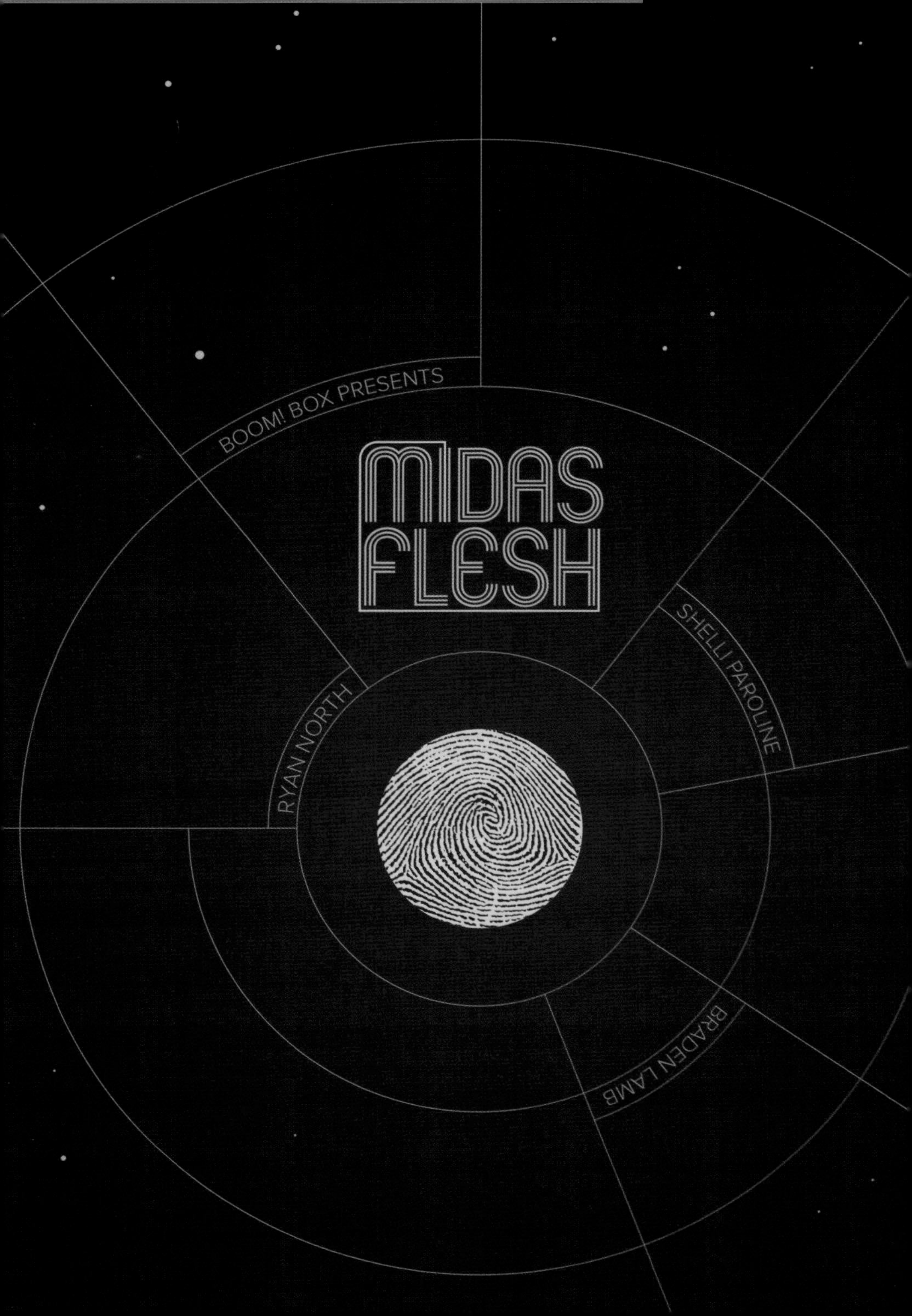
BOOM! BOX PRESENTS
MIDAS FLESH
SHELLI PAROLINE
RYAN NORTH
BRADEN LAMB

ISSUE ONE HASTING EXCLUSIVE COVER BY
CHRIS HASTINGS

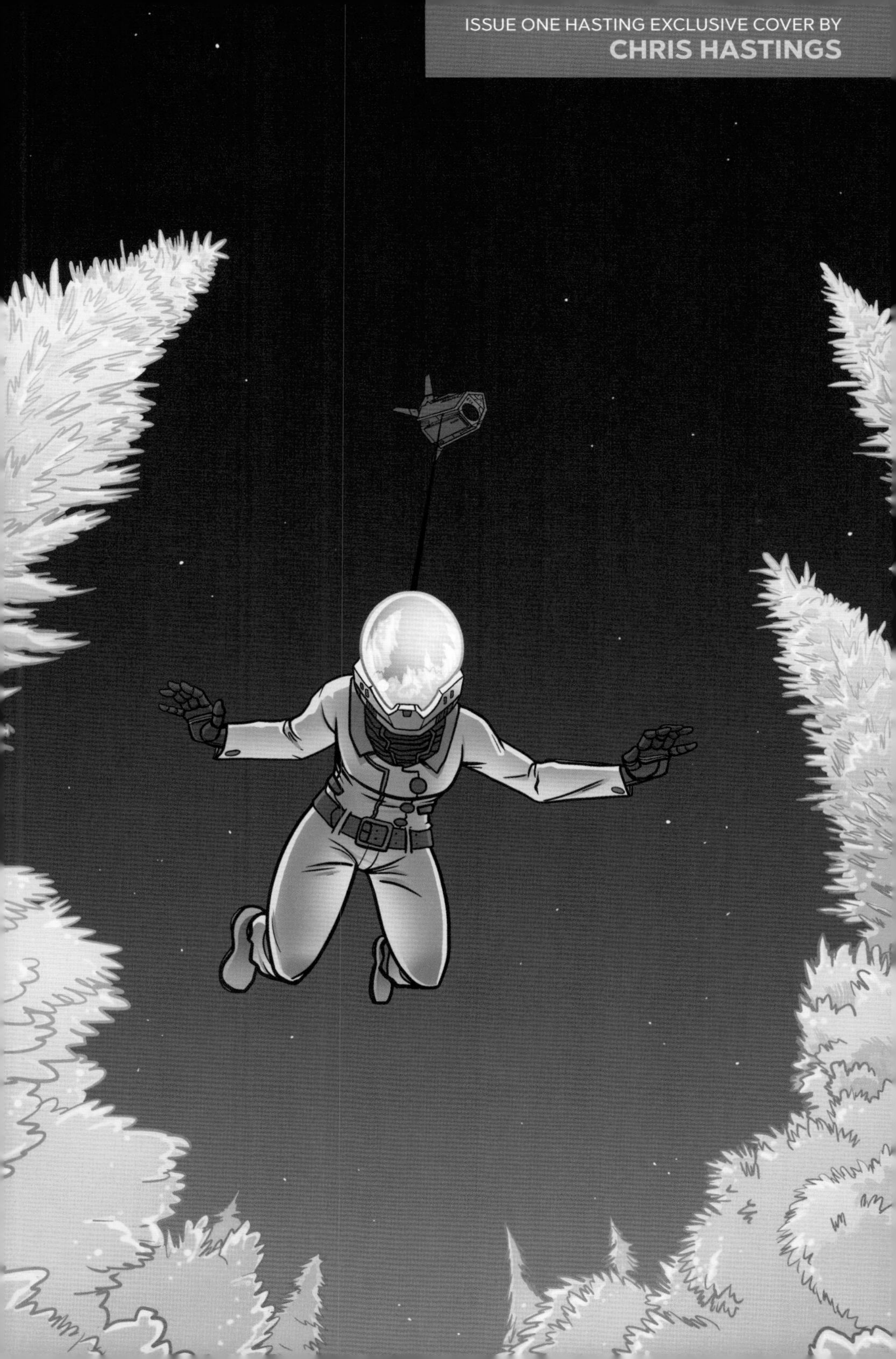

ISSUE ONE CARDS, COMICS & COLLECTIBLES EXCLUSIVE COVER BY
ROSEMARY MOSCO

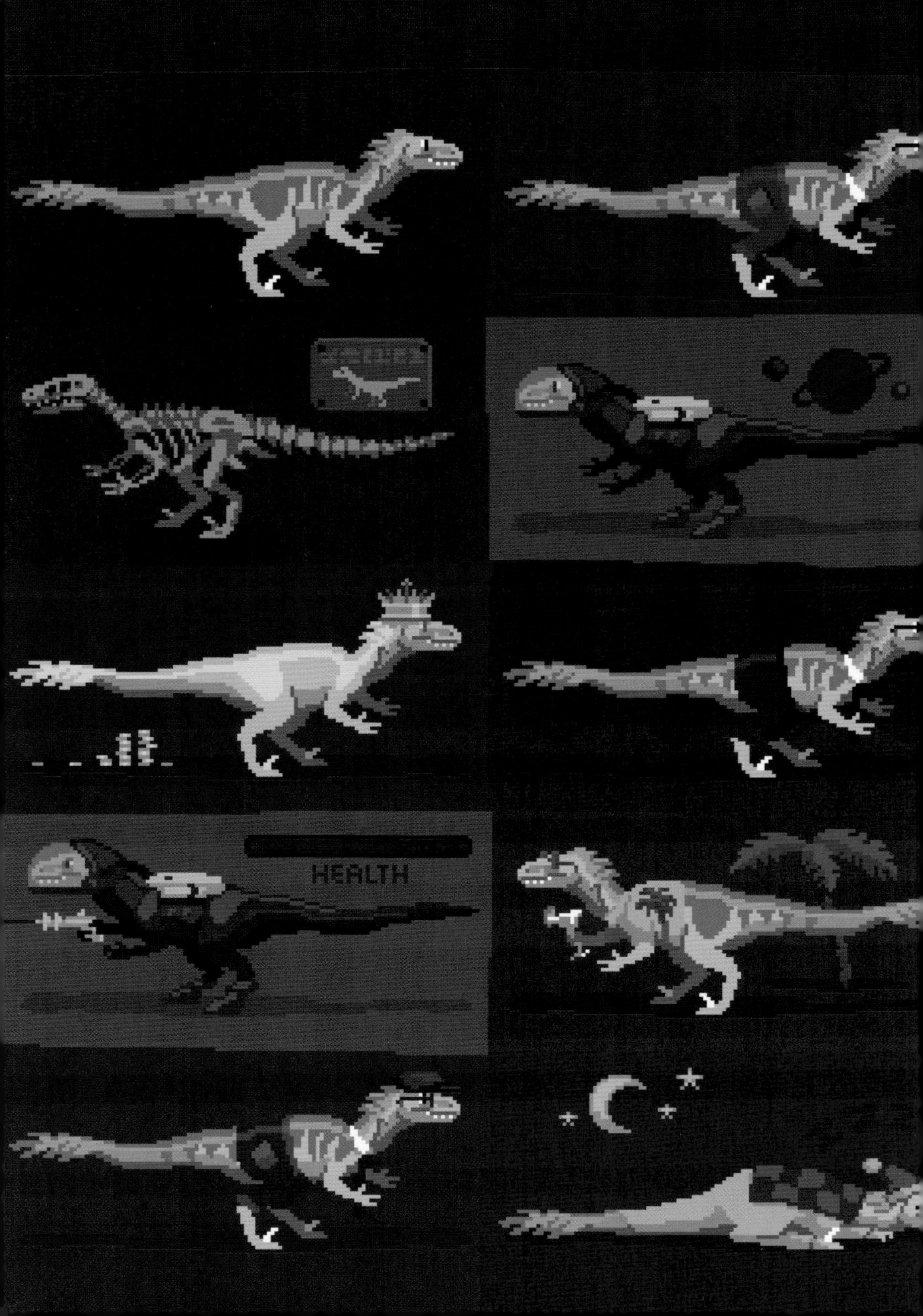
HEALTH

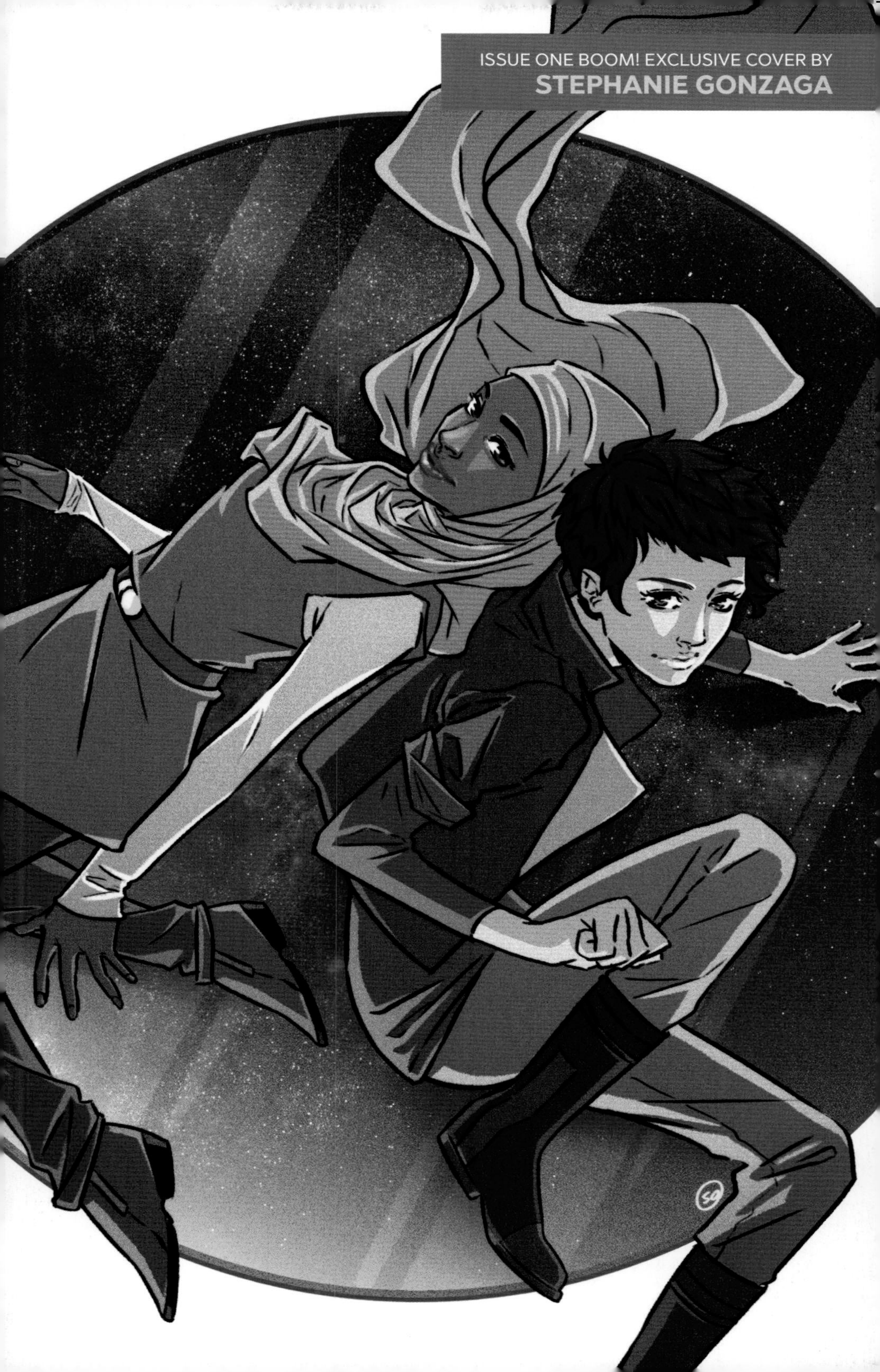
SG

ISSUE ONE BOOM! EXCLUSIVE COVER BY
STEPHANIE GONZAGA

ISSUE ONE SECOND PRINT COVER BY
JESS FINK

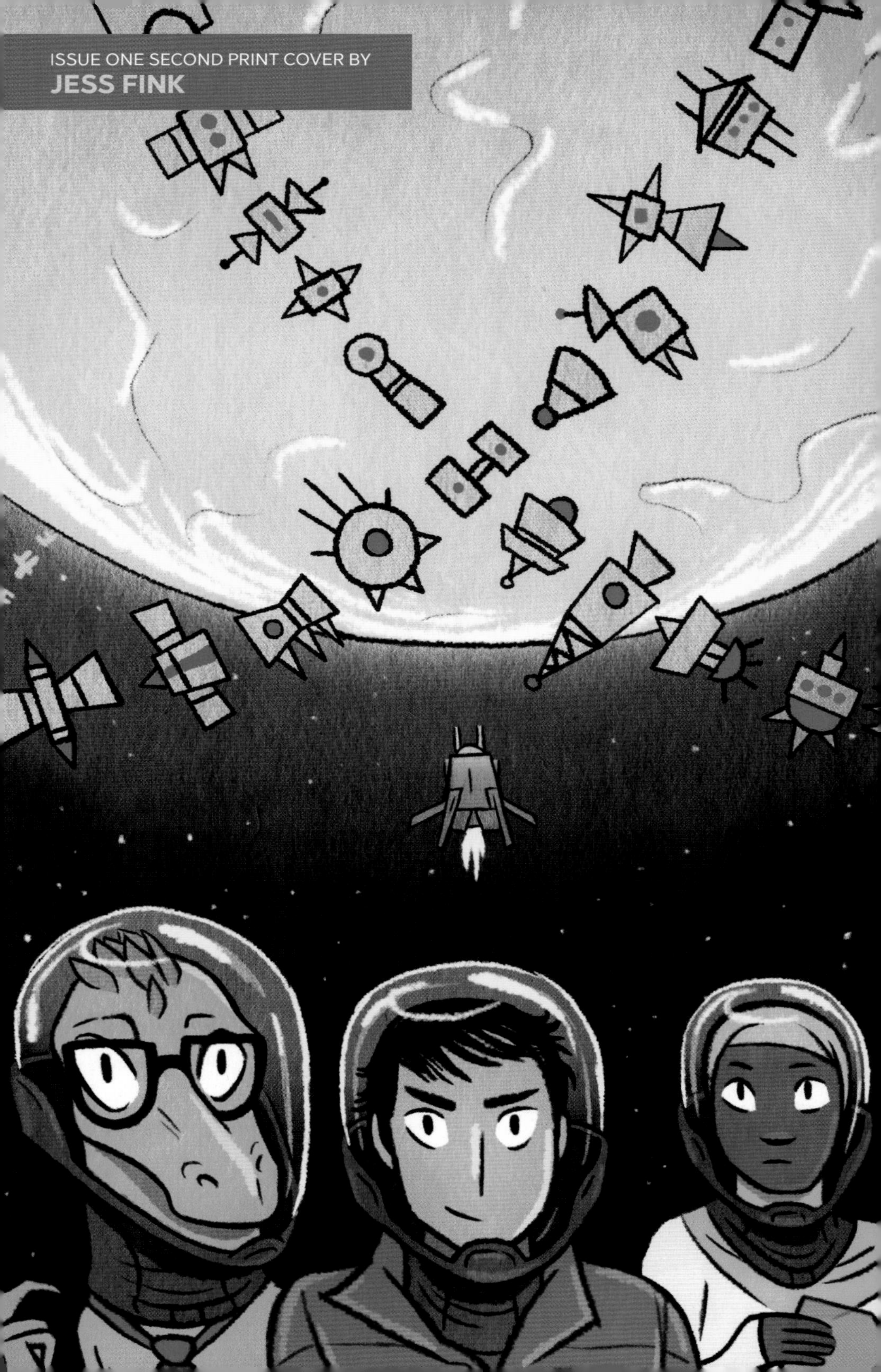

ISSUE TWO COVER BY
JOHN KEOGH

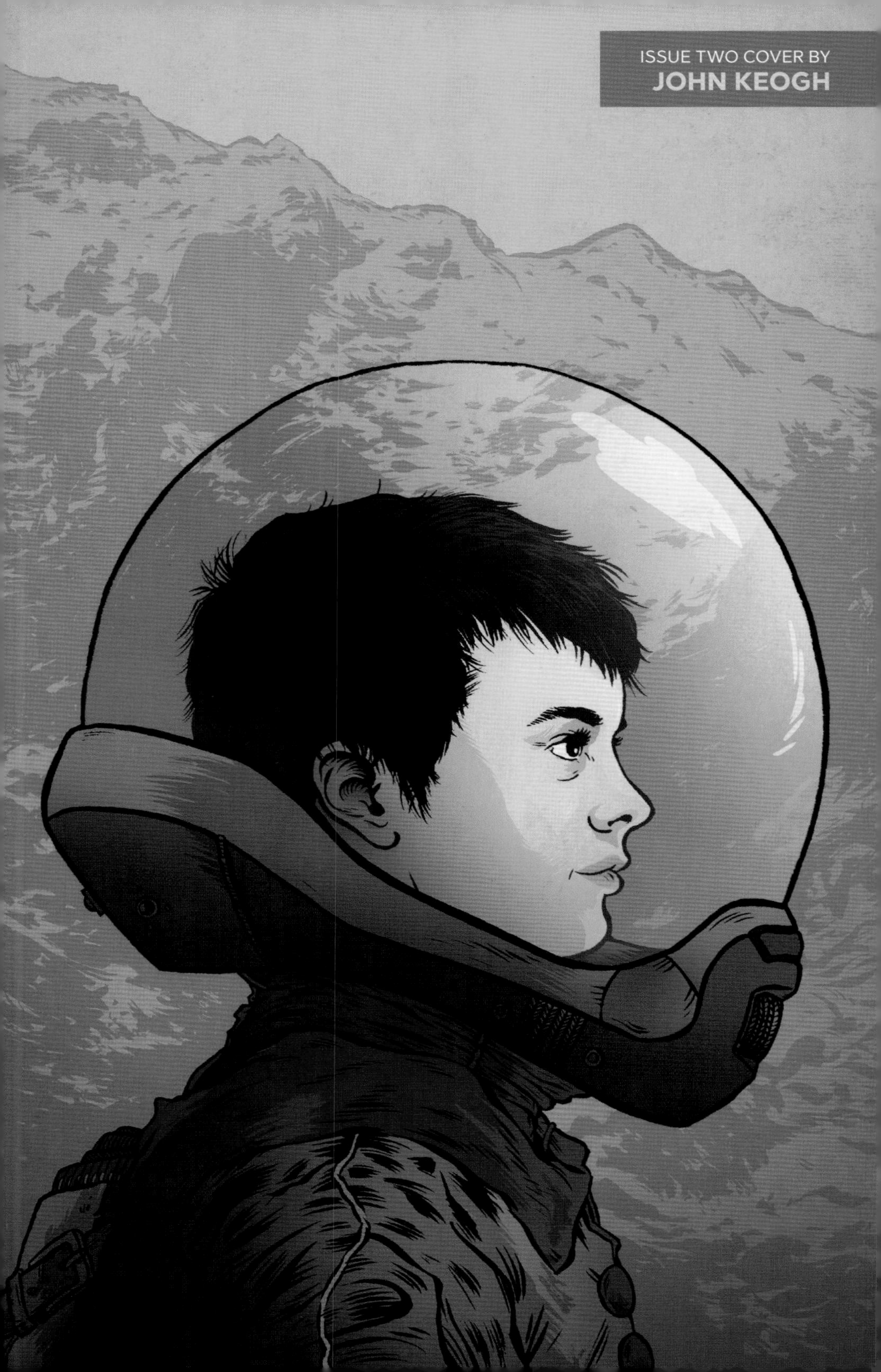

ISSUE TWO VARIANT COVER BY
AARON DIAZ

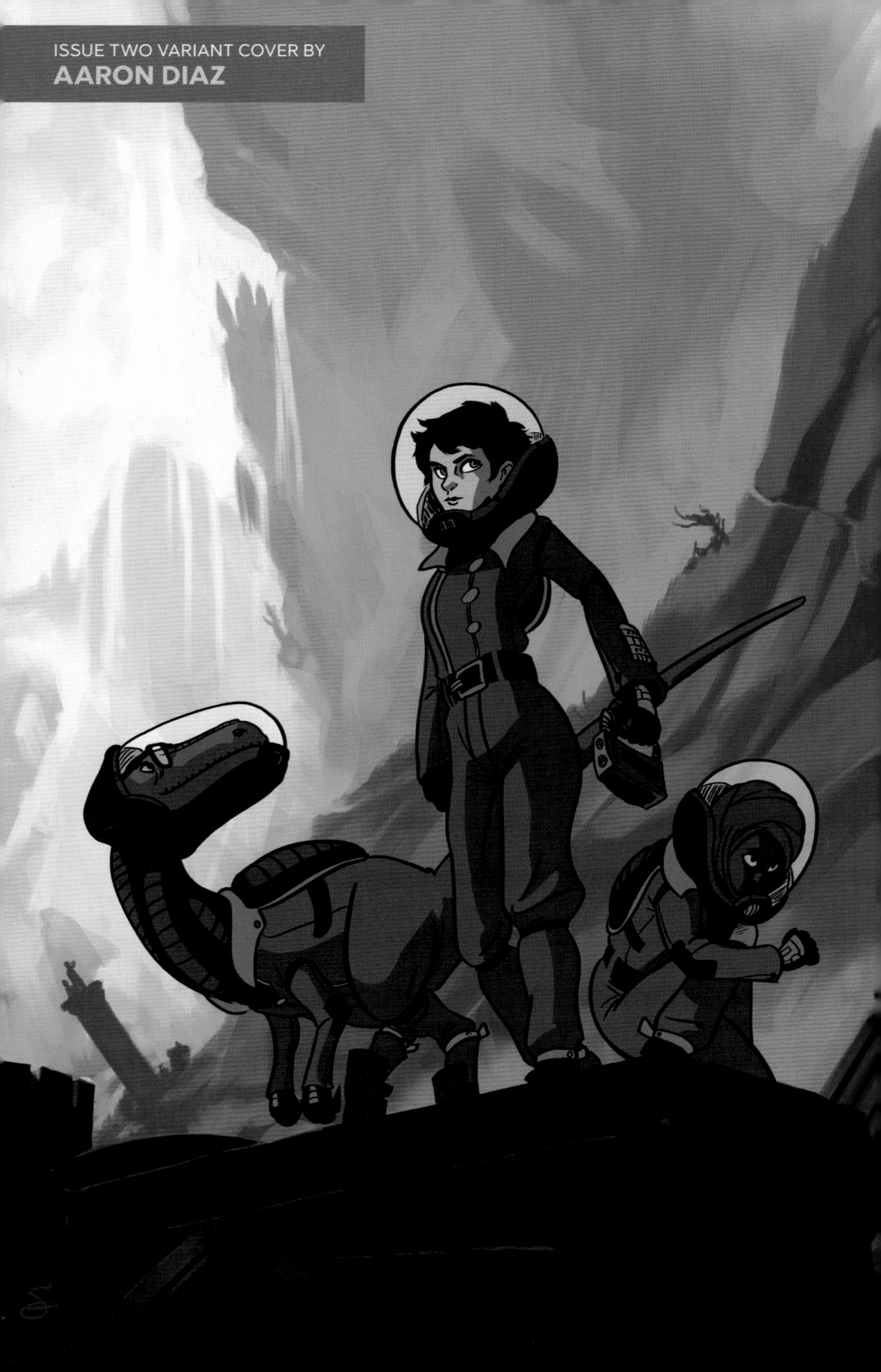

ISSUE THREE COVER BY
JOHN KEOGH

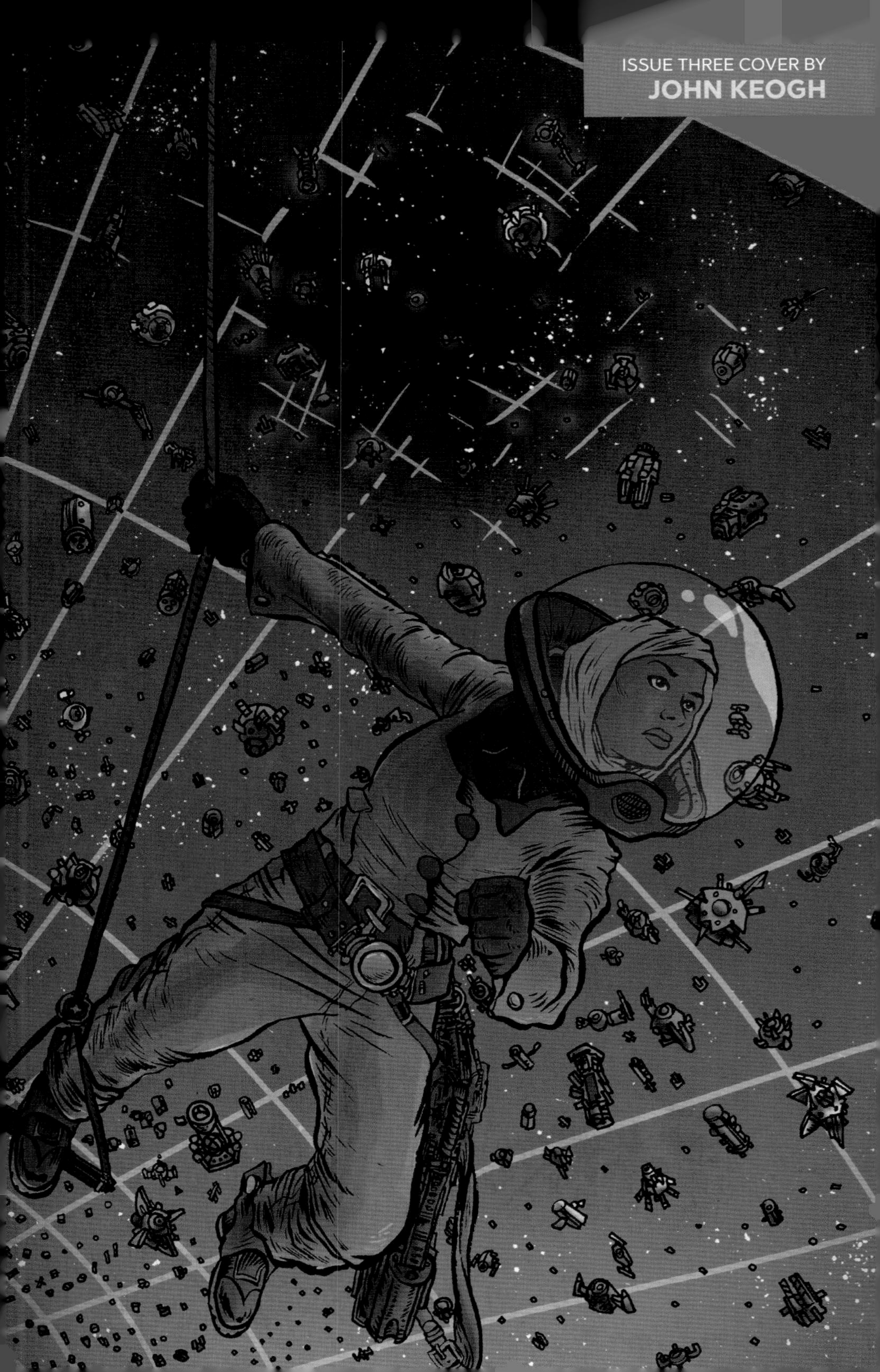

ISSUE THREE VARIANT COVER BY
KATE LETH

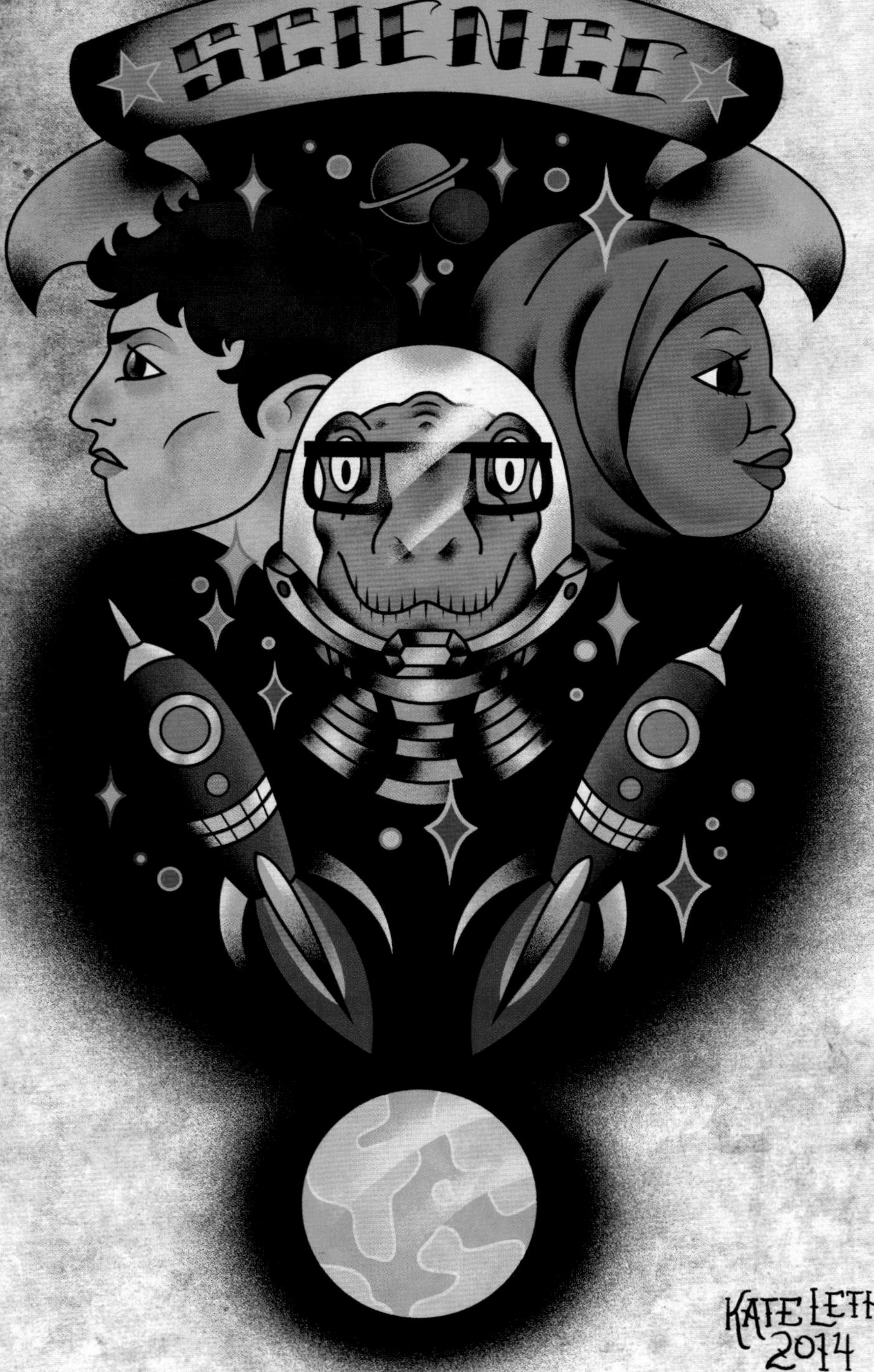
SCIENCE
KATE LETH
2014

ISSUE FOUR COVER BY
JOHN KEOGH

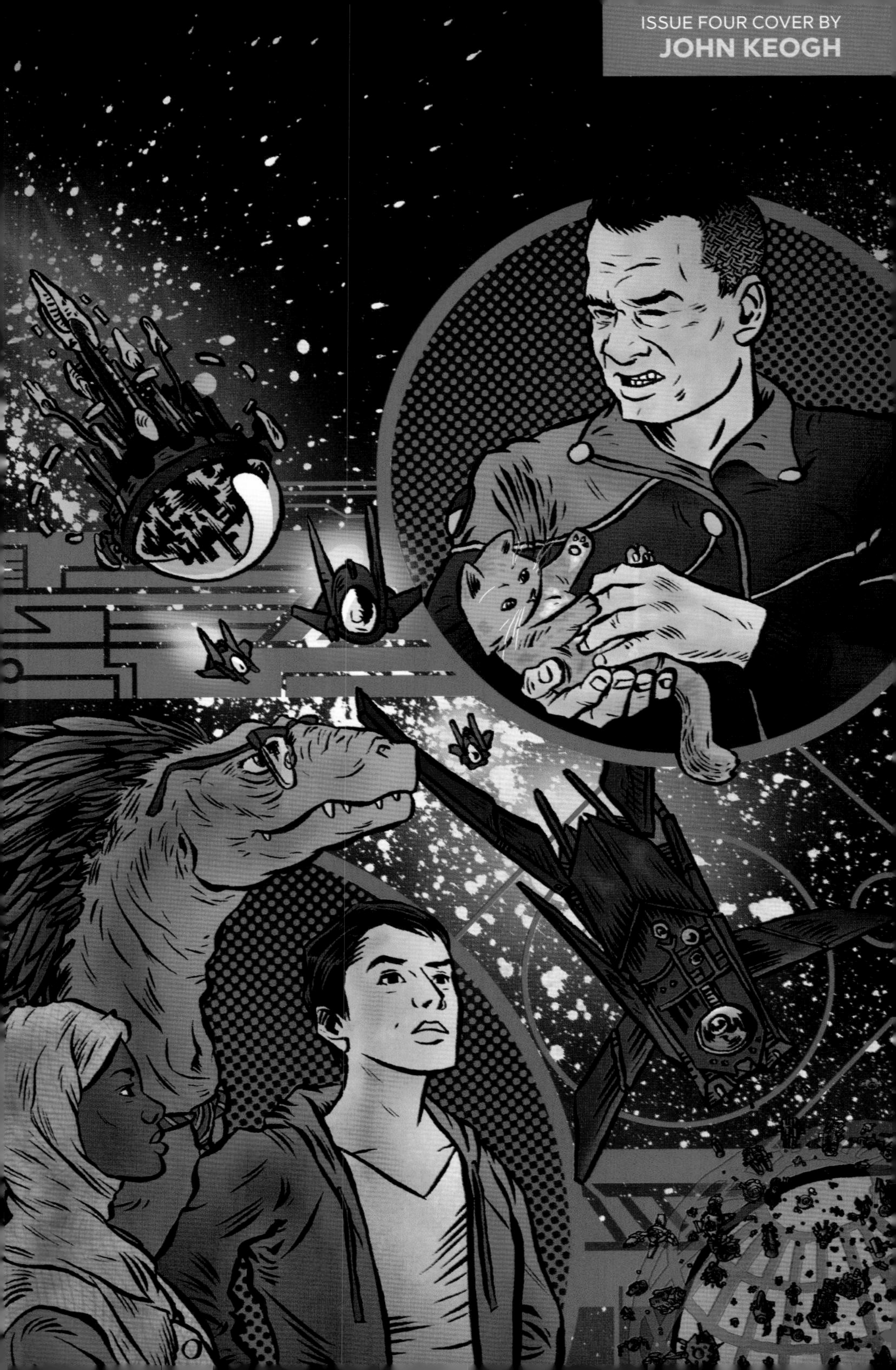

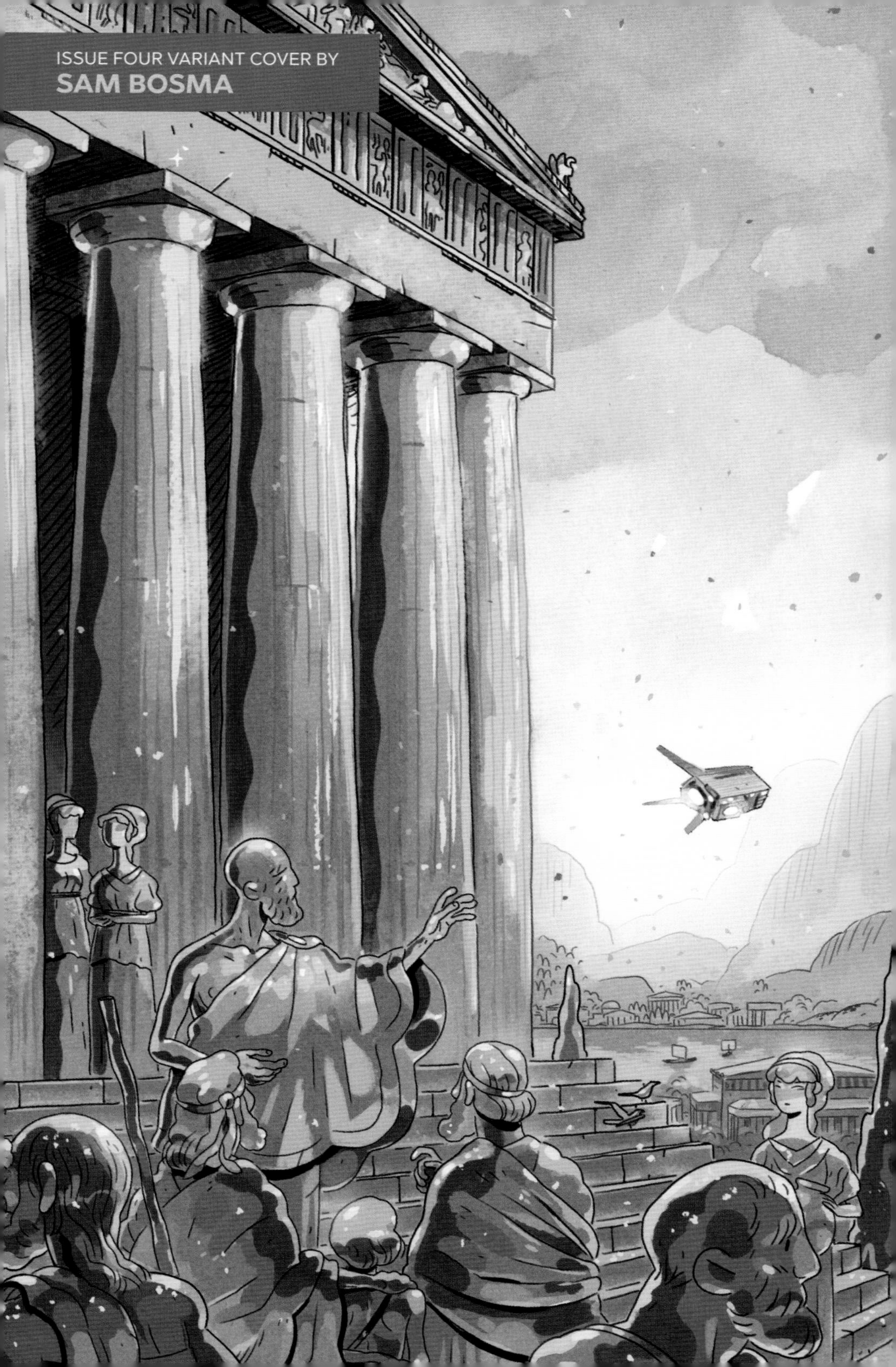

ISSUE FOUR VARIANT COVER BY
SAM BOSMA

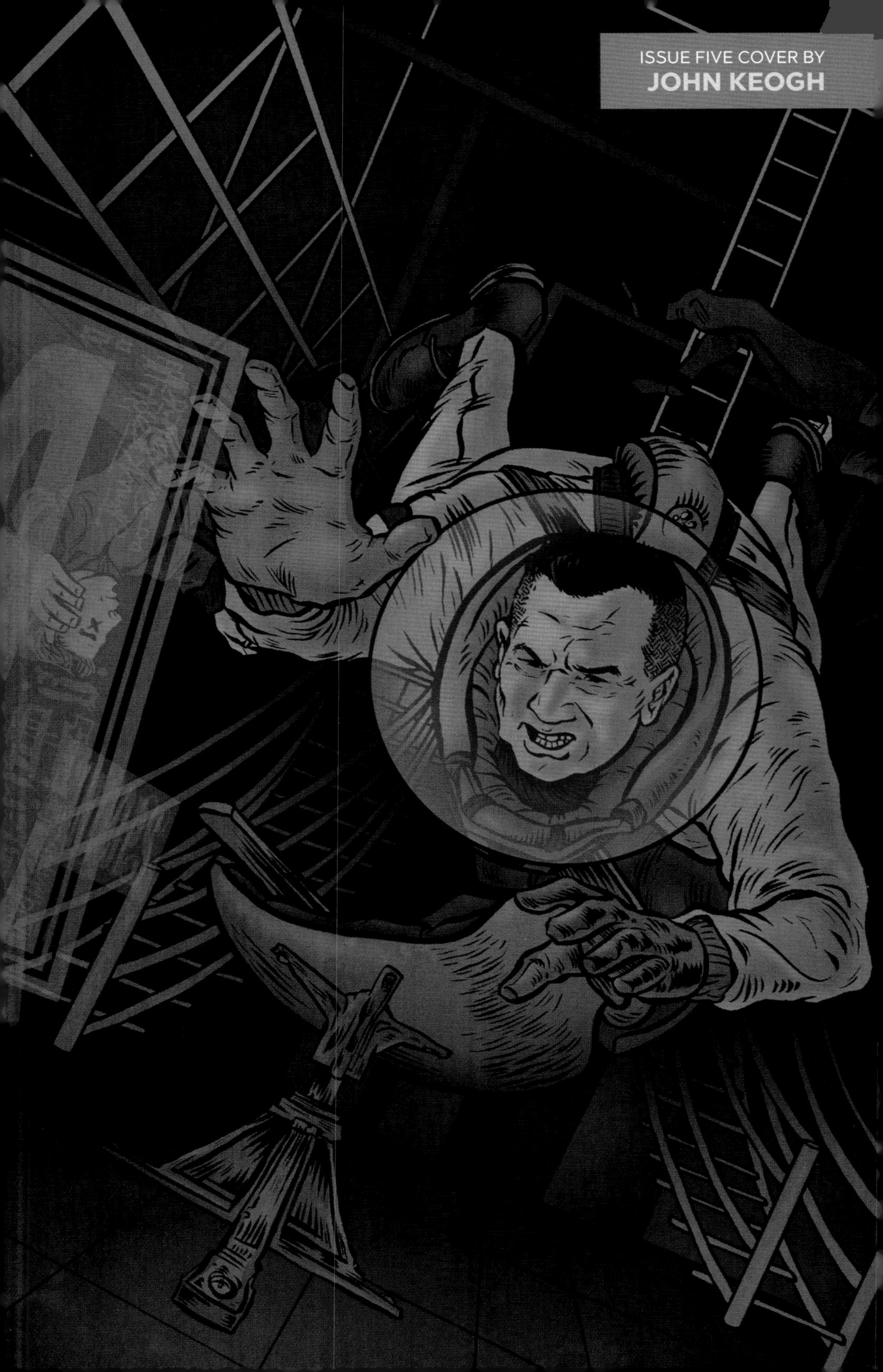

ISSUE FIVE COVER BY
JOHN KEOGH

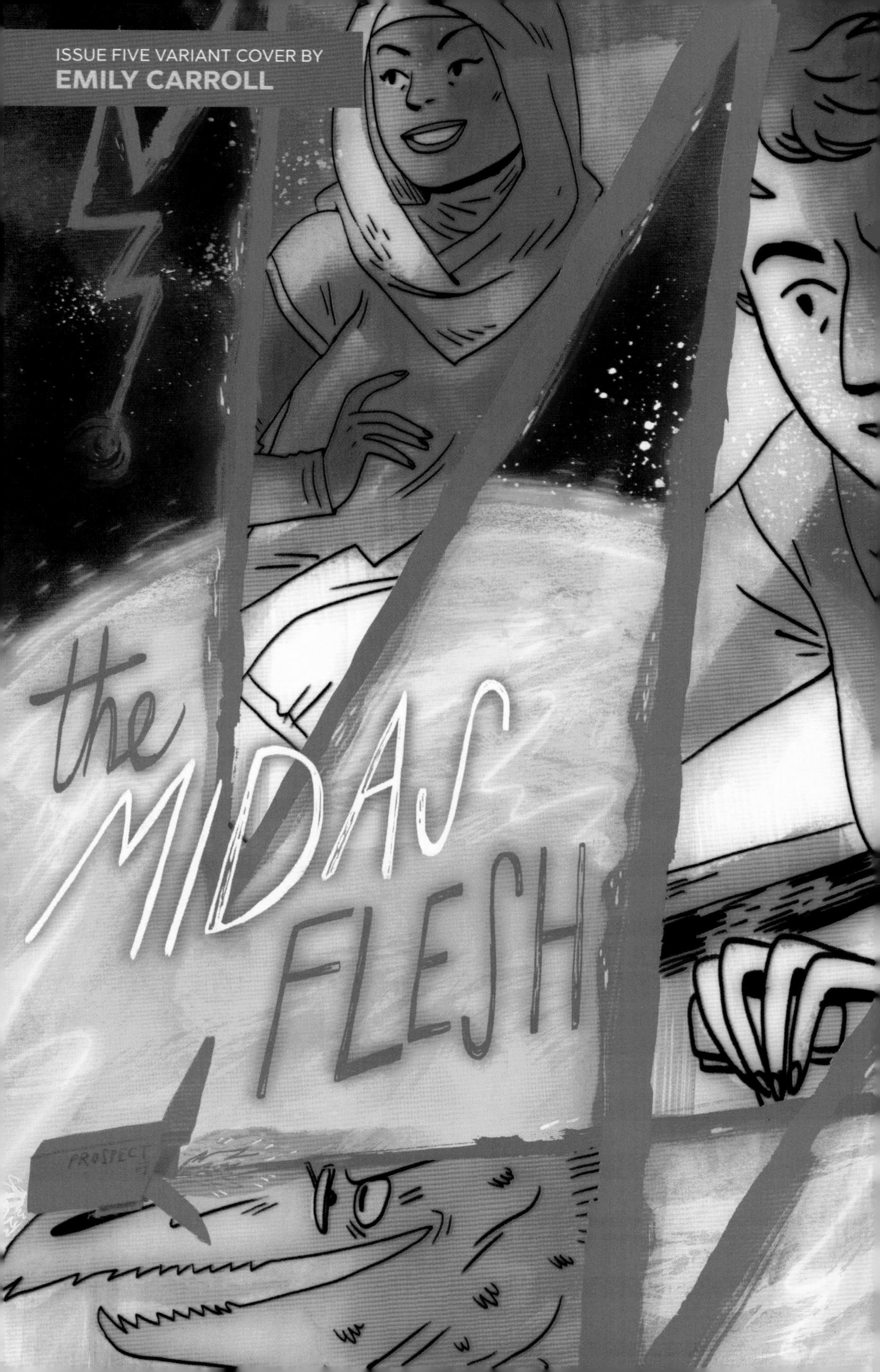
the MIDAS FLESH
PROSPECT

ISSUE FIVE VARIANT COVER BY
EMILY CARROLL

ISSUE SIX COVER BY
JOHN KEOGH

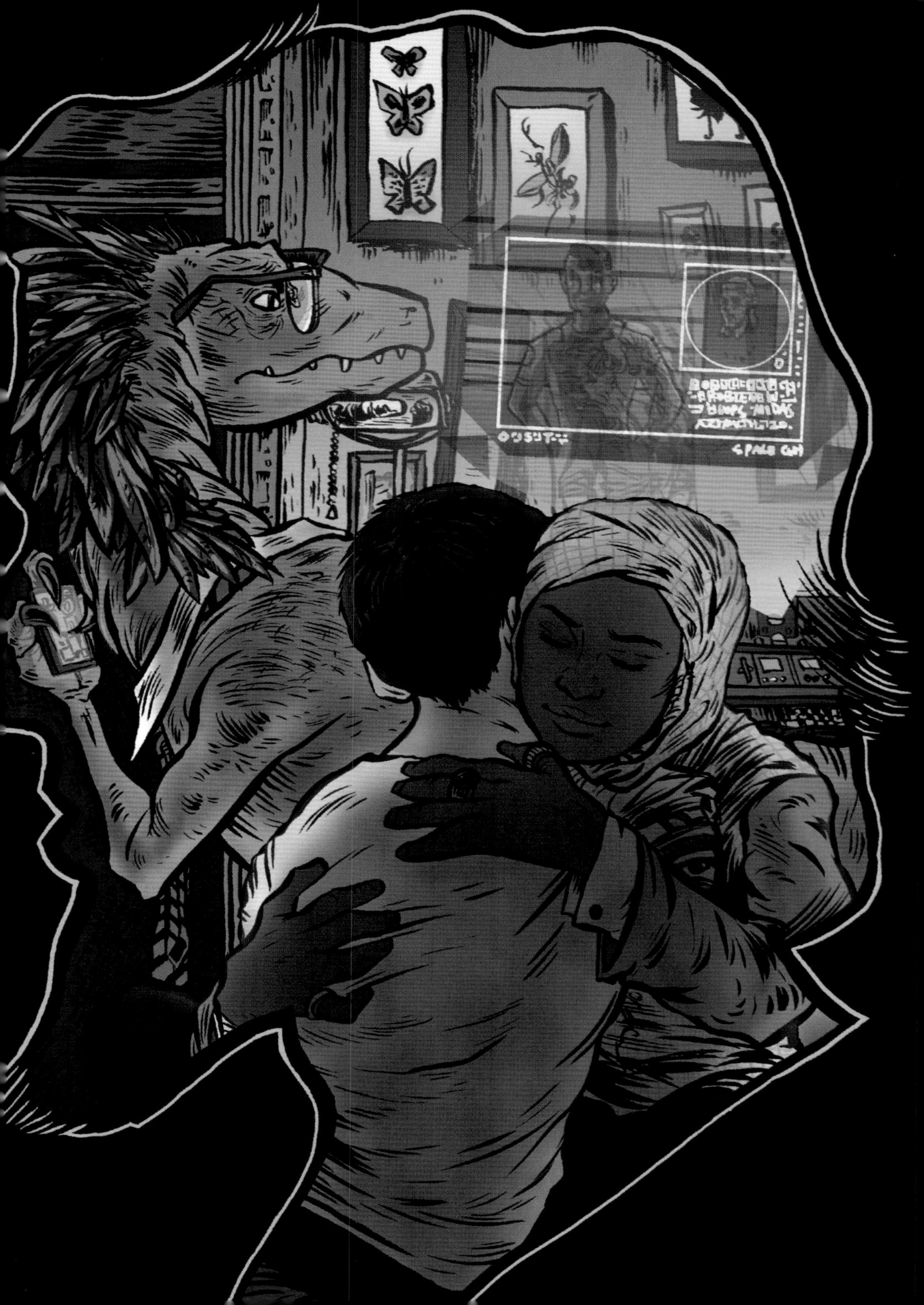

ISSUE SIX VARIANT COVER BY
DAVID MALKI

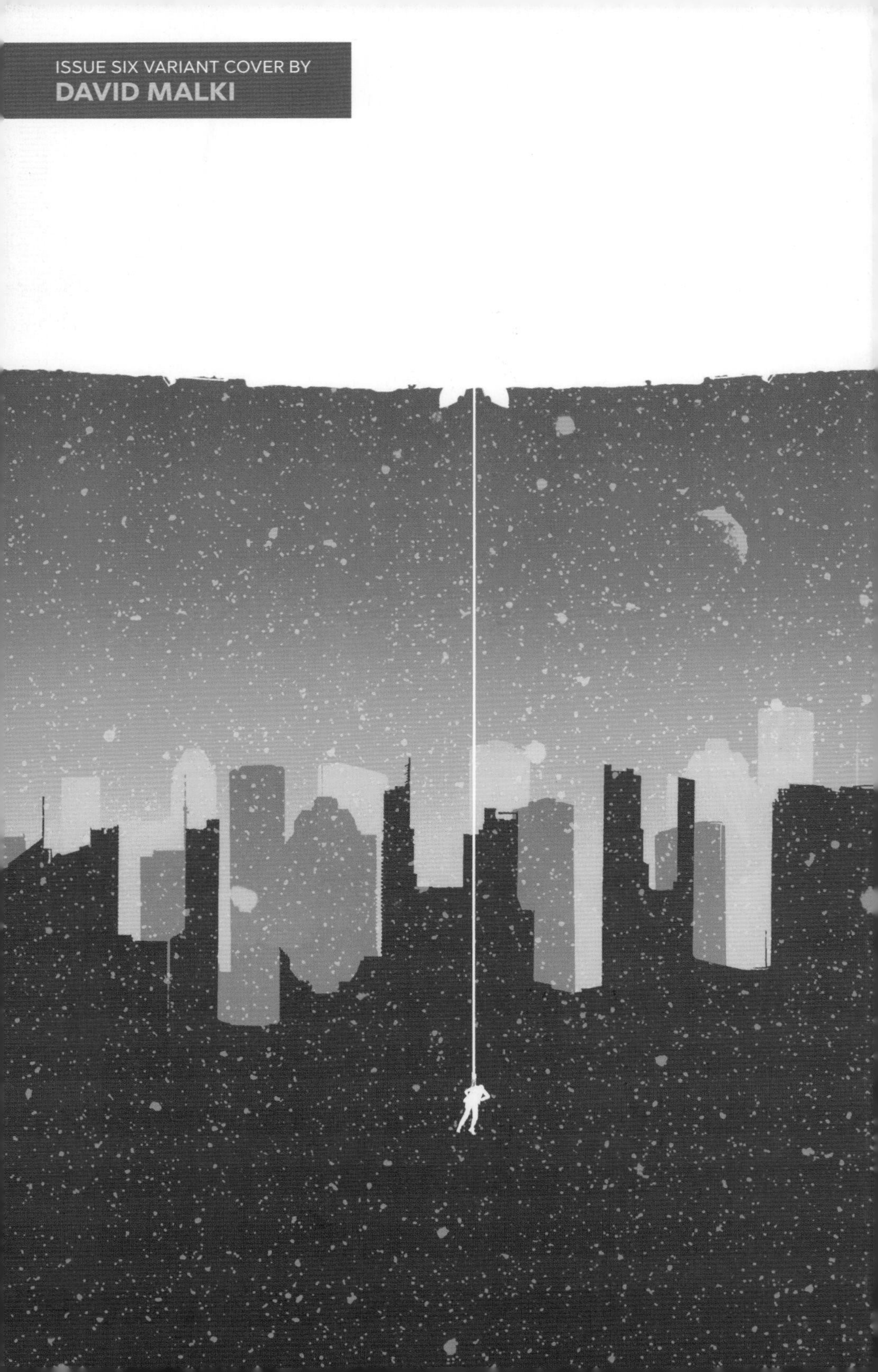

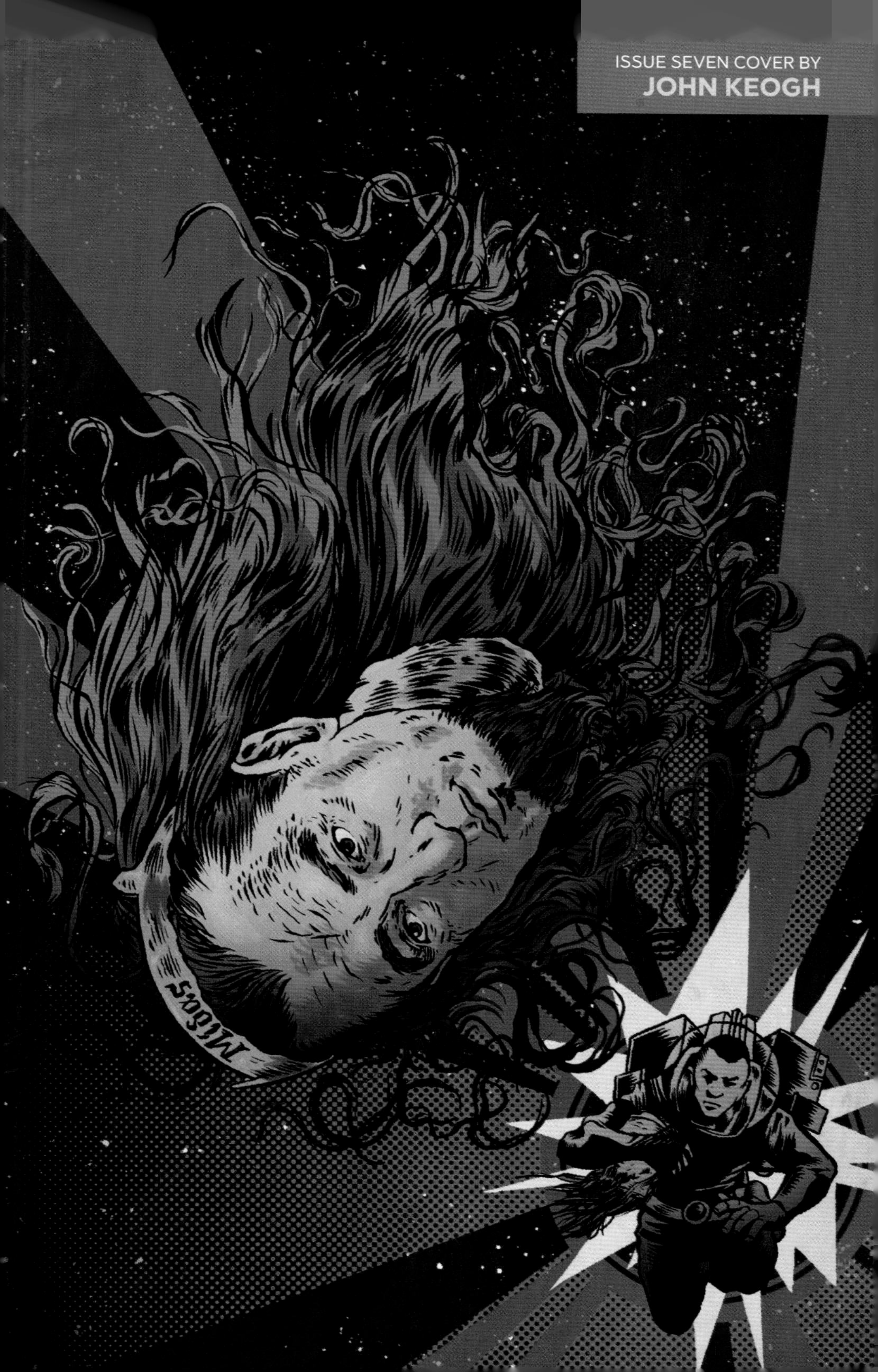

ISSUE SEVEN COVER BY
JOHN KEOGH

ISSUE SEVEN VARIANT COVER BY
DAVID HELLMAN

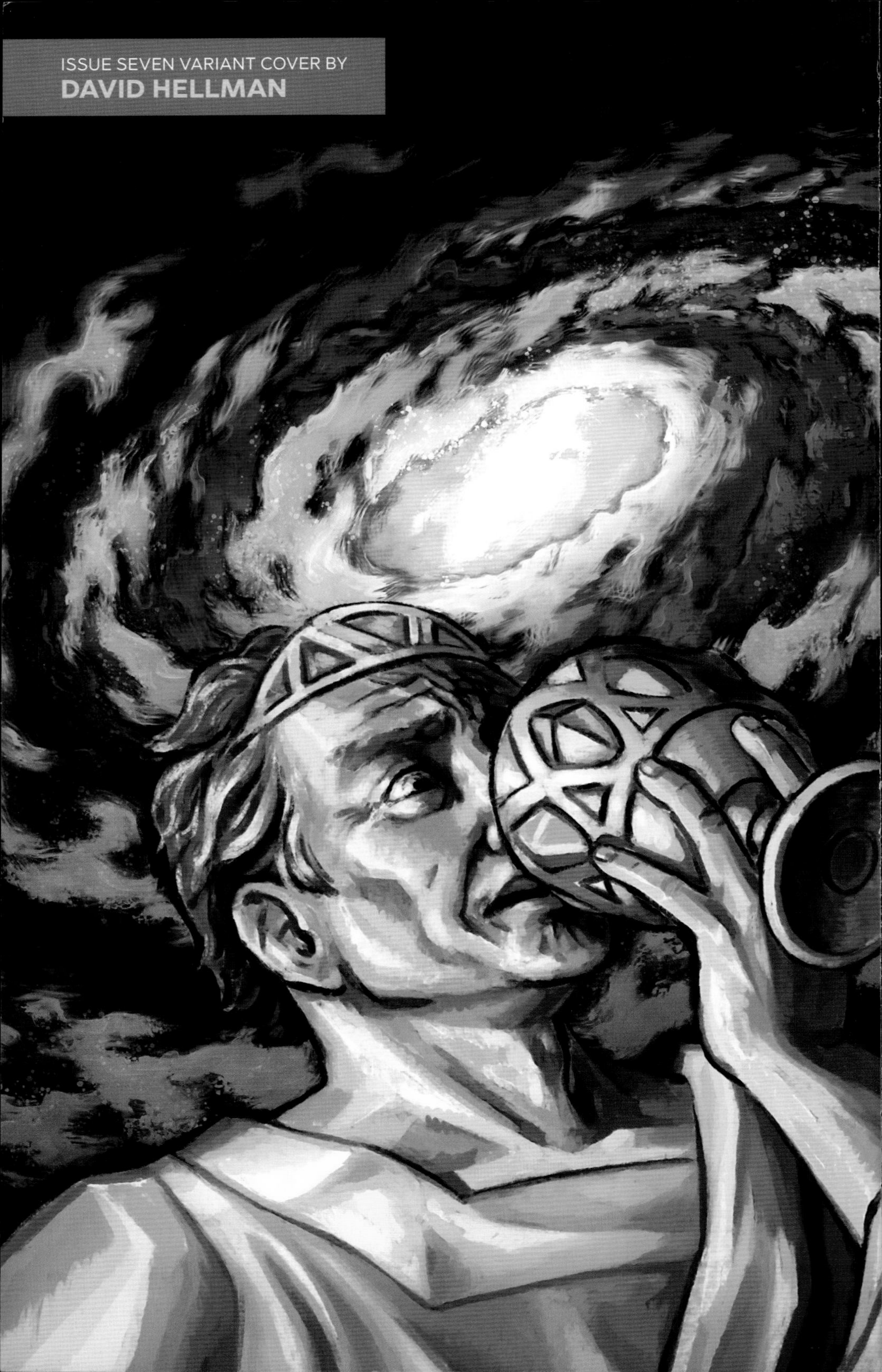

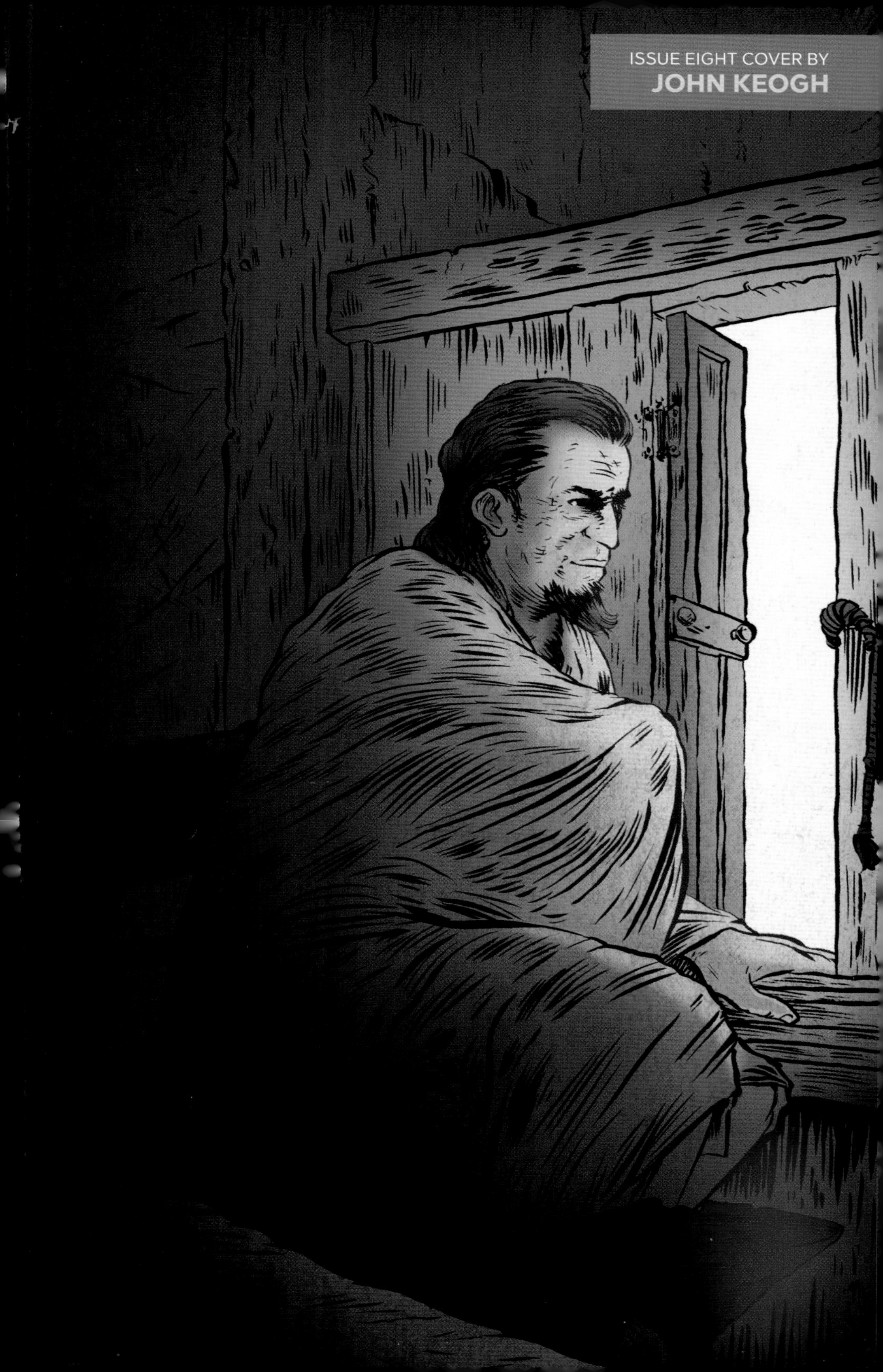

ISSUE EIGHT COVER BY
JOHN KEOGH

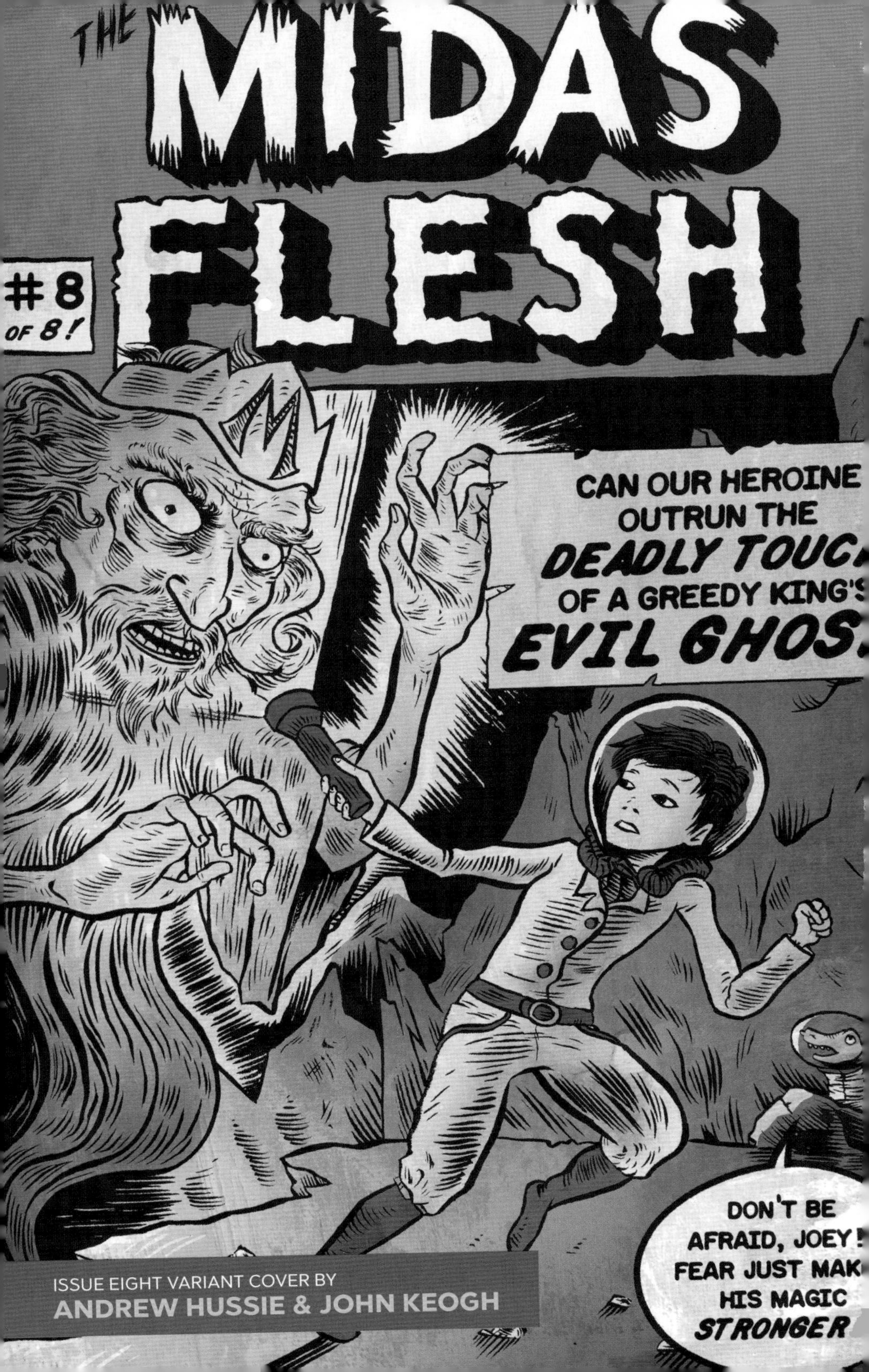
THE MIDAS FLESH
#8 OF 8!
CAN OUR HEROINE OUTRUN THE DEADLY TOUC OF A GREEDY KING'S EVIL GHOS
DON'T BE AFRAID, JOEY! FEAR JUST MAK HIS MAGIC STRONGER

ISSUE EIGHT VARIANT COVER BY
ANDREW HUSSIE & JOHN KEOGH

"MAXIMUM WARP TOWARDS THE FEDERATION HOMEWORLD. **PUNCH IT.**"

DISCOVER
ALL THE HITS

STEVENSON • ELLIS • WATTERS • ALLEN
LUMBERJANES
BEWARE THE KITTEN HOLY
NEW YORK TIMES BESTSELLING SERIES

Allison + Treiman + Cogar
GIANT DAYS
VOLUME ONE

RIBON • FISH • PEER
SLAM!
VOLUME ONE

Hope Larson • Brittney Williams • Sarah Stern
GOLDIE VANCE
Volume One

THE BACKSTAGERS

TYSON HESSE'S
DIESEL
IGNITION

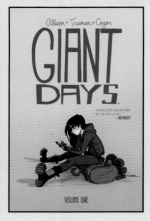

Lumberjanes
Noelle Stevenson, Shannon Watters, Grace Ellis, Brooklyn Allen, and Others
Volume 1: Beware the Kitten Holy
ISBN: 978-1-60886-687-8 | $14.99 US
Volume 2: Friendship to the Max
ISBN: 978-1-60886-737-0 | $14.99 US
Volume 3: A Terrible Plan
ISBN: 978-1-60886-803-2 | $14.99 US
Volume 4: Out of Time
ISBN: 978-1-60886-860-5 | $14.99 US
Volume 5: Band Together
ISBN: 978-1-60886-919-0 | $14.99 US

Giant Days
John Allison, Lissa Treiman, Max Sarin
Volume 1
ISBN: 978-1-60886-789-9 | $9.99 US
Volume 2
ISBN: 978-1-60886-804-9 | $14.99 US
Volume 3
ISBN: 978-1-60886-851-3 | $14.99 US

Jonesy
Sam Humphries, Caitlin Rose Boyle
Volume 1
ISBN: 978-1-60886-883-4 | $9.99 US
Volume 2
ISBN: 978-1-60886-999-2 | $14.99 US

Slam!
Pamela Ribon, Veronica Fish, Brittany Peer
Volume 1
ISBN: 978-1-68415-004-5 | $14.99 US

Goldie Vance
Hope Larson, Brittney Williams
Volume 1
ISBN: 978-1-60886-898-8 | $9.99 US
Volume 2
ISBN: 978-1-60886-974-9 | $14.99 US

The Backstagers
James Tynion IV, Rian Sygh
Volume 1
ISBN: 978-1-60886-993-0 | $14.99 US

Tyson Hesse's Diesel: Ignition
Tyson Hesse
ISBN: 978-1-60886-907-7 | $14.99 U

Coady & The Creepies
Liz Prince, Amanda Kirk, Hannah Fisher
ISBN: 978-1-68415-029-8 | $14.99

BOOM! BOX™

AVAILABLE AT YOUR LOCAL COMICS SHOP AND BOOKSTORE
WWW.**BOOM-STUDIOS**.COM